Praise for Charlaine Harris

'A first-rate mystery with special character . . . As convincing as it is surprising in the final revelation'
Washington Post

'Not many novels, and no mysteries, have shaken me as brutally as *A Secret Rage*' *Los Angeles Times*

'A series to savour' *Sun*

'Absorbing tension is maintained throughout leading up to a dramatic climax. Effective crime fiction' *Booklist*

'Harris writes neatly and with assurance, and she avoids the goo that makes equivalent books so sticky'
New York Times Book Review

'A home run the first time out' *Birmingham News*

'An author of rare talents . . . Harris artfully keeps the mask on the killer until the stunning conclusion'
Publishers Weekly

'*A Secret Rage* is a good mystery, well-written and compelling. I stayed up until 4:30 one morning in order to finish it . . . I don't want to give anything away by describing the climax and ending of this book, but it is certainly a powerful vision of women fighting together against a common enemy' *Boston Globe*

'Extraordinary. Powerful' *Library Journal*

By Charlaine Harris

STANDALONE NOVELS
Sweet and Deadly
A Secret Rage

THE AURORA TEAGARDEN MYSTERIES
Real Murders
A Bone to Pick
Three Bedrooms, One
  Corpse
The Julius House
Dead Over Heels
A Fool and His Honey
Last Scene Alive
Poppy Done to Death

THE LILY BARD MYSTERIES
Shakespeare's Landlord
Shakespeare's Champion
Shakespeare's Christmas
Shakespeare's Trollop
Shakespeare's Counselor

THE SOOKIE STACKHOUSE NOVELS
Dead Until Dark
Living Dead in Dallas
Club Dead
Dead to the World
Dead as a Doornail
Definitely Dead
All Together Dead
From Dead to Worse
Dead and Gone
Dead in the Family
Dead Reckoning
Deadlocked
Dead Ever After
A Touch of Dead
The Sookie Stackhouse
  Companion

THE HARPER CONNELLY SERIES
Grave Sight
Grave Surprise
An Ice Cold Grave
Grave Secret

Charlaine Harris is the bestselling author of the Sookie Stackhouse series, adapted for HBO as *True Blood*, as well as three other exceptional series – *The Aurora Teagarden Mysteries*, *The Lily Bard Mysteries*, and *The Harper Connelly Series*. She is married, with children, and lives in central Texas.

SWEET AND DEADLY

and

A SECRET RAGE

CHARLAINE HARRIS

An Orion paperback

This omnibus edition first published in Great Britain in 2013
by Orion Books,
an imprint of The Orion Publishing Group Ltd,
Orion House, 5 Upper St Martin's Lane,
London WC2H 9EA

Omnibus copyright © Charlaine Harris Inc. 2013
Sweet and Deadly Copyright © Charlaine Harris Schulz 1981
A Secret Rage Copyright © Charlaine Harris Schulz 1984

An Hachette UK company

3 5 7 9 10 8 6 4 2

A CIP catalogue record for this book
is available from the British Library.

ISBN 978-1-4091-2919-6

Typeset at The Spartan Press Ltd,
Lymington, Hants

Printed in Great Britain by Clays Ltd,
St Ives plc

The Orion Publishing Group's policy is to use papers that
are natural, renewable and recyclable products and
made from wood grown in sustainable forests. The logging
and manufacturing processes are expected to conform to
the environmental regulations of the country of origin.

www.orionbooks.co.uk

Contents

Sweet and Deadly   1
A Secret Rage   187

SWEET AND DEADLY

To Hal, who made this possible

1

She passed a dead dog on her way to the tenant shack.

It was already stiff, the legs poker-straight in rigor. It had been a big dog, maybe dun-colored; with only a quick glimpse, Catherine could not be sure. It was covered in the fine powdery dust that every passing vehicle threw up from the dirt road in the dry Delta summer.

In her rearview mirror she saw the cloud raised by her passage hanging in the air after she had passed, a cloud dividing endless rows of cotton. But the road was too poor to allow many backward glances.

She wondered briefly why someone had been driving so fast on the caked and rutted dirt that he had not seen the dog in time to swerve.

A sideways look at the cotton told Catherine that it would make a sad crop this year. The heat had lasted too long, unbroken by rain.

This land was Catherine's, had been her great grand-father's; but Catherine rented it out as her father had done. She was glad she did as she recalled her grand-father's irascibility in bad years, when she had ridden with him across 'the place,' as cotton planters called their acres.

She didn't remember the heat of those dim summers equaling the ferocity of this one. Even this early in the morning, with dawn not too long past, Catherine was beginning to sweat. Later in the day the glare would be intolerable, without considerable protection, to all but the swarthiest. To someone of Catherine's whiteness of skin it would be disastrous.

She pulled to a stop under an oak, killed the motor and got out. The oak was the only tree to break the stretch of the fields for miles. She stood in its sprawling shadow with her eyes closed, the heat and silence enveloping her. She wrapped herself in them gladly.

The silence came alive. A grasshopper thudded its way across the road from one stand of cotton to the next. A locust rattled at her feet.

She opened her eyes reluctantly and, after reaching into the car for the things she had brought with her, began to walk down the road to the empty tenant shack standing to one side of the intersection of two dirt roads.

The fields were empty of tractors and farm hands. Nothing stirred in the vast brilliant flatness but Catherine.

The sack in her left hand clanked as she walked. The gun in her right hand reflected the sun.

Her mother had raised her to be a lady. Her father had taught her how to shoot.

Catherine laid the gun on a stump in the packed-dirt yard of the tenant house. The bare wood of the house was shiny with age and weathering. A few traces of red paint still clung in the cracks between the planks.

It'll all fall down soon, she thought.

The outhouse behind the shack had collapsed months ago.

Under the spell of the drugging heat and hush, she made an effort to move quietly. The clank of the empty cans was jarring as she pulled them out of the sack and set them in a neat row across the broad stump.

She hardly glanced at the black doorless hole of the shack's entrance. She did notice that the sagging porch

6

seemed even closer to deserting the rest of the house than it had the last time she had driven out of town to shoot.

The dust plumed under her feet as she paced away from the stump. She counted under her breath.

A trickle of sweat started down the nape of her neck, and she was irritated that she had forgotten to bring an elastic band to lift the black hair off her shoulders.

The twinge of irritation faded as she turned to face the stump. Her head bowed. She concentrated on her body's memory of the gun.

In one motion, her head snapped back, her knees bent slightly, her left hand swung up to grip her rising right forearm, and she fired.

A can flew up in the air, landing with a hollow jangle under the steps rising to the porch. Then another. And another.

By the time only one can was left, Catherine was mildly pleased with herself. She dampened her self-congratulations with the reflection that she was, after all, firing from short range. But then, a .32 was not meant for distance shooting.

The last can proved stubborn. Catherine emptied the remaining bullets from the gun at it. She cursed mildly under her breath when the can remained obstinately un-punctured and upright.

It's a good time for a break, she decided.

She trudged back to the stump and collapsed, with her back against its roughness. Pulling a plastic bullet box from a pocket in her blue jeans, she set it on the ground beside her. She eased the pin from the chamber, letting it fall into her hand. She reloaded lazily, full of the languorous peace that follows catharsis.

When the gun was ready, she didn't feel like rising.

Let the can sit, she thought. It deserves to stay on the stump.

She was enjoying the rare moment of relaxation. She

laced her fingers across her stomach and noticed that they were leaving smudges on her white T-shirt. Her jeans were coated with dust now. She slapped her thigh lightly and watched the motes fly up.

I'll go home, she thought comfortably, and pop every stitch I have on into the washer. And I'll take a long, long shower. And then—

There was no 'then.'

But I'm better, she continued, smoothly gliding over the faint uneasiness that had ruffled her peace. I'm better now.

A horsefly landed on her arm, and she slapped at it automatically. It buzzed away in pique, only to be replaced in short order by one of its companions.

'Damn flies,' she muttered.

There sure are a lot of them, she thought in some surprise, as another landed on her knee. Attracted by my sweat, I guess.

That settled it. She would gather up the cans and go back to Lowfield, back to her cool quiet house.

Catherine rose and walked toward the dilapidated porch briskly, slapping at her arms as she went.

The flies were whirring in and out of the open doorway, creating a drone in the stillness. The boarded-up windows of the house and the overhanging roof of its porch combined to make a dark cave of the interior. The sun penetrated only a foot into the entrance, so the darkness seemed impenetrable by contrast.

She stooped to pick up the first can she had hit, which was lodged under the lopsided steps. The stoop leveled her with the raised floor of the house, built high to avoid flooding in the heavy Delta rains. As she reached for the punctured can, something caught at the corner of her eye, an image so odd that she froze, doubled over, her hand extended for the can.

There was something in that little pool of light penetrating the empty doorway.

It was a hand.

She tried to identify it as something else, anything else.

It remained a hand. The palm was turned up, and the fingers stretched toward Catherine appealingly. Catherine's eyes flicked down to her own extended fingers, then back. She straightened very slowly.

When she inhaled, she realized she had been holding her breath against the smell. It was a whiff of the same odor she had caught as her car passed the dead dog.

With no thought at all, she grasped one of the supports that held up the roof over the porch. Moving quietly and carefully, she pulled herself up on the loose rotting planks and took a little step forward.

A fly buzzed past her face.

The blinding contrast of sun and gloom lessened as she crept closer. When she reached the doorway she could see what lay inside the shack.

The hand was still attached to a wrist, the wrist to an arm . . .

It had been a woman.

Her face was turned away from Catherine. Even in the dimness, Catherine could make out dark patches matting the gray hair. She realized then what made the head so oddly shaped.

A fly landed on the woman's arm.

Catherine began shaking. She was afraid her knees would give way, that she would fall on top of the stinking thing. Her stomach began to twist.

She backed away, tiny shuffling steps that took all her concentration. Her arm touched a wooden support. She had reached the edge of the porch.

She turned to grip the support, then lowered a foot until it rested firmly on the ground.

She reached the stump and sat on its uneven surface, with her back to the tenant house. She stared across her land.

'Oh my God,' she whispered.

And the fear hit her. After a stunned second she scrabbled in the dust for her gun.

Her eyes darted around her, searching.

Nothing moved on the road, or in the fields; but she felt terrifyingly exposed in that vast flatness.

The car. She had to make it to the car. It was only a few yards away, parked under the oak's inadequate shade. All she had to do was cross those yards. But she was frozen in position like an animal caught in headlights.

The sheriff, she thought with sudden clarity. I've got to get Sheriff Galton.

With that thought, that plain plan, she was able to launch herself from the stump.

She opened the door and shoved the pistol to the other side of the car with shaking fingers, then slid into the driver's seat. Shut the door. Locked it. She managed to turn the key in the ignition before her muscles refused to obey her. Her fingers on the gearshift were too palsied to put the car into drive.

She screamed at her helplessness. She covered her ears against the ragged sound.

But with that release, her shaking lessened. She could put the car in gear and start back home to Lowfield.

2

There were two houses where the dirt road joined the highway. Catherine could have stopped at either and found help.

She never thought of it. In a fog of shock she had fixed her destination, and she would not stop until she reached it. She drove south on the highway without seeing anything but the concrete in front of her.

To reach the sheriff's office, she had to turn off the highway into the town. When she saw the familiar brick building sitting squarely in front of the old jail, Catherine felt dizzy with relief.

The lights inside the little building were on. Through the glass door Catherine could see the dispatcher, Mary Jane Cory, seated at her desk behind the counter.

It took an immense effort of will to unclamp her hands from the wheel, open the car door, swing her legs out, and force the rest of her body to follow them.

'Good morning, Catherine! I'll be with you in a minute,' Mrs Cory said briskly, and thudded out a few more words on her ancient typewriter.

In what later seemed to Catherine insanity, she kept silent and waited obediently. She leaned on the counter, her hands gripping the far edge of it to keep upright.

That silence alerted some warning signal in Mary Jane

Cory. She gave Catherine a second glance and then was on her feet her hands covering Catherine's.

'What's the matter?' the older woman asked sharply.

'The sheriff . . . I want to see the sheriff,' Catherine said painfully. Her jaws ached from long clenching.

'Are you going to faint, Catherine?' Mrs Cory asked, still in that sharp watchful voice.

Catherine didn't answer.

Mrs Cory switched her grip from Catherine's hands to her upper arms and called without turning her head, 'James Galton! Come here quick!'

There was a stir in the office that had 'Sheriff' on the door. The roar of the air conditioning covered the sound of Galton's quiet steps, but a khaki-covered elbow appeared in Catherine's range of view, propped on the counter beside her.

'You got troubles, Catherine?' rumbled a carefully relaxed voice. Catherine saw Mrs Cory's platinum head give a shake in answer to some silent query of Galton's.

Now that the time had come to deliver her message, Catherine found herself curiously embarrassed, as if she were about to commit a deliberate faux pas.

She turned her head stiffly to look up at Galton.

'There's a dead woman in an old tenant house. On the place.'

'You sure she's dead?'

Catherine's face was blank as she stared at him. 'Oh, yes,' she said.

'A black woman?'

'No,' she said, and felt the ripple of surprise. Lowfield white women did not get themselves dumped in tenant shacks.

'Do you know who it is?'

'No. No.' Her voice sounded odd to her own ears. 'She's covered in blood.'

Galton's face changed as she stared at him. He didn't look like the relaxed and genial Jimmy Galton who had been her father's friend.

He looked like the sheriff.

Catherine had assumed she could go home after informing the sheriff of her discovery.

She had, she soon realized, been thinking like a child.

Galton issued a few commands to Mrs Cory, who got busy on the radio and telephone. He gently but quite firmly led Catherine into his office, guided her to the chair in front of his desk, and then eased himself into his own battered chair.

'You want to go to the doctor for a tranquilizer?'

But the doctor was her father. He was dead.

No, she thought, horrified. No. She shook her head to clear her thoughts. This kind of confusion hadn't happened to her in a long time; she had thought it was over with.

'Want something to drink?'

'No,' she whispered.

He indicated his pack of cigarettes.

Catherine forced herself to reach for one and light it, while Galton eyed her intently.

He's trying to see if I can do it by myself, Catherine thought suddenly. Her back stiffened.

'Now, I'm going to ask you a few questions. You just take your time answering,' he said.

Catherine nodded briefly.

He was being kind in a stern way, but Catherine realized that the day would be longer than she had ever imagined when she arose early that morning to go target shooting.

Galton jogged her with a couple of questions. Once she got going, she gave a clear account of her morning.

There was nothing much to tell.

When she finished, Galton rose without a word, patting her absently as he passed into the outer room.

Catherine heard a shuffling of feet in the main office, a murmur of voices. Mrs Cory had called in the deputies.

Catherine looked down at her hands clenched in her lap. Her heavy dark hair swung forward, shielding her face, giving her a tiny corner of privacy against the open door.

The look of her twined fingers, the smell of the sheriff's office, and the scrape of official boots had ripped the cover from a well of memory. For a few moments she was not in Lowfield but in a similar police station in a similar tiny town, in Arkansas. She was not wearing blue jeans but the dress she had worn to work that day. Her parents had been dead for four hours instead of six months.

With a terrible effort, she wrenched herself back into her proper place.

I will not give way, she told herself ferociously. I will get through this and I will not give way.

She listened to Sheriff Galton's voice rumbling in the main office. He was telling Mary Jane Cory to call enough men for a coroner's jury.

She rode back to the shack in the sheriff's car. The car was bright green with gold lettering and a star on the side. She could see people glancing in as the sheriff drove past, then looking again as they identified Galton's passenger as Catherine Linton.

Though she had cut herself off from the mainstream of life in Lowfield, Catherine was fully aware that the talk would already be beginning. A month ago, it would not have occurred to her to care.

'Catherine,' Galton said.

She looked at him.

'Who rents your place?'

'Martin Barnes,' she said promptly.

She slid easily back into her silence. It had been her natural element for months; and even before that, she had not been what anyone would call talkative. Her room-mate in college had called her 'Sphinx.' It had become her accepted name on the small private campus.

She wished there was someone around to call her that now.

Martin Barnes. That was food for thought. Catherine supposed the person most familiar with that piece of land must be the most suspected. The shack was visible, but not obvious, from the highway. You wouldn't, Catherine decided, just glimpse it and say, 'Perfect place for this body I have on my hands.' But Mr Barnes can't have anything to do with this, she thought. He's – older than my father; he's a good man. Besides – she must have been raped. Why else would anyone drag a lady out to the country and bash her on the head?

But the woman's dress hadn't been disarranged. Catherine could see it clearly, pulled down around the woman's knees. A print shirtwaist dress, an everyday dress, short-sleeved for the summer. The kind of dress any older woman in Lowfield would wear to go to the grocery. Not a dress any woman would wear to die in.

Robbery, then? Catherine wondered. Had there been a purse at the woman's side? She couldn't recall one – and she could still see the body clearly. She shuddered, and her small square hands gripped her folded arms.

'Let me tell you the procedure, Catherine,' Sheriff Galton said abruptly, and she knew he had noticed the shudder.

She summoned up a courteous show of interest.

'First we secure the scene.'

The thought of anyone 'securing' the ramshackle tenant

house made her want to laugh, but she pressed her lips together and locked in the urge. Everyone thinks you're crazy anyway: don't confirm it, she warned herself. She inclined her head to show that she was listening.

'Percy here will take some pictures,' Galton proceeded with a matter-of-fact air.

Percy was the black deputy lodged in the back seat with a lot of camera paraphernalia. He was a solemn-faced young man, and as Catherine turned to look at him by way of acknowledging his entrance into the conversation, she felt an unexpected stir of recognition. Before she could place it, Galton rumbled on.

'Mary Jane's called the coroner, and he'll convene a coroner's jury at the scene. They'll hear your testimony and they'll give their finding.'

Then I can go home, Catherine thought hopefully.

'Then you come back to the station, make a formal statement, sign it.'

Damn.

'Then you can go home. I may have to ask you a few more questions later, but I think that'll be it. Until we catch the perpetrator. Then there'll be the trial.'

Trial opened up new vistas of trouble. It sounded pretty cocky on James Galton's part, too.

Catherine glanced at Galton's stern lined face, and suddenly she decided it would be a mistake to underestimate Sheriff James Galton.

The sheriff's car and the deputies' car following it turned off the highway onto the dirt road Catherine indicated. The sun was higher, the glare brighter than during Catherine's early morning venture. She had no sunglasses and had to lower the visor to shield her eyes. She was too short for it to help much.

'This your grandfather's place?' Galton asked.

'All of it.'

'All rented out to Martin?'

'Yes. For years. Daddy rented to him too.'

Catherine lit a cigarette from the battered pack in her pocket and smoked it slowly.

The shack at the crossroads came into view.

The weathered wood shone in the sun. It looked so quiet and empty that for a brief moment Catherine doubted what she had seen. Then she began shaking again, and dug her nails into her arms to keep from crying.

I'm not going in there. Surely they won't ask me to go in there, she thought.

'This the place?' Galton asked.

She nodded.

They pulled to a halt under the same oak that had sheltered Catherine's car. The sheriff and the deputy got out immediately. Catherine put out her cigarette with elaborate care. The black deputy opened her door.

She left the sheriff's car and began to walk down the road.

The sweat that had dried in the sheriff's cold office had formed a layer on her skin. Now she sweated again. She felt filthy and old.

She ignored Galton, the black deputy, and the other deputies from the second car. The dark emptiness of the doorway grew with every step she took. She imagined she could hear the drone of the flies already.

It was not just her imagination that she could pick up the smell when she reached the stump. She stopped in her tracks. The rising temperature and the passage of even this short amount of time had done their work.

She would not go farther.

'In there,' she said briefly.

The sheriff had picked up the scent for himself.

Catherine watched his mouth set grimly. She got some satisfaction from that, though she was ashamed of it.

The other deputies had caught up. In a knot, the brown uniforms approached the cabin slowly.

She could see the full force of the smell hit them. A wavering of heads, a look of disgust.

'Jesus!' one of them muttered.

The sheriff was eyeing the rickety porch with calculation. Catherine weighed about 115 pounds; the sheriff close to 185.

With a kind of detached interest, Catherine wondered how he would manage.

Galton scanned his deputies from the neck down, and picked Ralph Carson, who had gone to high school with Catherine, as the lightest of the group.

After some muttered consultation, Carson edged up on the porch, gingerly picked his way across, and reached the door frame without the porch collapsing. He looked in. When he turned to extend an arm to the sheriff, his face was set in harsh lines of control, and his tan looked muddy.

Galton gripped Carson's arm, and the deputy gave a heave inward. After Galton, the black deputy was hoisted into the shack. The others began to search the barren area around the house.

I guess I thought it would be gone by the time we got here, Catherine thought with a mixture of relief and dismay. Her tension drained away suddenly, leaving her sick and exhausted. She sat down on the stump, her back turned to the open doorway, which was now occasionally lit with the quick glare of flash bulbs.

A white and orange ambulance was bumping its way down the road. A deputy flagged it in behind the official cars, and two white-coated attendants and Dr Jerry Selforth, Lowfield's new doctor, jumped out. After exchanging a few words with the deputy, Selforth detached himself from the little group and came toward Catherine.

'Good morning, Jerry,' Catherine said with polite incongruity. He's excited by this, she thought.

'Hey, Catherine, you all right?' He massaged her shoulder. He couldn't talk to a woman without prodding, rubbing, gripping. Men he slapped on the back.

She was too tired to pull away, but her eyebrows rose in a frigid arch. Jerry's hand dropped away.

'I'm sorry you had to find her like that,' he said more soberly.

Catherine shrugged. 'Well . . .' the young doctor murmured after a beat of silence.

Catherine whipped herself into more courtesy.

'Your first?' she inquired, tilting her head toward the shack.

'My first that's been dead longer than two hours,' he admitted. 'Since med school. There's a pathologist in Morene that'll come help me.'

'They were better preserved in med school,' he added thoughtfully, as a short-lived breeze wafted east.

'Dr Selforth!' bellowed Galton from the interior of the cabin.

Jerry flashed Catherine a broad grin and trotted cheerfully away.

He certainly fit right into his slot in Lowfield, Catherine thought wryly. She had heard the ladies loved him, and after a residence of five months, he was first-naming everyone in town.

Catherine had not liked Jerry Selforth, who had taken over her father's practice almost lock, stock, and barrel, since the time he had laughed at her father's old-fashioned office in back of the Linton home. To her further irritation, Jerry Selforth had been much smitten with her black hair and white skin, and he had lengthened the business of purchasing Dr Linton's office equipment considerably, apparently in the hope of arousing a similar enthusiasm in Catherine.

Because of the dates she had refused, she always felt she had an obligation to be kind to him, though it was an uphill effort. Something about Jerry Selforth's smile said outright that his bed was a palace of delights that Catherine would be lucky to share.

Catherine had her doubts about that.

Time limped by, and the stump grew uncomfortable. Rivulets of sweat trickled down her face. Her skin prickled ominously, a prelude to sunburn. She wondered what she was doing there. She was clearly redundant.

She had felt the same way when other people, to spare her, had made all the arrangements about her parents' bodies. The sheriff in Parkinson, Arkansas, had been shorter, heavyset. He had been kind, too. She had accepted a tranquilizer that day. After it entered her blood stream, she had been able to call her boss at her first job, to tell him she wouldn't be coming back.

A flurry of dust announced new arrivals. Catherine was glad to have something new to look at, to break her painful train of thought. Three more cars pulled up behind the ambulance. The lead car was a white Lincoln Continental that was certainly going to need a wash after this morning was over.

As the driver emerged, Catherine recognized him. It was her neighbor, Carl Perkins. He and his wife lived in an incredible pseudoantebellum structure across the street from the west side of Catherine's own house. Its construction had had the whole town agape for months.

Catherine suddenly felt like laughing as she recalled Tom Mascalco's first comment on that house. Whenever he drove by, Tom said, he expected a chorus of darkies to appear on the veranda and hum 'Tara's Theme.'

Catherine's flash of humor faded when she remembered that Carl Perkins was, in addition to his many other irons in the town fire, the county coroner. The men piling out of the other cars must comprise the coroner's jury, she realized. She knew them all: local businessmen, planters. There was one black – Cleophus Hames, who ran one of the two Negro funeral parlors.

I wish I was invisible, she thought miserably.

She became very still and looked down the short length of her legs at her tennis shoes.

Of course, if I don't look at them, they can't see me, she jeered at herself, when she realized what she was doing.

But it worked for a while. The men stood in an uneasy bunch several feet from the shack, not talking much, just glancing at the doorway with varying degrees of apprehension.

It worked until Sheriff Galton drew all eyes to her by jumping from the cabin doorway and striding directly to Catherine's stump.

She had surreptitiously raised the hem of her T-shirt to wipe some of the sweat from her face, so she didn't observe the set of his shoulders until it was too late to be alerted. She had a bare second to realize something was wrong.

'Why did you say you didn't know her?' he asked brusquely when he was within hearing distance.

'What?' she said stupidly.

She couldn't understand what he meant. The heat and the long wait had drained her. Her brain stirred sluggishly under the sting of his voice.

Galton stood in front of her now, no longer familiar and sympathetic but somehow menacing.

He said angrily, 'You've known that woman all your life.'

*

She stared up at him until the sun dazzled her eyes unbearably and she had to raise an arm to shield them.

The cold stirring deep inside her was fear, fear that activated a store of self-defense she had never been called upon to use.

'I never saw her face. I told you that,' she said. Her pale gray eyes held his with fierce intensity. 'The side of her head nearest me was covered with blood.' Her voice was sharp, definite. For the first time in her life she was speaking to an older person, a lifelong acquaintance, in a tone that was within a stone's throw of rudeness.

She saw in his face that he had not missed it.

'You better think again, Catherine,' he retorted. 'That's Leona Gaites, who was your father's nurse for thirty-odd years.'

3

Catherine gaped at him.

'What on earth . . .' she stammered. 'Miss Gaites . . . what is she doing out here?'

Even through her shock Catherine saw some relief touch Galton's face. Her unalloyed amazement must have gone some way toward convincing him of her ignorance of the dead woman's identity. Her innocence.

My innocence? Her anger grew. It felt surprisingly good. She was so seldom overtly angry.

'Well, come on,' Galton was saying in a more relaxed voice. 'The coroner's jury is here. You have to testify.'

Catherine lost that portion of the day. While she automatically delivered her simple account to a ring of sober faces, she was remembering Miss Gaites.

The incongruity of seeing starched, immaculate Leona Gaites in such a state!

She must have given me a hundred suckers, Catherine thought, her childhood crowding around her.

The suckers had been a bribe to convince Catherine that Leona liked her.

It hadn't worked. Leona hadn't liked children at all.

So Catherine had disliked Miss Gaites, had not even accorded her the courtesy of 'Miss Leona.' She had disliked the way the starched uniform rattled when the tall woman walked, had disliked the hair that seemed set upon Miss Gaites's head instead of growing there.

Most of all, Catherine had disliked the pity she was obliged to feel for Miss Gaites, who had no family.

Her father had always praised his nurse highly to his wife and daughter, insisting with overdone joviality that Leona kept his office together. The forced note in his insistence told Catherine that even her amiable father could not find it in him to wholeheartedly like Leona Gaites.

Catherine remembered the tears sliding down Leona's square handsome face at the double funeral.

She shouldn't have died like that, Catherine thought, as she watched the coroner's jury being heaved across the porch and into the shack. A dog shouldn't die like that. Then Catherine remembered the dog's corpse she had passed that morning. The same person killed them both, she thought with surprising certainty. Driving too fast, to get away from what he did to Miss Gaites.

The coroner's jury viewed the body and came to the obvious conclusion. Murder, they found.

Catherine cast a last look at the covered figure, now bundled onto a stretcher borne by the two sweat-soaked cursing attendants, on its way to Jerry Selforth's eager knife.

As she watched the load sliding into the back of the ambulance, she saw one of the attendants gag from the smell.

Leona had always been so clean.

Catherine began to walk down the baked dirt road toward the sheriff's car. The coroner, Carl Perkins, fell into step beside her.

She looked at him with new eyes. Familiar people were no longer familiar. The anger and suspicion in Sheriff

Galton's face had shaken her out of taking for granted people she had known since childhood.

'Terrible thing,' Perkins muttered. He was obviously upset. His big hands were shoved into the pockets of his working khakis.

He must have been gardening when Mrs Cory phoned him, Catherine thought dully. She watched Carl and Molly Perkins working in their yard every weekend, provided she herself had remembered to have her hedge trimmed.

'Yes,' Catherine replied belatedly.

'I'm sorry for you, that you had to find her.'

There was real regret in his voice, and Catherine warmed to him. 'If I hadn't happened to shoot cans this morning—' she began, and stopped.

Perkins wrinkled his forehead inquiringly.

His eyebrows are too sparse to count, Catherine noticed. He's really getting old.

She spoke hastily to cover her stare. 'She wouldn't have been found for a long time, if no one had worked in those fields until—' 'Until the smell was gone,' she meant to say, but couldn't.

'You're right,' he said. He was angry: his voice sounded hoarse and strained. 'Wonder if Galton can handle this? All he's used to are Saturday night cuttings.'

They had reached the sheriff's car, where Galton was directing two deputies to stay behind and continue to search.

'Now, you come over and see us,' Perkins said earnestly. 'You've been a stranger since your folks have been gone.'

Yes, she thought. I've been a stranger.

'Is all your father's business tended to?' he asked into the blank wall of her silence.

'Yes,' Catherine replied, shaking herself. She would

have to say more, she realized after a second. 'Jerry Selforth bought almost all Dad's equipment. We were lucky to get another doctor in town so soon. Dr Anderson's so old that I know having Jerry take the practice is a relief to him.'

'It was a surprise,' said Mr Perkins. 'Not too many young men want to come to Lowfield.'

His bleak tone made Catherine raise her eyebrows. She didn't like Jerry Selforth much as a man, but the town had desperately needed him as a doctor. What had Jerry done to offend her neighbor?

Just then the ambulance started up, and the people by the cars had to step between them to let it edge by.

Catherine's thoughts flew back to Leona Gaites, and she scarcely noticed Carl Perkin's farewell nod as he went down the road to his Lincoln, in the wake of the ambulance.

The narrow dirt road became busy with flying dust and confusion as the accumulated vehicles reversed to point back to the highway. The cars formed a train like a funeral procession behind the hearse of the orange and white ambulance.

The black deputy was detailed to take Catherine's statement.

'Then head on over to Leona Gaites's house,' Sheriff Galton added when he was halfway out the door. 'Bring the camera.'

The young black man nodded briskly and turned to Catherine, who was huddled in a corner hoping she was out of the way.

'Miss Catherine, would you come over here, please?' he said, indicating a straight-backed chair by a scarred desk.

Catherine could tell from the set of Mary Jane Cory's back that she disapproved of this black policeman. The unnatural brightness of Mrs Cory's voice as she spoke to him contrasted sharply with the natural tone in which she spoke to a couple of blacks who entered the station as supplicants.

Catherine was beyond caring who took down her statement; but she was less comfortable with blacks in her own town than she was with blacks anywhere else. Upon taking up her life in Lowfield after her parents' death, she had found sadly that the old attitudes caught at her and strangled her attempts to be easy in an uneasy situation.

The deputy's name tag read 'Eakins,' Catherine noticed for the first time. Now she could place the familiarity of the man's face.

'Your mother is Betty, isn't she?' Catherine asked, as he rolled typing paper into the machine.

'Yes, Ma'am,' he said reluctantly, and Catherine felt a pit-of-the-stomach dismay.

Betty Eakins had been the Lintons' maid for years, until she had grown too old and arthritic to work any more.

Catherine had never called their maid anything but 'Betty'; and she had decided, after a year away in college, that that was a shameful thing. Catherine had not even known Betty's last name for the first years of the woman's employment. Catherine's visits home had been more and more awkward as her awareness of what lay around her became acute, to the point that Catherine was secretly glad when Betty grew too infirm to iron the Lintons' sheets. Catherine's parents had died before they could replace Betty with another maid.

'How is she?' asked Catherine. She had to say something, she felt.

'Mama's fine,' he said curtly. Percy Eakins's face rivaled Catherine's for blankness.

'She's a very old woman now,' he said more gently – whether out of fear of being rude to a white woman or

27

because he sensed Catherine's misery, she couldn't tell. She chose to regard his softened tone as absolution for the sin of having offended racially.

'I'll tell her I saw you. She talks about you all the time,' he said finally.

And their personal conversation was closed.

He took her statement in a meticulous professional manner, in question-and-answer form.

'Your full name?'

'Catherine Scott Linton.'

'Your age?'

'Twenty-three.'

'Place of employment and position?'

'The *Lowfield Gazette*. I'm the society editor.'

'Your present place of residence?'

'Corner of Mayhew and Linton.'

No one in Lowfield had ever felt a need for house numbers. The street her house faced had been named for her great-grandfather, when the town was bustling and the river was close. Now the river was two miles away, held in check by the levee, and Lowfield's population had not fluctuated appreciably in her father's lifetime.

'On the morning of July 11, what did you do?'

'I went out to some land I own, north of Lowfield.'

'For what purpose?'

'To practice target shooting . . .'

4

She came in the side door from the garage. Her coffee cup and the empty percolator still stood on the counter, waiting to be washed. The hands of the kitchen clock glided electrically smooth on their course.

She was almost surprised that the house was the same, so much had passed since she had left it that morning.

She stood in the middle of the bright tiled floor and listened. She had never done that before.

Catherine shook herself when she realized what she was doing, and started down the long hallway that divided the house, beginning at the kitchen and ending at a bathroom.

But she looked quickly into each doorway as she passed. She saw only the big familiar lifeless rooms, lovingly (and lavishly) redecorated by her mother. She paused in the doorway of the formal living room, where her parents had entertained, and suddenly recalled her father half-ruefully telling guests, 'Rachel's rebuilt this old house from the inside out.' It was the only room Catherine had changed.

At the end of the hall Catherine almost went right into her old bedroom. It's been months since I did that, she thought.

She went straight through the master bedroom to its cool tiled bathroom and shed everything she had on. She stepped into the shower, but not before self-consciously locking the bathroom door.

She had never done that before, either.

The shower was bliss. With cool water shooting over her, washing off the layers of dust and sweat, she was able to forget the shack for a few minutes.

She dried herself and combed out her wet hair slowly. She lay down on the big bed and hoped for sleep, but her body hummed with tension like a telephone line. Finally she quit hoping and got up, padding across the heavy carpeting to the closet and folding back a mirrored door to pull out a long loose lounging dress, pale gray and scattered with red poppies. She yanked it over her head and went down the hall to the kitchen, where she began searching the refrigerator.

Good. Beer. With one of those in me, I bet I can sleep. I'm glad Tom left some.

Armed with the beer and a fresh pack of cigarettes, Catherine wandered into the living room. She settled in her favorite chair, which she had pulled out of its original spot so she could look out the bay window. She had arranged beside it a heavy round table, and, some time later, another chair to keep the first one company. It was her own little base in a house too big for one person; a house still echoing with loss.

The old home across the street had been renovated into the town library. It closed at eleven on Saturday, so Catherine was just in time to see Mrs Weilenmann, the librarian, lock the front door. Mrs Weilenmann was the town wonder: an educated northern black woman, who spoke with no trace of the heavy accent white Southerners associated with blacks. And, rumor had it, Mrs Weilenmann, a widow, had acquired her name by marrying a white man. It was a bandage to Catherine's conscience that Mrs Weilenmann had gotten the librarian's job. The only wonder, as Catherine saw it, was that she wanted it.

I meant to go to the library today when I got back, Catherine recalled, glancing down at the heap of books on the floor as Mrs Weilenmann maneuvered her Toyota out of the library parking lot.

Catherine reckoned she had enough to read to last until Monday. And took a swallow of beer to celebrate that minor goodness.

A possible diversion occurred to her. She craned forward to see if Mr Drummond next door was holding true to form in his late-Saturday-morning grass mowing. But the lawn beyond the hedge that bordered Catherine's yard was empty. She was disappointed and puzzled. She faithfully witnessed Mr Drummond's ritual each summer Saturday. After a moment, she remembered that the Drummonds were still in Europe, and shook her head at her forgetfulness.

Perhaps she could move her chair to face a side window. She could look across Mayhew Street, see if the Perkinses were back at work in their yard.

It didn't seem worth the trouble.

I'll just sit and drink my beer, she decided. Maybe I'll think of something to do to use up this blasted day.

Her eyes fell on a half-finished book. She considered reading, but decided she couldn't concentrate enough. The book was a murder mystery. Not such a good thing to read today. Her mouth twisted wryly.

After a moment Catherine wriggled deeper into the big chair, stretching her legs to rest them on its matching ottoman. She drank some more beer. She was profoundly bored, yet very tense. She decided it was a horrible combination.

'Toes, relax,' she said out loud, suddenly recalling an acting-class exercise. 'Feet, relax.'

She had worked up to her pelvis when she was diverted by a car pulling onto the graveled apron at the end of the walkway in front of the house. She suspended her exercise in astonishment.

The car was familiar, but she couldn't place the owner. Not Tom, her only occasional visitor. He would merely stroll across to her back door from his own.

'It's Randall Gerrard!' she muttered. Her employer had never come to see her before.

She didn't realize the impact the beer had had on her empty stomach until she got up.

Instead of straightening up the pile of books, instead of fluffling out her damp hair, Catherine stared at Randall as he came up the walkway.

She itemized his heavy shoulders and thick chest, surprising on a man of his height. Especially surprising on a man who had, Catherine told herself, no butt at all.

The sun glinted on the thick reddish-brown hair of his head and beard, and winked off his heavy glasses.

How old must he be now? she wondered. Thirty-five?

She stood riveted and staring. Like a fool, she told herself when she finally roused. She had just begun to move when he knocked on the door, and she could only be grateful he had not glanced at the window.

'Please come in,' she said. The beer soaked her voice with a duchesslike formality. She blinked in surprise.

Randall's face, which had been grave, lit with amusement. She followed his glance down to her hand that had gestured him in with a gracious flourish. She saw, appalled, that she was still clutching the beer can. Her elaborate sweep had slopped beer all over her hand.

'Oh *damn*!' she muttered.

He said gently, 'Catherine.'

To her horror, that note of kindness tipped her into collapse. She began to cry. She twisted away to hide her face, covered her mouth to muffle the ugly sound. She hated for anyone to see her crumple.

A heavy arm went around her, and she instantly twitched away. But she didn't move when the arm firmly encircled her again.

She was somehow deposited on a convenient couch. She dimly heard footsteps crossing the floor and going purposefully down the hall. She looked up as Randall reappeared with a box of tissues. She blessed him mentally, and lowered her face. She was acutely aware of how dreadful she looked when she cried. As she cleaned her face, she felt the tears dry up inside her.

Catherine waited until she could hope that her nose had returned to its normal color before she brushed her hair back and looked sideways at him . . . and surprised something in Randall's face that amazed her, something unmistakable; though it had been a long time since she had cared to recognize it in a man's face.

Empty and giddy, Catherine felt a pleasant little jolt of lust. She had seen and thought too much of death to deny that positive celebration of life.

'Better?' Randall asked, with a fair assumption of gravity.

'Yes, thank you,' she answered with dignity.

He handed her the beer can. Catherine took a sizeable swallow. Her eyes were on his face – a Slavic peasant face, she thought darkly – as he looked around the room, zeroed in on her arrangement in the bay window. The soft chair with the dent her body had left, the paperback with a bookmark thrust inside, the lamp pulled over close to her chair surrounded by a litter of books: it looked like what it was, the habitual den of a solitary person. From where she was sitting now, Catherine thought, it looked pitiful.

'If you heard so fast,' she said hastily, 'then . . .'

An impatient knock on the back door finished her sentence.

'Tom,' Catherine said simply.

She was regretting the end of a promising moment as she went through the den at the rear of the house to answer the knock.

As she had predicted, it was Tom, her only full-time fellow reporter. His long lean frame bisected the doorway.

'Are you all right' he asked perfunctorily. His mouth had already opened to begin firing questions when Catherine cut him short.

'You might as well come on in the living room, Randall's in there,' she said.

Tom looked almost comically taken aback.

Catherine, bowled over by giddiness, nearly laughed as she preceded Tom into the living room.

'Hey, Randall,' he said casually, folding his length into an uncomfortable Victorian rosewood chair. Then he forgot to be offhand. 'The coroner's jury said murder, of course. And a *Gazette* reporter found the body! Jesus, what a story!' He yanked his fearsome Fu Manchu mustache so fiercely that Catherine thought he might pull the hair out.

'Calm down, Tom, it's not like there was another paper to scoop,' Randall said. He took his pipe from his pocket.

'Hey Catherine, is there any of that beer left?' Tom asked, sidetracked into showing Randall that he, Tom, had been there first.

'Three or four,' Catherine said. 'Randall, would you care for a beer?'

Randall accepted.

It seemed to Catherine that she took forever pulling out the tabs on three cans, pouring them, and putting the glasses on a tray.

Pouring them out seemed an unnecessary refinement, but she was determined to do everything right.

When Catherine came in with the beer, Randall and Tom were discussing rearrangement of the front page to handle the murder story. The paper only came out on Wednesdays, so there was plenty of time to think about it.

After she had handed the glasses around and resumed her seat, she realized the men were eyeing her with longing – for her story. Randall Gerrard and Tom Mascalco had print in their blood – the only thing they had in common, Catherine thought.

Randall had inherited the *Gazette* when his elder brother, for whom it had been intended, had shaken the dust of Lowfield off his shoes and headed for the fertile fields of Atlanta. In fact, Randall had abandoned a promising career doing something in Washington (Catherine couldn't remember exactly what), to come home when his father died.

However deep Randall's regret over that lost career might be, his raising had implanted in him enough of the newsman's passion for a story, and enough love for the Delta, to bend his will toward building up the *Gazette*.

Tom had worked for Randall for three months. He was younger than Catherine. The recent glut of journalism majors had made him glad to accept a job, even at the *Gazette*.

Tom was possessed, Catherine had observed, by a Woodward-and-Bernstein complex, which had led to some interesting clashes with Randall. Tom was restless with hunger for big stories, scandals. Catherine sometimes felt she had a tiger in her backyard since she had rented Tom her father's old office to live in.

'I'm all right, if you want to ask questions,' she said with a sigh. After all, she thought, I'm a newspaper person myself. In a rinky-dink kind of way.

'You sure?' Randall had the grace to ask.

'Yes.'

Catherine knew that Tom had only been held in check by Randall's presence. His pad and pencil had been ready in his hand when he knocked on the door.

In a clear monotone, she went through her story again. She wished it were more exciting, since she had had to tell it so often.

'Galton. Jerry Selforth,' Tom mumbled when she had finished, scribbling a list of people he wanted to interview.

'Who were her friends, Catherine?' he asked, pencil poised to write.

He looked up impatiently when she didn't reply.

'I don't know,' she said slowly, surprised. 'I don't think Miss Gaites *had* friends. She didn't go to church or to the bridge club, or anything like that. She told my father she saw enough people at the office every day to make her sick of them.'

And Catherine had to admit at that moment that her own attitude was much the same.

The thought of becoming a Leona Gaites frightened her.

'When was the last time you saw Leona?' Randall asked in his slow voice.

'When she helped me go through the things left in Father's office; things Jerry Selforth didn't want to buy. They had to be moved out of the house before Tom moved in. We put them up in the attic over there. Some old filing cabinets. I think a few other things.'

'Not since then?' Tom asked. 'I thought you had known her for years.'

'Yes, I have – had. But that doesn't mean I liked her.'

The two men seemed startled by this statement, which Catherine had delivered with bland finality. She returned their look impassively. They had not expected this from her, she saw. She really must have presented a skimmed-milk image.

'Have you talked to Jerry Selforth, Tom?' Randall asked.

'Just for a second. He hasn't done the autopsy. The pathologist in Morene won't get here till late this afternoon. From a preliminary examination, he doesn't think she was raped. She wasn't killed at the shack, either. She was already dead when she was dumped there. He thinks she'd been dead since early last night.'

'*Why?*' Randall asked himself.

Catherine's head swung up. She stared at him blindly.

A reason formed in her head. It caused her such pain that she couldn't recognize it for a moment. Something thumped and shuddered inside her. An enormous wound, compounded of deep grief and unreleased anger, just beginning to heal, broke open afresh.

'Did she have money?' Tom was asking. He sounded far away.

'Oh no,' Randall said. 'If she had, she kept it a secret and lived like a woman who has to be careful.'

Shuddering and screeching, about to be born.

'My parents,' Catherine whispered.

'What, Catherine?'

'My parents.'

'What did she say?' Tom's voice; an irritating buzz, like a horsefly.

A murmur from Randall.

'I thought they died in a car wreck.' Tom, clearer now.

'They were murdered,' said Catherine.

'And you think Leona's death ties in with theirs?' Randall asked quietly.

His voice steadied her.

'Oh yes, I think it has to be connected,' she said.

Tom looked bewildered, and angry about his bewilderment. They were talking about something he hadn't found out yet.

'Their car was tampered with,' she told him. 'They were on their way to spend the weekend with me. I was working at a weekly paper in Arkansas, my first job out of college . . . After they crossed the bridge into Arkansas, their car went out of control. Something—' and here Catherine, incurably machine-stupid, shook her head helplessly – 'something was loosened with a wrench, deliberately. The Arkansas police investigated the service station they had stopped at there. Sheriff Galton looked here.'

'They never caught who did it?' Tom was incredulous.

'No,' she said bleakly. 'How could they? Anyone could have gotten into our garage, Father didn't lock it. And it must have been done here. Why would a service-station attendant in Arkansas do anything like that? They were nice people . . . I met them.' She closed her eyes and leaned back against the couch.

She heard Tom rise, and knew it was because he was too excited to sit. I've made one person happy today, she thought.

'I'm going to call Galton,' he said eagerly. Without another word, he stalked out the back door.

She forgot him as soon as he was gone.

I've been waiting for this, Catherine realized. Somewhere in this little town he's been waiting, too, free and *alive*. Everyone forgot about my parents after a while. But now that he's killed again, he's drawn attention to himself. I've been waiting . . . She knew it now and was amazed she had not known it before. She was frightened to discover that this blood lust existed in quiet Catherine Linton.

But it was anger released. It felt good.

She opened her eyes to meet Randall's. He looked thoughtful.

'Go to bed,' he advised gently, and kissed her on the cheek. 'I'll come by tomorrow.'

She could hear him let himself out as she went obediently to the soft waiting bed. She didn't wonder at his sliding into the position of man to her woman, instead of employer to employee. She accepted the transition without question. As she turned over on her stomach and wrapped her arms around the pillow, she was able to forget her parents, forget Leona Gaites, for the moment before sleep swamped her.

5

Catherine slept dreamlessly until morning.

She woke slowly; saw early morning light seeping through the curtains, heard birds twittering faintly outside.

She felt weak but at peace, the way an invalid feels after a long and debilitating illness has passed its crisis. She turned on her side to peer out the gap in the curtains, and when she had absorbed what she could see of the morning, her gaze transferred to the curtains themselves.

They were an olive green to match the bedspread. It dawned on Catherine that she didn't like them, had never liked them. In fact, she hated olive green.

She would pick out new curtains, drive to Memphis and debate her choice with a saleswoman at an expensive shop.

I'll buy something light and striped and open-weave. I'll do it this weekend, she resolved. She swung out of bed and went to the louver-doored closet lining one wall of the bedroom. Her supply of clothes, most dating from her college days, barely filled one side of the vast closet.

And I'll buy new clothes, too, she thought. Shoes. She eyed her bedroom slippers with disgust. How could she have kept those for so long?

She went down the dim hall to the kitchen, looking forward to her breakfast. It wasn't until she saw the coffee pot, still dirty from the previous morning, that she remembered.

She sat abruptly on one of the bamboo chairs grouped around the breakfast table. She saw a hand lying in a pool of sunlight. Taking several deep breaths, she focused on the pattern of her robe until the worse had passed. With an immense and grim effort Catherine washed the coffee pot, filled it and plugged it in. From the pile of library books in the living room, she picked an innocuous biography of an Edwardian lady and sat at the glass-and-bamboo table reading the first paragraphs very carefully until the coffee had perked. After she had poured her first cup, she returned to the book.

She staved off the image of Leona's hand until she had finished three cups of coffee, two pieces of toast, and fifty pages of the lady's opulent childhood.

Then she moved to her favorite chair at the bay window and set herself to think.

If Leona's death was connected with the murder of her parents, what could the connection be? Leona and her mother had never been friends. So Leona and her father, nurse and doctor, must have seen, or found out . . . something to be killed for.

If that was so, if the two had died because they knew the same thing, had seen the same thing (whatever), why the gap in time between the murders? Catherine asked herself. Could Leona have been so difficult to kill that six months had lapsed before the murderer had had another chance?

She shifted restlessly. Hers was not the kind of intelligence that asserted itself in orderly trains of reasoning but the kind that mulled in secret and then presented her, so to speak, with a conclusion.

Instead of undertaking the calm application of logic she had set herself to perform, she found herself dwelling with resentment on the suspicion in James Galton's face when he told her that the dead woman was Leona Gaites. When Catherine's restlessness goaded her into the bedroom to begin dressing, she was still gnawing at the shock that suspicion had made her feel.

While she was brushing her teeth, Catherine decided she was arrogant.

Why should he *not* suspect her? In all the mystery novels she had read, the finder-of-the-body was suspect.

I never realized how much pride I take in being who I am, she thought. I expect my lineage to speak for me; I think 'Scott Linton' means 'above reproach.' The 'Catherine' – that's the important part. That's just me.

She looked in the mirror over the sink and surveyed the toothpaste surrounding her mouth in a white froth.

'Gorgeous,' she muttered. 'Like a mad dog.'

The word *mad* triggered another train of thought. Perhaps Sheriff Galton thought she was seriously crazy? Not just neurotic, but psychotic?

The anger she felt at the possibility was another confirmation, to Catherine's mind, of her own arrogance. She rinsed out her mouth with unnecessary force.

Of course, she brooded, she had reacted drastically to her parents' deaths. Who wouldn't? Especially when that loss was simultaneously double, untimely, and violent. A period of grief; natural, expected.

But people *had* begun to wonder – she had seen it in their faces, in their careful selection of topics – when the way she lived, holed up in her family home, became permanent. No invitations in, no invitations out. And by the time she realized how she had isolated herself, she had gotten used to it.

I've been working on it, she thought defensively.

The terrible jolts of the day before had shown her how far she had come and how far she had to go.

Like an arrogant fool, I didn't think anyone else would ever hold it to my discredit, she told her reflection silently (she was by now putting on her makeup).

Catherine glared at the mirror and made a horrendous crazy face at herself.

But Randall likes me, she reminded herself.

She picked delicately at the edges of that undeniable fact, half frightened. She mulled over the unexpected feeling that had passed between them.

Then she scolded herself, You're mooning like a fifteen-year-old. And she smoothed her face out and gave the mirror her best, her Number One, smile. It had been a long time since she had used it; it made her cheeks ache.

Instead of donning a long-ago boyfriend's football jersey, which lay at the top of the pile, she rooted deep in a drawer and pulled out something that fit quite a bit better.

The bells of the Baptist church were pealing for the eleven-o'clock service as she put in her earrings.

The church bell chimed in with the doorbell. Catherine opened the front door uncertainly, half doubtful she had heard it.

She had tentatively hoped it would be Randall. It was a dash of cold water in the face to see Sheriff Galton.

Oh, go away, she told him silently. I had gotten all settled, and here I am mad again.

'I'm sorry to bother you on a Sunday, Catherine, but I've thought of a few more questions I want to ask you.'

Galton looked as immovable as a transport truck.

Suddenly Catherine was no longer angry. She felt flat and depressed. She saw in James Galton the grinning man who had swept her to the ceiling in a deliciously frightening game, when he and his wife came to visit Glenn and Rachel Linton.

There was nothing fun about being frightened now. There was nothing fun about being the sheriff, either. James Galton's face had been sanded down with exhaustion.

'Please come in,' she said quietly, standing aside.

He sank down onto the couch with a barely audible sigh of relief. Catherine took the chair Tom had occupied the afternoon before.

For a minute or two they were silent. Galton was lost in some dark alley of thought. Catherine watched him, lit a cigarette, tried to relax. The feeling of being fifteen and in first crush had utterly died away, leaving her hardened, old, and alone. She resolved to behave like a normal, sane, balanced woman – a resolution that immediately made her nervous and fidgety.

'Well, I'll keep this as short as I can,' the sheriff began. 'I know you probably want to be by yourself' – and Catherine winced as her idea of her image in Lowfield was confirmed – 'but you know, Catherine, I don't enjoy this.'

She felt remorseful, receptive, and wary, all at once.

'Now, when you were driving to the shack yesterday, did you see anyone you know, anyone at all?'

Catherine reflected obediently.

'No. Well, yes I did,' she said, surprised. A blue pickup had been coming toward Lowfield as she was going to the shack. She remembered a friendly wave through a bug-spattered windshield.

'I saw Martin Barnes,' she said without thinking, still amazed that she had forgotten, especially since the sheriff had asked her who rented the land. Was she getting Martin Barnes in trouble? He was a pleasant not-too-bright man with a married daughter, Sally, who was Catherine's age.

Well, Mr Barnes is old enough to watch out for himself, Catherine decided with a new tartness.

'What was he driving?' Galton asked.

'His blue pickup. I don't know makes and models. But it was him; he waved at me.'

'Where do you reckon you were when you saw him?'

Catherine thought back. Her morning before she had entered the shack was blurry to her now.

'He was fixing to turn onto the highway, just as I was turning off,' she said. 'You know, there are a couple of houses there. One that Jewel Crenna rents. The other one's empty now.'

'The turn-off to the shack,' Galton observed mildly.

'Yes,' said Catherine and took a deep breath. Despite her every-man-for-himself resolution, she was still dressing things up. She didn't want to point any fingers.

Galton said intuitively, 'Catherine, *someone* did this. Maybe someone you know.'

'And maybe it was you,' whispered the silence that fell after he spoke.

'How long since you saw Leona?' he asked abruptly.

'Tom and Randall asked me that yesterday,' she said nervously. 'I honestly don't remember.'

Do drag in the word 'honestly,' she congratulated herself savagely. By *all means.*

'If you mean saw her around town,' she rattled on, 'I guess a couple of weeks ago in the drugstore. If you mean saw her to speak to, it was a few months ago – about three months – when Tom was going to move into the house in back, Father's old office. She called me—' Catherine stopped short.

'She called you?' nudged Galton.

'Yes,' Catherine said slowly. 'It was really kind of strange. Miss Gaites said she had heard that someone was moving into the old office, and she knew there were some things in there that Jerry Selforth hadn't wanted to buy. She wanted to know if I needed help moving them.'

Catherine remembered smothering her dislike, to preserve the false face of friendliness she and Leona had always worn when they dealt with each other.

A waste of time, Catherine thought now. And it had been funny-peculiar, her calling like that.

Catherine really had needed help getting those filing cabinets up the collapsible folding stairs that let down from the attic in her father's old office. And she had still been suffering from the 'be nice to Leona, she has no family' syndrome. So she had accepted Leona's help with protestations of gratitude.

Though why someone with no family would care to haul heavy things up flimsy stairs, any more than a person with seventy relations, is more than I can figure out, she said to herself.

'What did you talk about that day, Catherine?' asked Galton.

'Well.' She hesitated. 'The largest things that had to be moved were filing cabinets that Father kept patient files in. Some people still haven't asked for their files, to take over to Jerry's new office. Leona was saying how nice it was that some people were so healthy that they hadn't needed their records for such a long time; that now that the files were going up in the attic, it would be a lot of trouble when someone finally got sick and realized she had to have her records . . . I think I asked Leona if she had applied to be Jerry's nurse; and she said no, she had heard he had a friend who was getting the job, a girl who was going to commute from Memphis. That's all I remember.'

The sheriff's only response was a small movement of his huge hand. Catherine wondered if he had been listening. Then she thought clearly, He's trying to decide how to ask me something.

46

Catherine grew nervous at this hiatus and lit a cigarette. To break the silence, she asked quietly, 'How did she die?'

'She died in her house,' Galton said heavily. 'She was beaten to death. With something rounded and heavy; like a baseball bat.'

Catherine went very still and bit the inside of her mouth. Anything she could say would be inadequate.

'Catherine.'

Her eyes were blurry with tears of shock. She blinked and Galton came into focus again. She was warned by the sharpness in his face. Something important was coming up.

'Did you sell any of your father's equipment to Leona?'

If she had formed any idea of what Galton's question would be, that was not it.

'What? Why would Leona want anything from the office? I sold almost everything to Jerry.'

'What *didn't* you sell to Jerry?'

'Besides those filing cabinets in the attic—' Catherine made an effort to concentrate, but she was too confused to remember. 'Leona knew. She did all that, made the list for the lawyer. Father's estate. I was too upset,' Catherine said miserably. She had always felt some guilt for shoving the task off on Leona, though Leona had certainly been more qualified to do it. 'Maybe there's still the list of stuff for the lawyer? That you could check against what Jerry has now?'

Galton didn't comment on her weak suggestion, or explain why he had asked her, she noticed uneasily; but the mention of estates had given her something to chew on.

'Is there anything I ought to do? About Leona's house? Or about having her buried? She didn't have any kin, you know.' Catherine hated to offer, but knew she had to. It was the least and last thing she could do for Leona.

'Her lawyer, John Daniels, will handle all that, Catherine. She left a will. It's a few years old; and it's kind of surprising,' Galton said smoothly. 'She left everything – house, money – to your father. Now, I guess, it'll come to you. John Daniels says for you to call him.'

'Shit,' said Catherine. 'Is that what this is all about?' She was angry now, red hot. 'Come on, Sheriff! Leona didn't have doodly-squat. I know Father paid her what he could, but that wasn't all that much; and she hasn't worked since he died.'

'As a matter of fact,' Galton said calmly, 'Leona had quite a bit of money. But she was kind of informal about it. She had little wads stashed all over the house. The only thing she bothered to put in her checking account was her social security check and a little income from a pension plan she belonged to through some nurses' association.

'And,' Galton continued, his eyes searching Catherine's face, 'someone else besides me knows that. Sometime Friday night before you found Leona Saturday morning, someone took his time searching Leona's house: either before or after carrying her out to that shack on your place. Your inheritance is a little depreciated. Mattress slashed, chairs ripped open. But the money, and a few other peculiar things, are still there. Strange kind of thief. Didn't kill Leona for her money, but he looked mighty hard for something in her house after he – or she – killed her.'

Catherine shook her head. 'I don't know; no, I don't *understand* what you mean. If you think' – and her flame of anger flashed through the smoke of bewilderment – 'I killed Leona for money, I hate to say this, but you're crazier than I am. I can't believe we're sitting here talking about this. I've known you all my life. My father left me lots of money; my mother left me lots of money; there was insurance besides, and we – I own the land. In fact, I'm a rich woman. I did not bash Leona on the head so I could come into her bits of money. I did not search her house to make her death mysterious. And if you think I' – and the sweep of her hand down her body pointed out its smallness – 'could or would pick up a baseball bat or something, and beat a woman twice my size to death with it, you're just plain damn dumb.'

She sank back in her chair feeling clean. Something like a flushed toilet, she told herself bluntly and inelegantly.

Galton was eyeing her with amazement and a reluctant grin.

'I guess you let me have it with both barrels,' he said.

Catherine hoped he would add, 'Of course I don't think you had anything to do with Leona's murder.'

But he didn't.

'Why move the body at all?' she asked out of the blue. It was a point that had been bothering her. Moving Leona seemed an added risk. There was the chance that someone would see the murderer putting the body in his vehicle. And there was the undeniable conspicuousness of anyone at all being around and about in Lowfield in the late hours of the night. Though Friday night was comparatively busy, that didn't mean much.

'I've been thinking about that,' said the sheriff, sounding almost friendly. 'And I reckon whoever killed Leona was just trying to delay discovery of her body for as long as possible. She had plenty of neighbors. They would've noticed, after a couple of days of this weather, that something was wrong. But since she kept herself apart, they might not think about not seeing her for quite some time, if the body wasn't there to let them know.'

'Maybe someone just couldn't bear to see her lying there after she was dead,' Catherine said quietly, her hands running over the carved rosewood of the chair.

'And moved her so he wouldn't have to look at her while he searched. It had to be someone strong, didn't it?'

'Yes,' Sheriff Galton said, recrossing his legs. He shifted on the soft couch, and sighed. 'It was probably a man; maybe a woman, a tall woman, from the angle of the blows.'

She had never before been glad she was short.

'Or two people,' added the sheriff carefully. He lit a cigarette and leaned forward. 'You think to wonder what the killer was searching for, Catherine?'

She shook her head.

'Why, Leona was blackmailing people. She had another career going, but her main line was blackmail. We'll burn what we found so far – after we question the people involved. Just little pieces of nasty evidence she was holding for ransom; none of it criminal material. It's her other career that concerns us even more.'

After this revelation, Catherine was literally speechless. She could only wait for Galton to continue. His eyes were resting on her intently, and she felt her hands begin to shake.

'I have one more question to ask you, then I'll leave you to your Sunday,' Galton said heavily. 'Have you gone to Leona with . . . any kind of *problem*? Since your folks died?'

Catherine felt like a mouse being played with by a big old cat. Her thoughts were slow. She stubbed out her cigarette as she tried to recall, though she was sure she had never taken a problem of any kind to Leona. Her mind wandered. She tried to imagine herself crying on Leona's shoulder over some girlish difficulty, and decided that tears would have just rolled off that starched white shoulder.

When she looked at Galton again, she realized her long

pause had cost her something. There was once again a look of sternness in his face.

That's not fair, she thought despairingly.

'I would never take a problem to Leona,' she said. Her voice was as weary and watchful as Galton's. Even to her own ears, she sounded unconvincing.

'I thought it would be better if you didn't come down to the station again,' Galton murmured. There was a sadness, a regret, in his voice. He too was remembering the days he had swung her up in the air.

Catherine gave up trying. She had done her best, had cleared herself as thoroughly as she could. There was something, or perhaps several things, that Galton wouldn't tell her. He had obviously figured she would be more open in her own home, in a private conversation; he had made a concession to her in that respect. Somehow she had failed to meet his standards.

'I don't know what you want me to tell you. I honestly think' – Do drag in 'honestly,' Catherine! – 'I have told you what little I know. And I think what happened to Leona is directly related to what happened to my parents. I don't blame you for never finding out about them,' she added hastily. 'I know you were a good friend to my father.'

She had touched him on the quick. She wondered if she had meant to.

'I tried,' said Galton bitterly. 'You're damn right I tried! But I know why Leona Gaites was killed: she was a blackmailer, and something else too. And that doesn't have anything to do with Glenn and Rachel.'

He sat silent for a moment, visibly collecting himself. He looked so sad and worn that Catherine was unwillingly moved.

'You need some rest,' she said shortly.

'It'll be a while before I get any,' he said.

He rose, stretched, ambled to the door.

'Catherine,' he said, one hand on the knob, 'Why didn't you leave town, honey? What's kept you here?'

'You know, I've asked myself that just recently,' she said. 'I only found out yesterday. When I was telling Tom Mascalco what happened to Mother and Father. I want the person who did it to be caught. And I want him to be dead. That's why I stayed.'

'That Mascalco's a pest,' said Galton. 'His idea of his job is way too big. About that other, Catherine: it makes me sick to say it – you know how I felt about your folks – but I don't think we'll ever catch who did it. There's nothing for you here. You shouldn't have stayed – if you want unasked-for advice, too late.'

The complexity of being sheriff and suspect, family friend and bereaved daughter, tore at them.

'You be careful,' he said finally. 'I don't know what you've done, or what you know. I've known you to do some things that people thought were crazy. Well, in the Delta we've got a lot of crazies; known for it. Or maybe I should say *eccentrics*. Okay. But I've never known you to be bad or crooked. There's a lot of crookedness, a lot of badness, mixed up in this mess. So watch yourself, Catherine.'

He shut the door behind him.

She didn't know whether she'd been threatened or warned.

6

She was watching the sheriff's car back out into the street when her telephone rang. Maybe that's Randall, she thought.

'Catherine?'

'Sally?' Catherine asked uncertainly. She pulled out one of the bamboo-and-chrome dinette chairs and sat down heavily.

'Sure is, honey. I'm so sorry for you! You should have come and spent the night with us! I know you were scared out of your wits.'

How long had it been since she had talked to Sally Barnes? Sally Barnes Boone, Catherine corrected herself.

'I'm fine,' Catherine said, and made a face into the glass of the table. Once polite lies got into your blood, you never quit telling them, she thought.

'Well, I heard at church,' Sally was saying, 'and I just couldn't believe it . . . that poor woman! Daddy was so upset, that she was on that land he rents from you! He'd been riding the place that morning, but not close to that field, so he didn't see anything. I just can't imagine who could have done it. Someone from Memphis, I bet. Going through town to the fishing camps at the river.'

'I guess so,' said Catherine, who didn't think so at all. 'How is Bob?' She remembered, almost too late, that Sally had a child. 'And the baby?' A little girl, was it?

'Oh, they're fine, just fine. Chrissy's cutting teeth.'

'I know she's fretful,' Catherine said sympathetically. She had heard somewhere that this was the case with teething babies.

'Oh boy,' Sally answered feelingly. 'But I want to know about *you*. How are you? What have you been doing? I can't believe I never see you in a town this size!'

Because I have been taking care not to be seen, she thought to herself. I have been waiting.

She could hear a baby's wail in the background, on Sally's end of the line.

'Sally, thanks for calling, I really appreciate it,' Catherine said hastily. 'But really, I'm not scared. I just happened to find . . .' she trailed off. 'But it's not like it was in my *yard* or anything. I'll be fine. Thanks again. I can tell you need to go.'

The baby's wails were reaching a crescendo of pique.

'Chrissy, hush!' Sally said faintly. 'Bob, pick her up!' Sally's voice grew louder. 'Oh, Catherine, I better go, but you come see me real soon. I mean it, now!'

'Sure will. Tell Bob I said hello,' and Catherine hung up.

She absently noted that the top of the table was smeared. Her fingernails tapped along the glass as she considered what Sally had said. So Martin Barnes had lied to his daughter. He had said he had been out riding his place. Well, that was possible; every planter rode his acres, looking and assessing. But he had been near the shack where Leona's body was lying. And Catherine had the impression that Mr Barnes had not been driving from the direction of the shack but had pulled out from one of the houses by the highway. She tried to recall exactly what she had seen. No: she couldn't picture precisely where the truck had been before she passed it.

Catherine shook her head. It was a stupid lie that Martin Barnes was telling. She could see no reason for it;

he should have known she would report seeing him. Mr Barnes was a good planter, but definitely not the smartest of men.

Maybe he was the guilty one. If he was not the guilty man . . . her mouth twisted. This was loathesome. She wanted someone to be proved guilty; fast so no more suspicion would be attached to her. But she couldn't bear the certain knowledge that the murderer was someone she knew, someone whose face formed a part of her life. She had always known that but she had never been able to accept it. She couldn't think of anyone in Lowfield she imagined capable of beating a woman to death. Or of loosening an essential part in the car of the town's best-known and most-loved doctor and his wife.

Could it be that Lowfield contained two murderers? That the deaths of her parents and Leona were not related? Sheriff Galton clearly believed the crimes were separate.

A familiar tension, resulting from the suspense of watching and waiting, caused Catherine's muscles to tighten. She simply couldn't picture someone she knew plotting the horrible death Glenn and Rachel Linton had suffered.

Her hand came down flat and hard on the glass.

It left a print, and she retreated into wondering for the hundredth time why her mother had bought a glass-topped table. Catherine had gotten out the glass cleaner and a rag, turning with relief to the mundane little task, when she remembered telling Galton she was a rich woman. She shook her head again.

That was something you just didn't say.

The doorbell rang as Catherine was twisting her neck to look through a shaft of sun, checking to see if she had gotten all the marks off the table.

Does everyone in town want to talk to me? she

wondered crossly. For a well-known recluse, I'm having lots of company these days.

Molly Perkins, the coroner's wife, was standing with a casserole dish clutched in her hands when Catherine opened the door. Catherine had automatically looked up, and she had to adjust her sights down to meet Miss Molly's washed-blue eyes.

Miss Molly began instantly. 'I am *so* sorry you had such a *horrible* experience. I know you're upset. I won't stay but a minute, I just wanted to run this over to you. I knew you wouldn't feel like cooking.'

Food, the southern offering on the altar of crisis. Catherine was bemused by its presentation now. Finding a corpse must be close enough to death in the family to qualify.

'Thanks,' she said faintly. 'Please come in.'

'Well, like I say, I won't stay but a minute. I know you must be busy with company coming by and all.'

The plump little woman was trotting through the living room back to the kitchen.

'Company?' Catherine asked the air behind her.

But Mrs Perkins apparently didn't hear her.

Molly Perkins's whole body tilted forward when she walked, giving her the effect of charging eagerly forward at life. Her enormous bosom made her appear in danger of falling flat on her face at any moment, which had added a pleasant suspense to her company when Catherine was younger.

Placing the casserole on the kitchen counter, Mrs Perkins earnestly continued, 'I do hope you like gumbo. All these years up here, and I still cook Cajun. I always fix too much for Carl and myself. I just got used to cooking a lot while Josh was growing up. Can't change my habits now he's married and gone, I guess.'

56

'Thank you,' Catherine said again, determined to get a word in somewhere. 'And how is Josh?'

'We got a phone call from him and his wife Friday,' said Miss Molly happily. 'They're expecting. Carl is so excited. About that, and Josh is doing well in LA.'

'I know Mr Perkins is proud of him,' Catherine murmured. Her conversation with Perkins at the tenant shack was the only one she could remember that didn't feature Josh: his job, his wife (beautiful and of good family), and his brilliant prospects.

'I do wish they were settled here,' Mrs Perkins said wistfully. 'That's why we built that big house. Not many young people do stay in Lowfield, seems like.'

Catherine slid the gumbo dish back against the wall. She couldn't think of anything to say. As she remembered Josh, who was a few years older, the last thing he'd do would be to settle down quietly in Lowfield.

'I thought I saw a police car here this morning. I hope you haven't had any trouble?' asked Molly Perkins with a forced air of casualness.

So that was the 'company'; that was the purpose of this visit. The food, Catherine thought quickly, was an excuse to unearth interesting facts to relate at the beauty parlor.

'No,' said Catherine calmly. 'No trouble.'

Against the stone wall of Catherine's face, the little woman was visibly stymied.

'I guess Jimmy Galton has been mighty busy,' she said nervously.

'I imagine,' said Catherine.

The ensuing silence lasted a moment too long to be comfortable. Damned if I'll break it, Catherine thought.

'Well, I've got to be getting back; I hope you enjoy that gumbo.'

And Mrs Perkins trotted top-heavily to the front door, with Catherine again trailing behind.

'I got a post card from the Drummonds,' Mrs Perkins said abruptly.

'Oh?'

'They're in Florence, Italy. They'll be back in another week,' Mrs Perkins offered. 'They're having a wonderful time, they say.'

Catherine nodded.

'Well, I hope you enjoy the gumbo,' Mrs Perkins repeated desperately.

'I'm sure I will.' She noticed that Molly Perkins did not offer the quick hug and kiss that was customary on food-bringing visits.

'Can't let all your air conditioning run out the door!' Mrs Perkins concluded with artificial gaiety.

And off she trotted with an anxious backward glance at Catherine, who remained in the doorway with her arms folded across her chest until the woman had gotten down the walkway and turned right to cross the street to her own house.

When Miss Molly had entered the mansion's front door, Catherine slammed her own violently. 'Talk talk talk,' she muttered. Miss Molly had come to spy and pry, to report on Catherine's mental state and demeanor. And yet Catherine knew the pigeon-breasted little lady had also been genuinely worried about her well-being.

The phone rang as Catherine stood in the middle of the living room brooding over this duality in small-town life. She was bitterly sure the caller was not Randall: How could it be? That was who she wanted to talk to. She decided it was another sympathy call from some high school classmate she hadn't seen in years.

The irritating sound served to trigger the anger Galton and Molly Perkins had generated. Catherine said something that undoubtedly shocked the very curtains in her mother's living room. She had never in her life been able to take a telephone off the hook. The alternative was to leave the telephone. Catherine marched out her back door and across the lawn to Tom's house.

She pounded, rather than knocked, on the back door.

She was holding her heavy hair up off her neck, to take advantage of a slight breeze – maybe it would cool her down – when Tom answered. He was almost as surprised to receive a visit from Catherine as she was to be making one.

She had not entered the old office since Tom had moved in.

'Well, the landlady comes to call,' he said easily, opening the screen door for her to enter. 'Just come this way through the foyer, and don't scuff the marble.'

Catherine looked around as she went through the hall. Dr Linton's office had been a house before he bought it; now it was a house again. Her father had used the rooms at the back of the old house for examinations and storage. They were now Tom's kitchen and bedrooms. The living room had been Dr Linton's waiting room; now it had cycled back. Catherine took stock of the reversion.

'You recognize, of course, my furniture period – Modem American Battered.'

Tom's description was accurate. His couch and chairs were covered with mismatched throws, to hide the worst holes from sight – but not from sensation, as Catherine found when she sat down.

But the place was neater than she had expected. The couch, where Tom obviously had been lying, had a sad old trunk exactly centered before it to serve as a coffee table. On the trunk was a neat pile of magazines, a telephone aligned with the pile, and what Catherine supposed was a cigarette box beside a large cheap ashtray.

'You keep it nice,' Catherine offered.

'Oh, Mother Mascalco brought her boy up right,' Tom

said with a grin. She noticed that Tom wasn't sloppy in dress even on the weekend. He was wearing a sports shirt obviously straight from the laundry; and, amazingly, his jeans had creases . 'The bed, I have to admit, is not made. You wouldn't be interested in seeing the bedroom?'

Catherine shook her head with a smile. 'We wouldn't suit,' she said. 'Besides, what happened to your fiancée in Memphis? I thought one reason you took the job here was because you could drive up to see her on weekends.'

'She dumped me,' Tom said, with an attempt at lightness. 'Haven't you noticed that I've been lurking around here the past two weekends?'

Well, yes, she had noticed, kind of. But she had vaguely assumed he had fetched the girl from Memphis for some weekend housekeeping. Tom's visits to her house had been during the past two weeks, now that she came to think of it.

'Stuck here for nothing,' Catherine said, making a tactful effort to match Tom's light tone. 'Well, this job will look good on your résumé.'

'Yeah,' he said morosely. 'Want something to drink? Beer, orange juice? I have some milk, too,' he added apologetically, 'but I think it's past its prime. Or dope?' He opened the cigarette box, and Catherine saw that it held at least fifteen rolled joints.

'Yes to the beer,' she said.

'Turning into an alcoholic,' Tom said with a mocking shake of the head, as he unfolded his lanky frame from the low couch and went into the kitchen.

'You better watch out with this stuff,' Catherine called after him, putting the lid back on the cigarette box. She wandered around the room, then followed him to the kitchen. It too was neat, without being exactly clean. 'This little house sits in the county, you know,' she said 'and you'd have Galton to contend with rather than the town police.'

'You can't be serious,' he said incredulously. 'Why isn't the road in front of this house the city limit? There's only cotton fields on the other side of it! I feel like a planter every time I go out the front door!'

'I don't know,' Catherine said. She was looking around the kitchen, which her father had used for the shelving of medicines and supplies of plastic gloves and tongue depressors. The little stool Leona had used to get supplies from the top shelf was still sitting by the door. 'The line runs right through my backyard.'

Tom shook his head darkly at this piece of town planning, and Catherine wandered back out into the living room. The office – the house, she corrected herself – was as familiar to her as her own home, and it felt strange being a guest in it.

She sat down in the caved-in chair and leaned forward to see what magazines Tom bought. A photography glossy, *Playboy*, *Time*. The phone placed so neatly by the stack was a princess type. On the smooth back of the receiver Tom had pasted a list of phone numbers. It was not an extensive list. Tom was not integrated into the town's life yet, since he had been gone on weekends for the past months. Catherine noted that her own number topped the list. He really *doesn't* know any girls, she thought wryly.

But Tom was attractive in a long dark way, and Leila, the *Gazette* secretary-receptionist, had been giving him the eye ever since he started work. With the fiancée out of the picture, maybe Tom would wake up to Leila's adoring brown eyes.

'How did your dad stand having his office and house so close?' he asked as he handed Catherine her can of beer.

'The house I live in now was my grandparents',' she

explained. 'When my dad finished medical school and moved back in with them, they were already getting old. They had him late, and he was an only child. So he wanted to be close to them in case of an emergency, and my mother didn't mind living with them. This house was up for sale. So it was convenient to him.' She sighed. 'Things were different then. People would come at night—' and Catherine stopped dead.

She rose abruptly and walked straight to the door leading to the hall. She examined the door frame.

'Termites?' Tom asked silkily.

'Smartass,' Catherine said with irritation. 'No, look at this.'

He joined her.

'It's a buzzer, like a doorbell, and it rings in the master bedroom in my house. Dad had it put in so that if emergencies came at night, people could come into this waiting room and buzz him. I told you things were different then. He left the front door unlocked, only locked this door opening into the hall. I had completely forgotten about it.'

'My God, you mean I could ring for you?' Tom leered theatrically.

'Yes, but you'd better not!'

'It still works?'

'I guess so,' said Catherine, dismayed. 'Now don't go playing jokes on me, you hear?'

For a moment Tom looked as mischievous as an eight-year-old with a frog in his pocket. Then his thin lips settled into an unusual line of sobriety.

'No, I promise, Catherine,' he said. 'You've had enough shocks.'

'Thank you,' Catherine said with feeling. She sat back down.

Tom lit a joint. 'Sure you don't want some? Make you feel better,' he advised her.

She shook her head. 'Did you buy that here?' she asked curiously.

'Yes,' he answered, after he expelled the smoke he had been holding deep in his lungs. 'The other night. My first Lowfield dope run.'

'Not from Leona, surely?' Catherine asked impulsively.

'Christ, no!' Tom stared at her. 'What the hell made you think that?'

But Catherine didn't want to tell him that the sheriff had hinted that Leona had had something from her father's office – presumably medical equipment. She felt foolish for even thinking of Leona as a marijuana processor. Did you need medical things to prepare it to smoke? She could see Tom worrying over her rash question like a dog with an especially meaty bone.

'Come on, honey, you know something,' Tom coaxed.

He's sure not short on charm when he wants something, Catherine told herself. Tom had a convincing way of fixing his heavily lashed brown eyes on a potential source of information with melting effect; but Catherine had seen the trick too many times to be swayed.

'Save that for Leila,' she said callously.

'Leila?' Tom asked. 'What is this about Leila?'

His vanity, so badly bruised by his fiancée, was fully aroused. Catherine could tell she wasn't going to get out of answering his question.

'Oh, she likes you,' she said reluctantly, regretting she had introduced the subject. 'I can't believe you haven't noticed it.' But he hadn't, that was plain. He stroked his villainous mustache in a pleased way.

'She's a pretty girl,' he said thoughtfully.

'And just out of high school, and never been out of

Lowfield,' Catherine said warningly. Now shut up, she told herself. You've already made one mistake.

She didn't want to compound it by being fosterer and confidant to a relationship she thought would surely end in trouble. Tom was vain and immature; and Leila was too far gone on him before any relationship had even begun, and so very young.

Who am I, God? Catherine asked herself harshly. Quit predicting. You're not exactly the world's authority on men and women. How many dates have *you* had lately?

'Didn't you go out on Friday?' she asked Tom, changing the subject so she could stop feeling guilty. 'Have a date?'

'No,' he said sharply.

'I wasn't spying,' she said indignantly. 'I heard your car, and you know how hard it is to mistake any other car for yours.' (A defensive jab; Tom's Volkswagen was notably noisy.) 'I noticed it because I was trying to go to sleep.'

Tom relaxed in a cloud of pungent smoke. 'Sure you won't have some of this?'

'No,' she said impatiently.

'It's pretty good stuff for homegrown,' he said. 'No, I didn't have a date. I went out to buy this. It's not easy to set up when you don't know anybody. Took me forever.'

'Did you see – anything?' Leona had been killed Friday night, the doctors said.

'What do you mean?'

'I don't know, Tom. Anything?'

'You know what Lowfield is like on Friday night. I saw the high school kids riding around and around over the same streets. I saw the blacks who live out in the country coming into town to drink. I barely saw Cracker Thompson' (who was something in the position of the village idiot) 'riding around on his bicycle without any reflectors, wearing dark clothes. If that's what you mean by "anything." I presume,' said Tom, drawing out the words lovingly, 'you mean, did I see Leona Gaites dragged out of her house screaming, by a huge man with a two-by-four.'

Catherine shuddered. Though Sheriff Galton had told her that Leona was beaten to death, the reminder conjured up the same horrible pictures: Leona's outstretched hand; the flies.

Tom observed her shudder with bright eyes. 'Jerry told me that something heavy and wooden was probably the weapon, a baseball bat or something like that – the traditional blunt instrument. Anyway' – and Tom hunted around for his point – 'no, I didn't see "anything." '

Foolish, Catherine said to herself. I was foolish to ask. That must be good dope. Maybe I should have taken it. I could have had hours of entertainment just sitting and laughing to myself.

'But I might have,' Tom said suddenly. 'Maybe I can use that.'

'What do you mean?'

But Tom waved a hand extravagantly and laughed. Catherine eyed him as he slid lower in his seat. His spider legs were sprawled out in front of him. If he relaxes any more he'll pour off that couch, she thought.

'Tom,' she said uneasily.

'My lady speaks?'

'Don't . . .' she hesitated. She was not exactly sure of how to put it. 'Don't let anyone think you know more than you do.'

'Little Catherine!' He grinned at her impishly.

'I'm not kidding, Tom. Look at what happened to my parents. Look what happened to Leona . . . though the sheriff doesn't seem to think it's related.' She frowned, still not satisfied that the sheriff was right; though from his mysterious hints she knew there was something about

Leona's activities that Galton felt had led directly to her death.

'I know more than James Galton, that's for sure,' Tom said, with a whisker-licking effect. 'Guess who's selling dope in Lowfield?'

Catherine raised her eyebrows interrogatively.

'Jimmy Galton, Junior!' Tom laughed.

'Oh no,' Catherine murmured in real distress. If Tom knew that, who else did? All the kids in Lowfield, of course. Poor Sheriff Galton. Did he know? In his job, how could he avoid knowing? She wondered if Leona had known James Junior's occupation, too. And whether the wads of cash found in Leona's house were hush money paid by one of the Galtons to ensure she kept quiet. Money that was now coming to her, Catherine remembered, sickened.

'I wish you hadn't told me that, Tom,' she said bitterly.

'I'll comfort you, little Catherine.'

'The hell you will. I'm going home.'

'Oh, stay and have another beer.' And he gave her his charming grin. 'We can pool our resources.' His eyebrows waggled suggestively.

'Yeah, sure,' she said, laughing in spite of herself. 'Right now I don't feel like I have any resources to pool. Thanks for the beer.'

Tom made a gentlemanly attempt to rise.

'No, don't get up, you look like you'll fall down if you do. I know where the door is. See you tomorrow.'

'Yes,' Tom said cheerfully. 'I've got to write Leona's obit.'

On that happy note, Catherine shut the screen door behind her.

She had to lengthen her stride to hit the stepping stones that linked their back doors. The hedges between the houses joined the hedges running down the sides of the

66

yard, making an H of greenery. Her parents had planted it for privacy from the street on one side and from neighbors on the other; and to separate the office and home back-yards. It had gotten out of hand, and Catherine reminded herself, as she went through the gap planned for her father's passage, that she needed to take care of it.

I ought to do it myself, she thought. Then she looked down at her arms, too pink and tender from exposure to the sun the day before, and decided to hire someone.

What are these bushes, anyway? she wondered. She rubbed some leaves between her fingers, which of course told her nothing. She was trying to avoid thinking about the Galtons, Senior and Junior. Catherine stared at the growth blankly. I hate this damn hedge, she thought. I'll cut the whole thing down. Both yards are open anyway, and what do I do in the backyard that anyone shouldn't see?

The hedge was added to her mental list of things to change, which already numbered curtains, bedspread, clothes, and shoes.

It made her feel a little better, planning for the future.

When all this is over, she thought vaguely.

As she entered her back door, she heard the front door-bell ringing. No rest for the wicked, she told herself grumpily. What'll I get this time? An interrogation? A chicken casserole?

In this disagreeable frame of mind, she swung open the front door. Finally, her caller was Randall.

7

'Want to go out to the levee with me?'

'Okay,' Catherine said smoothly, dancing a little jig inside. 'Come in while I straighten myself up.'

She had only seen him in the conservative suits he wore at the *Gazette*. He was wearing khakis and a T-shirt. He looked incredibly muscular for a newspaper editor. He looked wonderful.

I am smitten, Catherine said silently as she gave her hair a hasty brushing in the bedroom. How long has it been since I was smitten?

She remembered as she touched up her makeup.

She had overheard the young man through her dorm window. He had been talking to a fraternity brother after he had deposited Catherine at the door.

'How was your date with Sphinx?' the fraternity brother had asked idly.

'Like dating Snow White. You never know if she's going to say anything, or if she does, what it's going to be; and you feel like she might have the Seven Dwarves in her pocket.'

He had never asked her out again; and Catherine had been too unnerved and hurt to accept a date for a long time after that.

But I'm not scared now, she realized as she dashed into the bathroom (wouldn't do to have to go at the levee).

She wondered, as she flushed the toilet, if Randall was so tempting because she had been so lonely for so long; because Leona's solitary life and death had forced her to wonder if she would be alone forever.

'I don't care,' she said out loud, zipping up her blue jeans.

She decided, peering in the mirror again, that she looked positively animated. The sun yesterday had taken care of her need for color. 'Though I wish,' she muttered, 'it had skipped my nose in the process.'

What the hell, she thought, stuffing her keys in one pocket and her cigarette case in the other. What the hell.

She had not been prepared to be so relaxed with him. She had heard talk of Randall all her life: her mother had been fond of his mother, though Angel Gerrard was considerably older. The two women, sitting companionably in the kitchen over coffee, had discussed their children; and Catherine, in and out, had heard (without caring a great deal, since he was so much older) of Randall's progress through college, graduate school, and employment with a congressman who was a Gerrard family friend.

Since Catherine had gotten a job at the *Gazette*, Randall had scarcely become more real. His presence had seemed so familiar, in a shadowy way, that she had never looked squarely at him. And during her first weeks of work, Catherine had been functioning automatically, in a state of shock. When her feeling had slowly returned, tingling as if her whole body had been asleep, she had come to know her coworkers bit by bit, but Randall had remained on the outer fringes. He was in and out of the office, selling advertising space, hiring delivery men, supervising the unloading of the enormous rolls of paper for the press: always busy. He was alert to the contents of his paper, writing stories himself when Tom and Catherine had too much on their hands. And always passing through.

He must be as used to hearing my name as I am to hearing his, Catherine thought, as they drove out of town in easy silence. This third-hand familiarity eliminated the need to exchange information immediately, as men and women usually did. Catherine became almost drowsy with comfort.

They were coming to the levee. The graveled road, which had been aiming through the seemingly endless level terrain of the fields, mounted to the levee in a sharp swoop.

She leaned forward a little, reliving the excitement she had felt at this abrupt climb when she was little and riding with her grandfather in his pickup. It had been as thrilling as a roller coaster.

Randall looked over at her and smiled.

A last lurch and they were on top of the levee. The graveled road on the top was barely wide enough for two vehicles to pass. On the river side, the green grass slope was scattered with cattle. It ran down to the trees that marked the edge of the marshy land bordering the river, though in places the slope rose again to modest bluffs that overlooked the water.

Some roads led down to fishing camps. Randall bypassed them, to Catherine's relief. The fishing camps were tawdry and depressing, with their ramshackle weekend cabins and litter of beer bottles.

'Where are we going, Randall?' she asked shyly.

'To the party bluff.'

She nodded. That was the right place to go today.

'I haven't been out there since I was in high school,' she said 'I hear they've put garbage cans out there, picnic tables. And some gravel to park on.'

'Yes,' he said 'When I was in high school, someone got stuck out there every spring. We would all be drunk as lords, scrambling around in the mud, trying to find wood to put under the tires. Our parents' cars, of course. Having to drive back into town in someone else's car, trying to get Danny at the Shell station to take his tow truck out there without phoning our folks.'

'Pooling your money to pay him,' Catherine murmured, nodding.

'Right,' Randall laughed, his memories chiming with hers.

They took the turnoff to the bluff. The road plunged down at what seemed an impossible angle. Catherine had a moment to think 'roller coaster,' and they charged down.

And down. The road, which disintegrated into a graveled track, began winding narrowly through choking undergrowth. The track had been built up to avoid flooding, but after any considerable rain, parts of it were under water. Since the weather had been so dry for so long, they didn't have to worry about that today. Catherine could see the roots of the trees sticking up like bare bones. Branches brushed the car. The road was roofed with interlocking greenery. Inside the car it was cool and dim.

Randall drove very slowly. The gravel had petered out, leaving only dirt, heaved and holed by the rain and then baked hard. The car rocked and shimmied.

After some twists, they began to climb again. The trees thinned, the driving was easier.

Catherine saw the shimmer of the sun on the water.

The bluff had been cleared of trees, leaving a large open area. There was a graveled turnaround, which Randall circled so that the car pointed back down the track. A couple of oil drums had been cleaned and placed in the clearing to hold garbage, and they showed evidence of heavy use.

'Much better,' Catherine said approvingly.

She and Randall didn't speak again until they had settled on the edge of the bluff. Below them the bank fell away gently down to the lapping water. The bank was concrete, old and broken in places, allowing the relentless Mississippi weeds to push their heads through the cracks. There was river litter, not human litter, scattered on the concrete – bits of wood and weed.

Catherine sighed. The bank of Arkansas was clear but tiny across the river.

She was content.

This was not like being with any other man. She couldn't explain to herself how someone so distant and so taken for granted could have switched positions so easily and naturally. She didn't want to explain, or worry, or wonder; or try to picture how he saw her. She was, for once, quite unselfconscious.

The swift and treacherous current swept a large branch downriver toward New Orleans. They watched it pass. The river spawned big sweeping thoughts that were best shared silently.

'Maybe a barge will go by,' Catherine said, after a time.

When she had been in her teens, a group of them would stand on the bluff and shout to the bargemen, their voices carrying across the river. The bargemen would sometimes sound the deep barge horn in reply.

'It's better at night,' Randall observed after a peaceful interval.

She remembered. The lights, shining over the dark water until the barge was out of sight around the bend in the river.

'We'll stay until one comes,' he said.

He inched back on his rear until he was behind

Catherine, his legs on either side of her. His thick fingers began to work gently in her hair, separating strands, combing them through. Catherine was catlike in her pleasure, her eyes half dosed, delight running down her spine.

'It's like a bowl, the rim of a bowl,' she murmured. His fingers brushed her scalp and she shivered. 'No beginning, no end. The river goes on and on. And kids come out to watch it in the night.'

'And barges come down with lights on.'

'The cotton grows,' she said, 'and they harvest it and plant more.'

'And there are the same roles to be taken in the town,' he said. 'Different people assume them. But they all get taken and worked, over and over – mayor, town drunk, planter. Newspaper editor.'

'Dogs get hit by cars,' she said, her voice sharpening, losing its drowsy dreamy pitch.

'And there are other dogs,' Randall said quietly. His hands rested in her hair, still, waiting.

'Other dogs,' she agreed after a moment, and his hands began moving.

She had almost lost their moment when she once again saw a large dun-colored dog lying by the side of a dusty road. But the continuity of the river, mirroring the continuity of their town, washed away that picture in its current.

They moved into the shade when Catherine's skin began to prickle. Randall lay under a dilapidated picnic table, reckless of ants and other interested insects. Catherine lay on her stomach on top of the table, peering down at him. She was not afraid of ants, not today, but she wanted to see his face.

'What did you do in Washington?' she asked lazily.

'I gave out the senator's press releases. I told people things. I leaked information on request.' He laughed.

'Did you want to come back?'

'Not at first. I had forgotten how it was. I was proud I was a citizen of the bigger world.'

'And later?'

'Well,' he said more slowly, 'I didn't resent the family-legacy thing after a while. Once I got back into living in Lowfield, it all seemed right and natural.'

'Do you miss Washington, and being in the center of things? A citizen of the bigger world?'

He thought. Catherine watched the ripple of his muscles as he put his arms behind his head.

'When I've been in Lowfield for a while,' he answered slowly, 'it seems like the center of things.'

'Can you see without your glasses?' Catherine asked solemnly.

'No,' said Randall and smiled. He took them off and blinked at her blindly. 'Do you get tired of writing up weddings?'

'They're all the same: only the names have been changed,' she said. 'I like it mostly. It needs to be done, and it keeps me busy. It makes people happy . . . Did you want to hire me?'

'I knew you could do it,' Randall said. 'I just wondered why you wanted to. Then I talked to my mother, who still has half-interest in the paper. She was absolutely sure that you were exactly what the *Gazette* needed. I think she had designs on you.'

Catherine raised her eyebrows.

'She was tired of my catting off to Memphis bars.'

'Oh.' Catherine blinked.

'Time coasted by, and I was busy and you were quiet and did your work and went home.'

Catherine said, 'Um.'

'And gradually, as I began to remember the reason I thought she wanted you at the paper, I began to look at you.'

'I didn't realize.'

'I know, and I was mad as hell. I said, "Randall, you're twelve years older than this girl, and you prance by her desk a dozen times a day, and she doesn't look up. When you talk to her, she just nods and goes back to work."' He opened his eyes to cock a look at Catherine. She kept her face still. ' "And she looks at you blankly," ' he said.

Catherine laughed.

'I practically doubled my running time in the evening and added five pounds to my weights.'

She reached down to touch his shoulder appreciatively.

'And I was scared to ask you out, because you were an employee, and how would you feel you could refuse? I didn't know how you'd react.'

'You came when I was in trouble,' she said 'I see you now.'

'This isn't how things usually go,' he said.

'I know.'

They saw their barge.

It swept around the bend in the river, majestic in the night. Its lights shone across the water.

Randall shouted, and the answering sound of the horn drifted, melancholy and beautiful, over the dark moving river.

'I have gumbo,' Catherine said, on their way back into town.

'It was contributed by Mrs Perkins; she's from Louisiana, and I'm sure she's an excellent gumbo cook.'

'Is that an offer?'

'Yes,' she said, shy again since they had left the levee.

'I'm hungry.'

The gumbo was excellent.

'Shall I stay?' he asked.

The weight of the next day descended prematurely. They would become employer and employee again. Then she couldn't stand herself for letting the thought cross her mind.

She was tempted to say yes, to get all the good out of this day she could, fearing it might not last, might never happen again. She had not trusted tomorrow for a long time.

She gambled.

'No, let's wait,' she said.

8

After the shock, fear, and joy of the weekend, Monday began badly. Catherine wanted to wear something she had never worn to the office before, in Randall's honor. But her closet held only the unexciting shirtwaists she had worn as a freshman in college, when girls still wore dresses to class. She had worn them all scores of times.

If Randall and I go out this weekend, I'll have to go to Memphis one evening this week and buy something to wear, she thought cautiously. I'm damned if I'll wear one of these.

She pulled on her least-faded dress, in a snit of anger at herself.

'Morning,' she said curtly to Leila Masham as she entered the *Gazette's* front door, which faced onto the town square. Her temper was not improved by the sight of long-legged Leila in a brand-new summer dress that bared Leila's golden shoulders. The girl flagged her down with an urgent wave, so Catherine had to stop instead of marching through the reporters' room.

Catherine expected inquiries about the weekend's big incident, but single-minded Leila whispered theatrically, 'Tom came in early this morning!' The girl's brown eyes were open wide at this unprecedented beginning to a Monday.

'He didn't have to drive down from Memphis,' Catherine whispered back, reminded of Leila's infatuation in time to stop herself from saying, 'So what?'

'Was *she* down *here*?'

'She' must be Tom's fiancée.

Leila would have to find out sooner or later.

'They broke up,' Catherine said expressionlessly.

She had given Leila the keys to heaven.

'Ooh,' Leila said, as if she had been hit on the back.

Catherine shook her head as she crossed the reporters' room to her desk. Tom was hard at work already, typing furiously, taking swift sideways glances at the notes by his typewriter. He acknowledged her with a look and a nod that said he didn't want to be interrupted, and hunched back over the keys. His long thin fingers flew.

'Such activity on a Monday,' Catherine muttered, whipping the plastic cover from her own typewriter. Then she realized that Tom was writing what would be the lead story, about Leona's murder. She paused with her hands in her lap, the cover clutched half-folded between her fingers.

I have a lot to do, and this can't get in the way, she told herself sternly. She stuffed the cover into its accustomed drawer with a resolute air, and pulled out a sheaf of papers from her Pending basket. As she flipped through them, she kept an ear cocked for Randall's voice.

Gradually, as she became caught up in her work, she forgot to listen. When that dawned on her, she thought, All to the good.

She was studying the layout of her society page – which she briefly sketched out as it filled up – when she realized with a jolt that Randall was standing at the other side of the desk.

I'm as bad as Leila, she thought ruefully.

'Movie in Memphis Friday night?' he asked.

She nodded.

'Won't you smile, Sphinx?'

She smiled.

As he walked through Leila's room into his office, she typed cheerfully, 'The mother of the bride wore beige silk . . .'

Catherine polished off two weddings with dispatch. She was glad she didn't have to actually attend the ceremonies. She usually dropped by the bride's house and extended her regrets, leaving a form to fill out that made writing the stories practically automatic.

Bridesmaids' names and places of residence, descriptions of everyone's dress, and details of the decorations at the short Southern reception. Groom's employment, bride's employment (this last recently instituted). Honeymoon itinerary.

Summer and Christmas were the wedding seasons. May was parties for graduates. Obituaries and children's birthday parties, anniversary celebrations and dinner parties, trips and out-of-town guests filled up the rest of the year. All of these appeared on Catherine's society page except the obituaries, which were scattered through the paper as fillers. Catherine wrote those as well – unless the death was unusual in some way, in which case Tom picked it up.

Leila buzzed Catherine's extension more often than any other. At the little paper, Monday and Tuesday were the busiest days, the two days before the paper came out, when people realized they had to contact her before the weekly noon deadlines. The *Gazette* was printed on Wednesday morning, distributed Wednesday afternoon.

This Monday was no exception. Catherine worked steadily through the morning, taking notes from callers and typing them up as soon as possible.

By eleven, her desk was an impossible clutter. It was

time to review what she had done and what she had left to do. Four weddings. One for this Wednesday's paper, three for the next issue. She carefully dated them. She had taken two more weddings back to the typesetter the previous Friday. She checked: yes, the accompanying pictures were attached to her new copy.

She put the copy in a basket and sorted through the other sheets of flimsy yellow paper. A little social note about the Drummonds' progress in Europe: that should please the old couple when they returned and read the back issues. A bridal shower. A baby shower. And two children's birthday parties. Catherine wrinkled her nose in distaste.

The last society editor had started this practice, and it was a sure-fire paper seller, but Catherine had always felt it horribly cutesy to write up infants' birthday parties. The stories were invariably accompanied by amateurish pictures taken by doting grandparents: pictures featuring babies sitting more or less upright in highchairs, often with party hats fixed tipsily to their heads. Catherine had long wanted to discontinue this feature, but in view of the papers it sold (every child having multiple relations who were sure to want a copy or two), she had never discussed it with Randall. The *Gazette* needed all the revenue it could get.

The Gerrard family was well enough off, but only because a wise forebear had made it legally impossible to put family money into the paper. Several generations of Gerrards had gotten ulcers achieving solvency for the *Gazette*.

One of the birthday stories for the upcoming issue was complete, with story written and picture attached. The other was written, but there was no picture. Catherine remembered as she read the first line of copy that this was Sally Barnes Boone's baby's party. It had been held at grandfather Martin Barnes's house; and Catherine recalled that Mrs Barnes had assured her that she would bring the picture in before Monday noon.

Catherine glanced at the clock. Damn, she should call. But she felt awkward about phoning the Barnes home. They might resent her telling the sheriff about Martin's proximity to Leona's dumped body. Barnes's wife Melba had a reputation for being unpredictable.

I guess she's one of those well-known Delta eccentrics that Sheriff Galton was so proud of, Catherine thought sourly. I'll wait until tomorrow, she equivocated. Maybe someone'll show up with the damn picture.

She hadn't had time to pay attention to what Tom was doing. Now she saw him through the picture window that made the repeaters' room a sunny fish-bowl. He was striding toward the courthouse, which sat in the center of the square, his camera in hand.

That meant he had already turned in his Leona Gaites story to Jewel Crenna, the typesetter. Catherine wanted to read it, and she had to take her copy back to Production anyway. She gathered up a sheaf of yellow paper and went through the swinging door to the big production room.

It was not exactly silence that met her as the backroom staff observed her entrance, but there was a definite, abrupt halt of activity. Catherine stopped right inside the door, surprised.

They want to ask me all about it, she realized after a second. No people on earth were as curious as people working in any capacity for a newspaper, she had found after she had started work at the *Gazette*.

Now Catherine straightened her shoulders, set her lips, and refused to meet the glances that sought to stop her.

Garry, the foreman, and Sarah, the senior paste-up girl, wouldn't have the face to accost her directly, Catherine figured rapidly, but she dreaded encountering Salton Sims, the pressman. He would ask anyone *anything* he wanted to know.

Catherine nipped quickly into the typesetter's cubicle. Jewel Crenna was hard at work and notoriously temperamental on Mondays and Tuesdays, so Catherine leaned against the wall behind her without speaking, and scanned Jewel's In basket. It was full to the brim with additions to ads, and last-minute amendments to stories Jewel had set the previous week. Catherine added her own sheaf to the pile and began searching the hook that held processed galleys of type. Jewel would have set Tom's story as soon as it came in, so the staff could read it.

Jewel glanced up once to identify the intruder in her bailiwick, and then her eyes swiveled back to the typed page held by a clamp in front of her, her fingers moving surely and with a speed that Catherine envied.

Jewel was a tall woman with suspiciously black hair and clear olive skin. She was a handsome woman with strong features and a tart tongue that knew no hesitation, a tongue that was widely supposed to be the cause of her two divorces.

Catherine had always had a sneaking admiration for Jewel, well mixed with a healthy fear. Jewel was an uninhibited shouter when she was irritated, and shouting people had always cowed Catherine completely.

Catherine skimmed through the justified type, getting the gist of Tom's well-written account. She raised her eyebrows when she found herself quoted. She hadn't said anything like what Tom had blithely invented. He must have felt free to take liberties since he was quoting a fellow reporter.

Oh well, she shrugged. The quotes were undoubtedly better copy than anything she had actually said; and they were truthful in content, if not in source.

She was so absorbed in reading that it was a while

before she realized that Jewel's fingers had stopped moving – an incredible event on a Monday. Catherine looked up to find Jewel facing her, broad hands fixed on her knees.

'I hope I haven't bothered you,' Catherine said instantly. She didn't want Jewel to let loose with one of the pithy phrases she used to blast disturbers of her peace. Jewel was aware that she was indeed a gem to Randall and the *Gazette*.

The whine of the press, stopping and starting as Salton Sims overhauled it, made Jewel's cubicle a little corner of isolation.

'I hear you told the police you saw Martin close to where they found that Gaites woman,' Jewel said abruptly.

'Yes,' Catherine admitted cautiously, wondering at Jewel's interest.

'Now Melba Barnes has got it in her head Martin was out at that shack meeting Leona Gaites for some fun, and found her dead,' Jewel said contemptuously. 'As if Martin would have anything to do with a plucked chicken like Leona Gaites! That Melba hasn't got the brains God gave a goat.' Jewel paused invitingly, but Catherine prudently kept her mouth shut. The light was dawning about Martin Barnes's presence on that road Saturday morning. He hadn't been riding his place at all: he had been at Jewel Crenna's house by the highway.

'Martin's a little upset about your telling Jimmy Galton you saw him,' Jewel said amiably. 'But he knows you had to do it; why the hell wouldn't you? Course, he was out to my place, not riding his land. Melba still ain't put two and two together – Martin and Leona, ha! – but she decided there was something fishy about Martin being out that morning. Up in the air she goes, stupid bitch! "Martin," I says, "just ignore her." When he comes home from church yesterday, she busts out crying and tells him now every-body's gonna know that he's cheatin' on her, how can she hold her head up, what about the kids (and them all grown), and so on and so forth.'

Jewel's voice had risen in a whiny and accurate im-itation of Melba Barnes. Now she resumed her normal robust tone. 'But I told Martin that Catherine Linton, she was smarter than Melba, she might figure it out; though of course,' and Jewel raised an emphatic eyebrow, 'she wouldn't tell no one. "She's a good girl," I said, "she's always kept her mouth shut tighter than a clam." '

Jewel gave Catherine a firm nod of approval and dis-missal, and Catherine silently replaced Tom's story on its spike and sidled out of the cubicle. She walked through the swinging door back into her own domain, knowing she had gotten a direct and forceful order to keep her nose out of Jewel's business.

Really, I think she overestimated me, Catherine thought with wry amusement as she rolled more paper into her typewriter. I don't think I ever would have thought of putting that particular 'one and one' together. There's a woman with nerve. She makes me feel like I just graduated from diapers.

Then Catherine frowned and let her fingers rest idle on the keys. Would Martin Barnes have paid blackmail to keep his affair with Jewel a secret? Jewel would have said, in effect, 'Publish and be damned,' but Martin Barnes was a different kettle of fish. Based on her limited knowledge of Melba Barnes, Catherine decided that if Melba had good grounds for divorce, she would take Martin for whatever she could get. And that would be a considerable sum.

Maybe Martin had gotten sick of blackmail. The pres-sure of trying to have a surreptitious affair in little Low-field, added to a bad relationship with a jealous wife, might have tipped Martin's scales toward violence; especially with the additional squeeze of having to pay hush money.

Sheriff Galton hadn't mentioned how much cash he had found in Leona's house. Had it all been blackmail money? How many people in Lowfield had secrets they would pay to keep hidden?

A week ago Catherine would have said, 'Not many.' But yesterday Tom had told her about Jimmy Galton Junior's drug sales. Today Jewel Crenna had told her she was having an affair with a prominent planter.

How many more people had mud tracking up their homes? And Sheriff Galton had hinted strongly at some other illegal activity the former nurse had engaged in.

It's a comment on how I felt about Leona, that I can accept the fact that she was a blackmailer, without being awfully surprised, Catherine reflected.

The swinging door rocked back and forth as Salton Sims, the *Gazette*'s press operator, came through. Salton approached everything at an angle, so until the moment he ended up at the side of her desk, Catherine had hopes she would be bypassed. Salton had appeared to be heading toward the filing cabinets.

'I missed seeing you when you was in the back,' he said cheerfully.

Catherine's heart sank. No escape. Salton was known and dreaded throughout the county for his complete tactlessness and his equally complete determination to have his say.

'Bet that ole Leona Gaites was a sight with her head bashed in,' Salton began. 'Bloody, huh?'

Catherine cast around for help, but Tom was still away at the courthouse.

'Yes, Salton, she sure was, and I'd just as soon not discuss it, if you don't mind,' Catherine said hopefully.

Salton stuck his hands in the pockets of his grease-soaked jump suit and grinned at Catherine.

'Well, you know what I say?' he asked her.

'I'll bet you're going to tell me.'

'Damn right! No one can call me two-faced.'

Boy, that's the truth, she thought.

'I say,' he continued, 'that it's a good thing.'

'Salton!' She shouldn't have been shocked, but she was. Out of the corner of her eye, she saw Leila come into the room and begin filing at the bank of cabinets. Maybe Leila's presence would inhibit Salton, who thought all females under twenty were sacred. But no such luck.

'No, Catherine, you just think about it. It was a good thing. Leona was a godless woman.'

'Godless?' repeated Catherine weakly. How long has it been since I heard anyone called that? She wondered. Only Salton would use that adjective.

'Sure, sure. I know for a fact, from a lady I won't name, that she killed babies.'

Catherine finally understood what Leona had used some of Dr Linton's equipment for. She glanced at Leila desperately and saw that Leila was shaken to the bone, staring in horror at Salton's broad face.

'I guess you mean that she performed abortions,' Catherine said slowly.

'That's what a lady told me,' Salton said with satisfaction.

'But they're legal,' Catherine protested. 'You can get them thirty miles away in Memphis.' Were they legal in Mississippi? She couldn't remember.

'Too many people from here go to Memphis every day,' Salton rebutted. 'Any kid from here who went to Memphis for a thing like that would be caught in a minute. And what teenager could leave here for two days to go to

Jackson, without their parents finding out what for and why?'

'True,' Catherine admitted.

'Well, back to that cursed old press,' Salton said happily, and wandered swiftly through the door, by some trick appearing until the last minute to be on a collision course with the wall.

Abortions. Wonderful. Abortion and blackmail payments: what a legacy I've inherited! That's where those medical instruments went: Leona was supplementing her Social Security.

Catherine caught herself bundling all her hair together and holding it on top of her head, a nervous habit she thought she had discarded with college exams. But she remained like that, both elbows out in the air, until she caught sight of Leila, whom she had completely forgotten.

Leila seemed equally oblivious of Catherine. She was still looking at the swinging door through which Salton had passed, her face so miserable that Catherine felt obliged to ask her if she was feeling sick.

'Listen,' said Leila urgently, then stopped to look back through the archway that led into the reception area. There was no one there, but Leila came and sat close to Catherine's desk. The girl was still clutching a handful of bills she had been filing.

'Listen,' she said again, and hunched over until her face was five inches from Catherine's. Catherine had to resist an urge to lean back.

'I'm listening,' Catherine said sharply. She had an ominous feeling she was about to hear yet another secret.

'She *did*,' Leila hissed dramatically.

'Perform abortions?'

'Yeah, sure,' Leila whispered. 'Listen, I know you won't tell on me . . .'

Everyone certainly seems to be sure of *that*, Catherine thought fleetingly.

'. . . but she "did" me. It's like Mr Sims says, how could I just tell my parents I was going to be out of town for two days?'

'When was this?'

'Five months ago.'

After Father died, Catherine realized with relief. Leona just kept some of the equipment when Jerry bought the rest. At least it wasn't while her Father was alive.

'I went up to Memphis and asked, but it was awful expensive.'

'Leona was cheap?'

'Oh, yeah, compared to Memphis. But I think she charged more later. I was one of her first.'

Catherine felt sick.

'I'm sorry, Leila.' It was all she knew to say.

'Oh, well.' Leila waved a polished hand to dismiss her former predicament. 'What I'm scared of,' she went on urgently, 'is the sheriff will tell, if he finds out. My parents, you know. I mean, what if Miss Gaites kept records?'

'Come on, Leila,' Catherine said tartly. 'She would hardly have a receipt file!'

Leila pondered that.

'I guess you're right,' she said. 'I mean, she was breaking the law. So she probably wouldn't have written anything down. And you had to pay her cash.'

Catherine imagined Leila trying to write a check for Leona's services and winced.

Leila, now that her immediate fear was banished, looked brighter by the second. She straightened her shoulders, leaned back in her chair, and gave her pink fingernails a once-over. Catherine was glancing at her notes surreptitiously, longing to return to something normal and humdrum, when the girl began to frown.

'How did you know about Tom's fiancée?' Leila asked abruptly.

'What?' Catherine made herself pay attention.

'Tom,' Leila prompted. 'When did he tell you?'

'That they broke up?' Catherine made an effort to remember. 'I guess it was yesterday.'

'He over at your place?' asked Leila, with badly feigned indifference.

'Oh,' Catherine said, enlightened 'No, I went over to his house' (that just made it worse, she saw instantly) 'and he happened to mention it in the course of the conversation.'

And I was trying to do her a good turn, Catherine reflected gloomily, as Leila shot her a look and rose from her chair. Leila returned to her filing, back pointedly stiff, slamming home the drawers of the cabinets with all her strength.

It seemed a good time to go to lunch.

9

Catherine spent the afternoon dodging conversations. She didn't want to hear any more secrets or opinions.

The entire staff was aware of her penchant for long silences, and when she gave minimal answers to direct questions she couldn't avoid, they got the point.

Finally Catherine caught up with her work. She had deposited with Jewel everything urgent she had pending, with the nagging exception of the Barnes's grandchild's birthday-party piece.

She had seen a couple of stories by Randall on the 'set' spike when she carried her own things back. In addition to turning out editorials, Randall had to report the occasional event, when Catherine and Tom were too busy to cover it. The *Gazette* simply couldn't afford another reporter, even though another pair of hands at a typewriter would often have been welcome, particularly in the fall when high school sports started up.

Catherine remembered the time she had had to cover a basketball game, during the hiatus between Tom's predecessor's departure and Tom's arrival. It had been a fiasco, and she shuddered to recall it, even months later.

Mrs Weilenmann, the head librarian, came in to give Catherine the schedule for the next month's special library programs. Catherine thanked her whole-heartedly for the neatly typed listing. (All too often, people brought in scrawls that Catherine had to type up to decipher.) In a gush of gratitude, she promised to place it prominently in the next issue, with a border around it.

'Catherine,' the tall middle-aged woman said slowly, after she had gathered up her paraphernalia to leave, 'I'm worried about you and your situation.'

Catherine stared blankly at Mrs Weilenmann's toffee-colored face. Mrs Weilenmann was intelligent, ugly, and charming; and Catherine had grown fond of her. But they had never had a really personal conversation.

'It occurred to me this morning,' Mrs Weilenmann said hesitantly, 'when I was getting the books out of the book-drop (and someone's hit it again; why can't people control their cars?) – well, it occurred to me that you are a little isolated now.'

Catherine couldn't think of anything to say, so she waited.

'Not – socially; I don't know about that. But geographically.'

'Oh?' murmured Catherine, mystified.

'Well, dear, I don't mean to make you nervous,' Mrs Weilenmann said in her peculiarly formal diction, 'but the Drummonds are gone, aren't they? Having a great time, I hear, but they won't be back for a couple of weeks. And the library is closed at night, in the summer, after six on weekdays; and for most of the weekend. So to one side of you and across from you, there's no one. And on the other side of you, the street. But no one can see your yard from the street, because of the hedge. And behind you, there's the hedge again, so the other reporter (he still rents from you, doesn't he?) can't see your back yard. And being single, I imagine Mr Mascalco isn't there often. At night.'

Catherine gathered her hair up in a bundle and held it on top of her head.

'I don't mean to frighten you. I guess this sounds like I'm trying to. Really, I think I shouldn't have said anything. But I hate to think of you alone in your house at night. Now I'm sorry I started this,' she finished in a distressed rush.

'What all this was leading up to (now that I've made a fool of myself by scaring you out of your wits) is that if you would like to stay with me, until this incident gets cleared up, I would love to have you.'

And in Lowfield that was, though Catherine could never compliment her for it, a remarkably brave offer from a black woman to a white woman. Not only was Mrs Weilenmann risking a shocked refusal, but, if Catherine accepted, Mrs Weilenmann would be extremely cramped in her rented crackerbox of a house – which was situated, like Bethesda Weilenmann, in a gray area between the black and white parts of town.

'It sure is kind of you to offer,' Catherine said slowly. 'I really appreciate it. But I think I won't take you up on that, unless I get scared.' That seemed inadequate, and Catherine groped around for another way to explain.

'You like being on your own,' Mrs Weilenmann said unexpectedly and accurately. 'I can understand; I do too. It isn't easy for me to be "company" even overnight. I like to leave and go back to my own place, such as it is.' Her face turned up in a smile. 'So I do understand. But if you reconsider, I have a cot I can set up, and it would be no trouble at all. You're a brave young woman, Catherine. And you're not stupid, not stupid at all.'

Catherine thought sadly that Mrs Weilenmann must have been very disappointed in many people, to be so firm in praising these paltry recommendations.

'Thanks for your good opinion,' Catherine said, and gave Mrs Weilenmann one of her own rare smiles.

'I'll see you, then,' Mrs Weilenmann said briskly, and headed back to her library.

Mrs Weilenmann's article would have an extra-thick border, Catherine resolved.

It had been a long day, even for a Monday. Catherine was covering her typewriter with a definite sense of relief as Tom walked in.

'I haven't seen you since this morning,' she said idly. 'Have you been working on the story about Leona?'

'Yeah,' Tom replied, one hand on the door. 'I took my basic story back to Jewel this morning, but I told her to expect additions. I've interviewed everyone who knows anything, and I haven't come up with a damn thing more than I knew this morning.'

'You've been doing that all day?'

'No. I went to the Lion's Club meeting, too, for their usual ham and potato salad fest and speeches. The lieutenant governor spoke today. And then I had trouble with my car. I'll have to take it into the shop again now.'

'Too bad,' Catherine said politely. 'See you tomorrow.'

She began walking to her car, which was parked across the street by the courthouse.

'Catherine!'

She turned and saw Randall hurrying across the street after her.

As she watched him come toward her, she realized she had been too busy all day to think about the date he had made with her that morning.

'How was today?' he asked.

'If you really want to know—' she said, and laughed.

'Salton been asking too many graphic questions?'

'Salton,' said Catherine, shaking her head. 'Salton says, and I have it from another source, that Leona was an abortionist. That explains something Sheriff Galton said to me yesterday.'

'Good God,' Randall said mildly. 'I had no idea we had a village abortionist.' He brooded for a moment. 'What did Galton say yesterday?' he asked finally, frowning.

'He asked if I sold to Leona, or knew she had, some things from Father's office. A sterilizer and instruments, I suppose, from what she seems to have been doing to support herself in her retirement.' Catherine's voice was arid.

'He thinks you knew? Aided and abetted?'

'Yes. Or alternatively, that I was a customer.'

Randall touched her hand.

'Oh well. I can't convince him different,' she said. '*And* that's not all.'

'More? You *have* had a busy day.'

'I'll tell you now. We didn't talk about this yesterday,' Catherine said, putting her purse on the car hood and leaning against the driver's door. He settled companionably beside her.

'Leona left her money, her house, the whole kit and kaboodle, to my father. Naturally, she had made this will before he died, and just never changed it. I wish to God she had.'

'You're the legatee now?'

'So it seems. Sheriff Gallon apparently thinks that constitutes a motive for me . . . and I guess it would, at that, if I didn't have some money of my own. I like money,' she said simply, 'but I'm not avid for more.' She paused to return the wave of Mrs Brighton, the mayor's secretary.

'But to keep to the track – Sheriff Galton didn't give me a figure, but it seems there was quite a lot of money stashed in that little house. Now, I can't imagine that many girls in Lowfield needed abortions. I think the bulk of it has to be blackmail payments.'

Randall nodded thoughtfully. She wanted to touch his hair.

'I have evidently been living in a dream,' Catherine went on quietly, 'because I am really – flabbergasted – that so many people in Lowfield were blackmailable, if that's a word.'

'Who? Did Galton name names?' asked Randall, looking at the ground.

Catherine was sharply reminded that Randall was a newspaper editor, in the business of spreading information. She became acutely uneasy at the way he was carefully avoiding her eyes. It was a moment of testing; she saw that painfully. Maybe I am brave, like Mrs Weilenmann said, she thought bleakly. She had opened her mouth to speak, when a new line of thought occurred to her. She asked, 'Randall? Not you? Blackmail?'

He looked sad behind his glasses. He knew as well as she that this was a test of faith that had come too early; she could see that in his face.

He took a deep breath. 'Not me,' he said. 'Maybe my mother.'

Catherine had tensed, afraid that they were going to shatter their fragile beginning. Now she relaxed.

'Miss Angel?' she said, incredulously. 'I thought she was made of iron.'

'She is,' he answered with a half-smile. 'But she has her chink. My father. He was a famous man, Catherine, at least in this state, and the newspaper is such a family tradition. Even a little weekly newspaper can become a name, when people like my grandfather and father run it. They were crusaders in their way. Brilliant men. Men who always had enemies.

'And my father, I've found out, once took a bribe.'

'You don't have to tell me,' she said swiftly, dismayed.

'Well, just the outline.' He took a moment to frame

what he wanted to say. 'The paper was losing money. Crusaders lose advertising revenue. Even though this is the only paper in the county, some people would rather rely on word-of-mouth, or advertising in the Memphis papers that everyone here takes, than pay money to the *Gazette*; at least while Dad was running it. And you know our family money was tied up by my great-grandfather; we can't pump it into the *Gazette*. So at a critical point my father accepted some money from someone running for office, to keep the paper going. The candidate didn't want one of his activities made known. My father was the only newspaperman who knew of this – activity.' Randall pulled off his glasses and rubbed his eyes.

Catherine was trying to hide her shock Randall's father had been one of her heroes.

'My mother found out after he died, when she went through his personal papers. I reckon she thought she had hidden all the traces, but I found them when I took over the paper, and I asked her about it. She told me, finally. And I know she would give anything to have no one else on earth know.'

Catherine felt honored that Randall had shown confidence in her.

'I don't think you should worry,' she said gently. 'I don't see how Leona could have known – unless your father told mine at his office, where she could have heard.'

'It's possible. They were friends. Close friends.'

'You've been brooding about this.'

'Not yesterday,' he said, with the ghost of a smile. 'But today, yes, I have. I heard rumors Saturday night, about Leona's – sideline. One of the deputies couldn't keep his mouth shut about the blackmail material and money they found in Leona's house. Or maybe Galton wanted that leaked, to stir things up and see what rose to the surface.'

'Miss Angel,' Catherine began, and faltered. 'You know

your mother better than anyone else, I'm sure. But from what I know of Miss Angel, I'd just out-and-out ask her if she had been paying Leona to keep quiet. Your mother's that kind of woman. I think if she'd wanted to do away with Leona, she would've shot her on the courthouse steps at high noon.'

'I think so too,' Randall said, and grinned at her. 'Now that I've spilled my guts, what about yours?'

With no hesitation, she told him about Jewel Crenna and Martin Barnes, and about Sheriff Galton's son.

Randall whistled.

'Sounds like the entire population of Lowfield might have had excellent reasons to want Leona dead.'

'I know,' Catherine said. 'I was so positive that the reason Leona died was the same reason my parents died. Now, I'm not sure.'

'Does it eat at you? Your parents?'

'How could it not? Vengeance sounds melodramatic, the very word . . . but that's what I want. I want vengeance.' She stopped. 'This may not be what you want a woman to say to you, or what you want a woman to be.' She clenched her fists and tried to pick her words with absolute accuracy. 'But at my core, where I really live, I want vengeance on whoever killed my parents. My mother and father should not have died like that. It has altered me.'

'I would wonder,' he said quietly, 'only if you didn't feel that way.'

They stirred, shaking off the grip of strong emotions, ready to turn to light things, normal subjects.

'Pick out a movie you want to see Friday,' Randall said. 'Early showing or late?'

'Late. We'll have dinner first, if that suits you.'

He opened her car door with an exaggerated flourish.

'I declare, sir, how kind of you,' Catherine said with an extravagant drawl and a simper.

Randall choked a surprised laugh.

'I am your servant, you sweet flower of Southern womanhood,' he responded instantly.

She gripped his hand for a second and then started the engine. She watched him walk back into the office before she pulled out to go home.

It was a lackluster evening. Catherine found herself wandering around the house in search of something to do.

I'm completely shaken out of pattern, she reflected. And a good thing, too. Not much of a pattern to stick to.

There was dust on the furniture, and the bathroom needed a thorough scrubbing. This lack of order made Catherine irritable, but she was too restless to begin clearing it up.

When she started putting the clean dishes back into the kitchen cabinets, she came to a stop as her hand fell on an unfamiliar shape. Mrs Perkins's casserole dish. Returning it was something concrete and necessary. She marched out her front door in a glow of virtue.

I'll thank her so nicely and be such a lady she won't be able to say a word about me, Catherine resolved.

The long summer day was fading as she left her house. She stopped on her doorstep to drink in the evening. The sky in the west was stained a dark strawberry-juice pink. The locusts were in full voice, their drone rising and falling in hypnotic rhythm. The humid warmth made her skirt limp against her legs, but the air was no longer stifling. As she moved on with a slower step, the grass rustled around her feet.

The streetlights were on. Catherine emerged from her yard onto the silent street, passing under the lamp at the corner. As she crossed the pavement, she barely bothered to glance right and left. It was a time for quiet in Lowfield.

She was embraced by the dusk, cast back for a few minutes into the time before Saturday, when she had felt shielded by the safety of her own town, street, and house, her unassailable heritage of land and good family.

Catherine sighed as she walked up the gleaming white concrete to the Perkins's pillared verandah. As she lifted the polished brass knocker, she returned to the present.

It was a signal of her intention to be formal that she went to the front door, instead of to the back as a good neighbor would.

Carl Perkins answered the door. Catherine had been expecting Miss Molly, for some reason, and for a moment she was startled as his thickened frame filled the doorway. She wondered how he could endure the long sleeves he always wore. As a gust of air from the house rushed out to meet her, she decided she understood his preference, at least in his own home. The air was not only cooled, it was refrigerated.

'Catherine Linton! Come on in,' he said, with no trace of surprise, only welcome.

He ushered her through the two-story entrance hall and into the living room. Miss Molly, dwarfed in the corner of an enormous beige couch, rose as Catherine entered. The little woman had some knitting in her hand, and she carefully set it down before she advanced to greet Catherine.

'I enjoyed the gumbo so much,' Catherine said, smiling her most correct smile and extending the casserole dish to Miss Molly, who looked mildly flustered.

'So glad you enjoyed it, just some leftovers really,' Molly Perkins deprecated properly. She took the proferred dish and went full tilt toward the back of the house, where, Catherine remembered, the enormous kitchen lay.

'Bring our neighbor some coffee,' Mr Perkins called after the dumpy retreating figure.

Catherine raised a hand in protest, but it was too late.

'Come on, have a seat. Been a while since we got to visit with you,' Mr Perkins urged.

She thought he was lonely. She managed another smile and sat reluctantly in a deep armchair facing the couch. As she sank farther and farther into it, she wondered how she was going to get up with any grace, with her short legs thrust out at such an angle.

Miss Molly came back in, burdened with a tray. Mr Perkins was on his feet in an instant.

'You shouldn't carry things like that,' he chided. 'Why didn't you call me?'

'I can carry this perfectly well, I'm not made of glass,' she scolded him.

Mr Perkins peered over Miss Molly's curly gray hair to give Catherine a wry shake of the head.

'How do you take yours, Catherine?' Miss Molly asked as she settled back on the couch.

'Black, please,' Catherine answered. 'I hope this wasn't any trouble for you.'

'No, no,' disclaimed Carl Perkins. 'We always have a pot on at night until we go to bed.

'I saw you through the window at the *Gazette* today,' he resumed, as Miss Molly poured, 'and I started to come in and speak, but you looked so busy I thought the better of it.'

'Mondays are mighty busy at the paper,' Catherine responded. She disliked being reminded of how 'on view' she was, with her desk right by the big window. It had bothered her when she first began working at the *Gazette*, but now she wasn't conscious of it most of the time.

Miss Molly handed Catherine her cup. A lot of wriggling was required before Catherine could work herself forward in her chair to reach it. Miss Molly's hand had a definite tremor, which didn't make the little transaction any easier.

Oh dear oh damn, Catherine thought. She wished she had just handed over the dish and gone right back out the door. Her intention of impressing Miss Molly with her sterling character and imperviousness to gossip seemed childish now.

Carl Perkins had just started to comment on the effect the rainless summer was having on the cotton when Molly Perkins's shaky hands caused an incident. His attention on Catherine, Mr Perkins held out a hand for his coffee cup. When Molly extended the cup to him, some of the steaming liquid spilled on his hand. For a long moment, as Catherine held her breath in sympathy for his pain, he kept his eyes on her face as if he felt nothing. Then Mrs Perkins's eyes teared as if she were going to cry over her mistake.

'Oh, Carl!' she said in a trembling, guilty voice. He looked at her, then down at the coffee that had run off his hand and stained the beautiful beige material of the couch.

Mrs Perkins somehow kept hold of the cup, rescuing it before it spilled completely. Then there was the fuss of Mr Perkins's retreat to the bathroom to put cold water and ointment on his burned hand, Mrs Perkins's agonized exclamations, and Catherine's attempt to leave, which was firmly crushed by Mr Perkins as he marched off to the bathroom.

As all this was being settled, Catherine passed from being uncomfortable to being miserable. She obviously disturbed Miss Molly for some reason; and she had no business sitting around frightening an old lady into burning her husband and staining expensive upholstery. But to extricate herself from this little visit without being out-and-out rude would have required more dexterity than Catherine could muster at the moment.

The scene jelled again as Mr Perkins entered and sat down as though nothing had happened, quieting his wife's attempt at yet another apology with a soothing, 'Now don't fuss any more, honey.' Mr Perkins was stoically controlling the pain he must have felt from the burn.

How kind he is to act as if it doesn't even hurt, Catherine thought. They must have a good marriage. They've come a long way together.

After Carl Perkins had come to Lowfield from Louisiana, he had climbed in the town and bought a business; then climbed more and bought more, with Miss Molly joining clubs right and left, working in the church, entertaining. The Perkins's only child was their son Josh. There were mementos of Josh everywhere: football trophies, baseball trophies, 4-H medals, and framed certificates. Catherine hadn't seen Josh in years. She recalled him as arrogant and insensitive, but intelligent in a graceless way. He had been one of Lowfield High School's golden boys.

Now he was married, about to become a father, and far, far away from Lowfield, Mississippi. Los Angeles, hadn't Miss Molly said?

Catherine was craftily preparing a lead-in to the subject of Josh, aware that little would be required of her if she could get Mr Perkins launched, when Mr Perkins himself jumped the conversational gun.

'I went to the Lion's Club meeting today,' he observed. 'Sure am glad I'm not running that outfit anymore. It's nice to take a back seat and let somebody else do the work.'

But you have to mention that you *were* the president, Catherine commented silently. She remembered that after the inaugural party for the Perkins mansion, her mother had said with despair, 'Self-made men are the proudest men on earth!'

'How was the lieutenant governor's speech?' asked Catherine brightly.

'He's campaigning now, so it was pretty agreeable,' Mr Perkins replied, smiling.

'What did he have to say?' Catherine murmured, relieved to have found such an innocuous topic.

'If he had had a lot to say, he wouldn't be lieutenant governor!' answered Mr Perkins cheerfully.

Catherine laughed without much effort. Mrs Perkins gave the tolerant smile of someone who had heard the same remark before.

The older woman had finally relaxed. She picked up her knitting and began to work on it expertly. Catherine saw that it was something tiny.

'For your grandchild?' she asked.

'Yes,' Miss Molly admitted with a proud smile.

'Josh and his wife say it'll be here in December,' said Mr Perkins eagerly, and Catherine had only to smile and nod for the next ten minutes.

'Of course, I had counted on Josh living here with us,' he wound down. 'Now Molly and me are just rattling around in this big house like peas in a hollow pod. I got all these businesses here, and no one to run 'em after I'm gone.'

Catherine felt sorry for the aging man, who had come to Lowfield practically penniless, her father had told her. Now there was no one to share the comfort of the easy years. The dynasty he had wanted to found had taken off for the golden coast.

Catherine rose awkwardly and evaded the obligatory urgings to stay, have more coffee, talk longer.

On her way out she passed a bank of photographs on a

wall. She stopped to comment on a wedding portrait of Josh's wife, whom she had never met.

'Very fine family,' Carl Perkins said with satisfaction. 'Been in Natchez forever.'

After Catherine agreed that 'Josh's wife' was lovely (what is the girl's name, Catherine wondered, or do they just call her 'J.W.'?), she was obliged to look at the rest of the pictures. Josh at all ages, in all varieties of sports uniform; Mrs Perkins with a prize-winning flower arrangement; Mr Perkins being sworn in to several offices.

One of the pictures had a duplicate in the files at the *Gazette*. Whatever past reporter had snapped it must have presented Mr Perkins with an enlargement. In the framed copy before her, Catherine saw him breaking ground for a new store. Heavy dark brows gave his rough face distinction, and upright shoulders lent an impression of vigor.

She looked at the man beside her now, and for a moment the hand of time lay heavy on her shoulder. Carl Perkins's skin had a curious patched look, his hair was thinning, and his eyebrows were almost nonexistent. His sleeve, rolled up for the bandage over the burn, revealed an arm marked by irregular dark spots. This pleasant hearty, proud man was going, bit by bit.

Miss Molly, in her own yellowed wedding portrait before Catherine on the wall, was small and smiling in her old-fashioned veil. Now her face was tracked with fine wrinkles. Instead of a wedding bouquet, she was clutching a bundle of knitting intended for a grandchild.

For a rotten moment, Catherine thought of the single gray hair she had pulled from her own dark head that morning, and remembered the tiny lines she had spotted at the corners of her eyes. She thought of Leona Gaites, grimly independent and dignified, performing cheap abortions in her little house and listening carefully for other peoples' cheap secrets, in order to finance an old age that would never come.

Then the room, gracious and overdone, came into focus again, and Carl and Molly Perkins were a kind couple with many years left to them – years that promised the pleasure of seeing in babies' faces traces of their own genes.

'Now you take care of yourself,' said Mr Perkins with a smile. 'Don't you go getting into any more trouble. Remember, we're always here when you need us.'

In the face of his kindness and concern, Catherine felt a sharp pang because of the fun she had poked at his ostentatious house. Her goodbyes were guiltily warm. Mr Perkins offered to walk her home.

Catherine said, 'It's just a few feet. No need to go to all that trouble.'

'Honey,' said Mr Perkins with sudden gravity, 'you, of all people, should know that things aren't safe around here.'

Without waiting for an answer, he stepped out onto the verandah.

It was fully dark now. No strawberry-juice stains in the sky, but blue darkness. The moon was full. The locusts were still chorusing throughout the quiet town. The streetlight at the corner of Catherine's lot seemed brighter against the full night.

And suddenly she was glad for the firm feet of Carl Perkins walking beside her, for the easy commonplace observation he was making about the need to repave Linton Street.

Then he said abruptly, 'You'll have to excuse Molly, Catherine. I know you noticed how shaky she is.'

'Is she ill?' Catherine asked gently. He doesn't need to explain, she thought Miss Molly believes I killed Leona, somehow. And she's scared of me.

'No, she's just plain scared.'

That fit in so neatly with her thoughts that Catherine stopped to stare at Mr Perkins. Was he going to tell her to her face that Miss Molly feared her?

Mr Perkins was waiting for Catherine to say, 'Of what?' When she didn't he stopped too, and looked back at her.

'Why,' he said, just as if she had supplied the expected words, 'she's scared for you.'

'*For* me?' Catherine asked cautiously. That preposition made a world of difference.

'Well, sure, honey. After all . . .' and here self-assured Carl Perkins floundered. 'I mean . . . several people close to you have . . .'

'Been murdered,' Catherine said impassively. I don't know but what I'd rather be a suspected killer than a potential victim, she reflected.

'Yes,' said Mr Perkins, as if the sad truth had to be admitted at last. 'If you knew why they died, it might be mighty dangerous for you.'

'I wish I knew,' she said slowly. 'Sheriff Galton said he thought the motives were separate.' She had no desire to talk about what the sheriff had found in Leona's house. Leona had been a blackmailer, an abortionist, and Catherine knew her father had been none of those things. She didn't think anyone who had known him would suspect for one minute that he had been involved in Leona's evil. No, Leona's brief life of crime had started after Dr Linton's death; and it was for one of those crimes, surely, that Leona had been killed. So the murders must not be related. That was James Galton's line of reasoning.

And I was halfway convinced of it too, Catherine thought. But the sheriff is wrong. I know he's wrong.

'I wish I knew,' she repeated, looking up at Mr Perkins under the streetlight.

He looked unutterably sad. 'I know you miss your folks,' he murmured, and touched her shoulder.

They began moving slowly through Catherine's yard.

'I hate like hell,' he continued, 'that Molly and I weren't able to be at the funeral.'

Stop, Catherine begged him silently. Even now, she couldn't endure her memory of that gray day.

'We tried to change our reservations, but it was so close to Christmas that it was just impossible,' he said.

'You went to see Josh out in California?' Catherine asked, trying to move him off the subject.

'Yes. Our plans had been made for so long; the airlines couldn't find other flights . . . it was just hopeless. I wish I had been here to help you settle your daddy's affairs,' he said with regret in his voice. 'But by the time we got back, Jerry Selforth had gotten himself all set up. Goddamn, Catherine, I'm sorry about your folks!'

The loss wasn't just mine, Catherine reflected for the hundredth time. It was everyone's.

They mounted Catherine's front steps.

'Thanks for walking me home.'

'Sure, my pleasure,' he said heartily. 'Want me to come in and check the house for you?'

'Oh, I don't think you need to do that.' She had locked the front door behind her when she left for the first time in her life worried about leaving it open for a brief period. She unlocked it now, and glanced in at the living room. 'See, all clear!' She attempted lightness.

'Okay,' said Mr Perkins, satisfied after scanning the undisturbed room.

'Goodbye now,' Catherine said. She stepped inside the house.

'Oh, heck.'

Catherine turned back.

'I been meaning to ask you ever since Christmas. Josh

wants his medical records. Does Jerry Selforth have every-thing of your daddy's?'

Damn Josh, she thought vehemently. He's got them wrapped around his finger for life.

This was a confirmation of the train of thought Randall had started in her head Sunday afternoon. In almost the same breath, even Carl Perkins could regret her parents' eternal absence and then move on to his son's record of vaccinations and measles.

'No,' she replied, suddenly exhausted and sick. 'It's probably up in the attic at the old office, since there's been no call for it since Father died. I'll get it for you.'

'No, no, don't worry about it now, Catherine.' Perkins seemed to realize the wound he had given. 'There's no hurry in the world.'

'Okay. I'll get it in a couple of days, maybe.'

He started down the walkway after clumsily patting her shoulder again with his bandaged hand.

She called goodbye after him. Her voice hung heavy in the living humid warmth of the night air.

Mrs Weilenmann had pointed out Catherine's isolation. Carl Perkins had pointed out that three people connected with her were dead. Despite her refusal of Mr Perkins's offer, she went through every room in the house before she went to bed.

'Thanks a lot, folks,' she muttered, as she locked herself inside her bedroom.

10

The multitude of Monday's revelations had worn Catherine down. She slept heavily, despite the Perkins's coffee, and woke groggy.

Tuesday, like Monday, began off-center. She overslept by ten minutes, an irritating breach of her workday morning routine. To make up the time, she had to scramble into her clothes while the coffee was perking, and skip a cup of that coffee. She promised herself to make up for it at the office, from the big urn kept continuously filled in the production room.

The telephone rang while she was making her bed. She was back on schedule and in a better humor, so instead of assuming that the call would be dire news, she predicted some mild disturbance, which was what it proved to be.

'My damn car's in the shop,' Tom said without preamble. 'Can you give me a ride to work?'

'Sure, come on over,' Catherine replied promptly.

This had happened before. Tom's ancient Volkswagen, noisy and battle-scarred, was subject to drastic breakdowns and expensive repairs.

Catherine was at the back door to let him in when he knocked.

'I was just about ready to leave, I'm glad you caught me,' she said, checking her purse to make sure she had her keys.

'No telling how much it's going to cost this time,' Tom said gloomily. 'I took it over to Don's Garage after work yesterday, and he said he'd bring it by this morning. Said it was nothing hard to fix, he could do it in a couple of hours.'

'That's what Don always says,' Catherine told him.

'Why?' asked Tom, outraged. 'If he had just told me he'd have to keep it, I could have called you last night.'

'He just likes people to leave happy,' Catherine said. 'That's the way Don is. I'm surprised you hadn't caught on to that by now, as much trouble as you've had with that car.

'At least,' she added as they walked to her garage, 'it'll be fixed when you *do* get it back.'

'I have plans for tonight, so he better get his ass in gear,' Tom said, folding himself into Catherine's front seat. She wondered, not for the first time, how he managed in the Volkswagen.

'I doubt he will,' Catherine warned.

Tom sulked all the way to the office. That was fine with Catherine, who didn't feel like idle chatter before nine o'clock at the earliest.

Leila was looking out the front window when Catherine pulled into a parking space miraculously open in front of the *Gazette* office. Usually the court-house people took all the good spots, arriving early to stake their claims. Her little triumph dissolved into a flat feeling when she saw Leila's face become woebegone at the sight of the two of them arriving together.

By the time Catherine and Tom came in through the glass door that had 'Lowfield Gazette' stenciled across it in gothic lettering, Leila was sitting rigidly erect at her typewriter behind the counter, pounding the keys furiously.

What a temper she's got, Catherine thought, passing

through the little reception room without a word. She wanted to go up to Leila and shake her by the shoulders.

She realized belatedly that Tom had not followed her into the reporters' room. She heard the whisper of voices behind her. It looked as if Tom and Leila were getting together. Maybe Leila was Tom's 'plans for the evening.'

Catherine made a wry face at her typewriter and then shrugged. The paper would go to press that afternoon, and would be delivered the next morning. There was a lot to do before the noon deadline.

She began checking over what she had written the day before. Jewel had left the proofs on her desk. Catherine had to proofread all her own stories, then pass them back to Production to be reread by Sarah, the paste-up girl, before she placed them on the page. Catherine got out her felt-tipped pen and settled down to work. Tom came in after a moment with a smug look on his thin face.

The feathers are sticking out of your mouth, she told him silently, and then was distracted by a cathedral-length bridal 'vail.'

Almost to Catherine's surprise, and certainly to her relief, the morning passed as quietly as Tuesday mornings ever did at the *Gazette*. The usual last-minute crises came up, but Catherine was braced for them. A bride's picture was flipped, so her ring appeared on her right hand. Catherine caught that and set it to rights. The weekly Dr Croft column was missing, and because of its great popularity with Lowfield subscribers, the search for it was a tense one. It was always pasted up days before the paper was due to come out, since it arrived set at the correct column width and had only to be cut off a sheet containing seven other Dr Croft columns, each one headed with a line drawing of the handsome and fatherly doctor.

'Dr Croft's Corner' had been unpopular with Catherine's father. Every time she read it, she recalled his indignation and impatience when two or three people came to his office after the appearance of each column, sure they had the disease Dr Croft had expounded on that week.

Catherine wondered for a moment whether Jerry Selforth had the same problem.

At last sharp-eyed Jewel found the missing column. The wax holding it to the page had weakened, and the fan had blown it under the paste-up table. Catherine, with dirty hands and knees after taking an active part in the search, rose from the floor and repaired immediately to the *Gazette*'s rather dreadful ladies' room to clean up.

Leila, she noted sourly, had kept her own golden limbs pristine by promptly recalling some bills that had to be sent out, at the moment the column was discovered missing.

Tom was slumped at his desk when Catherine emerged from the ladies' room.

'I must have called the sheriff's office ten times,' he complained, 'and I always get the redneck queen, Mary Jane Cory. "I'm sorry, Sheriff Galton is out. I'm sorry, Sheriff Galton is with someone right now." I keep hearing all these rumors about Leona's past, and I want a quote from him on that!'

Catherine considered. She was a little pleased to know something Tom didn't know. She thought, He'd throttle me if he knew I was withholding a tidbit from him.

She almost told Tom to go ask Leila about the truth of what he had heard, but she knew she would never forgive herself if she did. As long as he had heard the rumors, though. She had a mischievous impulse.

'Go talk to Salton Sims,' she said, pokerfaced. 'Salton knows something.'

'If I voluntarily talk to Salton, I *must* be dedicated,'

Tom said grimly, and set out, with pad and pencil in hand, to locate the pressman.

Catherine almost laughed out loud. But her little moment of mischief promptly fizzled when she glanced down at her desk and saw a hole for a picture on her sketch of the society page. The space hadn't been crossed by the large 'X' she drew whenever she sent a picture back to the offset darkroom.

'Omigod,' she said guiltily. She had forgotten to call the Barnes house to remind them to deliver their grandchild's picture for today's paper. She had picked up the phone to dial, casting a quick glance at the clock on the wall as she did so (it was an hour from the deadline), when Martin Barnes himself came through the front door and into the reception area.

Catherine heard Leila directing him to the reporters' room – not that he needed much direction, since Catherine was in clear view – and then the planter was advancing across the worn carpet to stand before her desk. Catherine was self-conscious because of the conversation she had had with Jewel the day before. She examined Mr Barnes covertly for signs of a romantic soul, but there he was: four-square Martin Barnes.

'How are you, Catherine?' he said mildly. 'Haven't seen you to talk to in a coon's age.'

Mr Barnes's weathered but still handsome face expressed nothing but polite pleasure. Before Catherine could say anything, he went on. 'I sure was surprised when Jimmy Gallon came out to my place yesterday. I didn't think it was so all-fired important that I was on the same road where Leona got dumped.'

Catherine fluttered her hand in a meaningless gesture. She wished she hadn't sent Tom off on a wild-goose chase to interview Salton Sims. She had a second to think,

That's what I get for being catty, before Barnes, slowly collecting his thoughts, began to ruminate again.

'I told him I was just out riding my land, same as I always do early in the morning,' Barnes said, looking at Catherine significantly. 'Well, little Catherine Linton saw me, Jimmy says, and right afterward she found something nasty, something mighty bad. Course, by then I had heard about old Leona Gaites at church, so it wasn't no surprise to me.'

Catherine could think of no conceivable response. Her reputation for silence was serving her well, she decided, for Barnes didn't seem to expect a reply.

'And I said to him, "Sure, I saw that gal."' Barnes went on slowly. 'I wondered at it, too, her being out so early on a Saturday morning. First time in my life the police ever come by my house to ask me questions. Parked in front of my house, for everyone to see.' He sounded mildly resentful, but Catherine couldn't decide whether or not the resentment was aimed at her. 'Melba 'bout went wild,' he added glumly.

She wondered if Jewel had had time to report their conversation of yesterday to her lover.

'First time the police have ever been at my house, too,' Catherine said, with a poor imitation of brightness. 'And the last time, I hope.'

From the corner of her eye, she saw Tom stalk into the room and cast a look of utter disgust in her direction. He threw his pad and pencil on his desk and walked directly out again. Catherine saw him lean on the counter in Leila's office, and heard the murmur of their voices.

No help from that quarter. Tom would happily let Martin Barnes talk her to death in retaliation for her sending him to Salton Sims to discover that Leona was 'godless.'

At least Barnes was smiling at her faint joke. He reached inside his pocket and drew out a photograph.

'Here's my picture of Chrissy for the paper,' he explained carefully. 'My first grandchild, you know.' The planter beamed.

Catherine eyed the picture. It was even worse than the usual run of photos handed in to the *Gazette* for such celebrations. For one thing, it was in color, which reproduced poorly in the *Gazette*; Randall couldn't afford expensive color ink. For another thing, the little girl was slumped sideways in her highchair at practically a right angle, and her stare was woefully blank: no cute smile, no expression at all. Little Chrissy's goggle eyes and gape were ludicrous in combination with the gay party hat, with its crepe pompon that had unwisely been strapped to the child's head.

'Cute kid,' said Catherine faintly.

'Looks just like her grandpa, Sally says.'

That triggered laughter in Catherine, who decided that Martin was maligning himself. He was still a good-looking man, and this baby – Catherine bit the inside of her mouth ferociously, to keep from bursting into unforgivable giggles.

'Thanks for bringing it in,' she managed, her voice only slightly choked. 'I'll take it to the back right away, so it'll be in the paper when you get it tomorrow.'

'We're looking forward to it,' he assured her earnestly. 'See you some other time, Catherine. I hope we don't meet out in the fields no more.'

Catherine looked up from the picture sharply, but Barnes was already walking out. He had to turn sideways to edge through the reception room, for the little area had become crowded during their conversation.

Tom was still leaning over the counter talking to Leila, Carl Perkins was standing nearby with a folder in his hands that must contain his enterprises' ads for the coming week, and, Catherine saw with a thud, Sheriff Galton was leaning against the wall with an air of infinite patience. Mrs Weilenmann was standing with Randall in the doorway of his office, deep in discussion.

When Tom straightened up from the counter and turned to see who was behind him, his whole body stiffened (like a bird dog, Catherine thought), as he realized that the object of his phone calls was within reach. Catherine couldn't hear what he said, but she saw Galton shake his head, smiling, as Tom's mouth moved nonstop.

Tom went on talking, and Galton shook his head again, with less of a smile. Tom was being persistent. As usual, Mr Perkins turned away, trying to appear uninvolved in their exchange. Randall and Mrs Weilenmann finished their talk, and, as the librarian worked her way out of the knot of people, Randall ushered Galton into his office.

It was the first time she had seen Randall that day. He caught a glimpse of her face and gave her a quick wave.

Catherine smiled back. Mrs Weilenmann, noticing her at the same time, assumed the smile was for her. She raised a hand in greeting.

As Catherine looked at the knot of familiar faces, her smile suddenly stiffened. One of these, she thought. Maybe one of these people . . . She saw an anonymous arm rising and falling, saw blood pouring through gray hair.

Why? she wondered frantically. Why? The nightmare was before her eyes again, all the more horrible in this hot sun-drenched, normal room. I'll face it, she decided. I have to face it squarely.

She looked at the worst.

Randall, who had the strength of an athlete. His reason: Leona's threats to expose his father's acceptance of a bribe. But, Catherine rebutted swiftly, he told me about that himself, when he certainly didn't need to. She then considered Randall's mother, Angel, for the same reason, but she knew Miss Angel was not physically strong enough to kill someone in the way Leona had been killed.

Sheriff Galton. His son was selling drugs. The shame of it would break James Galton, privately and publicly, if it became generally known. And Leona had had a habit of finding things out.

Mrs Weilenmann, that sad and misplaced woman. Her rumored white husband was supposed to have been a lawyer. Why would such a woman return to the South, where she was neither fish nor fowl? Catherine had always imagined that a long sad story was buried behind those dignified toffee-colored features.

Tom had resumed his conversation with Leila. If Leona had seen Tom buying dope Friday night . . . A drug conviction would bar him from ever holding another reporting job. Reporters were too thick on the ground now for any editor to have to consider hiring a risk.

Leila? Catherine almost dismissed Leila offhand. But to be fair, she paused to consider her. After all, Leila had admittedly had criminal contact with Leona Gaites. But, like Randall, she seemed to be cleared by that very admission. Of course, Leila's father was a pillar of a fundamentalist church. I just don't know what Mr Masham might do, if he knew his baby had gotten pregnant and had an abortion, Catherine thought.

And, of course, there were Martin Barnes and Jewel Crenna, the illicit couple.

This has gone far enough, Catherine told herself savagely, trying to arrange her face so it would have some semblance of normality for Mr Perkins, who had dropped off his folder at Leila's desk and was coming toward her. I could add Carl and Molly Perkins, Salton Sims . . . Maybe

I have blackouts and did it myself . . . Maybe the Drummonds aren't in Europe at all, but hiding out secretly in their house!

'Are you all right?'

Or none of the above, Catherine concluded before she looked up.

'Yes sir,' she said. 'I just had some bad thoughts.'

'I guess we've all had them lately,' Mr Perkins said sadly. 'Molly and I just wanted to know if you'd come over to supper at our house tonight. You can bring your boyfriend if you want to. Molly and I would sure like to get to know him better.'

'Know him better?' Catherine was sure her jaw had gone slack with astonishment. What was this new kite of rumor sailing through the Lowfield sky?

'Your tenant,' said Mr Perkins with a trace of uncertainty in his voice. He bobbed his head backward in Tom's direction.

'He's just my tenant,' Catherine said definitely. She smiled one of the killer smiles Southern women are taught. 'I'm so sorry I won't be able to come over tonight. I'm way behind on everything I have to do at home.'

'We're sure sorry you can't come,' Mr Perkins said, flinching almost visibly, unable to apologize for fear of getting in deeper. 'But if you get nervous about being on your lonesome, you just come right on over.'

'Sure will,' Catherine responded with absolute insincerity.

She watched her neighbor walk away. I guess I nipped that in the bud, she thought with some satisfaction.

The reception area had emptied while Catherine was talking with Mr Perkins. She was glad. She wanted no more talk, no more suspicion. She wanted to work and be ignored. She quickly delivered baby Chrissy's picture to the darkroom, earning a glower from the camera operator because of its late arrival.

Leila was at her desk humming as she stapled statements to checks when Catherine passed through on her way to lunch. The girl looked almost elevated, as if she had received a call to a higher duty. Tom was evidently living up to his image in Leila's eyes. Catherine paused, wondering what Tom was going to do about lunch, since his car was in the shop; but she saw him through the plate-glass window crossing the courthouse lawn, headed toward the sandwich shop on the other side of the square. She supposed he was getting lunch for himself and Leila.

Catherine decided to go home rather than buy a sandwich. She would definitely be a third wheel.

As she drove, she tried to remember what the refrigerator contained that she could fix quickly.

The only raw ingredient around was lettuce. After eating a limp and unsatisfactory salad, Catherine was assembling a grocery list at the kitchen table when the telephone rang. As she reached up to answer it, she wondered who would be calling her at noon.

The voice that came over the line was so choked as to be almost unrecognizable.

'What are you doing with Martin, you little bitch? What do you mean, getting him into trouble?'

'Mrs Barnes?' asked Catherine unbelievingly.

Her only answer was a few hiccuping sounds that could have been sobs.

My God, Catherine thought blankly.

'What are you talking about?' she ventured, into a silence so taut she imagined she could feel it vibrating. Melba Barnes, my fellow colorful Southern eccentric, Catherine thought wearily.

'I wanted to catch you at home, you little sneak, not

down at the paper office where your little friend Tom Mascalco could listen in and laugh at me, too.'

By now Catherine was recovering from her initial shock. Anger made her blood pump faster.

She had had enough.

Enough of Sheriff Galton's admonitions; enough of Jewel's hints about keeping her mouth shut, and Leila's nasty little confidences; enough mysterious half-threats from Martin Barnes; enough of the dark dealings of Leona Gaites.

In a careful low voice, she said, 'I don't know what the hell you are implying, Mrs Barnes. But I can tell you that I resent your tone and this entire conversation. Now if you have something to tell me, tell me and then shut up. Because if you ever repeat your suspicions to anyone else in this town, I will slap a lawsuit on you so fast your head will swim.'

Another awful hiccup-sob.

'What were you and Martin doing in that shack, anyway? You told the police you saw him out there. I saw him in your office today, through that big window. I saw him talking to you. I knew then be had been lying about riding around the place. I've known for a long time he's been carrying on, but I never thought it would be with a girl his daughter's age!'

Catherine closed her eyes and leaned against the wall by the telephone. Yesterday, according to Jewel, Melba Barnes had suspected Leona; today, it was Catherine.

'I can't believe this,' she said, unaware that she had spoken out loud, until Mrs Barnes gave a snort on the other end.

'Mrs Barnes,' Catherine said, in a voice so controlled and furious that she almost frightened herself, 'I have no interest in your husband at all. I have never met him anywhere by prearrangement. I passed him by chance on a dirt road Saturday morning.' Catherine had to resist a powerful temptation to tell her where her husband had been (Jewel should be the recipient of this blast, not me!). 'When Sheriff Galton asked me if I had seen anyone, I told him I had seen Mr Barnes. He was in his pickup and I was in my car. We were going in opposite directions. This morning he came by the office to give me your grandchild's picture to put in the newspaper. I think,' Catherine ended heavily, 'that you are crazy, and this whole conversation, if you can call it that, is disgusting.' Then she hung the phone firmly on the wall.

The whole thing struck Catherine as being so sordid that she shook her fingers, as if to shake off the dirt transmitted by the telephone.

Catherine Linton, femme fatale, she thought wryly, when she had become a little calmer. Leila thought Tom and I were lovers; Carl Perkins, too. Now Mrs Barnes thinks I've been screwing her dumb husband on the floor of a shack, with a dead woman beside us.

As she locked up the house, Catherine decided that today she didn't like anyone very much. She included herself in the group.

Leona's murder is like kicking over an anthill, she thought. Everyone is scurrying to get under new cover, treading over each other in their haste to escape exposure.

11

The afternoon went along quietly. The production staff was frantically busy getting the paper from the press and bundling up the issues to be mailed. The press broke down (it always did), and Randall had to change into a jump suit he kept handy, to help Salton Sims get it back into operation.

Few of the production troubles disturbed the reporters' room. Catherine was profoundly thankful. She felt she had had as much emotion, other peoples' and her own, as she could deal with for a while. She lay low deliberatly, not looking up from her desk at all, if she could help it.

The telephone didn't ring. People in Lowfield knew that Tuesday afternoon was frantic in the production department at the paper, and they generally supposed the reporters were busy too. In fact, the reporters regarded Tuesday afternoon as semilegitimate goof-off time.

When Catherine wasn't poking around figuring out column inches for the next issue, she was staring out the window by her desk, watching people come and go from the courthouse and the shops around the square. She was daydreaming, half-awake, lulled back into a sense of the continuity of the town by the normal sights of ladies coming and going from the grocery, storeowners and their customers chatting in front of the shops, and a town policeman working his way around the square with painstaking slowness, giving out parking tickets. The policeman was preceded by the usual flurry out of the stores and the courthouse as people saw him coming and hastily moved their cars to safety, or added more coins to the meters.

Catherine's thoughts inevitably drifted to Melba Barnes. She wondered what Sally would say if she knew her mother had accused Catherine, her high school buddy, of having an affair with Sally's father. Then she wondered what Jewel would say, and had an inward tremor of amusement as she imagined Jewel's pungent comments.

Catherine couldn't help feeling pity for crazy Melba Barnes. She tried to picture herself married and suspecting her husband of having a woman on the side. She couldn't quite think herself into it, but she felt a strong distaste at the idea.

It was the stealthy aspect of adultery, the sneaking and concealment in the face of someone close to you, that made it seem so . . . slimy. Though I suppose, Catherine reflected, the sneaking is more fun than the actual bedding down, for some people.

The extension on her desk buzzed. Catherine tucked the receiver between ear and shoulder; she was gathering loose paper clips to shove them into their original box.

'I'm sorry,' whispered a voice, and the line went dead.

Melba Barnes was apologizing as abruptly as she had accused. Catherine returned the receiver to its cradle. She wondered whether Mrs Barnes had ever called Leona and made the same accusations. Catherine wished she hadn't had that particular idea. Perhaps Melba hadn't stopped at words, with Leona.

No, quit it, Catherine admonished herself. When will I be able to stop assessing murderous potential in everyone I speak to? When will people stop wondering about my own potential for violence?

My life was so *simple*, she thought wearily. Now I'm operating upside down.

She was glad when Tom strode into the room, clutching a copy of the newly printed paper, half-wrathful and half-amused over a typo he hadn't caught in one of his stories.

A local girl had been elected Miss Soybean Products of Lowfield County – amusing enough in itself, at least to Tom. Miss Soybean Products was in law school, which had been misprinted 'lay' school. Catherine laughed over this bad joke until Tom threatened to throw water in her face.

'Extended hilarity,' Tom said sarcastically, when Catherine's giggles had finally trailed off, 'is just not your style, Miss Linton.'

That pomposity was enough to set Catherine off again. Leila, attracted by the unaccustomed laughter from Catherine's corner, appeared in the doorway and looked questioningly until Tom smiled at her.

Leila swept back to her desk, mollified, her bare legs looking revoltingly long and elegant to Catherine's envious eyes. Tom was transparently gloating as he watched Leila's retreat from a rear view. He hummed and whistled the rest of the afternoon, and wasn't as angry as Catherine had supposed he would be when he phoned the garage and found that his car wasn't ready. In a resigned voice, he asked her for a ride home.

'Of course,' she said. 'Is it time to go?'

'When are you going to start wearing a watch?'

'When I can remember to put it on in the morning,' she answered instantly.

'You never wear jewelry,' Tom observed with a note of disapproval. 'You ought to; you ought to wear silver. It would look good with your hair.'

Catherine mulled that over. If she was going to buy new clothes and new curtains and a new bedspread, to say nothing of her decision to cut down the hedge, why not some jewelry? She had always been so indifferent to it that her parents had stopped giving it to her.

I have nice ankles, she thought, peering at then. Maybe an anklet. Or were anklets hopelessly unfashionable?

And that was the most serious thought she had for the rest of the afternoon.

Sometimes on Tuesday afternoons she and Tom performed necessary housekeeping chores, like cleaning the darkroom or weeding out old files of pictures, but today neither was in the mood.

Tom kept up a pretense of occupation, in case Randall walked through, by pulling out the files containing the weekly columns. Every Tuesday, he made a little ceremony out of clipping the columns for the next issue. Catherine suspected he read the monthly allocation of comic strips in a single sitting. This little task could easily have been left to the production foreman, but Tom had somehow appropriated it when he came to the *Gazette*; and no one cared enough to take it out of his hands.

For the rest of the lazy afternoon, with the sun cutting through the venetian blinds across the big window, casting patterns on the floor, Tom read Catherine snips from the weekly columns ('Dr Croft,' 'Harry's Home Tips,' and 'Sandra Says') and from the mailed-in stories the *Gazette* received from state departments and the government.

Catherine listened with half an ear, smiled occasionally, cleaned out her desk at a snail's pace, and watched the bars of light and shadow shift across the floor. Randall came through once, filthy with grease and ink from the press, his pipe clenched between his teeth. He reached out to pat Catherine's hair as he walked past (Tom's back was turned, to show the boss he was busy), and Catherine dodged his grimy hand and laughed silently as he made a mock-threatening swipe at her face.

She was glad when it was time to go. She told Tom, as they drove home, that she planned an exciting evening of house-cleaning.

'Damn, I'd better clean my bathroom,' he said, suddenly anxious.

'Got a date with Leila tonight?'

Tom grinned and said, 'My lips are sealed. I have to protect the lady's good name. But I wonder how Randall feels about staff members dating each other.'

He looked at Catherine blankly when she began to laugh.

'I swear, you've changed,' he said huffily. 'It used to be as much as I could do to wring a smile out of you.'

Being turned upside down had brought the lightest as well as the heaviest elements in her to the top, Catherine decided, as she pulled into her driveway.

I guess when all this settles I might come out very different, she reflected.

'I never know *what* you're going to do anymore,' Tom grumped.

'I don't either,' she said. To their mutual surprise she patted him on the shoudler. 'See?' she said shyly.

'Where will you stop in your mad excesses?' Tom asked dramatically. Then he grinned at her and gave her hand a squeeze.

'See you tomorrow,' he said blithely.

She watched him stalk off across the lawn. He was pulling off his tie as he went. He cast a long narrow shadow across the grass.

In six hours he would be dead.

Catherine ate a brownie. There had been a coffee can at the back door when she unlocked it, a three-pound Folger's can full of brown bars. Even before she found the note inside, she knew they were from Betty Eakins, the Lintons' former maid.

The note, written on a ragged piece of paper, read, 'Miss Catherine, I thought you might like these right now. You use to. Come see me when you get a minute. Betty.'

Catherine's eyes prickled when she thought of ancient Betty walking all the way to her house on arthritic legs. Then she shook herself briskly. Probably that young deputy son of hers had brought Betty in his car.

The brownies were as wonderful as Catherine remembered; but not much of a meal. She reminded herself to go to the grocery store on her lunch hour the next day. She decided to drive to Memphis on Thursday evening after work, to begin her spending spree. If Randall was taking her out to dinner and to a movie Friday . . . She had to rouse herself from thinking about clothes, and Randall, to begin her belated housecleaning.

She started by cutting off the air conditioning and opening all the windows. The cessation of the humming of the central-air unit made the house suddenly very quiet. Outside in the dusk the locusts had begun their nightly drone. Catherine stood at a window listening, caught herself at it, and was angry; but she checked the three doors into the house to make sure they were locked.

Catherine began her cleaning in the master bedroom. She put on her oldest jeans for the operation; she never failed to get dirty while the house got clean. She scrubbed the bathroom methodically, and then set about dusting. The house was full of bookcases and her grandmother's bric-a-brac, so it was nine o'clock by the time she put away the dust rag and pulled the vacuum cleaner from its closet. The vacuum's businesslike roar filled the house with a satisfying sound, and Catherine maneuvered it around the rooms with unusual care, shifting the furniture laboriously to reach every corner and cranny.

Kitchen floor next, she decided as she looped the vaccum cord. And then I'll be through.

This evening was a little cooler than the one before, but her shirt was clinging to her back and her forehead felt wet by the time she had moved the chairs around the kitchen dining table.

The good thing about cleaning, she thought, as she turned on the kitchen-sink tap full blast, was that you could think about anything or nothing.

She chose to think of nothing, and the physical work was relaxing. But she was beginning to feel bored by the time she finished the tile floor.

She wrung out the dirty mop, rinsed, and wrung out the excess water again. Usually she put the mop out the side door to dry, but tonight she decided to put it out the back door. The last time, she had forgotten to bring it in for several days. In case she did that again, she wanted it to be out of sight from the street.

With a dirty kitchen towel wrapped around the mop to catch drips, Catherine walked quickly through the den and opened the back door to the night.

After propping the mop upright, she stood for a minute on the steps, looking up at the dark sky. It was cloudy; the stars were blotted out. Catherine hoped that meant rain, but the air didn't feel right for a shower. It was heavy, but not pressing.

As she stood with her face raised to the night sky, she heard a rustling in the grass.

She remained quite still. Her eyes, still turned skyward, no longer saw the blackness above them. They were blind with concentration. Everything in her was bent on identifying the source of the sound, so like that of feet passing through dry grass.

She thought of the light streaming from the open door behind her; of her outline, presented clearly to whatever was out there in the night.

In that interminable moment she was reminded of dreams she had had as a child, dreams in which danger threatened. In those dreams, she could never decide whether moving with elaborate unconcern or moving like lightning would save her. Some nights she tried one thing, some nights another. Which now? she wondered.

The sound was not repeated. Whatever was out there, beyond the pool of light from her house, was standing as still as she was.

Waiting to see what I will do.

What will I do?

If I move fast, if I show fear, it will be on me, she thought.

The watcher assumed the dimensions of the phantoms of her dreams, enormously big and perpetually hungry – and too awful to have to face.

She turned very quietly and without haste, opened the screen door and stepped inside her house. Very quietly and without haste she shut the heavy wooden door behind her. Then with fingers that were not at all quiet and were extremely hasty, she locked the door and leaned against it. She slid down the door until her rear hit the floor, and there she stayed until her breathing became more regular.

Should I call the police. To say what? I heard something in the grass and I'm scared, Sheriff Galton. I heard something in the grass . . .

And though she was sharply and clearly glad that no one would ever know she was doing it, she crept on her knees to the nearest window and huddled below it to listen.

A dry whisper in the grass. It had resumed movement.

She raised her head cautiously and peered through the

screen. In the light from the window, she saw a bird hopping through the yard. As she watched, it triumphantly pulled a bug from the grass and hopped away with its prey.

'Goddamn! Don't you know you're supposed to be asleep?' she asked the bird hoarsely. It was understandably startled and flew off, taking care to retain the bug even in its fright.

Catherine expelled a long breath and slumped against the wall. As she was about to give a self-conscious laugh at her panic, she changed her mind. It wasn't funny.

I don't care that I looked crazy as hell, she told her inward critic. I really don't care.

She sat there for a few minutes, letting her body calm down gradually.

'Oh boy,' she said. 'Oh boy.'

She had just scrambled clumsily to her feet when she heard a faint, curious buzz.

She turned her head to one side, trying to identify the source of that half-familiar sound.

The buzz came again, after she had hesitantly started down the hall to her bedroom in obedience to an obscure urging that told her it was the right place to go.

The second time she heard the sound, she recognized it.

It was the buzzer in her father's old office.

Someone's calling for him, but he's not here, she thought. He's dead.

Her skin crawled.

For a third time the buzzer made its rasping appeal.

'It's *Tom*,' she said out loud. Tom. Playing a stupid joke.

But he had promised he wouldn't. She couldn't recall him breaking a promise. He had been so serious when she had told him never to play a joke on her with the buzzer.

Something was wrong.

When she reached the master bedroom, she half expected to see her father's head rising sleepily from his pillow in answer to the summons from his office.

She stared at the place where the sound of the buzzer issued, by the bed on the side where her father had slept.

He's calling me, she thought. *Tom* is calling me.

The buzzer fell silent.

Tom, she told herself with an effort. Not Father.

'I am not a fool,' she said. She pulled open the drawer of her bedside table, grabbed her gun, and ran back down the hall.

Catherine didn't think of the fear that had just let go of her ankles. She was needed, and she had to go, to run, to get there before it was too late.

Out the back door. Fumble with the light switch that would illumine that terrifying yard. A quick scan after the light was on.

The yard was empty.

Running through the grass, avoiding the stepping-stones that would have tripped her in her haste. Through the hedge that seemed to clutch at her.

She was almost at Tom's back door when she saw that it was wide open. She stopped so suddenly that she wobbled back and forth, and had to struggle to keep her balance. A faint light glowed from the open rectangle. The door ajar to the hot night confirmed her feeling that something was horribly wrong. She held her gun ready.

Not even the eerie sound of the buzzer had been as frightening as that open door was. As she crept closer, she could feel the rush of cooled air escaping from the house.

She eased open the screen door as quietly as she could. It creaked a little and she held her breath.

The doors all along the short hall were shut. The faint glow was coming from the living room, and she was looking at it so fixedly that she failed to see the red splotches against the hall's white paint, until a thread trickled down from a larger splash. Its tiny movement, slow and hesitant, caught the corner of her eye. She stared at it and wondered if she could move.

There was no sound in the house except the hum of air conditioning behind one of the closed doors. The night, let in through the back door, held its breath.

Because she had to, she began to go forward, her hand against the wall for support. She snatched it away when it encountered wetness.

The hall resembled every nightmare she had ever dreamed. But the thing in the grass had gotten someone else instead of her.

As she moved closer to the light, closer to the living room, her scalp began to crawl.

'Tom?' she whispered.

The living room was a shambles. This disorder in what had been so neat struck her first. She didn't see Tom for a moment; then she saw his legs, his long thin legs, extending beyond the trunk that had served as his coffee table.

Without realizing she had moved, she was suddenly standing by him, looking down. He was on his back. He was very still, but blood was still running from his wounds. She watched a drop run down his cheek, over what had been his cheekbone. She watched it very carefully until it hit the thin carpeting and was absorbed in a larger stain.

'Oh Tom,' she said, and her fear was swallowed up by her grief. She dropped the gun on the trunk, knelt on the soaked carpet, and put her fingers to the pulse in his neck. It throbbed for a second that was a lifetime, and then the faint throb died.

There was a stillness about him, the total absense of

movement that belongs only to the dead, after even the tiny motions of breathing are extinct.

I'm too late, she thought. She could feel the blood soaking through the denim covering her knees. I'm too late.

He was only wearing his trousers, and Catherine wanted to cover him up. He would hate everyone to see him like that, she thought. He would just hate it. And no one should see his face; I should not have seen his face.

There was a tiny movement at the edge of her vision.

Her head snapped up, and she was staring into Leila's face. As she watched, that face stretched oddly.

'Oh Leila, he's dead,' Catherine said in an involuntary whisper. 'He just died.'

She rose to go to the girl, and Leila's silent scream came out in a weak strangled ache of a sound. Catherine reached out to touch her, then looked at her hand. It was bloody.

'Get away from me!' Leila shouted, her voice becoming unchained. She backed against the wall with her arms stretched out to repel Catherine. Then she realized she had put her back against a smear of blood, and her scream ripped the room apart.

Catherine suddenly realized that Leila thought she had killed Tom. She also absorbed the peculiar fact that Leila was in her underwear.

The sound Leila made affected Catherine like alcohol in a cut.

'Stop it!' she said harshly, but Leila kept on. Catherine's exasperation was heightened by shock. She felt positive joy in applying the classical method for dealing with hysterics. With no compunction at all, she hit Leila as hard as she could, and only felt a flash of dismay when she saw the girl stagger a few feet, from the force of the blow.

I didn't know I was that strong, she thought in amazement. I guess I've never hit anyone before in my life.

The blow did indeed silence Leila, but it didn't calm her in the least. Her terror was evident in her trembling body and distended eyes.

'I didn't do it,' Catherine said flatly.

But Leila was not in her right mind. Her eyes were empty of reason.

Catherine was irrationally angry.

'You stupid bitch! I didn't do this! I found him like this!'

Leila seemed to return to her body. She pointed a shaking finger at Catherine's bloody hands.

'From the hall,' Catherine explained. 'The buzzer sounded.' She pointed to the buzzer on the door frame. There was red spattering the wall around it. 'You remember the buzzer. To the house. That my father used. I think Tom hit it in the struggle.'

Leila looked where Catherine's finger was pointing. Her family had gone to Dr Linton. She nodded slowly, looking as if she finally understood. She deflated as fear of her own death left her, but she stared at Tom's legs, her complexion changing from ashy brown to green.

'Are you all right?' Catherine asked ridiculously.

'I'm going to vomit,' Leila muttered.

Catherine was thankful for her knowledge of the house, for she swung the girl into the bathroom and over the toilet just in time. Shivering now with reaction, Catherine sat on the edge of the bathtub until Leila emptied her stomach.

'I've got to call the police,' Catherine said.

'Not from here,' Leila pleaded. She was a limp ghost of herself.

'No,' said Catherine, her own stomach heaving at the thought of staying there.

Catherine's courage was fast seeping away. But the need to get the younger girl out of the house, the responsibility for someone in worse shape than she herself was, kept her mind moving.

'We have to go over to my house,' she said. 'Can you walk?' A stupid question, she reflected, because Leila will just dammit have to walk, whether she thinks she can or not.

'Come on,' Catherine said, 'if you're through throwing up.'

Leila got to her feet with some assistance.

Catherine awoke to another need.

'Clothes,' she said sharply.

Leila looked down at herself and turned from green to red.

I didn't know people could turn so many colors, Catherine thought.

'Oh, Catherine,' Leila began miserably.

'I don't give a damn,' Catherine interrupted, 'but I think no one else needs to know. Are your clothes in the bedroom?'

Leila nodded.

The bed was rumpled and Tom's shirt and underwear were set neatly on a chair. Leila's dress was on the floor, her shoes under it.

Dress, shoes. Underwear; Leila had that on. Hose? No, she didn't wear them. What else? Purse, of course. Purse. For an awful moment, Catherine thought that it must be in the living room, until she spotted it by the side of the chair. She scanned the little bedroom for any other traces of Leila, but saw none. It might not hold up, but it was all she could do. Then she remembered her own possession in the house. She had to go into the living room after all. She went directly to the gun, grabbed it, and ran out.

Leila was slumped on the edge of the bathtub.

'Here,' Catherine said crisply. She helped Leila into the dress and sandals and kept charge of the purse.

'Come on.'

She got Leila to her feet. Leila was by far the taller of the two. It was awkward for both of them, in a horribly comic way. Catherine put her arm around Leila's waist and Leila put hers around Catherine's neck. Somehow they supported each other down the spattered hall, out the open back door, and across the yard. They had to go slowly, tottering like two drunks through the gap in the hedge.

'I'm afraid,' Leila whispered, and the dark between the houses suddenly held ominous possibilities that Catherine had forgotten in her haste to leave the abattoir that had been Tom's home. She was hopelessly burdened. Leila and Leila's purse would make her too slow with the gun.

Catherine felt Leila begin to shake again, and heard the girl's breath become more like sobbing. They would never make it if Leila collapsed. Catherine was coming to the end of her strength. I will go mad if Leila screams again, she thought.

'Come *on*,' Catherine hissed through clenched teeth. Leila's arm around her neck was pinning her hair down, and the pain kept Catherine from panicking.

She had to use every muscle she possessed to haul Leila up the steps to her den. She dumped the girl on a couch and wobbled into the kitchen. She didn't sit down while she dialed the police, but leaned against the wall. She knew that if she sat down she would not be able to get up, and something still had to be done for the girl in her den.

By now Catherine almost hated Leila.

She said something, she never remembered what, into the telephone when it was answered at the sheriff's office. She hung up when an excited voice began to ask questions. Then she dropped her gun into a handy drawer. Before she returned to the girl, there was something she was going to do for herself.

She fumbled with the tiny Lowfield telephone directory, opening it with ponderous care to the 'G' page. She read the numbers out loud to herself and dialed with that same nerve-wracking slowness.

He answered the telephone himself.

'Randall,' she said, enunciating very deliberately. Then she was unable to speak.

'Catherine?'

'Randall . . . I wish you would come. Tom is dead.'

The silence was full of questions he was not going to ask yet.

'Tom is dead,' she repeated, and carefully hung up the phone, because she was afraid she was going to say it again.

She wondered what she had been planning to do next. Then she remembered Leila, and looked around the kitchen for something to take the girl. The most useful thing she could see was a roll of paper towels.

I think this is shock, she told herself. With precise movements, in slow motion, she picked up the roll of paper towels and began her slow trip back to the den.

As it turned out, the towels were a good idea. Leila had dissolved in tears by now, and she began choking out her story almost incoherently when Catherine reappeared.

Catherine handed Leila the roll, or rather simply thrust it into the girl's lap. She debated whether or not she could now sit down, and decided she could. She sat by the weeping girl and fixed a wide gray gaze on the pretty face now fuzzy with tears.

'We had a date,' Leila choked, 'but his car was in the shop, so I had to drive over to his place, but I parked the car a block away because I didn't want anyone to tell

Mama and Daddy, you know how people here tell your parents everything . . .'

Catherine automatically ripped a towel off the roll and stuffed it into Leila's hands. Leila looked at it as if she had never seen one, and used it.

'Oh, I loved him so much, and he was so good-looking . . . You know how it is . . . I just couldn't help it.' A pause for another application of the towel. 'And then when we were in bed, I mean, after it was over, there was a sound in the hall—'

I hope it was good for Tom, Catherine thought clearly. It better have been good.

'—and he got up and put on his pants, and he told me to stay quiet, not to move. He just whispered right up close to my ear, I was so . . . *scared* . . . "I left the damn door unlocked," he said.'

Leila turned her ruined face to Catherine, and her long hand gripped Catherine's frail wrist with painful strength.

'He went out and then I heard sounds, oh God, sounds. They hit the walls and came off them, out in the hall and then in the living room. I heard things falling and turning over. I thought there must be five people out there, I swear to God. And I couldn't keep quiet any more, I screamed. And I thought someone ran out of the house. So I waited for Tom to come get me. I thought he'd come in and say it had been a *burglar*. When he didn't come back, I thought he was calling the police. And I wanted to get up and get dressed before they got there. But I couldn't . . . I was too scared. I waited and waited, and I couldn't hear anything. So then I put my underwear on, as quiet as I could. I thought at least I could start getting ready. And then I heard the screen door. And it was you. I thought it was the man coming back. I guess it was a man. But I couldn't *wait* anymore. I had to see. I couldn't wait for Tom anymore.'

Sirens and lights outside.

The difference was that this time Randall was there, and his mother Angel. Randall only left Catherine once, to identify Tom formally. Angel made coffee and more coffee. And she greeted Leila's parents and led them to their weeping daughter.

Catherine observed dryly that Leila had recovered enough wits to protect herself: the girl edited her story to say that she and Tom had been sitting in the living room when they heard the noise of someone prowling, and that Tom has hustled her into the bedroom for her protection. That left open the question of why Tom hadn't called the police from the telephone in the living room, but Catherine decided that on the whole Leila had done well.

Then it was Catherine's turn.

She was holding an embroidered pillow in her lap. She remembered her mother's hands setting in the stitches. She had moved it from its place in the corner of the couch, so that she could jam herself into that corner as tightly as possible. The couch protected her right side and her back, and Randall was a solid wall on her left. Her fingers went over and over the embroidery her mother had worked on for hours. While Sheriff Galton asked her questions, her fingers never quit moving, in contrast to her face, which felt stiff, as if it didn't fit her skull very well.

Why had she not heard the screams Leila said she had given?

Because if Leila was shut in the bedroom, I wouldn't.

Why had she gone over to the house?

I heard the buzzer, he was calling me. I was too late. I heard a rustle in the grass, before the buzzer went off.

Why hadn't she called the police?

I thought it was a bird. I guess now it was – whoever . . .

She was grateful for Randall and his mother, but she

had gone where Randall could not reach her. She knew he was there, she felt his warmth and knew he was supporting her. She knew Angel was smoothing the way with cups of coffee and her mere presence, for Angel Gerrard, with her erect figure and carefully tended white hair, was a strong and influential woman and an impressive ally.

Catherine desperately wanted to reach out to them, to talk to them, to touch Randall's broad hand, but she could not. She looked at them from the corner of her eye. When they looked at her, she turned away: for suspicion hung around her like the heavy summer air.

She saw it in the eyes of the police, she saw it in the way Leila's parents carefully ignored her.

She heard one of the deputies ask Leila if the clothing Catherine was wearing now was the same she had worn when Leila saw her kneeling by Tom's body. She saw the deputy look at the blood dried on her knees, and at the smears on her hand.

No one would look directly at her face.

People might accept that she had happened to find one body, but not two, Catherine saw.

Not that she had been first on the scene two times.

Not that she had reported two murders. In three days.

The bruise forming on Leila's face, where Catherine had hit her, was examined by suspicious eyes. Leila had included the blow in her recital, and she had been quite graphic in describing how she was knocked to the wall by the force of Catherine's open hand.

Catherine saw very clearly that her frame was being reassessed with regard to its strength.

In a sideways glance, Catherine saw Angel Gerrard's back get stiffer and stiffer during Leila's account. A gleam entered Angel's alert brown eyes.

'I wonder how soon you can fire that girl?' Angel said

very quietly to Randall, when the room was momentarily emptied of all but the three of them.

'I won't wait too long,' Randall said grimly. There was a rough edge to his voice that Catherine had never heard before.

'Of course she was in bed with the boy,' Angel said briskly. She looked at Catherine for confirmation.

For the first time, Catherine met Angel's eyes directly. She nodded.

'I thought so,' Angel said. 'She's a pretty thing, but she has the brains of a gourd. I wonder that she manages to file things correctly.'

'She doesn't,' Randall said.

'Catherine,' Angel said sharply.

Catherine kept her face averted.

'Look at me, girl,' Angel said more sharply.

Catherine did, and felt as if she had gotten a shot of amphetamine.

'Did you hit that girl?'

'Yes,' Catherine replied.

'Good. Now wipe that guilt off your face. None of us thinks you had anything to do with this.'

Randall's arm tightened around her shoulders, and he gave her a little shake, as if to jog her circulation back into action.

She began to feel warm. The sluggishness of strain and fear were slowly draining away.

Sheriff Galton came in the back door. He looked haggard, years older. He seemed so ill that Catherine was on the verge of urging him to see a doctor, when she realized how ludicrous that would sound.

The sheriff dropped into a chair and looked at her wearily.

'Did Tom tell you that he knew anything about Leona Gaites's murder?'

'You know how he was,' she answered. 'He made big noises about digging into it and finding out something that you-all didn't know. But I don't think it came to anything?'

'You sure? He said nothing to you about finding something?'

'Not to me.'

'Well,' Galton muttered, passing a huge hand over his face, 'there's that marijuana in his house. Maybe something to do with that.'

Why didn't I remember to take that with me? Catherine thought. Then she remembered that Tom had bought the dope from James Galton Junior. She exchanged a quick look with Randall and hunched deeper in the sofa. Angel caught the exchanged glance, and rose to go to the kitchen to replenish the coffeepot.

'You know anything about that marijuana?' Galton asked her.

Now she was in a corner.

'I don't think Tom's death has anything to do with that,' she said.

'Am I going to have to search your house, too?'

'I saw it in his house when I went there Sunday,' she said. 'He told me he had bought it locally. That's all I know.'

The sheriff might not be admitting to himself what his son was doing, but Catherine could see that he knew. When he heard the word *locally*, he ran his hand over his face again.

'Where's Tom's car?' he asked abruptly.

'In the shop; Don's,' she said.

'It would look like Tom wasn't home,' Randall observed.

Catherine turned and looked at him. Sheriff Galton nodded slowly.

'Especially with the lights off, just the one light on in the living room,' Galton thought out loud. 'Maybe this was just breaking and entering that turned into something else when Tom came out of the bedroom unexpectedly.'

But his voice held no conviction.

'I overheard that the wounds are similar to Leona's,' Randall said expressionlessly. 'Is that true?'

'Yes,' said the sheriff. 'Very similar. But then, in any homicide by beating with a blunt instrument, they would be.'

A little idea began to trickle through Catherine's tired mind. But when she tried to focus on the tenuous thought, it dissolved. I should have let it alone, she thought. If I had let it alone, it would have formed.

'Drink,' said Angel firmly, putting a full cup on the coffee table in front of Catherine.

She looked up at the older woman, amazed that Angel could be immaculate at such an hour. Then her eyes filled with tears of gratitude that Angel had come to support her. Catherine shook her head angrily. I'm getting maudlin, she thought. She bent forward to pick up her coffee and to hide her face.

'Whoever did this would have been covered with blood,' Galton said, out of nowhere.

He looked at Catherine. Her eyes met his over the rim of her cup.

'I would not describe Catherine as exactly covered with blood,' Randall said with a dangerous gentleness. She felt his body tensing.

'No,' said the sheriff quietly. 'I see that.'

'Randall, do you have the Mascalco boy's home phone number? His parents' number, I mean?' Angel asked in the silence that had fallen.

'Oh. Oh God.' He thought. 'Yes, it's sure to be in the

file at the office. He was living with them when he applied for the job. I'll have to go down and get it.'

'You can give it to me,' rumbled Galton.

'I'll call them,' Randall said tightly.

'Then I don't envy you,' said the sheriff. 'I ought to do that myself.'

'He was my employee,' Randall replied.

'Okay, if you're sure. Tell them to call my office. I guess there's nothing more we can do here tonight. We've asked people for blocks around all the questions we can think of. No one saw a suspicious car, or any car except Leila's. No one heard anything, saw anyone. Well, come to the station tomorrow morning and make your statement Catherine.'

'Oh yes, I know the routine,' she said flatly.

Maybe by then I'll have another dead body to report, she told herself. Gosh, maybe someone will be dead on my lawn when I go out to the car tomorrow morning. That way, I could knock off two statements at once. People should hire me as a divining rod, to find bodies.

She realized she had to get some grip on herself, or she wouldn't be able to do anything the next day. Or for weeks. The black hole into which she had fallen when her parents died was waiting for her. An indescribable abyss of depression confronted her. She had only to take one more step and she would fall in.

The fear began to grip her. But fear would hurry her toward the hole faster than anything, if she let it overwhelm her. She wanted to lean against Randall with more than her body, but she knew from her experience during the weeks after her parents' death that this was something she had to fight through alone.

But Randall was there. When she came through, she would have a tenuous something at the other end. She hadn't had that before, and she had made it then. She would make it again. This time, if she won decisively, it might never happen again, she thought.

The police were gone. Angel was gone, after telling Randall without a twitch of an eyebrow that he would be staying with Catherine that night.

Only Randall and Catherine were left in the house, and it seemed empty with just two inhabitants, after the coming and going it had seen that evening.

In the house out back, there was fingerprinting dust, bloodstains, and silence. The blood, Tom's blood, would be dry now, and brown. Catherine could feel the presence of that house at her back. She wondered what she would do with it, the old house that had seen so many uses in its long life. Who would want it now?

Randall had gone to get the Mascalcos' telephone number after a long, quiet, tense discussion with Catherine. He had not wanted to wake the Mascalcos with the news that their son was dead. He had wanted to wait until morning. Catherine had only thought they had a right to know as soon as possible. It couldn't be withheld from them, she had argued. They would bitterly resent being called in the morning and learning their son had been dead for twelve hours.

Catherine had not learned of the death of her parents until she had gone back to her new apartment from her new job. She remembered the guilt she had felt at having been happily engaged in something else while their corpses were in a little funeral home in Arkansas. She remembered her anger that others had known the news, more important to her than to anyone in the world, hours before she was told.

Randall had yielded to her argument. She could hear his voice in the kitchen now.

But she realized, as she huddled in her corner of the

couch, that she should have said nothing to Randall, nothing at all. He, not Catherine, was the one who had volunteered to break the news. She should have left it up to him, since he had taken on the sickening responsibility.

She listened to the murmur of his voice and felt furious at her own interference. Her capacity for anger with herself was far greater than her capacity for anger with anyone else.

When Randall returned to the den, his face was gray with strain. He removed his glasses and rubbed the bridge of his nose. When he finally spoke, it was not about the conversation that had just taken place.

'Catherine, take off those goddamned clothes,' he said.

She gaped at him.

Then she understood. She rose without a word. In the bathroom she yanked off the bloodstained jeans and jammed them into the garbage can. She looked down at herself and saw that the blood had soaked through her clothes and dried on her skin. She stepped into the shower and soaped and rinsed, then repeated, until her hands and legs were white again and chafed with scrubbing.

Tom's blood, down the drain. Four people, down the drain. Gone. Snuffed out like dogs hit by careless cars, because they were in the wrong place at the wrong time; because they weren't aware of the danger until it was too late.

Randall would hire a new reporter. He would doubtless start looking the next day.

Jerry Selforth was prescribing antibiotics and setting broken arms, just as Dr Linton had done for years. He had a nurse who managed his office just as well as Leona would have. And Molly Perkins held the coffees for the bridge club every bit as well as Rachel Linton had.

Other dun-colored dogs were running through the

fields, coupling with bitches to ensure more dun-colored dogs.

That was the way life went on. The thought might even be comforting, after a few years. Many years. More years than I will live, she thought.

She sprayed herself with perfume, thinking the smell of Tom's death was still on her, and went out to join Randall.

He seemed to have recovered from the worst of his conversation with the Mascalcos. But for the first time, Catherine was fully conscious that he was twelve years older than she was. He had gotten out his pipe and was puffing away, looking more than ever like a muscular, misplaced professor.

'Can you sleep now?'

She shook her head.

'Neither can I. Let's go over it, if you can stand that.'

She waited. She owed him this, for having urged him to call the Mascalcos.

'Leona. No – your parents. The first ones.'

A fire ignited in her tired body. He accepted her conviction. He agreed.

'Your mother. Your father. His nurse. A reporter who said he was going to pry into their murders. This started with your folks. Glenn or Rachel, as the primary target?'

'I think . . . my father.'

'I agree. Something he knew as a doctor.'

'Not necessarily,' she said. 'He was a friend to half the county, and he inspired confidences.'

'Granted.' Randall knocked his pipe out in an ashtray. 'Do you think Leona could have killed your parents? Could she have been a murderer? How did she feel about your father?'

'Before she was a blackmailer and an abortionist, she

was a good nurse for my father for thirty-odd years,' Catherine replied. 'There was never anything between them, but I think Leona loved my father. I can see that now . . . Maybe I knew it all along.'

'Do you think she could have killed him, knowing she couldn't ever have him?'

'I don't think so. I think she was used to the companionship she had with him every day at the office. She would have been his nurse until he retired, and that was years away. And she lost her income when he died: Leona loved money, too. Last point, but not least, I don't think she knew how to tamper with a car.'

'That's disposed of, then,' Randall had tidied that argument away. Catherine realized that in his own way he was working off the grief and horror of Tom's death.

'So,' he muttered, 'we assume that Leona didn't kill your parents. Do we take for granted, then, that Glenn, Rachel, and Leona were killed by the same person, for the same reason?'

Sure, why not? Catherine thought crazily. She nodded.

'Okay. That would point to something they all knew. Considering the six-month lapse between murders, it would seem that for six months Leona kept silent about something she knew, while the murderer paid her blackmail money. Something Leona discovered after your father was killed, maybe when she got the office wound up . . . Or maybe she realized the significance of an event or a conversation later. Something your father knew in his professional life; or something told to him in the office, as a friend.'

Catherine mulled that over.

'I didn't express that well. Too many "somethings" and "maybes" . . . But do you agree?' Randall prodded.

Finally Catherine nodded. 'Leona was always at the office when my father was there,' she said slowly. 'Even when someone buzzed him late at night' – she shuddered – 'he would call her to come in before he even went over there. So she would have heard everything he heard, unless the conversation took place after he sent her from the room, while he talked with a patient after an examination. He would do that so she could prepare for the next patient, or pull files on whoever was in the waiting room. And all the files were accessible to her.' Catherine stopped to think. 'But with something like this, Randall, I can't imagine . . . We're presuming a critical conversation, a very personal and important conversation. Father would have sent Leona from the room. I know. He always knew when people were embarrassed or self-conscious about what they had, or suspected they had. His consultations with them were always private.'

'Couldn't she have listened at the door?'

'It would have been hard. There were always other patients around, and the office maid, and the receptionist.'

'Okay – difficult, but not impossible. However she did it, she found out. And Tom must have found out the same thing. You know what a gung-ho investigative reporter he thought he was. He wanted to solve this case before the police did. He told me so himself, Monday, while you were in Production.'

Again the little thought moved at the back of Catherine's mind, and again she tried to catch hold of it too soon. It melted away.

'I don't know,' she said uncertainly.

Randall looked at her questioningly.

'I would swear that during the past twenty-four hours he was thinking more about the breakup with his fiancée, and getting Leila to bed, than he was about Leona's murder,' Catherine said. She gripped the embroidered pillow and added, 'He was just a boy. He was younger than I am.'

Randall touched her cheek. They sat in silence for a few minutes.

Then he said, 'Just one more thing. If Leona knew who killed your father, do you think she would have kept quiet about it?'

'If she believed the person she was blackmailing was his murderer – she may not have known that, come to think of it – she might have figured, "Dead is dead. What good can this bring me?" Even if she loved him. Or she might have thought she was getting some kind of vengeance by blackmailing the murderer.'

Then Catherine added, 'I realize now that I never knew Leona, never understood her. At all.'

Randall stirred and looked at her. 'You should be in bed,' he said. 'Are you going to be able to sleep?'

She nodded.

'I'll sleep in here,' he said, thumping the couch.

'No.'

'Catherine,' he said gently, 'this isn't the right time.'

'I know that,' she said irritably. 'But you can sleep in my bed without being overcome by passion, surely, tired as we both are? Or you can have the other bed, in my old room.'

'Even as tired as we are,' he said, 'I think I'd better take the other bed.'

12

When she got up the next morning he was gone.

He had pulled the bed together, she found, when she peeped shyly into her old room. She was disappointed but a little relieved. She would have liked to see his head on the pillow, but her soul craved the solitude of her coffeemaking and reading at the table.

That might be a problem later, she thought hopefully.

He had left a note in the kitchen, propped against a full coffeepot. Bless him, she thought, peering at his spiky scrawl.

'Don't come in to work,' Catherine read. 'I looked in at you this morning and had to overcome a mighty temptation, but you need sleep more than anything else at this point.' She smiled.

She saw through the steam of her first cup of coffee that it was nine o'clock. She had to go to the sheriff's office to make her statement, but she was going to take her time. She needed to collect herself before facing Sheriff Galton.

Of course she would go in to work after that. She knew Randall would be run ragged if she didn't show up. No reporters, no one to answer the phone, since Leila undoubtedly would not come in. And that telephone would be ringing off the wall.

Yes, she would go to work.

After she had had some coffee and a few cigarettes, she realized there was no use trying to make anything normal of the morning. How deeply I'm embedded in my little rut she thought. A friend of mine died last night, while I was watching, and I try to drink my X number of cups of coffee, smoke X number of cigarettes, and stick to my piddling little routine.

She got dressed and drove over to the little brick building in front of the jail.

It was like her arrival there Saturday morning. To her horror, she began shaking as she pulled onto the concrete apron in front of the swinging door. She knew what she would see, and she saw it. There was Mary Jane Cory, typing, her unrealistic hair sprayed into an elaborate structure of swirls.

But the pattern was broken, after all, when the black deputy, Eakins, came out of the sheriff's office and approached her.

'Miss Linton,' he said reluctantly, his voice hardly more than a mumble. Catherine turned to face him and waited cautiously.

'My mother wants to see you.' Before Catherine could say anything, before she could tell him she didn't have any time that day, he went on. 'She wants to see you awful bad. She's been on at me about it for two days now.'

'What is it about?' She guiltily remembered the note in the can of brownies.

'She won't tell me. You know how stubborn and . . . old-fashioned she is.'

'Old-fashioned' must mean 'Uncle Tom,' Catherine decided. Yes, Betty was. It made Catherine as uncomfortable as it made her son.

I just can't cope with Betty's 'Miss Catherine's' this morning, she thought desperately. She was about to say no, when Percy Eakins gave her a pleading look it obviously hurt him to give. His pride was aching like arthritis on a rainy day, Catherine realized.

'I'll go after I make my statement,' she said.

Then Mary Jane looked up from her typing, and Catherine became caught up in the mills of the law.

Catherine's statement was longer and a little tricky this time (since she was concealing something, though it seemed a harmless thing to conceal), and she had time to notice that Mary Jane was no longer sympathetic. She was, if possible, even more briskly professional than usual. Her eyes on Catherine's face were cold and speculative.

Catherine realized for the first time that this might be the pattern for the rest of her life, unless the murderer was caught. There was not enough evidence to arrest her: there was only the coincidence of two dead people turning up in Catherine Linton's immediate vicinity. The sheriff knew she couldn't have physically accomplished the murders, she thought. But that would make little difference in Lowfield talk.

She was so depressed when she left the sheriff's office that she figured going to see Betty Eakins couldn't make her feel worse.

The black part of Lowfield was as close to a ghetto as a tiny town could get. Some of the streets were unpaved, and the children ran and played in them, only reluctantly moving aside for cars to pass. Some of the houses were clean, neatly kept, and sound; but most of them leaned and staggered, barely able to contain the life that spilled out of them.

Betty's house was at a stage in between. It was still upright, but it was beginning to slide. The paint was peeling, and the yard was growing wild.

There were no sidewalks, of course, and the street, paved perhaps twenty years ago, was narrow. Catherine pulled as close to the house as she dared, and hoped no other car would want to pass while she was inside.

Children gathered on the other side of the street to watch her get out of the car. They ranged in age from three to ten, Catherine estimated, and their clothing was in various stages of disrepair, ranging from neat-but-dusty to out-and-out rags. They were barefoot, smiling, and shy. She gave them a tentative smile. The shyest covered their mouths with their hands, but let their returning grins shine through.

She pushed through the burgeoning sunflowers in the yard and knocked on the doorsill. The wooden door was open. The screen door was almost off its hinges.

'Who that?' came a creaky query from the darkness of the house's back rooms. The shades had been drawn against the heat.

'Catherine,' she called.

'Miss Catherine!'

Betty's halting steps approached. Catherine could see her emerging from the kitchen. Betty must have been close to seventy-five. She was thin, bent, and gnarled. She was putting in her teeth as she walked, and was dressed in a formidably clean green and white housedress and white apron.

Catherine had never seen Betty without an apron on.

'Come on in! Come on in!' A chicken ran across the yard, and Betty made an automatic flapping gesture in its direction.

Catherine stepped into the room and looked around her for a place to sit. There was a sack of snap beans and a bowl half-full of prepared ones by a chair, so Catherine chose the sofa, which was covered by an old chenille bedspread, and lowered herself gingerly.

'You seen my boy this morning? He done told you I wanted to talk with you?'

'Yes, he did,' Catherine said. 'Thanks for the brownies. They were great. How are you feeling?'

'Getting old, getting old. My bones is hurting. But I reckon I'll live a while longer, make a few more batches of brownies.'

Betty took up the sack of beans, then put it down when she remembered she had company.

'No, go on,' Catherine said hastily.

Slowly Betty's hands returned to their work. Her head bent over the bowl. All Catherine could see was white hair braided and pinned in circles.

'Reckon I got to tell you something,' Betty murmured. 'You in trouble now . . . Reckon I got to speak up. I ain't told nobody, didn't want any trouble. But you my little girl. You in some kind of mess. I hear people talking.'

The two women sat quietly. Catherine couldn't think of anything to say, and Betty was thinking about what to say next.

'That boy that got killed last night, was he your beau?'

'No,' she said.

Betty looked up at her, relieved. 'You got a beau?'

'Yes. Randall Gerrard,' Catherine said firmly.

'Gerrard. I know Sadie who works for them. His daddy run the paper?'

'He's dead now. Randall runs it.'

'The Gerrards got money? Is he good to you?'

'Yes.'

'You know his mamma? She like you?'

'I think so.'

'I went to your mamma and daddy's wedding. Your daddy,' Betty said slowly. 'He asked me to come. He said, "You got to be there, Betty. It wouldn't be right without you."'

155

Betty was building up to something, rambling around the corners of what she really wanted to say. Suddenly Catherine was curious.

'They've been dead about six months now,' Betty said thoughtfully. 'Nobody asked me any questions then. I was glad. Percy, he was trying to get on working for the sheriff. Little Betty ran off to Detroit about then. Left me her kids to look after. I had the woes of Job, seemed like. So when your folks died, I just didn't think about something I should've spoken up about. But then, no sheriff come asking *me* questions. That would've brought it to my mind. I would've spoken up. But – I just had too many other things worrying me.'

Betty's fingers were moving steadily, breaking off the ends of the beans, then snapping them into pieces. Catherine watched the bowl fill up.

'But you in trouble now,' Betty muttered. Her fingers stilled as she reached a decision. She looked up into Catherine's white face.

'You got a little sun on you for once, didn't you?' Betty observed. She cleared her throat. 'Well, it was this way. I never did like Miss Leona. I know' – Betty lifted a dark hand to forestall an admonition Catherine would never dream of giving – 'it ain't up to me to like or not like. God made us all, we all got a place. But I didn't like her. I saw she didn't care for you or your mamma. So I watched her close, when she was in you-all's house. And even after I quit working for your mother, you know, I went and cleaned your daddy's office when the woman who worked for him got sick – or drunk, most often,' Betty said severely. She frowned over the erring maid for a moment.

'Here I am wandering,' she resumed. 'Well. About three days before your folks got taken, I was over to your daddy's office late in the afternoon. That Callie, she had been on a long one, but you don't care about that: it ain't the point of all this.'

Catherine reached up to wipe the sweat from her forehead, and found that her hand was shaking.

'Your daddy and some man was in the examination room.' Betty's eyes met Catherine's.

Catherine nodded jerkily.

'They was talking. They was raising their voices. I knew something was wrong. I *never* heard raised voices in your daddy's office before. It was late. Wasn't no one there but me and Miss Leona.' Betty's face went wry with dislike. She heaved a heavy breath and went on.

'I was mopping the second examination room. My door was open, but the door to the other room, where your daddy and the man was, 'course it was closed. I could hear voices, but not what they were saying.

'I seen Miss Leona come along the hall, you know how quiet she moved in them white shoes. She passed by the door of my room. I wasn't making no noise; I don't think she knew I was there. She was 'spose to be gone. I heard your daddy tell her to go on home, he had seen everybody. But then I heard her messing 'round in the medicine room, and I guess she heard the other man come in and was so nosy she had to find out who it was. She didn't like nothing going on at that office that she didn't know all about. For that matter, she didn't like your daddy doing nothing if she didn't know what it was and why.' And Betty shot Catherine a significant look with her yellowed eyes.

'What happened?' Catherine asked carefully.

'She was listening,' said Betty. 'She was listening at the door.' Betty's voice was flat. 'I knew that was wrong, your daddy wouldn't want that. Why else did he tell her to go home? But I couldn't *say* nothing.'

Catherine could understand that. Betty would never have said anything to Leona.

'I put down my mop real quiet, and I went to the door of the room so I could watch her. She was just drinking it in. Her head was so close to that door you couldn't have got a broomstraw between them.

'Your daddy put his hand on the doorknob and opened it a little to leave, or maybe to tell the other man it was time for him to leave. Miss Leona stepped back right smart then, she sure did. She went and hid in your daddy's office. She didn't go by me, you see. She didn't see me,' Betty emphasized. 'I stayed where I was. I was scared, by that time. Your daddy, he wasn't mad, he was just upset . . . But that other man, he was *mad*.

'Your daddy took a step out of the room, but he stood with his back to me and talked some more. He says – I could hear him then – he says, "You're going to have to face it. It's the law. I'm sorry, more sorry than I can say. But I have to report it. I got to tell . . ." This I didn't understand, Miss Catherine. Something about the government. Then he says, "You know things have changed, it's not like it used to be. After a while, you can come home. No one need know. And you'll feel a lot better."

'I didn't understand that part, either, Miss Catherine. The doctor said something about animals, some kind of animal. I don't remember the name of it. It was something they got in Texas, I know. I seen it on TV the other day, and when they call it by name, it was the same name. Begin with an *A*.'

Aardvark? Catherine wondered incredulously. She rummaged in her mind for another animal whose name began with an *A*. Nothing. She pushed that aside, for Betty was still talking.

'—I stepped back where I was. I didn't want your daddy

thinking I was listening in like Miss Leona. He went out the back of the office, all upset. He wouldn't have seen me if I'd jumped out in front of him and yelled. The other man, he came out after a minute. I heard him going down the hall and out the front door. So I didn't see him. I don't know to this day who it was. But Miss Leona knew, she saw him.'

'And you didn't tell anyone,' Catherine said.

'No. My Percy, my youngest, was worried about getting that job . . . Little Betty run off, leaving them poor kids. Your folks got killed. I forgot all about it until Miss Leona got herself killed. Then I heard you're in trouble, some folks think you did it. When you didn't come after I left you that note, I had Percy tell you I had to see you. All this may be nothing, Miss Catherine. But no one ever asked me. Now I think all the time. Remember, I can't go nowhere because of the arthritis.'

Betty plodded through her multitude of excuses again. Catherine believed her. It probably hadn't seemed very important to her, except from the standpoint of warning her to watch out for Leona. And no one had asked Betty any questions.

'How close did you say this was to my parents' death?' Catherine asked.

'Three days, I think. I can't call to mind the day of the week. But three days, maybe two.'

'And you're sure you don't know who the man was?' Catherine asked, knowing the answer.

'That's all I know, Miss Catherine.'

'I have to go now,' Catherine said shakily.

'Yes, ma'am.'

'Don't say that,' she said sharply. Then she collected herself. 'I'm sorry, Betty. I'm glad you told me. I'll come again when I can.'

'You bring that beau of yours by,' said Betty, more cheerful now that her mind was at ease.

'I will, Betty. Goodbye. Thank you.'

Catherine walked through the sunflowers in a daze.

The children were scattered in the street, playing an amputated form of baseball. Catherine automatically smiled at them, and drove out of the black section very slowly, to avoid chickens and children.

She didn't want to look in anyone's face right then.

She drove out of Lowfield a little way, just to the west of the highway where the last houses straggled to a stop. There was a small area full of trees, surrounded by a high metal fence. She turned into it, under the arch over the open gate, and parked her car in the usual spot. Beyond the fence, she could see a tractor in the fields. Except for that distant human, she was alone.

Lately she had not gone there as much as she had at first.

The headstones still looked new. The graves were neat. Catherine made donations to the church fund that paid the caretaker.

She had always liked it there, even as a child. She had read all the older headstones, and knew the more striking epitaphs by heart. It was always peaceful, always quiet.

She sat beside her family. Her parents were beside her grandparents. And her great-grandparents.

She sat beside them and cried.

When the big gush died down to occasional tears, and she was still shaky, but quieted, she walked through the cemetery. It was a good place to think without interruption.

She tried to picture Betty on the witness stand.
She couldn't.
She thought, *Antelope? Angus?*
Then she wiped off her face and returned to her car.

13

Catherine was immediately aware of the eyes. They peered from the door of the production room, and from the reception area. Two people were waiting there when she came in. They were obviously at a loss for what to do, without Leila at the desk to direct them. The door to Randall's office was shut, and the sound of typing came from behind it.

She felt a glaze harden on her face. She moved stiffly. One of the two visitors was an advertiser, delivering his ad for the next issue. He was startled by the sight of Catherine. Perhaps he had hoped to go back to the production room and have a good chat with the staff. Catherine took the ad and calmly assured him that she would deliver it herself.

The second visitor was the librarian, Mrs Weilenmann.

'I couldn't reach you at home,' she told Catherine. 'I just wanted you to know how much I'm – thinking of you.'

'Thank you,' Catherine said stiffly. 'I can't talk about it, please.'

Mrs Weilenmann patted her on the shoulder, then left.

Randall's door opened.

'I thought it was you,' he said. 'Come in here.'

She gestured toward the empty desk. 'I ought to be out here.'

'Mother's been handling it. She had to go out for a minute, but she'll be back.'

When he had closed the door, he held her to him. Catherine looked past his ear blindly.

He released her and looked into her face. She slowly reached up to touch his cheek.

'You should have stayed at home,' he said gently.

'No, no point in that.'

'Things here are pretty unpleasant,' he said.

He looked so depressed and so much older that Catherine was jolted into remembering something she had, incredibly, forgotten: that Randall feared Leona Gaites had been blackmailing his mother.

'Randall,' she said tentatively, 'surely you're not worried about Miss Angel?'

He looked at her uncomprehendingly.

'What? Oh, no. I did what you suggested. I just asked her. You were right. She said, "No, if Leona Gaites had approached me with any such proposition, I would have told her to publish and be damned, and that she was welcome to use my paper to publish in!" I can't understand now why I even worried about it. I guess just knowing we had a skeleton in our closet, knowing Leona had been taking advantage of skeletons to make money . . .'

'Is there something else you're worried about?'

'Aside from hiring Tom's replacement and wondering when I can expect that bitch Leila to come back, so I can get her to train a new receptionist?' he asked sharply. Then he shook his head. 'I'm sorry, Catherine. I'm just tired. I want all this to be over. I want this town to return to normal. I want to have time to see you in a regular relationship, without the stress and blood all around us.'

She wondered whether they would have become as

163

close, if it hadn't been for those very conditions of stress and blood. She thought not.

'We can't worry about that now,' Catherine said. 'We have to wait for this to end. Then there'll be time to lie in the sun and go back to the levee. There's something I want to tell you, something I just found out.'

Randall's extension buzzed at that second, and he bent over his desk to pick it up. He gave Catherine an exasperated look of apology.

While he spoke into the receiver, Catherine's gaze wandered over the collection of framed pictures and certificates covering the walls of his office. Four generations of Gerrard editors had occupied the room, so a great many of these mementos were yellowed. One piece of paper still white with freshness caught her eye.

'In appreciation of the services of Randall Gerrard and Dr Jerry Selforth,' Catherine read with difficulty, 'from the Junior Baseball Club of Lowfield County.'

I didn't know Randall and Jerry were coaches, Catherine thought idly.

She pictured Randall in uniform at the plate, hitting a ball over the bleachers, throwing down the bat and heading for first base.

Throwing down the bat . . . She stiffened. Before she could stop herself, another image arose: Randall's powerful arms swinging the bat at a blackmailing nurse, and at Tom. Maybe Leona hadn't approached Angel Gerrard. Maybe she had approached Randall instead.

You fool, she lashed at herself savagely. Don't you dare think for one minute . . . After all baseball bats are hardly rare or hard to buy.

But how accessible the weapon was to Randall. How easily he could obtain that heavy length of wood, if he needed a weapon.

She knew her judgment was clouded by physical

exhaustion and grief. She stared at Randall while he wrangled with the advertiser on the other end of the line.

If I'm wrong (and of course I'm wrong), he will never know I thought for one minute that he was connected with murder, she told herself.

Catherine lowered her eyes so they wouldn't meet Randall's inadvertently.

Maybe, just for now, I shouldn't tell him what Betty said, she reflected hesitantly. After all, her story is only confirmation of a half-baked theory of his, about Leona overhearing something at Daddy's office. It may not mean anything, right? And everyone who might have known something about this case is dead. Everybody but me . . . and Betty. Betty is the only possible living eyewitness to any portion of this whole chain of deaths.

Catherine realized she had just talked herself out of telling Randall about Betty's little story. She had reached a test of faith she couldn't pass.

Randall was still involved with his caller. Catherine tried to assume a natural expression and rose from her chair. When Randall glanced up inquiringly, she made typing gestures with her fingers. He nodded that he understood, and she eased out of his office. She moved toward her desk like an automaton and, once settled in her chair, folded her hands stiffly in her lap and stared at the wall. She was as miserable as she ever had been in her life.

When Randall's mother passed through the room, Catherine had to force herself to speak.

'Miss Angel,' she said in a lifeless voice, 'if you'd get me Tom's personnel file I'd appreciate it. I have to write a story.'

Angel eyed Catherine sharply and then nodded briskly. She brought Tom's file to Catherine's desk, along with Randall's notes from his conversation with Jerry Selforth and the sheriff. Randall had been prepared to write the story if she had not come in, Catherine realized dully.

She rolled paper into the platen, flexed her tense fingers, took a deep breath, and began to type.

'Tom Mascalco, 21, a reporter for the *Lowfield Gazette*, died Tuesday night as the result of wounds sustained in a struggle in his home.'

When the story was almost finished, she had to buzz Randall to ask when Tom's funeral services would be held.

'Friday,' he said wearily. 'Holy Mary of the Assumption, in Memphis. Ten o'clock. We'll have to go.'

It was the only time she spoke to him for the rest of the day.

During the afternoon, Sheriff Galton sent Deputy Ralph Carson to go through Tom's desk, to see if it contained any notes that might be regarded as clues. Ralph was courteous but remote. They might have barely known each other, instead of having dated off and on through high school, sharing hayrides, dances, and drinks. He was married now, with two children, Catherine remembered. But the gulf between them was far wider than the gap in time and circumstances.

He's definitely keeping his distance until he sees which way the cat jumps, she thought. But he has to be polite. After all, what if I didn't do it?

And provoking that courtesy, making him speak when he wanted to finish his job and leave, gave her an awful enjoyment.

The notes Tom had made on Leona's murder contained nothing that was not commonly known.

While Catherine identified items and notes to help the deputy, she also transferred *Gazette* material – sheets of columns and comic strips – to her own desk. She would have to handle that now.

As she gathered up the columns, she saw Tom leaning back in his chair, reading them with lazy interest, trying to decide which ones should be in next week's paper . . . pulling on his mustache, smiling, as he no doubt thought about persuading Leila to bed that evening.

For a moment her grasp weakened, and the sheets almost cascaded to the floor; but the next second she had hold of them again, and put them on her desk.

Then there was Tom's camera, in a bottom desk drawer. He had preferred to use his own, instead of the *Gazette*'s. It had film in it, she saw, and she realized she had to remove and develop the film before the camera could be returned to Tom's parents.

She thought of a question to ask Ralph Carson.

'About the house,' she said abruptly.

He looked surprised.

'The one Tom rented from me,' she explained. 'What can I do about getting it cleaned? His parents will have to get in there to get his things out. They can't see that.'

'Oh,' he said. 'Well, you could see if you could hire some prisoners from the jail to do it. Some trustees, maybe. They might be glad to do it for the money. Why don't you ask the sheriff?'

'I'll do that,' she said, and they continued their fruitless sifting. All they found were a couple of magazines that made Carson turn red and caused Catherine to lift her eyebrows. She pitched them into Tom's wastebasket.

It was just as well, she decided, that she had gone through the desk instead of someone else.

When Carson left, his hands empty and his face glum, Catherine sat down at her desk and looked around aimlessly. She had to do something.

Her eyes lit on Tom's camera. She would develop the film in it. No one would bother her in the darkroom.

The reporters' tiny darkroom was to the left of the door that led to the production department. Catherine grabbed up the camera, buzzed Angel to tell her she was still incommunicado, and dived into the little room, turning on the red light that shone outside when film was being processed. Now no one could talk to her for a good length of time.

The smock she wore to protect her clothes from chemicals was hanging in its usual place on a hook on the door. Tom's heavy denim work apron was beside it. On an impulse, she ran her hands through the pockets of the apron. There was nothing in them, and her mouth twisted in self-derision as she let it fall back against the door.

She pulled on her smock, snapping it down the front, and looked around the darkroom to make sure where everything was before she turned off the lights.

While the film developed there was nothing to do but wait. Catherine lit a cigarette and propped herself against the high counter.

This was the nicest moment of a jarring day. She lounged in the eerie red glow, safe from intrusion because of the light shining outside the door. The *Gazette*'s little darkroom satisfied her catlike fondness for small places.

The 'bing!' of the timer roused her from her reverie. She finished developing the film, her mind at ease and refreshed by the isolation and darkness.

Other places had big beautiful dryers, Catherine thought enviously. The *Gazette* had a clothesline and some clamps and a fan.

While the film was hanging from the clothesline, drying, Catherine switched on the light and examined the half-used roll of film. The pictures were, as she had supposed, Tom's shots of the Lion's Club meeting, featuring its guest speaker, the lieutenant governor. In reversed black and white, Catherine saw shots of a speaker at a podium, and men seated in rows at a U-shaped collection of tables, the plates in front of them showing up as black circles.

Somehow, Tom's last pictures should have been of something more memorable, Catherine thought.

He had been by far a better photographer than she, but he had been too impatient to enjoy darkroom work. She had often developed his film while she did her own.

He made me feel like a regular Martha, Catherine thought: and despite her weariness and confusion, the peace of the little room relaxed her so that she could smile at the recollection. She was beginning to assimilate the fact that Tom was gone.

She decided to enlarge all the shots. It would take up time, while keeping her busy with something she enjoyed. And besides, she was not a good interpreter of negatives. Tom had been able to run a look down the film and choose this one or that one, as the best shots. Catherine had to put much more time and thought into picking out pictures.

She let out a sigh and set about enlarging the five shots Tom had taken. *The Gazette*'s enlarger was old and cranky, had been secondhand when purchased. But she had always felt she had a kind of silent understanding with the enlarger. And sure enough, today it cooperated.

As Catherine rocked the pictures in the developing tray, she decided that there was something romantic about photography. She watched, enthralled, as the faces began to emerge from the solution.

There was a dramatic shot of the speaker, bent over the podium, one arm extended in a point-making gesture. And operating on the theory that faces sold papers, Tom had taken several shots of the assembled Lions listening, with greater or lesser degrees of attention, to the address.

There was Sheriff Galton, looking bored. These past few days had made an awful difference in the man. Catherine focused on the face beside his: Martin Barnes, obviously daydreaming, perhaps about Jewel and her little house by the highway, she thought wryly. The mayor's face materialized. He was staring at a roll on his otherwise empty plate, perhaps wondering if anyone would notice if he ate it (he had been battling his paunch for years.)

There was Carl Perkins, smiling broadly, either at the lieutenant governor's speech or at some private thought. Randall was beside him, pipe in hand. Then Jerry Selforth's smooth dark head appeared, his face all eagerness and attention. Jerry would marry a Lowfield girl, she decided, and stay there until he died.

When the pictures were ready, Catherine no longer had an excuse to linger in the darkroom. She emerged reluctantly, found Tom's copy of the story, and attached the picture of the lieutenant governor. She wrote the cut line and attached that. Then she typed in Tom's byline.

Once again she cast around for something to do.

There were the weekly columns she had lifted from Tom's desk. Clipping those columns was definitely necessary, and easy to do.

She got out her scissors and in a very few moments had cut out the comic strips indicated by date for the following week. The handyman column was easy, too. She imagined that the one about building rose trellises was suitable for summer, and her scissors snipped it out.

To prolong the little task, Catherine read all the Dr Croft columns. There were seven left in this batch. The one in the previous week's paper had been on appendicitis. Catherine remembered that it had made Tom a little nervous, since he still possessed his appendix.

Well, here was one on Crohn's disease. What about

that? Catherine scanned it and decided it didn't appeal to her.

Some of these are really exotic, she thought. Dr Croft must be running out of ailments. My father would be glad of that.

Then her eye caught the word *Armadillo*.

She read the column through once, twice. Pity and loathing made her heart sick.

When she was able to rise, she went to the darkroom and upclipped Tom's Lion's Club group picture. She unearthed photo files from ten years ago, five years, two years. She leafed through them and laid a number of pictures side by side.

She understood now why her parents had died, why Leona and Tom had been beaten to death.

Her father had been an innocent. Leona had been foolish, criminally and fatally foolish. Tom had just been in the way.

The day of her parents' funeral passed drearily through her mind again . . . And the day she and Leona had moved the filing cabinets into the attic of the old office. Leona hadn't taken a file from the cabinets that day, as Catherine had vaguely suspected after hearing Betty's story. Instead she had put something in; had hidden it there for safe-keeping.

She had to produce it at least once, Catherine thought dully. To prove she had it; so she could get her damned money. She hid it because she was scared he would break into her house to steal it . . . She wouldn't have had any leverage after that. Didn't Leona know how desperate he was? Or was she blinded by greed? Maybe she did see blackmail as a way to avenge my father's death. She paid . . . He did break into her house to steal it, and he killed her in the process. He came prepared to kill her,

171

with a baseball bat. What a convenient and appropriate weapon.

Catherine twisted her hair in a knot and held it on top of her head. She closed her eyes and thought of all the questions she had answered in the past few days without even being aware they had been asked. Her ignorance had caused Tom's death. That would be lodged in her conscience for the rest of her life.

Give the devil his due, she thought savagely. He didn't kill Leila. But then she was screaming, and he thought someone would come . . . Not enough time to kill Leila or search those cabinets . . . What a shock he must have had when she began yelling. It was bad enough that Tom was there, when he thought Tom was out on a date with Leila.

And of course he hasn't killed me, Catherine thought. He has tried every route in order to avoid killing me. He doesn't want to . . . He's *fond* of me. And he's probably very very *sorry* about Mother and Father. And Tom, my friend – too bad about Tom Mascalco. He was in the way. Of course, Leona asked for it.

Catherine shuddered.

Yes, very very *sorry* about Glenn and Rachel Linton.

It was a matter of pride and vengeance that she finish the thing herself. And a matter of habit: she had done things for herself for so long.

And then there was the fact that she had caused Tom's death. In the first place, she had given the murderer information indicating that Tom was an obstacle in his path; in the second place, she had not called the police when she had heard the rustling in the grass.

Her rational mind told her she had had nothing to do with the car troubles that had caused Tom to remain in the old office instead of going out with Leila; or with the couple's going to bed instead of using Leila's car to go to a movie, for example. But her rational mind also told her that words from her own mouth had led, however indirectly, to Tom's death.

Perhaps she could have saved Tom; nothing could have saved her parents.

When she thought again of the reason they had died, rage came over her. It had been gaining strength, quenching the pity and revulsion, while she sat brooding. The rage shook her as nothing had ever shaken her before. She felt as if she was being burned from the inside out.

She looked at the clock. She had forgotten about the time. Now she saw it was 5:30. Most of the staff must have gone by while she sat deaf and dumb.

Time to go, Catherine, she told herself.

She covered her typewriter and picked up her purse. She put the Dr Croft column on Randall's desk, in silent apology. She thought of trying to find him. She was sure he was somewhere in the building, maybe in the production room working on the press with Salton. But a rising sense of urgency carried her out to her car.

She drove the short distance home with special care. She didn't trust herself.

She was so fixed on her course that she was bewildered when she saw a strange car with two people in it parked in front of her house. She saw two heads turning to follow her car into the garage, and realized she couldn't avoid finding out who they were and what they wanted.

As she walked across the lawn to meet them, she noticed the Tennessee license plate on their car. A man and a woman, middle-aged, attractive.

It was hard for her to understand what they were saying. Her ears weren't at fault, she discovered slowly; their voices were choked and hoarse. The pretty dark woman, still young, with the red-edged eyes, was Tom's mother, Catherine gradually realized; and the man with olive skin and light hair was his father.

Catherine's ingrained training triumphed in her handling of these newly bereaved parents. She acted out of sheer reflex, rising out of profound shock. She simply could not think of how to ask them to go away.

'Won't you come inside?' she asked.

'We don't want to trouble you, but we would like to ask you some questions,' said Mr Mascalco.

'Of course,' she said blankly.

As she preceded the Mascalcos into the house, she felt as if she was walking through water. It was an almost physical sensation of pressure, a buoyant feeling of absolute unreality.

While the Mascalcos sat on the couch where Catherine had huddled the night before with their son's blood on her clothes and hands, she made coffee and carried it in to them.

The couple touched her so deeply that a little of her drifting sensation ebbed away. She felt her rage dissolving at the edges as she responded to their grief, their bewilderment at the death of their oldest child and only son.

Mrs Mascalco wept and apologized for weeping. Her husband sat with his arm around her, his face distorted with emotion.

They asked her questions.

I must be careful, she told herself repeatedly.

It would shock them, and they might well hate her, when they discovered their son had died not because he possessed information dangerous to the murderer but because he had rented a house from Catherine.

'We would like to go into the house,' Mrs Mascalco said finally. 'We need to get some of his things for the funeral. One of his suits.'

'No,' said Catherine sharply, jolted back into complete

awareness. They couldn't see the old office the way it was. She could hardly bear to think of walking through the spattered hall herself, though that was where she must go as soon as they left.

'His brown suit,' Mrs Mascalco said. 'A tie.'

'I want to see where my son died,' said her husband.

'No,' Catherine said firmly.

Tom's father, she saw, was passing from grief to anger, ready to take issue with anything.

Catherine got blanker of face and firmer of voice. She remembered what the scene of her parents' crash had looked like. She had seen the car, too.

She promised to get them the suit. No, not now, later. The sheriff had sealed the house, Catherine told them. She wondered, after she said it, if that was true.

Go, she urged them silently. Go.

But they wanted to know more details about the night before. They wanted to linger with Catherine. After all, she had been with their son when he died.

Catherine finally thought of offering them food, but she could think of nothing she had in enough quantity for three people. As if she could eat – but she would have to put up a pretense.

At last Mr Mascalco looked at his watch.

'My God, Elise, we have to go,' he said.

After many leave-takings, they departed, obviously puzzled by Catherine's increasingly tense manner. They couldn't reconcile the time and effort she had given them with the chilly, fixed blankness of her face.

'I'll get the suit tomorrow,' she told them. 'I'll send it up the fastest way I can.'

She took their address. Reassured by her sincerity, Tom's parents were finally out the front door and into their car.

After she made sure their headlights were pointing

in the right direction, toward the highway, she shut the door.

Headlights, she thought. It's dark. It's night.

She had to move, and move fast. The murderer would act tonight, too.

Perhaps the evidence had already disappeared from its hiding place. He would not have to wait very late. After all, he knew that tonight Tom really wouldn't be there.

Moving swiftly, clumsy in her urgency, she rummaged through a kitchen drawer for the extra keys to the old office. The police had Tom's, but she had a set of her own. While searching, she found her gun where she had thrust it the night before.

'Always check your gun before you use it,' her father had said.

She hadn't last night, but she did now. She had reloaded Saturday morning, before she found Leona's body. The gun was ready.

She had started out the back door when a new thought struck her. If anything happened to her – No, she said. Face it. If I am killed, no one else will know what I know.

She had left the Dr Croft column on Randall's desk, but she hadn't told him about Betty's account of the mysterious interview in Dr Linton's office shortly before the fatal accident. Betty's story was not essential, but it was corroborative – though Betty hadn't seen the man's face.

The only solid proof was in that file in the attic. She must at least tell someone else that it existed, and then move as fast as possible.

She went back to the telephone, and dialed the *Gazette* number. Randall answered.

'Listen,' she said. Then it was too much like her call the

night before. She had to wait for a wave of dizziness to pass.

'Catherine, is that you? What's wrong? Where are you?'

'I'm at home, Randall. I have to tell you something. Have you read that column?'

'Yes,' he said. 'I'm listening.'

'This is what I'm going to do,' she said. 'And why.'

'Wait for me!' he was saying almost before she finished telling him.

'No,' she replied. 'I have to go now.'

She hung up before he could say anything else.

The Mascalcos' departure had given her back her rage. She was across the moonlit yard, through the hedge, walking up to the back door. Carried along by her anger, she felt strong as a lion. But her body was telling her something quite different, she found as she approached the old office. She had to stop and wait for a wave of weakness to pass, before she could go on.

I should be afraid, she realized. I should be afraid.

She had to fit the rage somewhere in her tired body, shift it so it could be borne. It was threatening to dispose of her.

With difficulty she fit the key in the lock. The moonlight made her arms look eerily gilded. She thought of how clearly she could be seen if anyone was watching.

But still she was not afraid.

The back door swung open. The moon shone in on the white walls covered with dark splotches. A tiny shiver edged along her spine.

The attic door was in this hallway.

She switched on the light and looked up. There was the dangling cord. She laid her gun on the floor, so she could use both hands to reach it. But the old house was high-ceilinged, and she couldn't stretch far enough to grasp the cord.

Leona had pulled it down for her the last time she had gone up in the attic.

Catherine remembered the stool that had been in Tom's kitchen on Sunday. She went to fetch it.

At last she could reach the cord. She pulled, and the rectangular wooden slab that fit into the ceiling descended. She pulled out the flimsy stairs that lay folded against it.

The single railing was weak, and Catherine remembered worrying that it might give way while she and Leona were maneuvering the filing cabinets up those narrow folding stairs.

Almost as an afterthought, she picked up the gun. Then she ascended into blackness.

The only light in the attic was a bare bulb in the middle of the sloping roof. She yanked the string dangling from it, and the attic was flooded with light.

She had played there as a child. Then it had held trunks of her grandmother's old clothes. Now it only contained two filing cabinets, sitting close to the top of the stairs in the only area where a person could stand upright.

The slots no longer had labels, so Catherine had to go through each drawer looking for the file she wanted. There weren't many left. That helped. Few people were so healthy they hadn't needed to see a doctor at least once since her father's death.

Of course, the murderer hadn't dared to.

When she opened the second cabinet she found what she wanted in the top drawer. She saw immediately that this was the file she was looking for. It had been sealed around the edges with heavy tape. On one side of that tape, there was a slit.

Father did his best to keep Leona from finding out, Catherine thought sadly.

She slid the contents of the file through the slit that Leona Gaites had made in the tape.

She turned to the last entry on the medical record.

'Biopsy taken,' her father had written. 'Results: saw *Mycobacterium leprae*. Evidence of Hansen's disease.'

Carl Perkins was a leper.

'He didn't have to do it,' she whispered. She rested her head against the metal of the cabinet.

It wasn't readily infectious, Dr Croft had pointed out, deriding medieval prejudices. It needn't result in the deformities people associated with the word *leprosy*. It could be treated very effectively now. According to Dr Croft, researchers had found the nine-banded armadillo very useful in their tests to determine even better treatment.

Four people had died because of a man's fear of exposure – a family-proud man from Louisiana, where leprosy was endemic; a man who had established himself in the town and enjoyed its respect and admiration; a man who could not bear to see that town, and more crucially his precious, insensitive son (Josh the athlete; the baseball player) turn from him in revulsion.

Had her father ever realized how dangerous Carl Perkins was? Dr Linton had read up on the disease – had read books on how to perform the biopsy, how to look for *Mycobacterium leprae* – all to save his old friend Carl Perkins the humiliation of going to Memphis to a doctor he didn't know. Catherine could read that in the lines of the file, and she knew her father would do that for his neighbor. But her father wouldn't have flouted the law. Cases of leprosy had to be reported to the Public Health Service.

His eyebrows, Catherine thought. That's what happened to Mr Perkin's eyebrows. That was why he wore long-sleeved shirts. She shuddered as she recalled glimpsing the dark macules his rolled-up sleeve had revealed. That was why he hadn't felt the scalding coffee spilled on his hand. The feeling in the hand was gone, eaten away by a little bacillus.

She recalled her walk home in the dark with him. It was then that he had found out where the files were, under the pretense of needing Josh's. Mr Perkins had walked her home for her protection and safety, she remembered dully.

The next day, at the *Gazette*, he had checked to make sure she was not involved with Tom. Why? He would have killed Tom anyway, she thought Maybe he would have been *sorrier* if I had said Tom was my boyfriend . . . He had just heard Tom talking to Leila there in the office. I guess he did think Tom would be out of the house; if not with me, then with Leila. Did he hear Tom make a date with Leila? No, he must not have been sure, since he tried to get me to ask Tom to have dinner with them. If I had accepted, I guess he would have made some excuse to slip out for a while . . . Then he would have come here.

Catherine roused herself and shut the filing cabinet with a definite thud that marked an end. She tucked the file under her arm and switched out the attic light.

Time to go home and wait for Randall, who would be coming. It was all over.

She would tell him everything she had thought of that afternoon while she was staring blankly at the office wall. Carl Perkins had known far in advance that he would kill her father and mother. He had already made the plane reservations to visit Josh in California, because he didn't want to go to the funeral of two people he had murdered. A strange nicety. He had been upset when he found that during his absence Lowfield had acquired a new doctor much faster than anyone could have expected. The presence of a new doctor muddled the question of where the records would be kept and who would have charge of them. And then Leona Gaites stepped in, with the damning file. Who would ever know what had tripped her memory, what had made her search those filing cabinets while Catherine was downstairs preparing the old office for Tom's rental? How long Carl Perkins had paid for her silence, until, in the frenzy of a man driven too far, he came into her home and killed her . . . and after a desperate search found that the file was not there.

Where could it be?

Why, the old Purloined Letter ruse.

It was with the other files.

Or maybe he made Leona tell him before she died, Catherine thought for the first time, as she slowly descended the attic stairs.

Catherine slowly refolded the wooden stairs. As she was about to go out the door, she remembered she had promised Tom's parents she would send them his suit.

The bedroom had been left just as it was the night before. Averting her eyes from the rumpled bed, evidence of Tom's last moments of life and Leila, she searched through the closet until she found the suit. A matching tie was conveniently looped around the hanger.

She had turned out all the lights just before she heard the noise.

She froze with the gun in one hand, the file and suit encumbering her arm.

She didn't for one minute try to deceive herself into thinking it was Randall. She knew it was Carl Perkins.

He must have seen the light in the attic, from across the street. He knew what she had been doing. She had found the file for him. He still wanted it. He had killed four people to get that file and destroy it.

And she had left the back door unlocked, so Randall could enter.

It opened slowly.

She could see his silhouette against the moonlight streaming gently through the open door. She knew that her own white face was bathed in the same light.

'I never wanted this to happen,' said Carl Perkins.

Sorry. He was *sorry*. And he would kill her, in this house, where she couldn't run.

The pang of fear she had first felt when she heard the scrabbling at the door was growing. It would do her in, if she didn't act. It was already slowing her, she tried to summon up her rage, but it wouldn't come. She was swamped by the unreality of the situation. A man she had known all her life was prepared to kill her, end her existence.

She saw the long dark shape in his hand. It was Josh's baseball bat, she knew; discarded when Josh left behind him high school sports, Lowfield, and his father.

She must act now or she would *die*.

She threw Tom's suit in his face. She wheeled and ran through the dark living room. She was saved only by the stool she had left in the hall, and by her knowledge of the house. The stool tripped him up, and the suit blinded him for a second. The lock at the front door was familiar, and her fingers worked it automatically.

Then she was outside in the night. She was down the sidewalk before he came through the door.

She almost ran across the road and out into the fields, but the instinct to seek help made her turn left, round the corner, and run back toward the town. She ran between the side of her own house and the front of Carl Perkin's mansion. Would Molly Perkins protect her if she dashed up the sidewalk and slammed down the brass knocker? It was too risky to try, and her legs picked up their speed again after a brief hesitation.

Run, run, don't look back. Her breath was loud and ragged. She was lighter than Perkins; not very swift, but then he wasn't either. His arms were strong enough to wield a baseball bat but his legs weren't used to running.

Passing her front yard, the temptation to swerve in was almost irresistible. But she had left the front door locked, and it would take too much time to open it. Run, run farther, don't get trapped.

The gun. I have a gun.

It had just been something she was clutching along with the file.

She was now under the streetlight a block past her house. She wheeled, dropped the file.

Her knees bent slightly, her head snapped back, her left arm came up to grip her right forearm, and she fired. The sound ripped the night in two.

He kept running toward her.

He doesn't think I can hit him, she thought, with an odd cold rush of amusement.

She took careful aim and fired again.

She killed him.

For a long second she didn't understand the significance of the emptiness beyond the barrel of the gun. Then her arms fell to her sides. She straightened. For the moment of detachment she had remaining, she felt considerable pride in that shot. Her father would have been proud.

Then the detachment melted away forever, and she was Catherine Linton, shivering with cold in the oppressive heat of the summer night. The locusts were singing.

She walked toward the sprawled figure in the middle

of the street. She stood over Carl Perkins's body. The file, with its contents spilled out onto the pavement, lay forgotten behind her. She felt for a pulse she knew she would not feel.

Doors were opening down the street. There were shouts of alarm.

Then there was the sound of rapid light footsteps moving toward her. Molly Perkins was running down the street.

Catherine flinched away from the body, and took four rapid steps backward to stand under the streetlight. She turned away. She didn't want to see Miss Molly's face. She heard the sound of the woman kneeling by her husband's body.

Then she looked. Molly Perkins was gazing at the face of her dead husband. She did not look up at Catherine. There was no indication of surprise in the woman's posture; she had been waiting for her husband's death for a long time. Maybe her grief was all spent.

A car pulled up behind Catherine. She didn't move.

Running footsteps, heavier this time.

Randall held her to him fiercely.

She let out her breath in a light sigh. Her arms dangled uselessly at her sides, the gun still clutched in her right hand.

Then there were many voices, many footsteps. She kept her face buried against Randall's chest. There was a siren, and Sherriff Galton's voice. She didn't move.

Her fingers relaxed, and the gun fell to the ground, slid across the pavement, and went into the ditch. Her arms went up, anchored around Randall's waist.

In the noise and movement that disturbed the clear hot night they stood joined under the bleak glare of the streetlight.

The locusts sang.

A few miles outside of Lowfield, up the highway that led to Memphis, a little boy cried over his supper because his dun-colored dog had been missing for four days.

A SECRET RAGE

For Donna

1

Traffic noises and stinging smoggy air and men brushing against me. I marched through the stream of the city, looking purposeful, not meeting glances, in the style I had learned kept me safest.

Two blocks to go until I reached my apartment, two blocks to go until I could drop my street mask. I was wondering if I had any wine in my refrigerator when I saw the crowd gathered in front of my building. I was too angry to work my way to the back entrance, too anxious to reach my own place and indulge in some heavy self-pity. I waded through the crowd until I reached its center hollow containing the snag around which the debris had accumulated.

She was gray-haired and gray-faced. Her blood was still fluid and bright on the filthy sidewalk beneath her head. I had never seen a dead woman before.

'Miss Callahan!' a voice said at my elbow. My doorman was quivering with excitement.

'What happened, Jesus?' I asked. I tried not to look, but I caught myself flicking sideways glances at the dead woman.

'Kid grab her purse, threw her off balance, she hit the sidewalk, *thunk!*' Jesus' English was not perfect, but it was graphic.

'You call the police?'

'Sure. They be here in a minute. Ambulance, too. I saw the whole thing, I was a witness!' Then Jesus' face altered from sheer excitement to dismay. He had suddenly realized the inconvenience of involvement.

'Can you get me in the building?'

'Oh, sure, Miss Callahan.'

Jesus gave value for his Christmas tip. He waded into the crowd, elbows flying: a little tug pulling a much loftier ship into harbor. I was at least six inches taller than my doorman, but my fighting spirit was diminished by the day I'd had.

I reinforced Jesus' Christmas when I was safely inside the lobby doors, then began the stairs at a fast clip. I heard the sirens coming near, drowning out Jesus' voluble thanks.

I always took the stairs instead of the elevator, for the benefit of my leg muscles; but I regretted it by the time I reached my apartment. Reaction hit as I fished my keys from my purse. I worked the keys in the locks with clumsy fingers. Once inside, and after relocking, I pulled my hat off and felt my hair tumble down my back. I'd just jammed it on any which way at my agent's office; I'd been too upset to put it on properly. I took off my dark glasses (more protective camouflage) and headed for the refrigerator. Even my own apartment – everything in it beautiful to me, chosen with love, arranged with care – didn't give me any comfort today.

The afternoon was overcast, so my living room was dark. I didn't switch on any lights. The gloom suited my mood, and the wine suited my gloom.

I thought I would drink a glass, brood, and maybe cry a little; but my dark side drew me into my bedroom, to the waiting mirror. I sat on the stool before my so-aptly-named vanity. There I did switch on the lights. I took a second swallow of wine and then gave myself up to the mirror.

It was the same face.

Sometimes I didn't even feel I owned it. It had been grafted onto me. I lived behind it, and it earned my living. I took care of it; it took care of me.

My agent had just told me that it wasn't going to take care of me anymore. People were tired of it. There were newer, fresher faces.

But the face was still beautiful. I touched it with respect. Straight nose, high broad cheekbones, blue eyes, beautiful skin. Carefully drawn lips. Neat chin. Blonde hair to frame the whole assemblage.

And people were tired of this?

Yes, according to my agent.

'I swanny, Nellie Jean, some people shore are finicky,' I told my mirror. Then I turned away from it and buried my face in my hands.

At twenty-seven, I was overexposed and going down the other side of the hill. And I was lucky I'd lasted the years I had, my agent had told me today, shaking an elegant copper fingernail under my nose for emphasis.

'If you didn't have some brains, you wouldn't have lasted this long. Quit while you're ahead. I'm your friend.' ('Right sure, uh-huh,' I muttered through my fingers now.) 'Otherwise, I'd let you drag on and on and get every little cent I could. I'm doing you a favor, Nickie.'

I swung back around and stared into that mirror for five minutes. And I made myself admit she had been my friend and had done me a favor.

I was sick of my own vanity and how easily it could be wounded. It was what came of living off my face.

'You have other irons in the fire, Nickie,' my agent's voice retold me in my head. 'You're burned out on this business yourself; I know. I can tell. The camera can tell. And you can't tell me you love the camera like you used to.'

Before I turned from that mirror, I made myself admit that everything she had said was true.

So that was that.

I switched on a lamp in the living room and put on my reading glasses. I turned to my solace in times of great trouble – Jane Austen. I could open any chapter of any book of Jane's and immediately feel more peaceful. Tonight, Jane worked almost as well as she usually did; but I had to put a box of tissues on the table beside the lamp. I caught myself wandering, thinking bitterly that at least the woman on the sidewalk had no more woes; and I slapped my cheek in rebuke. Melodramatic, foolish.

I buried myself in the troubles of Miss Elinor Dashwood, until I felt able to sleep.

By next morning my common sense had raised its head. I woke up with a mild hangover from crying, set the coffeepot to perking, and did my exercises while I waited for it to finish. Since I was no longer a model, I treated myself to butter on my toast. I riffled idly through the morning paper to find a mention of the woman on the sidewalk, and found she had rated one brief paragraph. I wasn't surprised.

Since I'd had more unbooked days in the past year than I'd cared to notice, I was accustomed to free time. But now that I knew that part of my life was over, I felt jangly, at loose ends. The once-weekly cleaning woman had done her job while I was gone the day before, so I hadn't even straightening up to do. I scanned the titles in my bookshelves, trying to find something worth rereading; I had to save Jane for crises. Nothing seemed to strike a chord.

It occurred to me that I could try reworking one of my own novels again, but I felt too drained to be creative in a major way. My eyes roamed around the room for something that looked fruitful. The only item that held instant appeal was the blank notepad I kept by the telephone.

I love to make lists.

A grocery list? Not sufficiently enterprising. After a thoughtful moment, I decided that this morning was a prime time to Count My Blessings. I sharpened a pencil and set to.

1. Nice apartment, good location; but lease due to be renewed

2. Money in the bank, money invested, and a smart (and reasonably honest) financial counselor

3. Two brilliant novels that have been unaccountably rejected by dimwitted publishers

4. Friends. My agent, a couple of other models, a photographer or two, and some bona fide beautiful people whom I suspected would prove to be in the fair-weather category – and, of course, Mimi

5. Furniture and books

6. Jewelry

7. Clothes

8. Brains, undisciplined

I hesitated. I wanted to make as long a list as possible, but I really couldn't include my mother among my assets. And the only male-female relationship I had going was casual to the point of boredom. I finally settled on:

9. Southern background

10. Fair education, as far as it went

Surely there was something else? But after a moment's brooding I couldn't come up with anything.

The list as it stood wasn't bad, however. I could be proud of achieving financial security at twenty-seven, right? Modeling had been good to me, if not good for me.

The phone interrupted my pleasant contemplation of my bank account. I reached for it absently, my pencil still tapping the list, itching to write '11.'

'Nick?' The voice had the remote buzz of long distance.

'Mimi? It *is* Mimi!' I said delightedly. 'Hey, I was just thinking about you.'

'It's me all right. Hey, honey, how are you?'

'Mimi, I'm so glad to hear your voice. Just talk for a while, and let me hear that accent.' Sometimes I felt I lived in a land of squawking blue jays. The sound of home gave my ears a rest.

'Well, I called to talk, so I might as well. Listen, Richard left me and divorced me. I mean, we're divorced.'

'Whoosh.' I made a hit-in-the-pit-of-the-stomach sound, an exact evocation of what I felt. 'Okay,' I said after a second. 'I've absorbed that.'

'Good,' she said, and started crying. 'I haven't. After one of those painting trips of his, he came home for one day, and he said – while I was changing the sheets, can you believe that? – he said, 'You know, Mimi dear, this just isn't working out for us, is it? If you aren't petty enough to contest it, I think I'll go to Mexico or somewhere and get a quickie divorce.''

'Just like that?' I asked weakly.

'Nickie, I assure you. Just like that.'

'Has he come back to Knolls?'

'Oh no.' The temperature of Mimi's voice dropped to freezing. 'He's in Albuquerque. Since he needed some of the stuff he left, he wrote me. He's living with a *fantastic* woman who makes her own jewelry. She's never in her life cut her hair. She can,' Mimi said venomously, '*sit* on it.'

My nose wrinkled. 'Good God, Mimi. That alone should tell you something about Richard. Never cut her hair? Yuck.'

'You won the bet,' Mimi said.

'What? What bet?'

'Remember the bet you had with Grandmama?'

'Oh. Oh, hell. How'd you know about that?'

'She told me while she was in the hospital. She was sort of weak and wandery towards the end, you know, but she still thought that was real funny. She told me that even if I got divorced right away, she owed you five dollars because Richard and I had stayed married more than two years. She told me to be sure I gave you your money.'

I entertained myself with a pleasant fantasy of stringing Richard up by his – toes. If he'd had the sensitivity of a table, he'd have realized he was dealing Mimi a blow on top of an unhealed wound. Celeste, Mimi's grandmother, had died only five months ago. I'd been very fond of Celeste; she had been my substitute grandmother, since all my grandparents were dead. Mimi had been especially close to Celeste.

'Well, I guess I'll be all right,' Mimi was saying unconvincingly. 'I just wanted to call you to cry on your shoulder. I expect I didn't love him anyway. He was really awful selfish. But good-looking, wasn't he? Oh, Nick, I feel so durn old! I've been married and divorced twice now, and I'm only twenty-seven.'

I was feeling pretty old myself, so I couldn't whip up the energy to give Mimi a pep talk.

'I've wailed enough now. How are you?' Mimi asked. 'Tell me you're raking in money from modeling, and some big publisher gave you a huge advance for your book, and you're dating a beautiful man who's single and rich and good in bed.'

'Ho ho ho,' I said nastily. 'I'm washed up as a model; my agent dumped me yesterday. I have writer's block, following rejection by three major publishers. The only man pursuing me with any enthusiasm is my landlord, because he wants me to renew my lease.'

Thoughtful silence.

'Hmmm. Were you serious, in your last letter, about wanting to go back to finish college?'

'I've thought about it,' I admitted cautiously. 'Why?'

'Then why don't you come live with me and finish school at Houghton?'

I pantomimed amazement for my own benefit, staring at the receiver and holding it away. Then I pressed it close to my ear again, lit a cigarette, and quit fooling. 'Are you serious? You're serious.'

'I mean it,' Mimi said. 'I'm selling my house. I can't stand to live in it anymore, after two bad marriages. I'm moving into Grandmother's house, she left it to me. I had planned on selling it, but I just haven't been able to bring myself to actually list it with a realtor. Then I thought yesterday, "Aha! I'll just move into it myself!" I'll be a lot closer to campus, and I've always loved that house.'

'Me too,' I said, and the memories began to crowd in. The high ceilings, the large rooms . . .

'—but you know, it's real big. We wouldn't fall all over each other, and you could go to Houghton. I have furniture and you have furniture and we ought to be able to fill up the house between us.'

'What happened to all Celeste's furniture?'

'Oh, she left different pieces to different people: the great-aunts, Cully, Mama, and Daddy. After all, I got the house. Can I have the top story? I've lived in a ranch style so long. I want to be up in the treetops and climb stairs.'

'You can have whatever you want; it's your house,' I said unguardedly.

'Yahoo!'

What had I done? I couldn't possibly . . . I opened my mouth to retract, but then I snapped it shut. I pinched myself. I listened to Mimi's beautiful southern voice running on and on. I ached to see her. I imagined hearing only that accent around me – no more squawking blue jays. I thought of the old woman dead on the sidewalk. I imagined walking down the street *unafraid*. I remembered my agent's copper fingernail waving in my face. I thought of the heap of typing paper lying pristine in my top desk drawer, and I wondered if the discipline of study and the stimulation of reading other writers would give my writing a better chance of success. I thought of clean air, and space, and jonquils, and Mimi's laughter. Knolls, Tennessee.

I'd been desperately homesick, and I hadn't known it until this moment.

'Do you really mean it?' Mimi was asking anxiously.

'Why not?' I said, after one more second's hesitation.

'Oh, when? When?' she asked jubilantly.

'Let me get to work on it.' I ripped the list of my assets off the pad; it had lost its interest. I began a new one: lease, movers, Con Ed, Bell, post office. The pad was filling up even as I spoke.

Over all those miles, Mimi said accusingly, 'Nickie! Quit making one of your lists and give me a time estimate! I have to move my own stuff, too!'

'I'll call you back tomorrow,' I promised. 'Can I have that bedroom by the stairs?'

'You can have any room in the house.'

When I hung up, I was tingling with excitement. Out of New York. A complete change. I took a moment of peace before the scurry began, to think of how I would arrange my furniture in my bedroom-to-be – the big one off the hall on the ground floor. It was difficult to visualize it empty.

When Mimi and I had spent the night with Grandmother Celeste, we had always had that bedroom off the hall. We'd slept in a beautiful four-poster. Every night we'd crawled into that bed we'd felt like princesses; safe and beautiful and destined for everlasting fame. In the summer, we'd switch on the fan and watch it circle against the ceiling. In the winter, there was a beautiful old handstitched quilt that Celeste's mother had made . . . Even as we grew older we still felt the same about that bed.

All those years and seasons.

We had met, Mimi and I, when we were fourteen – thrown together as terrified roommates at Miss Beacham's Academy for Girls in Memphis. I was from a small town in northern Mississippi. As our yearbook put it, Mimi 'hailed' from Knolls, Tennessee, east of Memphis. Her christened name was Miriam Celeste Houghton, which I decided was beautiful and romantic. I disliked my own, Nichola Lynn Callahan; I thought it sounded like my parents had wanted a boy.

Mimi Houghton had Background. In Knolls, there was a Houghton Street, a Houghton Library, and of course, Houghton College. Fortunately, I didn't know any of this until Mimi and I were already close friends.

Mimi had come to Miss Beacham's because her mother, Elaine, had gone to school there. I had been sent by my father, to keep me away from my mother, who was becoming an alcoholic.

I don't know if Father was right to send me away or not. My mother's drinking began to increase after I left home, as if my presence had been holding her in check. But I guess she would have accelerated her drinking in time anyway. I try not to criticize Father in hindsight. He meant to protect me from ugliness. Then, too, the fights between Mother and me outweighed the pleasure he got from my company when I was home. He was a plain and straightforward man. He didn't understand that the bitter scenes did not happen because I didn't love my mother but because I did love her.

I suppose Mimi had explained my situation to her parents, Elaine and Don. They always made me welcome.

As my home gradually became a place to fear, a haunted house, I began to see my parents for only a couple of days each short vacation, maybe a couple of weeks during the long summer breaks. After my duty times at home, my father would drive me to Mimi's. At first we were close on those drives; but as time passed, a silence fell between us. We couldn't talk about the thing that most concerned us. He dreaded what he would find when he returned home. His hours at his law office lengthened and lengthened. He became well-to-do and far too busy. He probably suspected the condition of his heart, but he never mentioned it to me or my mother. Aside from making a will, he didn't prepare for the cataclysm at all.

When I was a senior at Miss Beacham's, my father died of a heart attack in his office. Six months later, my mother remarried. The tragedies were too close. I didn't absorb either of them for years.

I went home once following my mother's remarriage. I hoped she needed me despite her new husband, Jay Chalmers. The second day I was home, my mother left to attend some bridge-club function. Thank God the builder had installed sturdy doors with sturdy locks. I had to stay in the bathroom for two hours, until Jay passed out. (He drank, too.) It was mostly dirty talk, and a clumsy attempt to kiss me; but quite enough, from an older man, to terrify a seventeen-year-old. Though he hadn't managed to lay a finger on me, I felt dirty and guilty; I was very young. That evening, I packed my bags and made Mother take me to the bus station. I trumped up a story about having forgotten some school committee meeting for which I had to return early. When Mimi came back from her own weekend at home, I told her what had happened. Then I threw up.

I'd always planned on going to Houghton College with Mimi. Since the college had been founded by her great-grandfather, naturally she had been enrolled from birth. But Mother and Jay were spending Mother's portion of what my father had left as if there were no tomorrow; and since I wouldn't inherit my share till I became twenty-one, I had no money of my own yet. His own shame and guilt having crystallized into hostility, Jay told me there just wasn't enough for Houghton's steep tuition. So I enrolled in an obscure, cheaper college, living carefully and earning a little extra from modeling for department stores and regional magazine ads, as I'd begun doing at Miss Beacham's.

One of the store buyers casually remarked that I should go to New York and try my hand at professional modeling. The idea took hold. I needed a change, and at that point college meant very little to me. I was about to turn twenty-one; and I'd be receiving a small steady income from investments my father had made in my name, plus a moderate lump sum.

I vividly remember calling Mimi in her dorm room at Houghton to tell her about my resolution. She was stunned by my courage. I was, too. It was the bravado of sheer ignorance. Even now, it seems amazing to me that the city didn't chew me up and spit me out.

For the first two months, my heart was constantly in my mouth. Where I came from, New York qualified as a synonym for hell. It had the glamour of hell, though.

Inadequately armed with a little money and a short list of names, I scuttled through the streets of the Big City.

Luckily for me, two of those names on my list paid off. A former fraternity brother of my father's helped me find a place to live, fed me some meals and some invaluable advice, and withdrew his hands when I shook my head. A connection of the buyer's steered me to a reputable agency who liked my looks.

And I caught on. Within a year, I was able to move out of the hole I'd been sharing with three other women, into my own place. I slowly acquired the most beautiful furniture and rugs I could afford: that was very important to me. I bought books. I began to write a little myself. I imagine I was trying to refute the 'beautiful but dumb' image that clings to models.

That year was a golden year. I was given up utterly to the mirror.

Toward the end of that year, which had been a big one for Mimi too, I returned to Knolls for her first wedding. The groom was a down-home good ol' boy she'd met at Houghton.

In a moment of absolute insanity, I picked an outrageous dress to wear to the rehearsal dinner. I was far too full of myself as a glamorous model. That dress was the most serious social mistake I had ever made.

I brazened it out, though I almost began screaming the fifth time I heard Mimi's mother murmur, 'Well, you know, she *is* a New York model.' (Elaine was defending Mimi, not me.) I realized that for years I would be 'that friend of Mimi's who wore that dress to Mimi's rehearsal dinner.' I knew my home ground.

I drank too much that night, rare for me with Mother's example before my eyes. And I alternated sulking with self-reproach all the way back to New York.

At Mimi's second wedding – the good ol' boy had lasted

eight months, Mimi's mother talked the marriage to death – I wore a completely proper, even severe, outfit. Even after the passage of two years, I wasn't *about* to forget my lesson. It did help a lot; I read that in the approving smiles and extra pats on the shoulder, the little nods the ladies gave each other. But my redemption had less exposure than my damnation, since this was a much smaller wedding, of course. It was 'solemnized' in the living room of Celeste's big house.

Since Mimi was coming down the stairs alone, having vetoed attendants altogether, I sat with Celeste. We skirted our fears for Mimi (we didn't like Richard, we had decided after a little conference) by laying bets on how long the marriage would last. Celeste bet on Richard's doing something unforgivable in the first two years. I laid my money on Mimi's pride and gave it three.

The marriage dragged on for almost four years; and when Richard decamped to Albuquerque, Celeste posthumously owed me five dollars.

2

As a child, I'd always imagined that the Memphis airport looked like champagne glasses cast in concrete. I still thought of it that way, though I was now far more familiar with champagne glasses.

It was a pleasure to be in it again, a delight to see Mimi waiting for me as I emerged from the gate. We held each other tight with a pure joy I had almost forgotten.

When I stepped out of the terminal, I knew I was home. There'd been tinges of fall in New York. It was hot as hell, full summer, in Memphis. I began sweating as we loaded my bags into the trunk of Mimi's Chevrolet. The sweat became the signal of homecoming. I took a deep lungful of the heavy humid air that clings to the skin like a soggy body stocking.

After the initial shrieking and hugging and inquiries about my trip, Mimi and I were a little shy with each other. To get past the inevitable period of adjustment to each other's physical presence, Mimi told me about the changes in Memphis. The Peabody Hotel had been reopened. The population had grown. The crime rate was up. Elvis Presley's death had gradually made Whitehaven, suburban site of Gracelands, a traffic nightmare and a tourist trap. But Memphis would always be dear to us from our years at Miss Beacham's.

'And Knolls?' I asked. 'How many Seven-Elevens now?'

'One bona fide and two imitations. Quickie Snackie Pickies, or Stomp 'n Grabs, or some such abominations,' Mimi said sadly. 'And a Burger King, and a Hardee's, and two McDonald's – I guess because of the college. But they can't come close to the campus,' she said in clear triumph. 'It's all residential for blocks. Zoned, by God! Signed, sealed, and delivered!'

Getting Knolls zoned had been Mimi's latest battle. No one had ever seen the need before.

'Maybe a little inconvenient for students without a car,' I suggested, pokerfaced.

'Tough luck,' said Mimi callously, scanning her entrance to the expressway with care. And quite rightly: Memphis drivers tend to have very individual styles.

She expanded on the zoning battle when we were safely heading east. The whole brouhaha had been set off – the gauntlet flung down – when Mimi had discovered a restaurant owner was trying to buy one of the very few rundown houses close to Houghton College, with the vile purpose of converting it into a so-called student hangout.

'With an *amusement arcade*,' Mimi told me grimly.

When I laughed, she stared at me indignantly before she began laughing too. At that moment, I felt we'd never been apart.

Mimi is a sort of hybrid, like a lot of young southern women. Like me. She is part carefully bred elitist, though she tries very hard not to be, and she is also a partisan who believes fervently that women are equal to (or better than) men in most ways. The clash and combination of these two parts of Mimi have produced an unpredictable woman. I never knew which half would win out in any given internal argument between the two parts of my friend. I only knew that the partisan side had an awful habit of vanishing when Mimi cared for a man. Mimi was always the most traditional bride and wife imaginable.

Blushes, deference, hot suppers every night. In one of my stupider moments, between husbands one and two, I had – gently, I thought – pointed this out to Mimi. It took her three weeks to forgive me.

'Did my furniture get here okay, really?'

'Very few scratches,' she reassured me. 'One broken bowl, one dented tray. Duly entered on the little form. They like to have never found the house, though. The driver told me that everyone he asked kept telling him it was "just down the street a little bit look for the big magnolia." He'd never seen a magnolia, can you believe it? I went on and arranged all the furniture, so you'll just have to tell me if it doesn't suit you.'

'I imagine it will.' The thrill of saying 'I imagine' again! And Mimi had actually said, 'They like to have never.' I couldn't stand it, I was so happy. Superficial, I know, but signs I was home.

I took a deep breath. 'How are you all doing?' I asked proudly.

Everyone in New York had felt obliged to say that to me. They had completely misunderstood the term, always using it as singular. I'd corrected people at first until I found they thought that was even funnier. After a few such laugh fiestas, I had omitted it from my conversation consciously.

'We're all fine,' Mimi answered casually. 'Daddy had a summer cold last month, but he's okay now. Mama's joined the DAR, which I should've expected, I guess . . . at least it keeps her busy and out of my hair. And Cully's settled in okay. All he could find was a weentsy garage apartment, but he flat refused to move in with our parents. Which was smart of him.'

My smug contentment vanished. 'Cully?' I said stiffly. 'Settled in where?'

'In Knolls.'

'You didn't tell me.'

'Well, with all my own news, I guess I just forgot. He's been back about a month now, I think.' Her voice was overly casual.

With an effort, I closed my lips on more questions. I would find out about Cully later. It was ridiculous of me to react so strongly.

Now, I wanted to look out the windows at the fields rolling by; cotton and soybeans. Some rice – that was a new development. I soaked up the sights like a sponge: the chickens loose in the yards of the tenant houses, the earthen sidewalks lined with Coke bottles or tire halves, the horizon unbounded by concrete and brick, the late-summer limpness of the foliage.

We whizzed by a grove of pecan trees that abutted a beautiful house. Its front yard would have contained my apartment building.

The landscape grew more and more familiar. I grew easier with every mile. Every sentence began, 'Oh, there's . . . !' The John Deere place, the bait shop, the wonderfully named Maubob Motel (Maureen and Bob Pitts, proprietors), Grandma's Sizzlin' Steaks, Grace Funeral Home . . .

By the time we were into Knolls, any doubts I had had were gone. When we pulled into the driveway of Celeste's old home, our new home, I had put them behind me, along with New York City.

'A girl got raped here this summer,' Mimi said suddenly.

I looked over at her. I had been stroking the cats in perfect peace. She was sprinkling oregano into the pot of sauce bubbling on the stove.

'Here?' I was surprised.

'Yes, here. On the campus.'

Since Mimi was a Houghton, no doubt the location of

the attack seemed almost as deplorable to her as the fact that it had happened.

'At night?' I saw a snag on my index fingernail and rummaged in my purse for a file.

'Yes, of course.' It was Mimi's turn to sound surprised. Knolls might endure the shame of an occasional rape, but certainly not in *broad daylight*, I gathered.

'White girl?' And I pinched myself, hard. I'd fallen right into the same old pattern. The first question, always the first question, when anything had happened to anyone, be it wreck, kidnapping, assault, sudden death, or a win in a sweepstakes: *Are they white? Is she black?*

'Yeah. A freshman student named Heidi Edmonds. She wanted to get in a few courses before the fall semester began.' After tasting the sauce, Mimi added a pinch of salt.

'I don't know why a crime always seems so much more evil if the victim is virtuous,' she said thoughtfully, 'but it does, doesn't it? Heidi was everything in her high school, Nickie. Valedictorian, Honor Society, National Merit Scholar. The kind of student we love to get. Since I'm on the admissions board, I'd seen her application. And I'd met her at one of those punch-and-cookies receptions.'

So Mimi knew the girl. Heidi Edmonds's little tragedy began to have flesh. I shifted on the breakfast-nook bench to make more room for the cats; Attila and Mao praised me with purrs for my intelligence. Mimi, finally satisfied with the meat sauce, turned and propped one hip against the stove.

'It's so good just to see you sitting there,' she said.

'It can't look as good as it feels.'

But the warm moment passed when Mimi's face tensed again. She really wanted to finish her story. 'She was on that sidewalk that meanders through the gardens. It goes indirectly from the library to the women's dorm area –

you remember? It's been years since you were on campus; I keep forgetting.'

I did remember, vaguely. I nodded.

'Then of course you remember how tall those camellias are? They're old as the hills, and just huge, and they grow on both sides of the sidewalk there. She had a big armful of books, because she'd been studying at the library until it was about to close; nine or thereabouts. It hadn't been dark that long – you know how long it takes to get dark in the summer. But it was dark.'

It was dark outside now at half past seven, with the season coming to a close. The secret night outside the bay window suddenly made me anxious. I got up to close the three sets of blinds covering the sections of the window. I didn't want to hear any more. But Mimi, I decided, would think I was selfish and callous if I cut her off.

She had always been a good storyteller. Her thin hands and dark eyes worked together to illustrate her narrative.

'. . . he was in the camellias, or just beyond. He came through the bushes and grabbed her from behind. She dropped all her books and papers, naturally. That's how they found her – a couple looking for a place to smooch. They wondered why there were books all over the sidewalk.'

'She was *dead*?' I thought of gray hair and red blood against a dirty sidewalk. The woman had not crossed my mind since Mimi's phone call. I felt goose bumps tighten the skin of my arms.

'No, no. Unconscious. Evidently, when he grabbed her, she fell and hit her head on the concrete. He'd dragged her off the sidewalk into the dark. And raped her. And slapped her around a little bit.' Mimi's voice had gotten crisper and crisper, as it does when she's talking about difficult things. 'Maybe – I think – he was trying to bring her to, so she wouldn't miss anything. Her face was pretty badly bruised.'

The muscles of my own face tightened and pinched. Beaten in the face. What if someone had done that to me in New York, when I was just starting out?

'I went to see her in the hospital – representing the college, you know. The dean of women was out of town. Jeff Simmons – you won't remember him, he's the college president now – he kept saying that since I'm a woman, it would be better for me to go than him.' Besides pity and anger, Mimi's mouth showed a certain distaste. 'A dirty job he just dumped on me.'

I made a face, to show I'd registered the cowardice of Jeff Simmons. Yet I thought that he might have been right.

I started to ask Mimi what had happened to Heidi Edmonds afterward; if the police had been kind to her, and so on. I was curious, finally. But alerted by the hiss of the boiling water, Mimi had turned back to the stove to break up the vermicelli.

'To tell the truth,' she said over her shoulder, 'I kind of wondered if her folks would sue the college for negligence.'

'Did they?'

Mimi dropped in a handful of pasta. 'Never even mentioned it,' she answered absently. 'Her father turned out to be a minister. I've gone over and over it, the whole incident, trying to see how Houghton could have prevented what happened. But I swear I just can't think of anything we could've done, Nick. The sidewalk was well lit. The actual distance the girl had to walk wasn't that far. And she could've called one of the security guards to walk her back to the dorm. That's in the brochure for freshman women. Not that I think any of them have ever done that, because this has always been such a quiet town. But it is possible to have an escort if you want one.'

I mentally filed that fact. I would begin attending Houghton in a few days. Maybe I would be working late at the library some nights.

I had to ask one last question. 'She couldn't identify the guy?'

'She never saw his face,' Mimi answered tersely.

The goose bumps spread to my chest. Celeste would have said someone was walking on my grave. I lifted the orange tabby, Attila, and hugged him for the comfort of his warm fur. He wriggled indignantly out of my arms and stalked to the kitchen door, loudly requesting that Mimi let him out.

And I watched Mimi double-lock the door behind the cat's retreating tail.

That one small act told me how much Mimi had taken to heart what had occurred in the late-summer darkness on Houghton campus. I could not remember a house in Knolls ever being locked, all the years I'd visited Mimi.

We talked half the night. We'd faithfully written and called each other during all the years of separation; but even communication as constant as ours didn't equal face-to-face conversation.

Mimi rehashed Richard's defection. I decided that though she was sincerely grieved, mostly her pride had suffered. Mimi had always been the leaver, not the left, even when she'd had to scramble to get out the door first.

And naturally, I in turn rehashed the mortification of being an old face after a few years in the limelight; though I'd never exactly been a top model, I'd had my share of magazine covers.

Well, a few, anyway.

The second novel I'd shakily put together in my steadily increasing leisure time had actually gotten a very long letter of rejection from one publisher. As I explained to

Mimi what a good sign that was, and she grew excited about that rejection, I realized how much I had needed her.

The evening was just a little cool, courtesy of a light breeze that puffed the curtains inward. My furniture had been arranged with Mimi's sure hand around the huge (by New York standards) living room. Mimi had given me the ground floor bedroom I had requested. It lay off the hall running from the living room to the kitchen.

Celeste's was not a grand house but a large old family home. All the rooms were big, with the original high ceilings. When Mimi mentioned having to turn on the furnace in a few weeks, we thought of the probable heating bill and exchanged grimaces of dismay.

Mimi yawned, crumpled an empty cigarette pack, and pitched it toward the wastecan. Siamese Mao intercepted the pack with a lightning paw and began batting it around between my rugs. Those rugs looked beautiful against the hardwood floor, I noticed with pleasure.

'Want to hear about Cully?' Mimi asked.

'I guess so.' I kept my gaze carefully fixed on Mao. 'Rachel's consented to live in little old Knolls?'

Cully's wife had strong and strange ideas about the South and small towns. Rachel was from New York. I'd seen them a couple of times when they'd come up to visit her family.

'He and Rachel just got divorced, too. The Houghton children don't have a very good batting average when it comes to staying married.'

So Cully was divorced. I set my teeth against asking why she hadn't told me before. But there were some questions I couldn't repress.

'Why did Cully come back here? Weren't they living in Memphis? What happened?'

'He was living in Memphis. And he came back here to

lick his wounds, like me. Except I have so many, I have to stay here all the time.' Mimi laughed halfheartedly. 'There's nothing like living in a town with a college, street, and library named after you. Anytime you have an identity crisis, you can just turn around and there's your name. Your *generic* name, anyway.'

I pitched her a cigarette when she looked around to see if another pack was within reach. She caught it as gracefully as Maò. Mimi is always deft and quick. She is small-boned and dark, with black hair she wears like a lion's mane. She looked fragile that evening, and vivid, in a brilliantly patterned caftan. Mimi has never been afraid of strong colors.

'As to what happened, to answer your second – or third? – question. My theory about Rachel is that she was just doing an anthropological study about southern tribal customs. When she had enough material, she gave Cully the old heave-ho. I never understood that marriage, anyway. Of course I have a theory about that too. I think Cully was searching for Mother's opposite.' Mimi squinted at me through her smoke and jabbed the air to point out her own wisdom.

'Expound?'

'Oh. Well, Mother is still beautiful, resolutely unintellectual, committed to the social graces, and she's as conventional as they come. Her religion is being gracious. Rachel was – plain, to put it nicely. She'd gotten heavy into stuff like *The Dialectics of Sex*. And her idea of fancy entertaining was to pour some wine in the spaghetti sauce.'

I laughed; I couldn't help it. Mimi's thumbnail sketches were an element of our intimacy. She had always sworn that no one else would remain her friend after hearing how nasty she could be.

'What Cully *missed* seeing,' she said, carried away by the flow of her theory, 'was that they are *both* bitches.'

'*Shame* on you, calling your mama that,' I said out of duty, though my mouth was twitching.

Mimi tried to look properly ashamed. She had weather-vane reactions to her mother. There would be truces, sometimes for months, during which the two thought alike and got along very well; but inevitably an explosion would come – always when the partisan in Mimi was ascendant. The warfare never came completely into the open; it was a suspenseful guerrilla variety.

'By the way,' Mimi said more soberly, 'the college has hired Cully as a counselor for the students, and he's setting up a private practice. Don't holler nepotism, or at least not too loud, okay? A full two weeks before Cully decided he wanted to leave Memphis, our last counselor had some sudden health problems and told us he'd have to retire.'

I was having my own thoughts. 'Maybe Cully thinks I'm like your mother, and that's why he's always had such a thing about ignoring me,' I ventured.

'Why didn't that occur to me before? I'll bet that's it. I can see a strictly superficial resemblance. Now there he is, a psychologist; and he's never figured all this out. Here we are, mere amateur analysts, and we have the whole thing solved in seconds. You're beautiful, and the image of the model is that she's a brainless nitwit. And you were brought up to have social graces, even though you may have lost them up north, I don't know.' Mimi gave me a very wicked look. 'So that might very well be.' She picked up Mao and tickled the cat behind the ears. Attila, who had come back in, glared at this favoritism from behind a plant stand.

'I think you've just had this thing about Cully all these years because he's different around you.'

'It is very true, Mimi-my-friend,' I said heavily, 'that your brother has always been "different" around me.'

When other boys were going to absurd lengths to bump into me accidentally, when other males were calling every dorm at Miss Beacham's until they found mine, when men were generally behaving like fools in my presence, Cully had stood resolutely untouched by The Face. Even worse (though less surprising) was his matching lack of interest in what lay beneath that face.

So I had had a mission since I was fourteen. My mission was to make Cully Houghton notice me. Since I am in most respects a normal healthy person, that ache of piqued vanity had subsided in recent years. I had recognized it for the childish thing it was. But the ache wasn't entirely gone. I had just begun to assess my power, and use it, when I met Cully Houghton. He had been my first – and for a long time, my only – failure.

'More power to you, if you're still attracted,' Mimi said suddenly. 'He needs someone. He really tried with Rachel. It just didn't work.'

'Do you remember the expression on Rachel's face when I walked into your rehearsal dinner in that dress?' I asked.

'Are you still brooding about that?' Mimi said incredulously. 'That was years and years ago.'

'*You* can say that. You've never been on the receiving end of the polite freeze.'

'Water under the bridge,' Mimi said grandly. 'And we'd better go to bed. You've got an appointment with your faculty adviser at eleven-thirty tomorrow morning. Barbara. Dr Barbara Tucker to you, lowly student.'

'Faculty adviser?'

'You've forgotten the ropes. She'll be your shepherd. Help you pick your schedule, approve your courses, et cetera. I zapped you through admission, but you have to pick out your courses and times, and Barbara should know by tomorrow how many of your hours from Elbridge have transferred.'

'Look, Mimi, did you have to ram me down the college's throat?' I had known Mimi could get me admitted in time, but I had worried that scrambling in under her wing might make my presence resented.

'No, ninny. You had good grades, very good grades. Don't worry so much! There's been a slump in enrollment, so there was room for you. Even with the slump, there's no extra dorm room or parking spaces – those have been at a premium for years. Since you don't want either, they were practically panting. You'll like Barbara. I do. She's been here several years, and she's really fitted in well. She just got tenure. By the way,' Mimi added delicately when I was halfway to my room, 'you have to pay your fees this week. How's the money situation?'

'I'm a well-to-do woman,' I told her firmly. 'Don't even think of filthy lucre. I'm chipping in on the house expenses, of course. We'll have to sit down and work that out tomorrow.'

'I think you have a fan,' she remarked dryly.

I looked down to see Attila sitting before me, great green eyes fixed on my face in an unnerving stare. When the big cat was sure I was watching, he flopped over to expose a wide creamy belly and said, 'Rowr.'

'Don't be surprised if you have company tonight,' Mimi warned me. 'He's been sleeping on your bed ever since I set it up.'

I observed Mao as she slept curled on Mimi's lap. Mao was a fancier's cat, fine-boned and graceful and purebred. I looked back at huge tawny Attila, who had the glow of mockery in his eyes and a generally self-satisfied expression. Since I didn't bend to scratch the proferred expanse of stomach, he rolled to his feet and began rubbing himself against my legs. I hoped there wasn't any unflattering significance in the cat's preference.

But I told the bathroom mirror that birds of a feather flocked together, before I crawled into bed with the cat.

I lay awake for a while, mulling over my good fortune. Just as I was drifting off to sleep, I thought about poor little Heidi Edmonds. I couldn't even recall the face of the dead woman on the sidewalk in New York. I could lose her in the city. But in little Knolls, I couldn't forget the tragedy of a girl I'd never seen.

I sent a wish for her recovery and well-being out into the ether, drowsily tickled Attila behind the ears, and blanked out with my hand still resting on the cat's broad back.

3

I'd always regretted that Celeste's house didn't actually face the campus, whose landscaped gardens made a beautiful view; but the house stood only half a block away from the college's southwestern corner.

I borrowed Mimi's car for this first trip to the campus, since I didn't want to arrive for my appointment dripping with sweat. I should've realized the unfamiliar strain of driving would make me even more anxious than I already was. I bit my lip until I turned safely into the college's main drive. The campus was fully as impressive as I'd remembered – green and welcoming, if slightly frazzled near the end of the fierce summer.

With a glance I checked the campus map spread on the seat beside me, to verify the location of the English department. The college grounds were empty and quiet – in a dreamy calm before the storm of freshman students soon due for orientation. I saw the occasional parked car, so a few staff members had to be tucked away somewhere. But workers on the grounds crew were the only living souls I glimpsed.

I slid the Chevrolet awkwardly into the first parking lot I saw. I'd walked about ten feet when I realized, from a further study of the map, that I could have parked much closer to the English building. I hesitated for a moment, but it didn't seem worth the extra strain of maneuvering the car again. The gardens were always worth a visit, anyway. I shrugged to myself and set off down the concrete path.

Houghton's gardens were quite famous. When Mimi's great-grandfather had founded the college, he had planted them as a combination public service/tourist attraction. Photographs of the camellias and roses in bloom were always prominently featured in Houghton publicity material. It was easy to see why Houghton was a popular site for outdoor weddings. The sidewalk I now followed led through the heart of the gardens and emerged to one side of the library, crisscrossing other paths.

The foliage was dusty but lush, and the grass had been trimmed to a carpet texture. The day lilies were blooming, their rich orange flaring brilliantly against the dark green. It was good to see so much flora after New York. I bent to run my finger lightly over the curve of a petal. I felt a sort of grateful relaxation deep inside me. I knew the name of almost every plant; my mother had been an avid gardener before she turned to drinking.

I recalled all the times Mimi and I had sauntered through these gardens as teenagers, pretending we were real college coeds. At least that part of Mimi's dream had come true, though she'd been unfortunate in other ways. Now I was going to make it happen for myself. A real Houghton College coed. How young those kids were going to seem to me.

Thinking of the young faces that would soon surround me reminded me again of one Houghton student I would never meet: Heidi Edmonds, achiever, whose adventure had ended in getting raped and going back home defeated. As I strolled around a curve and arrived face to face with the library, I realized I was on the path where she'd been attacked. I turned to scan the camellias, the sidewalk; and then snorted at my own stupidity. But it did seem such agony should have left some mark. I saw only the lazy charm of the gardens, and heard only the whir of a bee touring the day lilies. Somehow that was more unnerving than a commemorative plaque would have been.

For the benefit of the bee, I suppose, I glanced down at my watch and stepped out a little faster.

The immense double doors set in the center of the ground floor led into a vaulted central cloister, cool and very dark after the glare outside. As I peered through the dimness, searching for some sign of stairs to the second floor, I wondered if the original Houghton architect had toured medieval monasteries right before he'd been commissioned for the job.

There were halls leading off to the right and left; they were empty. After some fruitless searching, I became absurdly frantic. Where the hell had they hidden the stairs? I wasn't going to impress Dr Barbara Tucker if I turned up late. I took a few tentative steps forward, peering from side to side. My wooden heels made little tap! tap! echoes on the stone floor. The building was quite silent otherwise.

To my heartfelt relief, one of the enigmatic doors in the corridor to my right opened. A man came out and walked in my direction. (I'd been quite prepared to bellow for help if he'd turned the opposite way.) As he drew nearer, I saw he was about thirty-eight, with a slight belly preceding his legs and a tonsure fringed by blond curly hair.

'Excuse me,' I said, louder than I'd intended.

He jumped. I felt embarrassed.

'Can I help you?' he asked politely, after he'd located me in the gloom.

'You're going to think I'm awfully stupid, but I just can't find the stairs.' I winced. I was simpering. I hadn't simpered for years.

He laughed and came closer. I could make out a patrician nose and the slight suggestion of a double chin. I mentally prescribed laying off the sweets and starches for a few months.

'I think the architect wanted to hide something as mundane as stairs,' he said. 'I'm Theo Cochran, the registrar. Don't feel stupid. I tell an average of twenty people a year where the stairs are. There, see?' He pointed to the right. After a second, I was just able to discern the balustrade. It was composed of the same stone as the wall, and blended into it perfectly in the pervasive gloom.

'Oh,' I said flatly. 'Well . . . thanks a lot.' Come on, Nick, manners. 'I'm Nickie Callahan. You probably just processed my transcript.'

'Oh. Mimi Houghton's friend.'

Distinct lack of enthusiasm. Having an influential friend is not always a plus.

Theo Cochran stirred himself, probably remembering that influence. 'We're glad to have you with us here at Houghton, Miss Callahan.'

'Thank you,' I said again. 'I'm sure I'll be in and out of your office in the next week or so.'

'So will the entire student body. The first week is always hell,' the registrar said more pleasantly. He seemed to look forward to hurling himself into the fray. 'Goodbye, now.'

'Goodbye.' I started climbing the stairs, my heels clattering. I resolved to remember to wear rubber-soled shoes to classes in this building.

I looked down the stairwell and saw the bare tonsure of the registrar moving away down the hall into the darkness. His progress was relatively silent. He must have made the same resolution.

It was impossible for me to blunder any more, since room 206 was just a few feet to the right at the head of the stairs. I checked my watch again. On the dot. I twitched my skirt and gathered myself in general.

'Come in,' called a midwestern voice after I knocked.

'I'm Barbara Tucker,' said a slim auburn-haired woman as she rose from behind a desk covered with every imaginable form of printed material: books, notebooks, forms, memoranda, catalogues. I blinked. The office seemed dazzling with light after the cavern below.

'Nickie Callahan,' I said too heartily. I shook Barbara Tucker's hand and took the only scarred wooden chair that wasn't overflowing with books and papers.

The woman sat down, pushed her glasses up on her slight nose, and smiled at me. Her features were plain, but her skin was beautiful. I decided I liked her on the spot. I liked her smile, I liked the books stacked everywhere, I liked the plants that flourished in the two slitlike windows. I beamed back at Barbara Tucker in approval. There are some women who dislike and distrust me at first sight, on principle. She was not going to be one of them.

'So, you decided to leap back into the academic battle, Miss Callahan.'

'Call me Nickie. I decided it would be a good idea to finish, and the time was right.'

'Good decision. I remember Mimi told me you were a model, but I think I would have figured that out anyway.'

I had to make it clear I was not a dilettante. 'I used to be a model,' I said carefully. 'Now, I hope, I'm an English major.'

'Okay, we'll start you on the road to a degree today,' Barbara Tucker said briskly. She pulled my file from a crammed metal tray. 'What's your goal? Do you want to teach?'

I took a deep breath and plunged. 'No, I'm going to be a

223

writer,' I said, and couldn't stop myself from making a deprecating face.

Barbara brushed back her bangs and looked thoughtful. She didn't ask me how I planned to eat and pay the rent on a writer's erratic earnings; and she didn't laugh. She did smile again, suddenly. 'You'll be the Don Quixote of the English department,' she said. 'Let's get you started.'

For forty-five minutes we went over the hours I'd accumulated at my first college and made out a list of courses I wanted and courses I was required to take as an English major – certainly not a synonymous list. Finally we hammered out a schedule I thought I just might be able to handle.

But I kept reminding myself I'd been over six years away from the academic routine. As Barbara signed forms, I blew out a sigh of relief and apprehension.

'You're certainly going to be an interesting addition to the student body,' Barbara commented cheerfully.

'Does Houghton have many older students?' I asked.

'Not that many, but you'll have some company, don't worry. And the older students we do have almost always make higher grades than the average-age student. They seem to have a better idea of why they're going to college.'

That was heartening. I wondered again how it was going to feel, seeing those nineteen-year-old faces surrounding me. 'I'll probably be a mother figure,' I said ruefully.

Barbara whooped. 'Believe me, Nickie,' she gasped. '*No one* is going to think of you as a mother figure.'

'What's all the merriment?' asked a voice behind me. I started, then twisted in the chair to look.

A man had stuck his head through the gap left by the partially open door. Now he looked as though he felt extremely foolish. 'I'm sorry, Barbara, I didn't know you had anyone in here,' he apologized.

'Come all the way in, Stan, and meet Houghton's newest sophomore-and-a-half,' Barbara invited.

The man smiled a little shyly and edged into the room. He was a few years older than Barbara, whom I'd placed at around thirty-five. His neat brown beard was well salted with white and his face was seamed. He managed to look comfortable with himself.

As Barbara performed introductions (his full name was Dr Stanley Haskell), I got the firm impression that the two were a couple. They shared the ease that comes of intimacy and long association; and Barbara seemed not the least disturbed when his eyes stayed glued to me.

They were obviously going out for lunch together. I quickly thanked Barbara for her time and gathered up my papers. Since Dr Haskell was going to be instructing me in Chaucer (at eight o'clock Mondays, Wednesdays, and Fridays), I told him I'd see him in class and took my departure, my heels tap-tapping again down the stairs.

As I pulled the Chevrolet cautiously out of the parking lot, I spotted the two English professors at a stoplight at the edge of the campus. They were laughing. The sun was shining. I beamed idiotically to myself. Ah, love!

Mimi's narrow driveway led around to the back of the house, where it formed a wide apron, affording room to turn around; but she'd asked me to leave the car out front, since she meant to use it. I parked across the street from the house. The yard sloped up from the sidewalk, so I had to climb steps up to the yard, and then more steps up to the wide porch that girdled three sides of the house.

Panting a little from the heat and the stairs, sweating like a pig, I flung open the front door with that silly smile still pasted on my face – and there stood Cully.

. . . I was fourteen again. A tall, thin, black-headed boy, a lofty senior in high school, slipped into the chair opposite mine at the Houghtons' dining table. Hazel eyes summed me up and dismissed me.

'This is Mimi's brother, Cully,' Elaine Houghton had said proudly. Mimi kicked me because I was gaping like a fool. I was abruptly sick, stricken with first love; and those light-brown eyes with little green streaks were utterly cool when they rested on me . . .

Mimi wasn't in the living room to kick me now, so I did the job myself – mentally, of course. Cully's eyes were just as cool now, though the rest of him had changed a little. He was still very tall and too slender, but a little gray streaked the black hair of his head and mustache. There were a few wrinkles at the corners of those eyes. His cheekbones and arched nose jutted a little more sharply; the parentheses from nose to mouth were deeper.

'Hello, Nickie,' that mouth said calmly.

'Hi,' I said, and slung my notebook down on one of the couches. 'Where's Mimi?' Charm and grace, that's me.

'She and Alicia Merritt are in the kitchen planning the party.'

'Alicia! What party?'

'Your party,' he said, and relaxed enough to smile faintly.

Now that was interesting. Cully had been very tense.

'Mimi just decided she wanted to celebrate your arrival and have a housewarming at the same time,' he continued.

We stood in uneasy silence for a moment.

'By the way . . .' He hesitated for an awkward length of time, and I stared. Cully *always* knew what he wanted to say. 'I'm sure coming back here fitted in with your plans, but I'm glad you did come back to town and move in with Mimi,' he finished.

Surely not for the sake of my beaux yeux.

The slap and the stroke, or the stroke and the slap. Cully had never said an unmitigated thing to me in our whole acquaintance. *I'm sure you came back to Knolls for your own, doubtless selfish, reasons, but I'm also glad it's what my sister wanted and needed.*

One thing I could say for Cully – he'd always adored Mimi, and the feeling was mutual. Now, I decided, Cully was angling toward something. But I wasn't going to bite.

Things had never, never been simple between us.

'I'm glad too,' I said briefly. 'Now when, and where, is this party going to be?'

'Friday night, here. I'm going to bartend.'

'I'm glad to hear that,' I said sincerely. Mimi had never mixed a decent drink in her life. Then my mind started racing. Friday was two days away. Some of our moving boxes were still strewn through the house. I was itching to make a list of things that had to be done. I began rummaging through my purse for a pencil and a pad.

'Listen, as long as we're alone . . .' Cully began, capturing my undivided attention.

'Yes?' I fixed my eyes on his. That usually either frightens men or inflames them. One of my photographers, a romantic, had said that my eyes were exactly like opals – a compliment that had pleased me no end, of course.

Just as a little voice inside me was protesting that I had promised to stop using my face as bait – and I'd told that little voice to shut up – Cully went on: 'I want you to watch out for Mimi.'

I was back in the real world, with a thud.

'I'll tell you something in confidence—' He broke off as Alicia Merritt and Mimi blew into the living room.

I had to jump and scream and embrace Alicia in the accepted fashion. If I'd done less, she would have thought I wasn't happy to see her. Alicia was refreshingly the same, her accent still one of the heaviest I'd ever heard. Her voice dripped magnolias and molasses. When she exclaimed 'You sweet thing!' the product sounded like

'Yew sweeet thang!' I held our former schoolmate at arm's length to take a survey.

'You look great, Alicia,' I said. And I meant it.

Her short hair was more golden than God had made it, and curlier; but her figure was definitely her own, and still tempting as a ripe peach. Alicia had the happy face and assured manner of someone who has seldom in life denied herself an impulse – someone who has pretty nice impulses, that is.

'How's Ray?' I asked, when I decided we'd gushed enough. Mimi beamed in the background.

'Oh, he's just fine, Nickie. He still has that same old job, though, and he's on the road all week. At least he comes back home on the weekends. I'm glad I'm not the jealous type!'

'You don't have anything to worry about,' I assured her.

'Oh, I'm fat as a butterball,' Alicia protested untruthfully. 'And you're still long and thin and totally gorgeous. It must be staying single that does it.'

I'd forgotten Alicia's little needles, the way you tend to forget little faults in otherwise nice people. For a second, this little barb almost got to me. I was off guard and back in the ambience of girlhood, and I actually found myself defensively totting up the proposals I'd received. Shame! If I'd been alone, I would've slapped myself for my regression. As it was, I had to clamp my mouth shut: I had been on the verge of retorting, 'Oh, Alicia, I'm just so *picky!*'

'Where are you all living now?' I said instead, and promised myself something nice for my restraint. Earrings?

'Didn't Mimi tell you?' Alicia gave Mimi a look of mock reproach. 'We bought the house two doors down from here, the other side of Mrs Harbison, oh I guess about a year ago. So I'll get to see a lot of you! When I have a second, that is,' she added, to my relief.

'Are you still in every club in town?'

'*And* on a bunch of college committees, too. Got to support the old alma mater, and I have to do *something* while Ray's gone!'

Alicia's energy was something of a legend. Underneath all the gush and flutter, which apparently she found necessary to assume, Alicia was actually a very efficient woman. Mimi had told me that in college Alicia had invariably made the dean's list. But if Ray's fraternity brothers mentioned that achievement to her, she would blink and giggle and tell them it must have been a fluke.

'You know,' our old friend was saying now with a great display of roguery, 'Mimi was on every board at Houghton, and they finally gave up and started paying her for it. I'm just hoping that some day this town will give *me* a salary for running it!'

'You sure deserve it,' I murmured. I was tiring already. It had been a long time since I'd met Alicia broadside.

'Ray and I are going to start working on a baby,' she told us cheerfully. 'He says that'll keep me at home, if nothing else will. He thought buying our own house would do that too. But you know, I had the whole thing done over in no time.'

'I don't doubt it for a minute,' Cully said with a smile that robbed his words of any sting.

Alicia looped her purse straps over her shoulder and moved to the door. 'Nick, I'm just thrilled to death you're back in town to stay. We'll see you at the party Friday night. Ray'll be back in time, and we'll be here with bells on. You call me, Mimi, you hear? If you need any help!'

All at once she was gone, leaving us standing in a daze, as if a tornado had passed close by.

'Still the same,' Mimi said with a grin of half-admiration, half-regret.

I nodded. 'What's all this about a party?'

'Oh, just some people you met when you used to stay with me, and some of the people from the college,' she said smoothly.

'Like the entire English faculty?' I asked with suspicion.

'Oh, don't worry! Just the ones I really know and like. I'm not trying to butter anyone up for you.'

'Oh. Okay,' I said, feeling some doubt. 'When is this going to be? What kind of party?'

'It kicks off at eight, and from the length of the bar list, it's going to be a drunken brawl,' Cully interposed. 'Listen, Mimi, are you sure this is everything you need from the store?'

A list I hadn't gotten to make. I eyed it sadly. Then I realized that Cully was going to the grocery for us, and I felt a jolt of amazement. I just couldn't imagine Cully Houghton doing something as tedious and universal as wheeling a cart through the supermarket to buy groceries. It occurred to me that I had perhaps been idealizing Cully a wee bit all these years.

'I'm sure,' Mimi said firmly. 'Listen, are *you* sure you've got the bar list?'

'Right here.' He pulled the edge of another list from his pants pocket to prove it to her.

'Good. Thanks, Cully, that'll save us time. We've got to get cracking on cleaning up this house, and we'll have plenty for you to haul off to the dump, starting tomorrow.'

'Maybe I should try to borrow Charles's pickup?'

'Good idea. Drop by his office and see if he'll need it. Generally he just uses it on weekends.'

There was a little something about the way Mimi smoothed her hair . . .

'Charles?' I asked, after Cully had left.

'Oh, you'll meet him at the party. I've known him forever,' Mimi said nonchalantly.

Right. Uh-huh. Here we go again.

But I swore to myself I wouldn't say anything. Mimi was always prickly in the first stages of any attachment. There are some lines even a best friend – or especially a best friend – shouldn't cross. I'd upset Mimi in the past with my criticism of her choice of men, before I'd gotten wiser. That was why Mimi was being so clamlike with me now.

I withheld my sigh until I reached my bedroom. Then I heaved it to the mirror, as if I were practicing 'Exasperation' for a pantomime. We'll just see about *Charles*, I told myself grimly while I changed into my oldest cutoffs and my T-shirt with the paint stains. Reserve judgment, Nickie.

Mimi had excellent taste in clothes, furniture, jewelry, and (of course) friends, but she completely lost that taste when it came to men. Husband Number One had at least been harmless; Mimi had just gotten tired of packing ice chests with beer for fishing trips and whooping it up at fraternity parties. Richard had been more dangerous; an effete would-be painter who lived on an allowance from his parents – who could well afford it, granted. But he too had never denied himself an impulse, and his impulses, unlike Alicia Merritt's, were apt to be rather nasty. There'd been others she hadn't married, of course. I remembered best the cadet who had painted a glowing picture of an army officer's wife's life, and the budding rock star who'd wanted to have a baby (via Mimi) and name the child Acidstar.

At least apprehension about Mimi's latest involvement temporarily smothered my curiosity about what Cully had been going to tell me before Alicia and Mimi had come into the living room. I had the distinct feeling that whatever it was, it was something unpleasant.

For the remainder of that day and the bulk of the next two I hadn't time to think of anything but Comet, Future, and Glass Plus.

After we'd taken the kitchen apart and put it back together, we turned our attention to the long living room that extended the width of the front of the house as the kitchen extended the back.

Mimi had tentatively arranged my heavy desk and bookcases in the empty dining room across the hall from my bedroom, but the living room was so scantily furnished that we had to move them back out to fill one corner. My two couches and chairs, which had filled my apartment in New York rather tightly, looked like an island perched around the fireplace at the right side of the living room. In despair, we lugged down a couple of chairs and a table of Mimi's that blended with my stuff well enough. The result was passable.

Then Cully began to haul boxes and other moving debris, and we began to cook.

Of course Attila and Mao went wild in this maelstrom of upheaval. They'd scarcely had time to adjust to the move from Mimi's former home. The cats dashed between our feet, pounced out of odd corners, and got shut in closets for indefinite periods. Thursday evening, when I called the two to supper and only Attila responded, Mimi leaped from her chair as if she'd been electrocuted and pounded up the stairs at full speed. She returned in a minute, her nose red with incipient tears, clutching Mao to her chest.

'I just remembered the last time I'd seen her she was asleep in my underwear drawer, and then I pictured myself putting the wash away and shutting the drawer without even thinking about it,' she explained in a shaky voice. 'Oh, God, she could've suffocated!'

To Attila's intense indignation, Mao had an extra treat for supper that night. Mao accepted her close brush with death quite placidly. In fact, when I asked Mimi if the cat had been frantic when she opened the drawer, Mimi told me rather stiffly that Mao had still been fast asleep.

Cully was a great help; which, like his grocery shopping, surprised me – until I realized that he'd never watched *me* lift a finger to do anything practical, either. When he and Rachel had dropped by my apartment on their infrequent visits to Rachel's family in New York, I'd of course had the place spotless hours beforehand.

I volunteered to go to the dump bins with Cully on Friday morning, since his load was especially heavy. I perched up high in the pickup that the mysterious Charles (whose last name I discovered to be Seward; occupation, lawyer) had obligingly donated. It had been years since I'd been in a pickup. I felt very down-home.

'We ought to have a beer in our hands and country music on the radio,' I told Cully as we bucked along the dirt road that led to the county landfill. It was good to get out of the hot kitchen.

'It *is* kind of fun,' Cully admitted cautiously. He was shifting gears with a certain macho air that tickled me. I had a feeling that if he'd been alone, he'd have been going 'Brroom, brroom,' pretending to be a cross between Mario Andretti and the Marlboro man.

When we got to the dump and Cully had let down the tailgate, I heaved garbage bags with tremendous panache.

'That's the one with all the cat litter and the broken glass in it,' he protested when I grabbed the gathered neck of the last bag.

I gave him a scornful look. Since Cully was not only a man and a southerner but also a jogger, he tended to be smug about his superior strength. Pooey on you, Cully! I'm tall and I exercise every day – well, almost every day – and I'm not going to play clinging vine.

My training in the control of my facial muscles came in handy. I managed to swing the bag off the tailgate and onto the pile of dumped garbage with the requisite gusto, but I was glad Cully had to shut the tailgate. That gave me a moment to hop back into the pickup and have a blissful second to relieve my anguish by some down-home cussing.

I let out a few more unprintables when I discovered I was bleeding. Some of the broken glass had pierced the bag, and me. I believed the cut was small; but as hand injuries will, it bled profusely, and I couldn't be sure. When Cully climbed in beside me, he may have had the hint of a smile on his face, but it vanished (fortunately for him) when he saw the blood.

'Charles has a first-aid kit in the glove compartment, since he takes this pickup when he hunts.' He reached across me, his arm touching my knee, and pulled out the kit.

I was angry and embarrassed. 'It's just a little cut,' I said through tight teeth.

Cully was already pulling a gauze pad from the kit. He pulled my arm over as if it weren't attached to a body. Dabbing carefully, he blotted the blood with the gauze. His eyes flashed sideways once, but his look bounced off mine and back to the cut.

It came to me that Cully was a wound healer. That was a beautiful trait in a psychologist, or a brother, or a bosom friend; but fairly dismaying in an object of lust. If I could manage to survive a pretty bad car accident, I conjectured, I might even rate a kiss.

'What did you start to say to me that day that Alicia

was over at the house?' I asked, just to remind him that I was indeed at the end of my arm.

'Oh.' He was absurdly intent on the little cut. He got out a bandage and ripped off those irritating strips of paper that guard the adhesive. 'I just wanted to tell you to be sure to lock up at night, and just sort of watch out in general for Mimi.'

I frowned. 'Maybe I'm being dense, but why?'

'Well, she's been through a lot lately; Grandmother and Richard and all.'

Mimi was about as frail as an innerspring. Though Cully might not see her that way; after all, he was her dearly beloved and only brother. There's more here than meets the eye, I told myself wisely, and twirled an imaginary mustache until Cully looked up and caught me.

'What on earth are you doing?'

'There's something you're not telling me,' I parried.

He straightened and looked thoughtful. I wondered if I could have my arm back, since it was obvious this was not going to be one of those electric movie moments when the hero suddenly gives way to passion after touching the girl, usually when she's dismounting. I didn't have a horse to slide off of; the best I could do was cut my hand.

'No,' Cully decided out loud. He bent back over my cut, meticulously applied the bandage, and handed my arm back to me.

'No, what?' I asked nastily. My muscles were aching from the weight of the garbage bag, the cut began to throb, and there were about seventy-five things I had to do before I could retire for my much-needed preparty nap.

'It wasn't important anyway,' Cully said, and started the pickup bucking along the road.

We were halfway home when I turned to him and said with absolute honesty, 'Cully Houghton, you are one of the most aggravating and frustrating people I have ever known.'

He looked considerably surprised, as well he might. I think it was the first time I'd ever said something really personal to Cully.

'That's interesting,' he said after a moment.

We didn't speak again; but oddly enough, the silence wasn't uneasy. I blocked him out of my mind, and I was half asleep by the time we got home.

Attila was pressed in a hot purring bundle against my leg when I woke up. He'd definitely adopted me, which showed sheer ingratitude to Mimi, who'd found him as a starving kitten and fed him to his present enormous size.

He sat on the toilet lid as I showered and dried my hair. The sound of the blow dryer made him nervous, but he tolerated it to satisfy his curiosity. He even endured my tuneless humming, the closest I will ever come to singing. The nap and hot shower had banished the worst of my soreness. The cut looked clean and small. I felt refreshed and in a mood to party. I tickled Attila under the chin, and he followed me to my vanity table to watch me put on my makeup.

I was thinking sweet thoughts about little furry friends when (via the mirror) I observed Attila carefully and deliberately shoving one of my earrings over the edge of the table. He tried hard to look innocent when he realized I'd caught him at it, but the look didn't come off.

'You're going to have to learn my ways,' I said grimly, 'if we're going to cohabit. *Bad cat*!' I whacked him on his broad beam.

He instantly bit me and began purring like a chain saw.

We stared at each other.

The cat's schizophrenic, I concluded. I knelt to grope under the bed for the earring. (Of course it had bounced under the bed – don't they always?) Attila descended from the vanity with a thud and dived under the bedspread to see what I was doing. He spotted the gleam of gold a split second before I did and quickly sat on my earring. We stared at each other again. It looked like a Mexican stand-off.

Fortunately for one of us, little Mao stuck her head around the door to investigate my room. Attila was off the earring in a flash, pursuing the smaller cat with yowls of fury.

Dressing went more smoothly after his departure. Soon I was all ready except for the top layer, and that required some thought.

Before going upstairs for her own nap, Mimi had advised me on what to wear: 'Something that doesn't show a whole lot of boob. Wait till they get to know you, for that. But don't condescend, either; they'll all know where you've lived and what you've done for a living.' As if I needed that advice, after my never-to-be-forgotten gaucherie years ago.

Now I searched through my closet nervously, sliding hanger after hanger across the rod in search of something absolutely appropriate. It suddenly occurred to me how ludicrous my anxiety was. I recalled some of the parties I'd dressed for in New York. Some – not a lot, but some – had been the kind that got written up at great length and talked about for years.

Unfortunately my old ego boosters (Famous People I've Drunk With, Publicized Parties I've Attended, Beautiful Men I've Dated) didn't seem to weigh an ounce now I was back home. They might as well have been social distinctions on the moon, for all they counted here and now. I gave myself the green light on being nervous. I had every reason to be.

I finally lighted on a dress that mingled every shade of

blue and green and covered my chest pretty thoroughly without being in any way virginal. I pulled it on and got everything settled. Then I turned around in front of the mirror and looked over my shoulder. My partially bare back told me my tan was holding up pretty well.

'Great!' Mimi applauded from the doorway. She was wearing true red and she looked like a million dollars. She came and stood beside me, and I revolved to look at our reflections in the mirror. We had gazed into many mirrors together across our friendship's span of thirteen years. I liked this reflection better than any I'd seen.

We were as sharp a contrast as ever – Mimi small and dark, myself tall and fair. Some of the arrogance was missing in the way she stood and held her head; it had been pared off by the divorces. Some of the self-conscious power vested in me by my face had been knocked off my shoulders. Mimi was not so wild and willful. She was not so trusting, either. I was less defensive; and I knew now I would never conquer the world.

I don't know what Mimi was thinking during that long moment. Maybe her thoughts were traveling the same road as mine. But somehow I was convinced that she saw us as we used to be; not as we were.

She put her arm around my waist and hugged me close, then loosed me to lift my hair on my shoulders and re-arrange it in a drift she liked better.

'Let's get this party rolling,' she said briskly.

I blinked, and the moment was gone.

4

Parties in Knolls started (and ended) earlier than I was used to. About eight-thirty I decided that the entire population of the town was crammed into Mimi's house. At least the entire *white* population of Knolls – some things hadn't changed much in the years I'd been gone.

Aside from their uniform skin color, our guests ran the narrow gamut of Knolls society. There were friends of Mimi's with their husbands in tow, women I vaguely remembered, most of them giddy with the excitement of a night off from the kids. There were plenty of college people. I met the cowardly college president, Jeff Simmons, and found him charming. He had a beautiful head of wheat-blond hair for which most women would've sacrificed their microwaves. And there were people un-aligned with either college or society cliques, whom Mimi just knew and liked. Town and gown and independent.

I hadn't been to see Mimi's parents yet, so I was glad to see them come in the door. Sleek, dark Elaine was still one of the most attractive women I've ever known. She swept me up in a carefully loose embrace and brushed her cheek against mine, bombarding me with questions it would take me a week to answer. Not that Elaine intended to stick around and listen if I did. She was wearing a beauti-ful dress that revealed a lot of still-prime cleavage. If

Elaine subscribed to Mimi's dictum, the people here tonight must know Elaine very well indeed.

Elaine's husband Don was close on her heels, as always. I hugged Mr Houghton with far more enthusiasm. I'd always been very fond of him, a fondness compounded both of pity and of gratitude for his kindness. I believed it was not easy to be married to Elaine, and I sometimes thought it couldn't be too easy to be Cully's and Mimi's father. In social situations Don was always overshadowed by his family. But he did have his own flair; Don could make money, and he was shyly proud of that, I'd discovered years ago.

'How's the man with a finger in every pie?' I asked lightly.

Mr Houghton looked pleased and embarrassed and altogether like a great teddy bear. He'd lost some hair and gained some weight since Mimi's last marriage, but his face wasn't deeply lined and he still had a bounce to his walk.

'Well, I can't complain,' he admitted proudly.

I led Mr Houghton over to the bar, where Cully mixed his father a gin and tonic. They shook hands with an odd formality, but they looked glad to see each other.

'What are you up to now?' I asked in a whisper.

'Well, Nickie,' Don began slowly, taking a sip of his drink, 'I've bought me a restaurant.'

'Which one?' This was sure to be a secret. In addition to owning a big insurance agency, Don was a silent partner in many Knolls businesses.

Don whispered back the name. I recognized it as one of the few good restaurants in Knolls.

'You demon,' I said with a grin. 'You're going to own this town before too long.' Don loved that kind of talk; he grinned like a twelve-year-old with a frog in his pocket.

We chatted for a while, and at first I enjoyed it

thoroughly. But as usual, Don (bless his heart) began to bore me just a little after a while. I caught myself looking wistfully at guests I hadn't had a chance to visit with.

Mimi whipped up to rescue me in a swirl of red.

'Daddy! You let Nick talk to other people. You can have her over to lunch soon and hash over old times. There's Jeff Simmons over there. You better go tell him that Houghton needs some more insurance, after that awful thing this summer!'

Her father obediently headed in Jeff Simmons's direction, his face becoming purposeful as he thought of business.

'You've always been such a favorite of Daddy's,' Mimi told me as she whisked me away. That pleased me, of course; Mr Houghton had always been a favorite of mine, too. But this evening, as we'd talked, I'd caught a little gleam in his eye that was quite unwelcome in the father of my best friend.

I shrugged to myself. Oh, well, Don had always been an appreciator of women. He bragged about Elaine's looks all the time, as if he were personally responsible for her attractiveness.

Mimi introduced me to white-haired Mrs Harbison, our next-door neighbor, who immediately assured me she'd 'just dropped in for a minute.' Mrs Harbison's minute stretched to twenty as she filled me in on the details of her widowhood. Her house was as large as this one. I wondered how the old lady managed by herself. As I listened, I found out. Mrs Harbison had few free moments. She gardened, kept the house up, canned, embroidered, played mahjong, and was active in the church. And she took some pains to find out what church I belonged to.

It had been so long since anyone had asked me that, I hardly knew what to say. I'd forgotten that this was always one of the first questions to be settled in the

South. I remembered I'd been an Episcopalian once upon a time. I breathed a sigh of relief when Mrs Harbison turned out to be a Baptist. She couldn't enlist me in any of her church organizations, and she was a little disappointed about that. To my dismay, she told me she'd be sure and tell a mysterious Mrs Percy that I was in town. I assumed Mrs Percy was Mrs Harbison's Episcopalian equivalent, and I shook in my shoes. Church-minded ladies are as incontestible as gravity.

Mrs Harbison finally wandered off home. I made my way back to the makeshift bar where Cully presided. We'd borrowed two sawhorses, laid some planks over them, and covered the whole with a tablecloth now sadly stained with spilled cola and bourbon.

'Got any Blue Nun left?' I asked.

'Coming right up,' Cully said, and poured me a glass. He looked at me a little doubtfully, and I thought he was remembering that long-ago rehearsal dinner when I'd had too much to drink. I looked him straight in the eye and gave him the smile that had formerly cost so much per hour. For a gratifying second he looked stunned. I decided to leave while the going was good.

'See you later,' I called gaily, and wriggled through the crowd to join Barbara Tucker and Stan Haskell by the mantelpiece. They were standing close together and alone, looking like a pair of shy sheep. It was obviously my duty as a cohostess to cheer up this corner of the party.

I bellowed at Stan and Barbara over the noise of the room and got them livened up. Soon another Houghton professor wandered over and began to deliver a neat character assessment of his department head. I fixed my face in attentiveness, but my mind drifted. I listened to the party booming all around me. This was my first southern party in years, and I began to notice a difference in it. The voices were certainly as boisterous, the throats as dry. Of course these voices had a different cadence, for the most part; some Houghton people from the North and Midwest added variety. But many of the topics of conversation I could hear were the same – the president, the economy, children, personalities.

But there was a difference. Finally I had it. Most of the people I'd known in New York were on their way up or already there, in one of the most competitive cities in the world; a city in which making the grade locally meant making the grade all over the world.

Incredibly, these people at this little party in Knolls, Tennessee, were more assured. They had a place; and by God, they knew it. With the exception of the imported college people, the crowd in Mimi's living room was inter-related, interbred, and interdependent. And with rare exceptions they would always be accepted in the place they'd been born to, no matter what any one of them did.

That had its advantages and disadvantages, like any other given condition. But this evening, in the flush of successful party-giving and the warmth of homecoming, that assurance seemed almost divine. In this society I felt an incredible safety that I'd felt nowhere else. I sank back into it as if it were a soft couch. Back in the fold. No need to prove myself. My struggle in New York seemed ludicrous.

Barbara shouted something in my ear then, and I snapped to. I couldn't make out what she was saying, but I did hear enough to tell her she was acquiring a southern accent. Barbara laughed so much that I realized she was certainly appreciating the liquor. She was flushed with the heat of packed bodies and a good dose of bourbon. Stan, her Chaucerian lover, looked mildly embarrassed by Barbara's noisy good cheer, but it appeared he was matching her drink for drink. Maybe later in the evening I would get to see shy Stan Haskell let his hair down. What a prospect.

Right now he was gesturing wildly to someone beyond my left shoulder. I twisted to see who it was. My rescuer from the cloister of the English and Administration building was making his way to our little group.

'Nickie Callahan, Theo Cochran,' Barbara introduced us. 'Nickie, Theo is our registrar at Houghton.'

I beamed at Theo. 'We already met, in the dark,' I told Barbara. Barbara laughed immoderately again.

Theo smiled and nodded to me, then craned toward Barbara. He was looking rather handsome this evening, in his Roman senator/well-fed way. 'Congratulations, Barbara! On the tenure!' he said. 'I haven't seen you since I heard.'

'Thanks, I'm celebrating! Where's your wife?'

Theo pointed toward the farthest corner of the room. His wife seemed to be the intelligent-looking woman wearing a dress that would have made any designer throw up.

'How's Nell?' Barbara asked. I must have looked blank. Stan bent over to tell me that Nell was Theo's little girl. I nodded. There was that special inflection in Barbara's voice that signaled a delicate subject, so I sobered my expression appropriately.

'She's doing as well as we expect,' the registrar told Barbara through stiff lips.

And that was the end of Theo's stay in our company. He stood there the second longer required for courtesy, then nodded curtly and moved off to rejoin his wife.

'You shouldn't have asked,' Stan told Barbara. I got the feeling that perhaps I should edge away. Stan was obviously more than a little aggravated with Barbara.

She accepted his irritation as just. 'You're right, that was dumb. Nell's his little girl, Theo's only child,' she explained to me. 'She has leukemia.'

'Oh, that's horrible!'

'He doesn't like to talk about it at all. It was really stupid of me to ask. But I *do* want to know how she's getting along and show some concern. It's okay to talk to Sarah Chase about it – that's his wife's name – oh, didn't you go to Miss Beacham's?'

Bewildered by the abrupt change of subject, I nodded.

'Theo's wife is Sarah Chase Beacham.'

'Miss Beacham has relatives?' I said in amazement.

'Well, a brother anyway,' Barbara said. She was beginning to smile again. Stan took her glass and his own to get a refill, but I shook my head when he gestured toward mine. 'Sarah Chase's father is Miss Beacham's brother. He's in education too. I think he's dean of men at Pine Valley Methodist College, and Sarah's brother is a high school principal somewhere, and she herself used to teach. But with this illness of Nell's – well, Sarah Chase just had to quit work. She's changed beyond recognition. She's older than you, so I doubt she was at Miss Beacham's when you and Mimi were.'

I peered over at the woman again, trying to recall her face. Now that I knew her story, I thought I detected the lines of care, the grayness, that marked her features prematurely. But I didn't think I'd seen Sarah Chase Cochran, née Beacham, before. When Stan returned with two full glasses, I took my leave and began circulating through the crowd. Mimi made her way toward me with a man in tow. He was tall and solid, with heavy blunt features and a sensuous mouth. Her face looked more alive, more animated, than it had since I'd come home.

'Nickie, this is Charles Seward, young lawyer-about-town,' she said lightly. 'Charles, Nickie Callahan, my oldest and dearest.' But I noticed that while one small hand lay relaxed on his arm, the other hand at her side was clenched in a tight fist. She was afraid I'd judge him as harshly as I'd judged the others.

She fluttered off immediately after the introduction, a technique of hers with which I was familiar. I called it (very much to myself) 'Make Them Seek,' and I'd never been sure if the practice was conscious or unconscious on her part.

'I've heard a lot about you, Nickie,' Charles Seward said pleasantly.

He couldn't know that was my least-favorite conversation opener, of course. I ordered myself to overlook it and find some pluses in a hurry.

The young lawyer was tall, even taller than Cully, so I knew he was a recent arrival. (Late for Mimi's party – a minus, unless he had an acceptable excuse.) He was quite an attractive man, I thought. His brown hair was prematurely thin on top, but that gave him an air of gravity becoming to a man of law. His light-blue eyes looked even lighter against his deep tan.

'Have you known Mimi long?' I asked cautiously. I can converse in platitudes as well as the next person.

'Long enough to wish I was living here with her, instead of you,' he said. Right to the heart of the matter.

'Whoosh,' I said, and rubbed my stomach.

'I've been waiting four years for that creep Richard to leave. Before that I waited for Gerald to leave. What do you think my chances are?'

'There's nothing like getting down to brass tacks,' I muttered. Why hadn't he stuck to platitudes? 'Well, do you think you could hold off until I finish college?' I asked half-seriously. 'I just moved in, and I hate the thought of changing addresses so soon.'

'Sorry,' he said, without a trace of sincerity. 'I tried to catch hold of Mimi after she divorced Gerald, but I bided my time, since I thought she needed some breathing space. That bastard Richard hopped in and whisked her off before my eyes. I told myself then that if I got a chance, I was jumping in with both feet. And I have. And I'm sticking.' He looked unnervingly determined.

Mimi's bruised ego made her a pretty susceptible woman right now. I hoped Charles Seward was the right man for her – because with his looks and his flattering determination, I figured Mimi might be a goner.

Charles grinned at me suddenly, and I blinked. If he wasn't so set on Mimi . . . I could see the young lawyer's attraction, yes indeedy.

'Well. Moving right along, are you a native son of Knolls?' I asked.

'Born and bred. Good family: father, mother, two sisters married to good men. Went to law school, joined my father's firm. All set. Now all I need is a wife just like Mimi.'

Now *that* was a fixation. The Houghton children seemed to inspire them, I observed to myself. I glanced involuntarily across the room to Cully.

'Good luck,' I said. I didn't know if I meant it or not. At least Charles Seward came from Mimi's world – a plus. He saluted me and plunged into the crowd, surely in search of Mimi.

Make Them Seek.

I stared thoughtfully after him and wished my wine glass was full.

'What do you think?' asked a voice somewhere over my head. Cully stood very close behind me. How had he gotten here so fast? He handed me a full glass and took my empty one. He must have taken a mind-reading course for his doctorate.

'I think his chances are good,' I said soberly. 'Do you like him?'

'Fairly well. He's a little too hearty for me. I haven't been impressed with Mimi's husbands so far . . . Charles

247

is several degrees better than Richard or Gerald. Mimi didn't much like my wife, either. It looks like a pattern.'

It was fortunate that someone hooted for Cully to return to the bar, since I had no idea what to say to that I'd already opened my mouth to try, though; and it wasn't wasted effort. Alicia Merritt flew up to me, and we shrieked at each other for a while. I also got to visit – a little – with her husband, Ray, whom I dimly remembered as the boy who'd called Alicia every night long-distance while we were at Miss Beacham's.

Ray was a light-complexioned, sandy, solid type: Alicia's paperweight, I thought, inspired by the wine, He didn't seem overwhelmingly glad to see me. He'd always been one to mistrust the different, I recalled.

After the Merritts joined Jeff Simmons's coterie, I went back into general circulation, from time to time going down the hall to the kitchen to get more munchies for the table.

About midnight, the crowd seemed to be thinning out. Time for the babysitters to go home, I guessed. Cully had abandoned his post to talk to his father and Ray Merritt. Elaine was being mooned over by a youngish bachelor coach from the college. Mimi's red dress wasn't hard to spot; but Charles Seward wasn't looming over her, to my surprise. When we met by chance in the kitchen, Mimi told me rather proudly that he'd be working all weekend on a court case for Monday, and had left to plunge back into his preparations; so I mentally excused Charles for being late. Stan and Barbara said a slightly tipsy goodbye, and it seemed that Theo and Sarah Chase Cochran had already left. I'd never gotten over to her corner to meet Theo's wife, and I chided myself. As I was totting up the remaining guests, I saw Elaine neatly detach herself from the young coach and collect Don.

My facial muscles were aching from my hostess smile.

I rubbed my cheeks as I surreptitiously began to check nooks and crannies, tracking down the glasses that people leave in such odd places. I took a few back to the kitchen as unobtrusively as possible, and there was trapped by a professor who wanted to talk about the Romantic poets, apparently with a view to getting my mind on the general subject. After I smiled him out the front door with a hearty handshake, I found a few more glasses and plates and exchanged chatter with a few more people.

So when I considered it later, I decided it was about forty-five minutes after the Houghtons left that the phone rang. I happened to be blotting up a ring on the hall phone stand, an old-fashioned arched one built into the wall. I lifted the receiver automatically and said hello.

'Nickie? Nick?'

Elaine Houghton. 'Yes, ma'am?'

'I have something kind of nasty to tell you, now. You and Mimi lock up extra careful tonight, you hear? A friend of mine who rents her garage apartment to Barbara Tucker just called me, and the police are over there. Barbara Tucker got raped tonight.'

'But she was just here,' I said stupidly.

All the party drained out of my system. I found myself staring at the ring on the painted wood as if it were proof the news wasn't true. 'Maybe she just got burglarized?'

'No. There's an ambulance,' Elaine said crisply. 'Besides, the police told my friend Marsha. I'm quite sure. Goodbye, now.' She hung up.

I was close to the improvised bar just inside the living room. Cully was there, for once making himself a drink. I wobbled over to him and put my hand on his back. He turned sharply.

'What?' Then, more urgently, he said, 'Nickie! What's wrong? Who was that on the phone?'

'Oh, Cully. Oh, Cully,' I said out of a fog of alcohol,

exhaustion, and shock. 'Poor Barbara. He's gotten Barbara Tucker.'

Mimi had sensed trouble with her built-in hostess antenna, and she arrived at the bar in a swish of red, her face stern at the spectacle of two people being upset and serious at a party. So I was able to tell them both what Elaine had said.

I thought of the woman on the sidewalk in front of my apartment building in New York, and wondered what was so different here, after all.

5

Eight o'clock in the morning was a horrible time to schedule anything, much less Chaucer. I was almost stumbling on my way to the English building, trying desperately to wake up and look alert. I wanted to start briskly and keep the momentum going.

All the dreariness of registration, fee payments, orientation, book buying, had led to this first full day of classes. I was actually beginning the completion of something I'd quit years before.

Since the registrar's office was situated on the ground floor of the English and Administration building, I passed Theo Cochran's open door on my way down the hall. The fluorescent light was gleaming on his bald head. He looked up as I passed and gave me a little wave. It was nice to see a friendly face among the herd of strangers, all depressingly younger than I.

To say I was nervous was an understatement. Mimi had been giving me rah-rah speeches for days, after I'd finally admitted how scared I was about learning to study all over again, being pitted against younger minds, handling the workload poor Barbara had so cheerfully assured me I could bear.

Right classroom? I checked the room number on the door against that on my schedule. Right classroom, yes indeedy. I hesitated for a second. Then I grabbed my courage with both hands and pushed open the door – to be met by an audible gasp from a little guy wearing a Led Zeppelin T-shirt who was sitting in the first row of desks. That exaggerated gasp focused everyone's attention on me. I stared back at their smooth faces. Had I done something wrong?

'Wow!' said cocky little Led Zeppelin just as loudly as he had gasped. 'You are some *kind* of woman, woman.'

From sheer relief I started laughing, and after a second the others joined in. Even Stan Haskell chuckled from his post by the desk.

I sobered when I saw him. My amusement disappeared abruptly, as did his when he saw me watching him. He was grayer. The summer had gone from his face as surely as it was fading in Knolls. In a week, Barbara's shy lover had passed to the other side of middle age, too early and too fast.

I pitied him and I was angry with him; but I had resolved that on Mondays, Wednesdays, and Fridays from eight to nine he was going to be Dr Stanley Haskell, my professor in Chaucer, period. I had to take this class. I had my own life, I told myself. My own goal. I had to stop thinking about Barbara Tucker. So I slid into a desk, whipped out a pen, and opened the virgin notebook I'd labeled 'Chaucer.'

Mimi, bless her heart, was ready with a glass of wine when I got home. I'd been studying in the library until five-thirty, when hunger rousted me out. Mimi's big push had been in the previous weeks, when she'd been assembling committees, organizing the year, and smoothing ruffled faculty and staff who ran atilt during the anxious preopening month. She would have a brief lull now, she had explained.

'How'd it go, Nick?' she asked sympathetically.

'Oh boy, oh boy. I'm going to have to work my tail off, Mimi.' I threw myself down on the couch and accepted the wine gratefully.

'Well, you knew that.'

'Sure. But knowing and doing are two different kettles of fish.'

'Did you see Stan?' She settled opposite me, and Mao arrived to jump in her lap.

'Yes, first thing this morning.' I told her about my resolution.

'You're going to have to do that, all right. But what a bastard. I just can't think of any other word for him, Nick.'

'Well . . . yes. But I don't think he dropped Barbara like a hot potato because he's a *basic* bastard. Do you see what I mean?' Attila materialized on the arm of the couch. I took a long sip of my wine and tickled the cat below his chin. He began cleaning my knuckles ardently. Maybe he'd missed me today? More likely he was hungry. 'You know I don't know them well, not nearly as well as you do. But I think he just *can't* talk about it to her. And if he can't talk about that crucial thing, they can't have a relationship. He can't even stand to see Barbara, he can't face any part of what happened to her.'

'Why not?' Mimi had been especially sensitive to disloyalty ever since Richard left her.

'I guess he just can't.' I lit a cigarette. 'When I saw them together I thought they were a matched set, and you say they were in love for at least two years. But I guess Stan's just weak, or something.'

'Like it was her *fault!*' Mimi interrupted.

'I'm not defending him,' I said gently. 'I'm just trying to understand, because I need to. I have to stay in the class.'

'I'm not mad at you. I'm sorry,' she said. 'But you know how broken up Barbara is, and Stan acting like this is all she needs, right? Now is when she needs him most. Now is when he bows out. Remember how she kept asking?'

I didn't want to remember our visit to Barbara. I'd suffered with, and for, Barbara Tucker as much as our limited acquaintance would allow, since I'd so naturally liked her at first meeting. Now I was weary of the pain and fear her situation had given me.

But I couldn't help remembering. I heard again her bewildered voice asking Mimi if she knew why Stan hadn't been by. That had been the day after the rape, when Barbara was still disoriented and in pain.

When Stan had dropped her at the door, she told us, they'd both been sleepy from too much to drink. Stan started back to his own place to collapse. Barbara had climbed the steps to the front door of her garage apartment as usual – probably making a lot of noise, since she was clumsy from the bourbon.

The man had already broken in the back door. He was waiting for her in the dark. When she'd reached to turn on the light, she had instead touched an arm.

We could scarcely bear to hear it, but Barbara went on and on in a shaky voice. She had finally fainted. After the rape. When he hit her on the jaw.

But it wasn't over when she'd come to. It wasn't over for a while. Now it would never be over; never. That was what had shaken me to the core, so painfully that I'd recoiled from Barbara. What had happened to her could not be mended, healed, shoved aside, bought off, glossed over. It was irreparable.

In New York, I'd known women and men who'd been robbed on the street or burglarized. But by chance I'd never been close to anyone who'd been the victim of a personal and violent attack by another human being.

Like Heidi Edmonds, Barbara had never seen her

attacker's face. She hadn't the slightest idea of what he looked like: eyes, hair, build, or anything.

But he had called her Barbara.

Mimi and I agreed later, once we'd gotten home and calmed down a little, that his knowing her name might mean a great deal, or nothing at all. If he'd been stalking her (Stalking? In *Knolls*?), he'd have easily found it out. On the other hand, he might be someone she knew well. She seemed sure of it. And that was so unthinkable that we just blotted it out.

6

Two months went by while my thoughts were turned to my books. Those weeks were so full of adjustments and assignments requiring all my concentration that the outer world just had to get along without my participation.

Alicia dropped by from time to time, and we went to dinner at her house. Ray seemed to like me more now that I was doing something as ordinary as finishing college. Whenever I talked about my life in New York, though, those pale eyes would flicker.

Mimi and I met Cully at the Houghtons' for a Sunday brunch. It was an uncomfortable meal. Mimi and Elaine sniped at each other from the underbrush, and Don still had that gleam in his eye that made me uneasy. Cully, too, was at his dryest that day. He said his counseling load at the college was much heavier than he'd expected – a lot of freshman students were already having qualms about attending college at all. They were homesick. He and I seemed to have established some kind of truce. The talk and feel of things between us was easier and more relaxed. I caught him watching me at odd moments, and developed the notion that he was beginning to see me as a rounded human being, not just a beautiful dodo. But that was the only bright spot of the meal.

I decided to ruin the day good and proper, so I called

my mother. She'd been to church, come home, and started drinking. Jay wasn't there. She tried hard to sound sober, but I knew she wasn't. However, she was proud of my going back to college, and she managed to ask correctly after the Houghtons and send a polite message to them. Mother also said one curious thing. She told me, quite out of the blue, that she hadn't told Jay where I was.

I was going to have to think about that.

Before I went to sleep that night, I decided that Jay might have dropped a hint to Mother, God knows why, that he'd gotten rough with me all those years ago. It also occurred to me that it had been a long time since I'd known Mother to hold off drinking long enough to get dressed and go to church. I tried to cancel that thought; I pinched myself in punishment. I would not hope.

Time ran through my fingers as my life with Mimi settled into a comfortable routine. Having two separate floors to live on made that much easier. We didn't collide in the bathroom, we didn't keep each other awake with lights or music or studying. Our most serious disagreement was the great debate about when to put the garbage out – the night before pickup was due, so we wouldn't have to surge out in our bathrobes at the crack of dawn, but the dogs often got it; or early in the morning, in which case the dogs still might get it, but not if we watched to shoo them off. We solved this knotty problem by alternating garbage duty instead of sharing it.

Because of our lavish cooking I gained four pounds, which Mimi swore became me. I thought I looked like I'd swallowed a cantaloupe.

Attila became quite possessive. He cuffed Mao unmercifully when the smaller cat ventured too close to me. I grew used to studying with a heavy load of tabby on my lap. When I was alone, I discussed things with Attila in disgusting baby talk. Mimi overheard me a couple of times and made graphic gagging noises.

Occasionally I heard from New York friends. Their phone calls seemed like communications from a foreign land. I was sliding back into my own. My speaking cadence slowed. I didn't wear camouflage on the street. My manners resumed their former polish. My way of thinking reverted (a little) to the labyrinthine.

But mostly I studied. I had to. If I wasn't reading, I was writing: not the novels of my dreams, but essays and term papers of one kind or another.

I dated a friend of Charles's once or twice. He was nothing worth working at, just good for a mildly pleasant evening; for one thing, he talked about duck hunting too much. But our double dates gave me a chance to observe Mimi with Charles. To my relief, she showed distinct signs of finally having developed a streak of caution and a sense of her own rights.

Sometimes she sang in a fair-to-middling alto as she got ready for a date, and sometimes she had that exalted, melted, 'in love' look. But more often she seemed thoughtful. I was glad to see that; I hadn't brought myself to like Charles yet though I was trying. And I did not, repeat did not, criticize him to Mimi. But perhaps she sensed my anxiety. He was courting her at such a furious clip that I'd become semiseriously concerned about finding another place to live in Knolls, in case Charles really did succeed in sweeping her off her feet and to the justice of the peace. Housing in Knolls was no idle concern. Because of the shortage of dormitory space, every doghouse and garage in town was rented during the college year. Barbara Tucker had had an awful time finding a place to live after she got raped. She just hadn't been able to stand her garage apartment any longer.

Poor Barbara. She was the only specter on a horizon I found full of promise, and she was becoming a very faint wraith. I was truly busy, desperately busy; and the tiny tremor in her voice reminded me that I should, must, treat her specially. She was of the walking wounded. She marched down the sidewalks of Houghton very swiftly, and very alone. Stan's defection had proved permanent. From a comment she dropped during one of our rare meetings, I got the idea she was seeing Cully professionally, and I hoped my surmise was correct. Cully's calm, restraint and precision would be comforting to a woman in Barbara's situation, I thought.

Talk about Barbara's rape was no longer current in Knolls, partly because neither Heidi Edmonds (the first victim) nor Barbara had ever been figures in the mainstream of town life. According to Mimi, the feeling prevailed that the rapes were a campus problem – though plenty of residents strolled through the gardens, and of course Barbara's rape had happened off-campus. The scare had hit hard only among faculty wives and town women who worked at the college. These women watched what went on around them more carefully, and many installed extra locks. The female students went in pairs after dark, at least while the fear was fresh.

Mimi and I were conscientious about locking the doors every night and I tried to do all my library work before I came home to supper. We decided we were doing everything we reasonably could to make ourselves safe. I distinctly remember the phrase 'fortress mentality' coming into our conversation when we discussed security measures.

On the whole, this was a pleasant and rewarding period in my life. I loved it. I was living in a place I wanted to be, doing what I wanted to do, spending time with a friend I cherished. I was slowly making more friends. The ladder was gone; I didn't have to climb it, or scrabble to keep my place on it anymore. I seldom turned on the bulbs of my mirror for that dark close examination.

Late October had never seemed so full of golden light.

7

I was jerked out of sleep so suddenly and violently that the shock robbed me of breath. A hand was clamped over my mouth. If I had had any air, I would have screamed.

'Don't make a sound,' whispered the figure that was only a darker part of the darkness filling the room.

That figure was not Mimi or Cully or anyone who had a right to be there. In the worst moment of my life I knew clearly what was going to happen.

I couldn't breathe, I had to breathe. I lifted my hand to knock his away, let me *breathe!*

'Don't move, I have a knife,' he whispered.

He held it up into a shaft of moonlight he was careful not to cross. I saw the blade, as he wanted me to.

Oh my God I'm going to die.

And I imagined the blood soaking the sheets, and God bless Mimi, she would find me. I was going to die and I wanted to live.

My heart was pounding so erratically and loudly that I feared a heart attack, too – fear was going to kill me, fear and the knife, fear or the knife. This was my end; this secret dark and hideous incubus was going to end Nickie Callahan, and my God I couldn't breathe.

There was hate filling the darkness around me, hate trickling down that shaft of moonlight. I was sick from the hate and the fear.

He moved his hand and I gasped air, air, oh Jesus, let me live! The hand had risen to gain impetus for the smashing blow it delivered to the side of my face. I choked on blood and pain.

'Be quiet,' he warned me, and then he hit me again. And again.

Sometime before the fifth blow I was still conscious enough to begin to hate, for my hate to match his; conscious enough to want his death for the death he was dealing me.

I heard the ordinary sound of a zipper rasping.

He put the extra pillow over my face and he raped me.

I twisted my head to one side under the pillow's smothering pressure and breathed wonderful air for the minutes I had left. My arms were locked protectively across my chest. I could feel his head brushing them. I wrenched my mind away from my body. I loathed the thing that lay on me. What was happening bore no relation to anything I'd experienced before. This was not sex but punishment. He hated me. He was going to kill me. And I couldn't move to defend myself. If I moved I would surely die, and there was a chance, some kind of chance, there *had* to be . . . *a chance that I would live* . . . if I stayed still.

The incubus owned my life.

Where was the knife? Somewhere it was waiting to slide into me, between my ribs, ripping me, violating me in another way. Both his hands were occupied *(don't feel, Nickie)*, the knife must be somewhere in the tangle of sheets.

But I couldn't move to find it.

My heart pounded erratically, on and on, frantically wanting an end to this. I knew the end would be soon.

Then it was over. He was off me, and I heard a fumbling in the dark as he zipped up his pants. My silent screams had compounded into such a noise inside me that I could barely hear the things he was whispering. I was glad of that. I had reached the bottom of humiliation and helplessness.

He hit me again, body blows now; over and over, and I thought it would maybe be better if he went on and used the knife. The fear would be over, the pain would end. I was going to die soon. There was no chance of my living. I could feel that rage, taste it in the blood in my mouth – my rage and his. He surely wouldn't let me survive to hate him this much.

He bent to my ear, bent to the air gap under the pillow. 'I might come back, you superior bitch,' he whispered. 'Think about that. I might come back.'

I suddenly realized that he meant to leave me alive this time – alive. This bastard was going to *permit* me to live; and I hated him, it throbbed in the blood pumped by my exhausted heart.

'Don't move, or I'll kill you, Nickie,' he whispered again. 'Do you understand?'

I nodded somehow; he must have seen the pillow shift.

Then a funny sound. It came to me that I was hearing gloves sliding onto hands.

A final 'Don't move.' I felt a stir in the air.

I was going to live.

He was leaving.

If I had gotten up, and to the window, perhaps I could finally have seen him. I couldn't move. Nothing could get me off that bed. My muscles were locked, and fear was still shrieking through my veins and arteries.

I had survived.

I stared into the darkness from under the pillow wet with my blood – but not my lifeblood. The fact that I was going to live filled the universe under that pillow.

But he might come back even now. I sensed he was

gone; but he might be back, he might be just in the next room. Had he meant immediately? Or had he meant some night in the future?

Oh God I can't stand it if he comes back. I can't survive it again.

There was not such a thing as time. There was only breath after breath, one more breath that I had lived, then another . . . In. Out. Not dead, I'm not dead, alive alive alive. In. Out.

There came a breath when I was convinced he was gone.

In one convulsive shove I threw the pillow from my face and the chilly night touched my face. I stared into the dark corners of the room. Even the shaft of moonlight had vanished, covered by clouds.

It was really over. It had really happened. I smelled of it, to my sick disgust. I had lived through it. And I had to have help. I managed to roll. I stretched my arm. I found the switch on my bedside lamp.

Light. Blessed light, emptying the room of shadows that might hold him. He was truly gone; I would truly live. I was filled with an intense shock of astonishment.

Now. If I could get up. I looked down at my body and shuddered, feeling more naked than I had thought it possible to feel. There was damage. He must have worn a ring; maybe he'd put one on especially to cause more damage. I felt as sorry for my body as if it were a separate thing, not a part of me. My mind pitied my body for what had happened to it. It had to be covered, poor bleeding raped thing. I had to reach the closet to cover up that bruised body. I didn't want it to be naked anymore, ever.

But the closet was a few feet away. Need drove me. I swung my legs over the side of the bed, bringing them together in a tight protective parallel. Holding on to the bed table, I stood. I swayed for a second and caught myself. I shuffled forward, my knees trembling, and turned the handle of the doorknob. Opened the closet. My robe, my winter robe, the long one that closed up to the neck, that had a sash that I could tie tightly; that was what I wanted. It took me a long time to find that robe and get it on. I had to rest before I started for the hall. If my knees would just stiffen; come on, please, legs.

Raped. Oh Jesus God, *raped.*

I hadn't left the door to the hall closed when I went to bed. It was closed now. I opened it with infinite effort. It swung in silently, disclosing the blackness of the stairs and hallway.

And I wondered if Mimi was still alive.

The terror started all over again. My hand independently found a switch and pushed it up. The stairs leaped into light. Attila was huddled in a mass of wild-eyed panic on the landing. His tail twitched as he stared down at me. I couldn't climb the stairs; I tried to lift my foot to the first step, and failed.

'Mimi,' I whispered. Louder, Nick, I told myself.

'Mimi,' I said raggedly in a voice I didn't recognize as my own. I felt fluid running down my thighs. I gagged.

Then I screamed, 'MIMI!'

An uncertain sound upstairs. Then a whole series of little thumps, a door opening. Attila turned his crazed eyes upward.

Alive and unhurt, Mimi appeared at the head of the stairway, buttoning her bathrobe. She stopped on the landing when she saw me. I stared up at her.

'Oh no,' she said quietly. She brought her hands up to cover her mouth. 'Not – oh, Nickie. Not you.'

The tears that started down her cheeks ran over her hands. She jumped when she felt the wetness, dropped her hands to grip the banister, and crept down the stairs to me, hand over hand on the wood, like an old crippled woman. When she was level with me she looked at my face, into my eyes, and shuddered. I didn't feel anything, anything at all. I knew that would end, soon. And there was a lot to do before it ended.

'Call the police,' I mumbled. Something was going wrong with my mouth. My knees gave way and I sat on the stairs. 'Call them right now.'

She moved past me. The cat streaked past her heels, mad with all this abnormality, wanting out. Away. I huddled close to the banister and crossed my arms over my breasts, pressing the bathrobe more tightly around me. I could feel blood moving down my cheek and couldn't – wouldn't – lift a finger to stop the ooze. I focused on the front door, directly across the expanse of living room from me. Soon a lot of people would be coming through that door. I dreaded the unknown process that was about to be set in motion; I dreaded the questions; I dreaded, most of all, the faces.

But my hate matched his. No matter what it cost me, I would endure anything to catch the man who had done this to me. Before the pain blurred my thoughts, I realized, with an eerie clarity, that nothing I had ever done in my life – nothing – could justify the punishment that had been meted out to me.

It didn't hurt my cause that the house I lived in was Mimi Houghton's; that I was white; and that I had visible wounds to show. Even so, I was surprised by the Knolls police department. They were neither naive nor inefficient. The first car arrived within two minutes of Mimi's call. These were patrolmen. After a quick question as to whether I needed an ambulance, they began to search the house and the block. Then came the detectives, two grave middle-aged men in sports clothes with faces like road maps of unpleasant scenery.

They held some kind of colloquy with Mimi, and she vanished into my bedroom. When she returned, she squatted in front of me and took my hands.

'Come with me for a second, Nickie. Can you get up?'

Confused, but not caring enough to ask any questions, I let her lead me to the empty room across from my bedroom. She had a pair of underwear balled up in a bathrobe pocket.

'Honey, you have to put these on, okay? They're going to have to keep them and send them in to the lab.'

I had to lean against the wall while Mimi tugged them on. She saw my torso. She had to sit down for a second, and she sobbed, deep racking gusts of air. I stood propped against the wall and observed her.

She got up after a minute. 'Now, we're going to have to go outside, but the police will be with us,' she said unevenly. She put her arm around me and I leaned against her, my own arms still crossed over my chest. One of the detectives came to my side as we crept through the living room and out the front door.

'We're going to see my doctor,' Mimi explained carefully as they maneuvered me into a strange car. 'For the evidence, and because you're hurt, okay?'

I nodded. If I had tried to speak, I would have started screaming and never stopped.

The examination I had to endure, I did endure. I clenched my teeth while the doctor treated the cuts and clucked over the forming bruises, then told me I had no broken bones and only two loose teeth, which was some kind of miracle. The doctor recommended a visit to an optometrist to have my eyes checked, told me I'd have one shiner, and then got out some kind of kit to collect evidence for the police.

In a nervous effort to make small talk, to fill the silence as I stared at him, he explained that he'd examined the student, Heidi Edmonds, the past summer; and also Barbara Tucker two months ago. The police had supplied him with some kits in case the rapist struck again. He'd gone to a training school, he told me, to learn how to use them.

I had a horrible vision of myself posing for an ad for rape evidence kits, an ad designed for some law-enforcement journal. I would be posed holding one and smiling, sitting on the examining table with an avuncular doctor patting me on the back. A stern and determined policeman would be visible through a partially open door into the hall.

I suddenly realized I was still in my bathrobe. Mimi was somehow in blue jeans, though I'd never been aware of her leaving my side to dress.

The doctor told me it wasn't necessary for me to go to the hospital, but if I wanted to check in for a couple of days of observation, that might be best.

'No.' I would not have more people staring.

While I lay on my back on the cold examining table, I spied a clock on the wall. I realized, with a jolt, that it registered four o'clock in the morning. When had I been awakened by that hand over my mouth? I'd gone to bed around ten-thirty. Mimi had been out with Charles Seward; I vaguely remembered hearing her come in, but I had no idea of the hour. I'd gone straight back to sleep.

By the time the doctor had finished, the night was thinning toward dawn. We rode back in the detectives' car. We walked into the house to face more activity than we'd left. I saw men in my bedroom, dusting for prints. For the first time, I noticed that the screen was not on the window I'd left ajar when I went to bed – a window that looked out onto the encircling porch.

That must be how the man had entered my bedroom. It had not occurred to me to wonder before. While I was sleeping, in my own bed in my own home, he had stood there watching me through the window and then carefully removed that screen and entered.

I had thought I could sleep with an open window on a cool fall night. Despite Heidi Edmonds, despite Barbara Tucker.

There it was, the thing I was guilty of: I'd left a window open. I stood convicted of not fearing enough.

'There have been two rapes,' I said informatively to the detective helping me get to the couch.

He jumped. It was the first time I'd spoken since the doctor's. 'Yes,' he said. 'Maybe more. Some women won't call us, you know.'

'Is this the same rapist?'

'After we've talked to you some more, we'll have a better idea. Oh – later we'll need your bathrobe, too, Miss Callahan. I'm sorry.'

That was okay with me. I never wanted to see it again after this night was over.

Their questions had been few and brief so far, only aimed at determining how close the rapist might still be to the house. They'd decided right away that a doctor had to come first.

Mimi left the room. I faced the detectives on the opposite couch. Other policemen were coming up to report things in whispered conferences.

Then Mimi was back beside me, holding a glass of water and a handful of pills. 'You have to take these,' she said.

'What for?'

'Um, in case he had a disease,' Mimi said wretchedly. 'Dr Cole said I had to make sure you took them pretty soon.'

I had informed the doctor, in a very terse exchange, that I wouldn't become pregnant from the attack. I was on the pill. The very idea of pregnancy had filled me with such loathing that I almost vomited. Now I had to make sure I wasn't diseased. I took two of the pills from Mimi, swallowed them, drank, and shuddered. Then two more. Every time I thought I was through, Mimi handed me more. While I swallowed and shuddered, the detectives began questioning me, their voices quite neutral. I was grateful for that briskness; it helped keep me from collapsing.

And suddenly I became conscious. If it was possible to be walking and talking in a state of unconsciousness, I had been. I could remember my conversation with Mimi's doctor, but not his face, or his office, except the clock on the wall. I stared at the two detectives, seeing them individually for the first time. They had different faces, I observed. They were not interchangeable, as I would have sworn minutes earlier.

'What are your names?'

They looked startled, and glanced at each other.

'Tendall,' said the gray-haired one.

'Markowitz,' said the heavier man with brown hair.

They waited for me to tell them why I'd asked, or give some kind of signal. They were eyeing me warily; they were unsure of what I might do next.

'He called me Nickie,' I said. 'He knows me.'

I had to tell them everything: every word, every act. And I had to hold myself very tight to get through it.

'I can stand this,' I assured Mimi, apropos of nothing. 'I lived through that. I can stand this.'

Then my awareness began flickering again. It was like drifting in and out of anesthesia. At one point I became aware that the pills were all gone and the glass of water was empty. I must have finished taking the capsules. I took Mimi's hand. Until she gasped, I didn't realize that I was gripping it with unbearable force. When the detectives were asking me the most delicate questions ('And did he – uh – experience an orgasm?') I heard a nagging sort of noise that bothered me, and I glanced around vaguely to find its source. It was Mimi; she was crying.

I didn't want to cry. I was never going to cry . . .

And I went under again, only coming back to myself when a door slammed. Mimi was standing in front of me and the house was empty. I was in a different bathrobe.

'What time is it?'

'Six o'clock,' she answered. 'The police are all gone. They asked me to bring you to the police department tomorrow afternoon – today – to take pictures.'

'Pictures?'

'Your bruises and cuts.'

I began to laugh. I'd been photographed for years, for my beauty. Now I was going to be photographed for my cuts and bruises. 'How much will they pay me per hour?' I gasped.

Mimi collapsed on the couch beside me and began laughing too. Then she began crying. I watched her curiously, my legs carefully parallel, my hands folded neatly in my lap. 'I'm never going to cry,' I told her.

Wisely, Mimi didn't respond to that. 'You're going to bed in my room,' she told me.

The thought of going to sleep, of being vulnerable again, made me begin to shudder. I'd been trembling since I'd crawled from my bed hours ago, but now violent muscle spasms began to shake me. 'I can't get up the stairs,' I said helplessly.

Mimi looked as though she was at the end of her resources. 'Do you think you can sleep on this couch?' she suggested finally.

'Not alone, I can't be alone.' The very idea made the shudders intensify. I wanted desperately to bathe, to be *clean*, even more than I wanted to rest. As soon as the idea occurred to me, I knew I couldn't sleep until I washed the uncleanliness off me, the filth he had left. 'I have to bathe,' I told Mimi.

'I'll help you,' she said with instant comprehension. 'We'll have to use your bathroom, though.'

That meant passing through my bedroom to get there. 'I can do that,' I mumbled. It was increasingly difficult for me to articulate. I could tell Mimi was having a rough time just understanding me.

'Okay, here we go,' she said bracingly. She put her arm around me to help me rise.

I read the utter exhaustion printed on her face. 'I'm sorry, Mimi,' I whispered.

'Shut up, ass,' she said. 'I can't cry anymore.'

I kept my face turned away from the mirror over the sink.

We got me into the bathtub, a tub filled with the hottest water I could stand. I didn't realize how many cuts I had until I sank into the water. I became fully aware as soon as I submerged. I hissed at the sting. But my God, it was a blessed thing to wash. I dipped my head down in the tub as the simplest way to clean my hair. The water became so soapy with repeated latherings that Mimi finally drained the tub and turned on the shower attachment to rinse me off.

After the bath, my mind was more at ease. I felt cleaner inside and out; perhaps a particle of what I'd undergone had been washed away. Some of my cuts had reopened in the water. Mimi bandaged them. Then she found my nightgown and helped me into it. It had been a long time since I'd worn one, and I only knew where it was because I'd unpacked so recently. Mimi looked a little surprised when I asked for it.

'I'll never sleep naked again,' I said flatly. 'I don't know how much of this will stay with me, but that is one thing I do know I will never do again.'

Finally, finally, I was ready to stretch out on the couch, with Mimi ensconced on the one opposite. It was daylight. A few cars were moving on the street. The world had come alive again after the death of the night.

I knew when I put my head on the pillow that I wouldn't be able to sleep. I would mime it for Mimi's sake, since she was obviously at the end of her rope. I would keep watch over us.

The next second I was asleep.

8

When I awoke there was a man standing over me. I drew in my breath to scream.

'It's all right, Nickie,' Cully said urgently. He knelt beside the couch. 'It's all right. It's me.'

After a moment my pulse slowed, my breathing eased. 'Better in a minute,' I whispered. We waited.

I could tell by the slant of the sun across the floor that it was afternoon. Cully was wearing blue jeans. I wondered why he didn't have a suit on, and realized it was Saturday. I felt slovenly in my wrinkled nightgown. I wrapped the light blanket around me as firmly as I could and swung my legs to sit up. My breath whistled in sharply. Movement brought pain. I stared at a dust mote dancing in the air until I had adjusted to this pain.

Cully observed me silently. He sat on the couch beside me. I knew what my face must look like by now; I turned it to him. Directly, deliberately, for once with no artifice, I looked directly into his eyes.

I watched his own face change. I had finally gotten to Cully. The wound healer saw a massive gash in a human being he knew.

I watched him search for something to say. Cully, the articulate psychologist, was struggling for words. I waited, full of unused anger, my eyes fixed on his face.

He'd never been a toucher, by inclination and by

training. But when the words didn't come, he touched me. He searched out a square inch of my face that wasn't damaged and he kissed it very gently.

I remembered thinking once that I would have to survive a bad car smashup to rate a kiss. Well, I'd done it. I turned from him, ashamed of my anger. It shouldn't be focused on him, of all people. He was the one man in Knolls I could acquit of being the rapist. No matter what the circumstances, I would have known Cully.

'Where's Mimi?' I asked quietly. It seemed an eerie echo from two months ago.

'Trying to calm Mother down. They're in the kitchen.'

I told him bluntly that I didn't want to see Elaine.

'I know. We'll try to keep her out.' Then he said tentatively, 'I think I'm going to move in here for a while.'

I felt a vast indifference. During the long night my edifice of pride and independence, my integrity, had collapsed after the voice had come from the darkness. Today another structure, called Cully, had slid to the ground. All the feelings I'd built up around Cully's image seemed to crumble in the space of five minutes. For the first time in fourteen years he was just Cully, Mimi's brother, comforting a female he'd known for years, his little sister's best friend.

Now I was a grown woman with no girl left. No structures at all, and I had to start all over again.

I didn't know the first thing about the man at my side. And I wondered for a bleak moment if I really knew Mimi. I suspected I didn't even know myself.

I had no frills left.

At this illuminating and painful moment, Elaine Houghton went out of bounds and swept into the living room, Mimi on her heels with hands outstretched as if she were thinking of physically restraining her mother.

*

Today I looked at Elaine bare. I'd always tended to think of her as a one-dimensional comic-book villainess. Of course, she was human – perhaps not a good mother, but capable of moments of generosity and sympathy. Elaine squatted before me, took one of my hands in hers, and said, 'Nickie, I'm so sorry this happened to you. It upsets me no end that this has happened to you in our little town, while you're Mimi's guest.' To her credit, she did no more than clench her teeth and swallow hard when she got a close-up of my face.

That's Elaine, I thought. Really sorry it happened at all, but even sorrier that it happened in Knolls in a family home. Obviously Cully had inherited his 'slap, stroke' technique from Elaine. But almost in the same instant I realized I was being grossly unfair. Elaine had undoubtedly been scared out of her wits. Her daughter had been only yards away from a terrible crime, and perhaps had escaped being its victim only by being on the second floor of the house.

'I know you'll want to leave us now, and you've only been here a few weeks. Please don't think badly of us.'

'Leave?' I said blankly.

'I hardly imagine you'll want to stay here,' she said in surprise. 'I mean, with everyone knowing . . . you'll be more comfortable where nobody knows.'

'Why?' Fool that I was, I really couldn't imagine why. How could I get the support I needed, if no one around me knew me? Where should I go? Home to Mama, who would cry over me and then get drunk? Home to my stepfather, good old Jay?

Elaine began to lose her assurance. Her dark bird-wing brows contracted. 'Why, Nickie . . . Who could you date here? I think you've learned an awful lesson, the hard way, bless your heart, but surely you'll want to start all over again somewhere else.'

The three of us stared at her. Elaine rocked back on her haunches, a hard thing to accomplish in a ladylike manner in a skirt; but she managed.

Cully said, 'Mimi, do you understand what Mother's saying?'

'Yes,' Mimi answered wearily. She rubbed a hand across her forehead.

'What?' I asked. 'What's she saying?'

'She means no one will want to date you here, since you're damaged goods now,' Mimi answered. 'I think she's hinting that you somehow brought your rape on yourself.'

Elaine had drawn herself up. She was not used to face-to-face challenges. She was not used to open contempt from her daughter. She wasn't sensitive, but she would have needed a hide of iron not to feel her children's exasperation and dislike at this moment.

'Not exactly "brought it on yourself,"' she protested. 'It's letting them think they're equal, welfare letting them have anything they want without having to work for it or pay for it. And the clothes girls wear now.'

'No,' I said. 'I don't believe this.' I leaned back against the soft couch and shut my eyes. But there was a sinking feeling in the pit of my stomach.

'You probably just smiled at one on the street and they just thought it was an invitation.'

If Elaine Houghton felt this way, surely others would too. Elaine had never had an original emotion in her life. I hoped her comments would just evaporate; but they stuck to my skin, they congealed. I had more to face than I had imagined.

'Mother, go away,' Cully said quietly. I could feel his arm muscles tense.

'Mrs Houghton,' I said, opening my eyes and leaning forward painfully. 'Listen to me. You're Mimi's mother, and I don't want to be rude to you. But you have to understand how I feel. What happened last night . . .' I drew a breath. 'Getting raped . . . was in no way my fault. If I'd walked down the street buck naked, I would still in no way deserve what happened to me. I am not ashamed. If my purse had been snatched, you wouldn't be saying what you've been saying. This was . . . another crime, a nastier crime. An act of hatred. But it was not my fault any more than a purse snatch would be.'

As I mumbled this lengthy speech through swollen lips, I probed myself for the truth of what I was telling Elaine. I was formulating my thoughts as I spoke. It was true. I was not ashamed. But it was also true that I was horrified that even strangers to me would know approximately what had passed in the dark of my bedroom. It was sickening to conjecture that some people would look at me and try to picture my rape; perhaps secretly enjoy that picture, or think it served me right, in some mysterious way. There are a lot of black crevices in the corners of sympathy. Last night I'd fallen into one that had widened into an abyss.

'I don't know if you can see this,' I said to Elaine and to myself. 'But the man who raped me wants me to be destroyed by what he did. He wanted to hurt me; and he did. I couldn't do one damn thing about it. But he wants me to keep on hurting. I can do something about that. I *won't give him the satisfaction*.' My fingers were clenched in fists by the time I finished. I meant what I said down to my bones, I meant it more than I've ever meant anything.

'Well,' Elaine said briskly, 'I think you're making a mistake, Nickie.' She rose in one graceful movement and brushed her hands against her skirt. Washing herself clean of me. 'You would forget a lot faster if you moved away. But you're a grown woman, and Mimi owns this house, so I guess there's nothing more I can say.'

But of course there was. Elaine was deeply shaken, not

only by the anger of her children but by what she must have seen as a NOW diatribe delivered by, of all people, a former model. Elaine's face was red; she was holding down her voice with an effort. 'I personally feel you should get out of town and try to put this behind you. And may I add, Don agrees with me.'

Mimi and her brother exchanged glances. Mimi had long ago told me that her father agreed with everything Elaine said, to keep the peace and because he loved her. He just did what he wanted after he'd completed his lip service.

'When you get over this being brave to impress people' – and Elaine glanced pointedly from me to Cully – 'you may take my advice.' Her face twisted with genuine passion. 'Honey, how are you going to pass them on the street? Knowing one of them raped you? They'll all talk about it, you know. How will you be able to stand it? I bet half the niggers in town know who did it, but will they tell? Oh no, not on one of their own.'

In the North I'd become accustomed to racism being more cleverly cloaked, among my chic acquaintances. I'd temporarily forgotten Elaine's earlier ranting about 'welfare' and 'taking things for free.' Now I understood what she had meant all along. White men wouldn't date me because a black man had raped me, she thought.

'Mrs Houghton, the man who raped me was white. I don't know anything else about him; but I do know that he was not black. I know from the voice.'

That shocked Elaine more than anything else I could have said. She stared at me in utter disbelief. Then she obviously decided I was making my rapist white out of rampant liberalism. 'You poor child,' she said, and marched out the door.

'What can I say?' Mimi cried. 'Nick, I'm so sorry.'

'I wonder how much of what she said is true.'

'Nothing!'

'A little,' Cully said. Mimi made a violent gesture of protest, but Cully raised his hand to silence her. 'You're going to notice changes in attitudes,' he told me steadily. 'But mostly it'll be because people won't know how to express sympathy to a woman who's just been through a rape. They'll be uncomfortable, because they won't know whether you want to talk about it, or maybe couldn't stand it being mentioned. It's almost like . . .' He thought for a moment. 'Like you had an enormous green wart on the tip of your nose. No one here would ever dream of mentioning it to you, out of kindness and embarrassment. Even if you had that green wart removed, people *still* wouldn't say anything – for fear of admitting that it had disfigured you before.'

I nodded. I could remember how it bad been, when this had been the only country I knew. And I remembered, with shame, how uncomfortable I'd been when I talked with Barbara Tucker. I'd put her misery at arm's distance. I was guilty of more than an open window after all, I decided.

'Men, especially, may be uncomfortable,' Cully continued, still speaking in his steady professional voice, but with his eyes averted.

Thanks, Cully. I'd already figured that out.

'They may feel guilty that one of them did this to you. Maybe they'll feel uneasy about how you're going to react to other men now – dating and sex and so forth.'

'Gosh, it's great having a psychologist in the family,' Mimi said savagely. She mimed gap-mouthed admiration.

'I need to be forewarned, Mimi,' I said. 'I'd never . . . naturally, I'd never thought of all this.' Others were certainly going to invest a lot of emotion in my tragedy.

'You haven't exactly had time,' she said briskly. 'Now, I think you ought to try to walk around some, so you won't get stiff. The doctor wants to see you again this afternoon and take some x-rays of your ribs, just to check, and the police want to take pictures. We have to make a dentist appointment, too.'

I didn't want to see anyone at all. I didn't want my face recorded. I wanted to stay in the house. I wanted to get dressed and study. I wanted to do anything normal, anything routine, to keep from remembering the night before. But there was my brave speech to Elaine Houghton to live up to. I rubbed my forehead. There was a gap, I thought, between my intentions and my desires. There was more to face now than I'd faced the night before, when I had seen the thread of my life held in someone else's hands.

The thread of my life was in my own hands again. I was *alive* to face those problems.

Gratitude raced through me for the precious life I had kept. I looked at the sunlight drifting through the curtains. I looked over at my books, piled on the desk on the other side of the room. I was deeply grateful to God that I would be able to open those books again.

I would pay a price for my life. I might lose some of the friends I'd just begun making, lose them in a welter of embarrassment and misunderstanding. But what did that matter if I was still alive?

At that second, I felt I would never lose the wonderful awareness that everything was new for me. I had thought my eyes would never see the world again. I decided I would never take for granted any action my live hands could perform. I looked at those hands, saw the veins still working to purify my still-circulating blood, flexed the muscles that worked so miraculously. I watched the bones move under my skin.

That glory, that beauty, didn't ebb, even when I stood painfully, even when Cully helped me hobble out to the kitchen for the most delicious bowl of Campbell's chicken noodle I'd ever tasted.

Cully explained something to me later that day.

'I started to tell you twice, once the day I first saw you and again when we were on our way back from the landfill. I have a friend on the police force, a guy I used to hang around with in the summers.' Cully, like Mimi, had gone away to school. 'He told me that when Heidi Edmonds got raped, the police thought it was a fluke. A transient, or maybe a boyfriend no one knew about who got carried away. But then they began hearing rumors that another woman had been raped and just couldn't report it. And then another.

'So, my friend figured it wasn't a fluke. There really was a rapist in town. He got the police chief to come to me, with the idea I could give them some directions to look in. But there wasn't anything I could tell them that was helpful. I started to warn you, twice. But both times I decided I'd just frighten you more than I'd get you to be alert. I figured you'd be on your toes anyway, since you'd lived in New York. And after Barbara got raped, I didn't think I needed to say anything.'

It wouldn't have made any difference, and I told him so. His face relaxed. 'Cully, even if I'd locked my window, which I only *might* have done if you'd warned me, the police told Mimi the locks on those windows are so old a ten-year-old could get in. Don't ever think of it again.'

I hope he didn't. I never did.

Sunday was another out-of-kilter day. After the bustle and appointments of the day before, it felt empty. Empty for me, anyway; Mimi was kept busy answering the telephone. No one, apparently, wanted to come by, because they weren't sure what shape I was in. But they wanted to express concern. Mimi said most of the callers sounded frightened.

I hunched on the couch, hearing the reassuring murmur of Mimi's voice in the background. I stared in front of me with an awful emptiness echoing through my whole body. *Emma* lay open on my lap, but I never turned a page. This crisis was too evil for gentle Jane.

I had always been healthy, so physical pain was new to me, and shocking. I couldn't move without a reminder of what had happened to me, though it was never far enough from my thoughts to make that necessary. The rape happened to me over and over again, that Sunday.

I discovered many things.

I discovered that pain requiring vengeance is very different from accepted pain. The misery of my father's death now seemed equivalent to the coldest grimmest day of winter, perhaps after an ice storm, when every forward step is shaky. But this pain had pinned me in the middle of the forehead, branding me with a sizzling V for victim.

I discovered I wanted to know his face. I wanted to seize that face in my hands and rip it, cause pain, draw blood. I wanted to say, 'See! *This* is what you did to me!' I wanted to hang him naked and conscious in a public place, and say again, *'See! This is what you did to me!'* And I would never be able to do it.

But still I wanted that face, and I swore to find it. I swore before I went into the bathroom to look in the mirror for the first time.

I discovered then that my face was finally my own. I would never see or think of it as a separate thing again. I would also never again think of myself as beautiful. Even after the skin healed, even when the bruises faded.

I wanted to know his face.

*

I went back to classes on Monday. It was the hardest thing I'd ever done.

Two days had started the healing but made the discoloration of the bruises more lurid. At least my clothes covered my ribs and stomach. If any student at Houghton College, any resident of Knolls, had wondered who the rape victim was, they would wonder no longer.

That was why I had been beaten; so everyone would know.

As I left the shelter of the house, it occurred to me that any man I saw, any man I knew, might be the one who'd done this to me. He could examine his handiwork; he would be pleased with what he'd done to my face.

And he might be furious that I was apparently going to go on with my life. As that new fear occurred to me, my courage faltered. I clasped my books closer to my chest, as if they could protect me. My feet dragged. I was desperately tempted to turn back to the house, to hide myself from his eyes.

'No no no,' I swore out loud, and slapped my chest with the books. Going back to the house today could easily – so easily – be the first step toward shutting myself in it for the rest of my life. I would not, could not, do it. That would give him what he wanted, on a platter. I'd felt that in his rage.

But more than that I did not know. Even under a requestioning by the tired detectives, I couldn't think of anything tangible to tell them, except that the man was white, solidly built . . . his weight had not been light on me; don't think don't think . . . and he had said he might come back.

'Common threat. Don't worry about it. They never do,' Detective Tendall had reassured me. He hadn't looked at me as he said it.

Never? Tendall was fudging just a wee bit, I decided. Just a wee bit. So as not to scare me.

Here came a girl, a student. I was approaching her and would pass her. I looked neither to the left nor the right. I heard the sharp gasp as the girl went by.

Beautiful sidewalk, white and even.

In a few hours my classes will be over and I can go back home legitimately, I thought. I will study and I will take another shower and I will not think about Friday night. I will take a pain pill and I will sleep without dreams.

During that longest walk to class, as I caught the faces of those who passed me from the corners of my eyes, a film of that night played over and over in my head: the hand clamping over my mouth, the pillow over my face, the beating, the rape, the pain in Mimi's face. Over and over, as my feet moved forward, I relived that night. The projector in my mind was running that movie continuously, and I had no means to switch it off. I wondered if I would always watch that movie; the audible tortured thudding of my own heart on the soundtrack, the visual shaft of moonlight, the intangible presence of death.

I must've seen it ten times before I reached my classroom. I glimpsed Theo Cochran during one of the intermissions. He nodded to me silently, solemnly, from his desk beyond the open door to his office. He knew. I nodded stiffly back, the screen jumped, the movie sped on.

My tunnel vision was serving me well. But I felt the silence in the classroom as I entered; so different from the silence of admiration that had greeted me the first day. Led Zeppelin T-shirt wouldn't whistle at me now. I sat like a stone at my desk. I heard the sound of the class bell, then the belated footsteps of Dr Haskell, half a minute late as he'd been ever since the first day. Those footfalls stopped short in the doorway. He had seen me. Then they resumed at a staccato pace to his lectern, and he entered my tunnel of sight. He was white. Every line in his face was deeper, all those grooves and seams etched into the flesh. He started to say something. He looked away.

Go on and speak, I begged him silently. Mention it. If you acknowledge it, it won't be so bad.

But the Stan Haskell who couldn't tolerate seeing even his lover after she'd been assaulted wasn't going to speak. To borrow from Cully's simile, he was going to pretend he didn't notice the gigantic green wart on my face.

That might have made some women feel better. It scared the hell out of me. If other people pretended it hadn't happened, I'd be left alone watching that movie in the dark.

'In our last class . . .' Stan Haskell began jerkily.

And there I was. Alone in the dark. A restricted audience; and no popcorn.

Barbara Tucker was waiting for me in the hall after class. She flinched when we were face-to-face. I was getting used to that. She drew herself together and laid her hand on my arm. I felt movement on either side; my classmates were departing very slowly, passing me reluctantly, as if they wanted to stop. Stan Haskell had brushed by as soon as he could, casting one unreadable glance at us.

Gradually I became surrounded by people, as though Barbara and I had formed a dam to hold back their flow. We were all quiet for a long moment. Then the chunky blonde girl who sat to my right in class said, very formally, 'I don't want to intrude on your privacy, Nickie, but you have my complete sympathy, and I hope they catch whoever did it. And I hope he resists arrest and I hope they shoot him dead. For Dr Tucker, too.' She said this in one breath, touched me gently on the shoulder, and marched off down the hall. There was a chorus of 'Right' and 'Me, too,' and then a loud and shrill 'Kill the son of a bitch' from my dear Led Zeppelin T-shirt.

'Sisterhood, Nickie,' said a tiny girl named Susannah with great earnestness. I tried to smile, which caused a cut on my lip to open and bleed. The militance that had filled the hall altered to sick horror.

'Thank you,' I mumbled, so the poor things could go.

Barbara's hand on my arm began to urge me toward the women's bathroom. She awkwardly pulled a tissue from her purse with her other hand and dabbed at my lip as we reached the door. We sat on a hideous brown couch. Barbara gave me a cigarette and lit it. Her face twisted.

'For God's sake,' I said furiously, 'don't cry.'

'Neither of us needs that, I know,' she said. She gulped a few times. 'Okay. Do you think there's any chance they'll catch him?'

'Minimal, in my case. No fingerprints. No one saw anything, least of all me. Except maybe Attila the cat. It was too dark.'

'Same here. The first thing the police asked me was, "Is he black?"' Barbara said grimly.

'White. I could tell by the voice.'

'Me, too. I think I'm so damn fair-minded. But you know, that's the first fear I had when he grabbed me. Is it a black? The great racist bogeyman rises again.' She brooded over that for a moment while she put out her cigarette with a vicious grinding motion. 'What's made this thing a nightmare for me is how Stan hasn't been able to handle it. I haven't seen him away from the college since it happened.'

Right now, I didn't give a tinker's damn about how Stan Haskell was handling it. I was worried about *me* handling it.

'He can't deal with it at all,' Barbara continued. 'I can't fathom his attitude. He's a caring man, he surely believes in the equality of women, but he can't come to terms with me being raped at all.'

'Cully says some men are just embarrassed,' I offered. Then I remembered that I'd suspected he was counseling Barbara, that he must have formulated the advice he'd given me from his experiences with her.

There had been a flatness in my voice that had penetrated to Barbara. She flushed. 'You have enough problems without me burdening you with mine,' she said.

I realized I was doing it again. Shoving her off. 'Barbara,' I said, 'we share something pretty unique. I can say this to you, I think. Screw Stan. Let him grow up on his own. He's not tough. We are. We're here. We're going on. Not all men are like him. You've lost something that must have been pretty wonderful. But we're here, alive.'

She sensed what I was saying, but it didn't satisfy her, of course; I'd had no right to expect it would.

'Anyway,' she said finally, 'I couldn't go to bed with him, or anyone, now. Maybe after a long time. With care. A lot of care.'

That hadn't been a prime concern of mine, since I hadn't any partner. But I suddenly wondered how that was going to be for me.

We had been wandering through our separate fears for a couple of minutes when Barbara roused herself to ask me how I was physically.

'No broken bones. The dentist tomorrow – I expect a lot of dental work. The eye doctor said Saturday that there wasn't any permanent damage to my eyes, just bruising. I'm sore, and stiff, and I hurt like a sick dog. But I'll get over all that. Mostly, I'm just mad. Barbara – do you hate?'

She flipped the clasp of her purse open and shut a couple of times. She pushed her glasses up on her snubby nose. At last she looked at me directly; I saw something naked behind those glasses.

'For the first time in my life, I frighten myself,' she said.

'I know exactly how you feel. What can we do about it?'

'There must be something. I'm torn up inside. Sometimes' – and she pushed a wisp of hair behind her ear – 'I can't believe that I can walk and talk and teach class and tell people good morning . . . and all the time I'm carrying this terrible cancer inside me.'

'We can pool what we know. We can think, we can figure.'

'The police are professionals at that.'

'It happened to *us*.'

'I'll tell you one thing I know that I don't think the police took much stock in. He knew me. He didn't just know my first name. He *knew me*.'

I took a deep breath. 'He knew me, too.'

'All right,' Barbara said with a briskness she hadn't displayed in a long time. 'We'll do it. Think about everyone you know. Write names down.'

'I'll make a list,' I said. This was going to be a different list from any I'd compiled before. 'We'll compare. It's a pity Heidi Edmonds isn't here at Houghton anymore.'

I straightened up. I felt my shoulders brace. Even probably futile action was better than no action. In my heart I was quite sure that the trained, professional police would do the best job possible. And in New York, our plan would have seemed laughable. But here in Knolls . . .

'I think mad is a good way to take it,' Barbara was saying consideringly. 'The little girl – she really was, you know – who got raped last summer; she got *sad*. Heidi was one of Stan's students. He told me she became so frightened she wouldn't even go to the bathroom without someone to go with her.'

'Oh, I'm scared all right,' I said grimly. 'It takes an hour and sometimes a pill to get me to sleep. Then I keep waking up. But going away isn't the right thing for me. It may yet get to be too much for me here, but I'm going to try to stick it out.'

'I have to stick it out here, I have no option,' Barbara said. 'The job. Speaking of the job, I have to go meet a class.' She gathered together the paraphernalia teachers and students carry with them everywhere. 'If you ever need me, call me. Anytime.'

We clasped hands briefly and tightly. When I left for my next class, I felt better. I was not alone in that darkened room anymore.

And I made it somehow through the rest of the school day.

When I got home, a locksmith was putting new hardware on all the windows and doors. Mimi was following him from room to room, a cigarette lit but disregarded in her hand. I was appalled by my mental estimation of the cost of this. I cornered Mimi to tell her I'd pay for it. With one terse phrase she turned me down. When the locksmith left a check tucked in his pocket and a smile on his face, Mimi asked me if I was ready to move upstairs with her. I'd been sharing her king-size bed for the past two nights; she had been as restless as I.

'No,' I said. 'I'll keep my bedroom. And sleep in it, starting tonight.'

'That's crazy,' Mimi said bluntly. 'There are two rooms upstairs you could have. All it'll take is a little time and muscle.'

It was foolish of me to insist I would sleep in my own bedroom. Sheer bravado, rather than courage. Having determined I wouldn't let this get me down, I was bull-headed enough to persist in any resolution, however ill-reasoned. I should've made some concessions to myself, given myself a little leeway. I should have known my life would never again be exactly as it had been.

'With all those locks you put in,' I insisted, 'no one in the world could break in unless he was a professional and had lots of undisturbed time.'

'Then, Miss Martyr,' she said tartly, 'Cully's going to sleep in the dining room right opposite your bedroom.'

'There's no need for . . .'

'Just cut out this heroine stuff,' Mimi said. Her voice soared high and thin. I saw her hands shake when she lit another cigarette. 'You may be willing to be an iron woman, but my God, I'm *scared*.' Even the cats, sleeping together peacefully for once, lifted their heads at the warning note in her voice. I felt very small: as my father used to say, 'knee-high to a grasshopper.'

'Mimi . . . I'm sorry. I've just been so set on overcoming this thing that I hadn't thought about how you must feel.' I shut my eyes (they were watering) and bit my lip. Which of course promptly bled.

'Okay, you don't have to flagellate yourself,' she said unevenly. 'You have enough on your plate right now. You're doing great. Just don't carry it too far. I want Cully to move in for *me*. And he wants to. Just for a while, okay? Charles wanted to move in instead' – and her mouth turned up in a lopsided smile – 'but I told him the town had given us enough attention as it was. Besides being good for us, I think the move would be good for Cully.'

'What do you mean?'

We had migrated into the kitchen. Mimi began washing dishes. She paused in her task, her hands immersed in the soapy water. She sucked in her lips, a sure sign that she was thinking heavy thoughts. 'Cully is a psychologist, but that doesn't mean he's immune to the syndromes he treats in other people,' she said finally. 'I think he's probably very good professionally. He's always in control, he always knows what he wants to say. And he can keep so calm and detached. Boy, is he good at detachment!' Mimi screwed up her face expressively, and I laughed a little. I picked up a dish towel and began drying.

'I bet lots of people think he's a cold fish,' she continued soberly. 'But he's not underneath. He's as vulnerable as anyone else; and maybe more tender than average. Rachel's leaving him hurt, just as bad as Richard's leaving me. But I wailed and cried to you, and now it doesn't ache quite so much.' Mimi's crooked smile lit her face. 'Cully, now, hasn't wailed and moaned at all. Mama thinks that means he's glad to "get shuck" of Rachel. Well . . . he may have fallen out of love with her, but he had shared a life with her, and he had a lot of pride involved in that marriage.'

'Being a psychologist wouldn't help in that situation,' I said as I put the glasses away in the cabinet. 'You'd feel like everyone was saying, "Ha, ha, look at the pro who can't even counsel his own marriage back into shape."'

'Exactly.' Mimi nodded vigorously, the dark cloud of hair flying. 'So Cully really needs to feel all male and effective right now, and I do want him here. I think it's a good thing for all of us. Really, won't you sleep a little better with a man in the house?'

'I think, frankly, that I'd sleep better with a shotgun in the house. But since I'm not about to buy one and have no idea how to fire one if I had it, Cully will have to do.' I imagined briefly how Cully would react if he knew he was running second to a shotgun. Then I handed Mimi the last dirty cup and saucer and headed toward the living room to try to read my assignments. My body was reminding me at every step that it had been abused, and the damn movie was still playing. Studying wasn't going to be easy, but I had to start sometime.

'Hey,' called Mimi as I reached the door. I turned.

'I just want you to know, you're a great woman. Now don't come hug me or anything,' she added hastily as I took a step forward. 'Or I'll cry again. But I just wanted to tell you that. You should already know I feel that way, but sometimes I want to tell people things I'm sure they know.'

'I love you very much, Mimi,' I said, and left the room. My eyes were watering again.

9

So Cully moved into the house, in a limited way, the next weekend. Since Celeste had left the dining room suite to a niece, the room opposite mine was already empty. Mimi and I had made an exploratory trip to the attic in search of furniture for Cully's room and had discovered a bed set that apparently had been stored up there for years. We managed to haul the mattress halfway down the stairs, but I was too sore to get it any further. Fortunately, at that point Alicia breezed in. She willingly helped Mimi drag the mattress out into the backyard to air. Until her arrival, our labor had been a hasty chore of sweat and curses, and pain for me. With Alicia on the scene the old house rang with giggles and a stream of comments flavored with her heavy accent.

'I hope you all have a beer in the icebox to pay me for that!' she gasped, after the box springs had followed the mattress out into the yard.

'Sure,' I said. 'We have two six-packs left over from the party.' I creaked into the kitchen and bent stiffly to peer into the refrigerator. The bruises on my torso and face were assuming a fainter but wider spectrum of colors now that most of them were almost healed. I had all the hues of a sick rainbow. The deepest cuts were still scabbed, a healthy but hideous development.

It was a temperate early November day. The sun,

294

radiant in a clear sky, was a blessing, not the curse of full summer. The leaves were turning in a halfhearted southern way; a light breeze fluttered them from the oaks. There was peace in that day, and calm; I think we all felt it as we sat on the porch drinking our beers.

'Is Cully going to see his private patients here, Mimi?' asked Alicia idly.

'No, he'll go back to his apartment for that.'

'Good. You don't want those folks coming in and out here. I reckon it might be one of them that did this to Nickie.' Alicia inclined her head toward my bruises.

Mimi's eyes met mine in surprise. 'Why do you think that, Alicia?'

'Oh, it stands to reason,' she said calmly. 'Any you-know-what who can do a thing like that' – and she crossed her expensively trousered legs tightly – 'has got to be sick in the head.' Alicia stared out over the serene backyard where Celeste had spent so many hours. The roses were still blooming, but reluctantly, tired of the task. Mao was industriously stalking an oblivious cardinal. 'Not that that's any excuse. You hear all the time about criminals with four and five convictions getting back out on the streets in no time. Remember Cotton Meers, out on work release two years after he shot his ex-wife's boyfriend? And us – the people who pay the taxes that pay those judges – we're the ones out here with 'em. We pay over and over. Not them, not the criminals. Oh no, they're sick and they have to be *cured*. Pooh. Some people are just *bad*. Born bad. Not sick – evil. Cure them, hell. They should be *removed*. Like rabid dogs.'

I'd heard this view before, of course. Reactionary as it sounded, there was a lot of truth in it. I couldn't deny that the man who'd raped me was genuinely sick; of course he was. Any man who could do what he'd done to a woman who couldn't defend herself, a woman totally unwilling, was sick. Did I want him treated, rehabilitated, freed? Did I pray, if his problem was plain and pure evil, that he'd find the Lord? No-siree. I wanted him to hurt. I wanted him to *suffer*. If that couldn't be arranged, I was willing to settle for just plain death. Nothing like an experience with face-to-face violence to provoke a gut reaction, I thought. And my gut reaction was definitely eye for eye, tooth for tooth. At the same time, and at risk of sounding pompous even to myself, I admitted that a big dose of this vigilant-ism would ruin my country.

'You know,' I began, after Mimi had fetched three more beers, 'I wonder if the kind of man who'd do this would ever voluntarily go for help? I doubt, myself, that he's among Cully's patients. Maybe he can justify, in his own heart, what he did to me. He must be able to.' I was thinking of this for the first time. 'Otherwise, how can he live with himself?'

'He probably didn't even give it two thoughts,' Alicia said with disgust. 'Don't you waste your time trying to understand an animal like that. Besides, I read two maga-zine articles that both said rapists have the lowest cure rate of any offenders under treatment. Animals.'

Animals don't rape – only men rape; but I decided to let that point go by. I knew what she meant.

'How do you feel about what happened to me, Alicia?' I asked curiously. Alicia gave an impression of trans-parency, but I'd discovered just now that her true feelings were very different from what I'd expected. Civilized Alicia had let her savage vein show.

She stirred uneasily in her chair. I realized I'd asked a northern question; or not so much northern as un-southern. Her lips were disapproving. But the beer, or the sweetness of the cool day, or us being women together, made her answer honestly. 'I'm scared to death,' she said bluntly. 'I'm scared to death. You know I'm by myself most of the time, with Ray on the road so much. Why did it have to happen to you, so close to my house? If it had been a nigger woman in the subdivision' – I noticed Mimi wince – 'well . . . that kind of thing happens all the time down there. It was bad enough with that little girl this summer, worse when it was Barbara Tucker. But then it had to happen two doors down from me – to someone I've known for years.'

After all this directness, Alicia covered her face with her hands, to let her features re-form behind them. She sighed, uncovered, and looked directly at me for the first time that afternoon. 'Sometimes I think I'm just *mad* at you since it did happen to you – not to someone I can forget about,' she said. We stared into each other's faces for a long moment. Her blue eyes dropped; she sighed. 'There, I've gone and said it and probably hurt your feelings, and that's not Christian. You shouldn't have gotten me in a corner, Nickie. I'm real fond of you, but you shouldn't have gotten me in a corner. You just forget what I said. You have other fish to fry than worrying about what I think. I'll just go on with all my committees,' she said, making a wonderful wry face, 'and run this town till I have a baby.'

She reassumed her brightness like a favorite sweater. 'Got to run, now,' she said cheerfully. She rose, gathered up her beer cans to deposit in the kitchen on her way through the house, dropped a sudden kiss on the top of my head, and breezed away.

'I did wrong,' I told Mimi.

'You didn't do wrong. Your crisis just spread. The old "stone in the pond" image. They always do, crises. It's not just yours. It's everyone's.'

'That makes me feel guilty.'

'Then you are a true southerner, despite your Yankee ways,' Mimi told me solemnly.

We both laughed, startling Mao's intended victim, who gave a wild squawk and flew away. I realized it was the first time I'd laughed in a week. Mao looked at us reproachfully; Mimi promised him an extra dollop of 9-Lives at supper. Then Cully's car pulled in beside Mimi's on the gravel apron, and he emerged with an armload of clothes. The afternoon melted away in toting, lifting, and arranging.

After supper (I made chicken-fried steak, one of Cully's favorites, in his honor) we pulled on sweaters and returned to the porch to watch the dusk. Darkness was closing in faster and faster as the year drew to a close. After we had settled in the lawn chairs, due to be stored for the winter, none of us spoke. We were three people who had known each other for a long time and were enjoying each other's silent companionship, the evening, our place in the world. For the first time, I thought that true peace might come to me again, that the even glow of my life before the rape might resume.

In the next two weeks Cully began adjusting to us, and we to his male presence. (That meant, chiefly, that we remembered to be dressed when we left our rooms.) Since he wasn't due in his office at the college until nine, he went out to jog at seven-thirty every morning. I had the bathroom all to myself to get ready for my eight o'clock class.

Houghton's committees were recovering from their beginning-of-the-term exhaustion and churning with projects. Mimi was spending hours on the telephone at work and at home, reminding people to attend this or accomplish that. If I listened, I could hear her every evening while I studied in the living room. I'd never understood exactly what Mimi did, but her job title was College Coordinator. As she explained it, she had to know what every club and committee on campus planned in the way of activities and projects, allot them a date and room for meetings and whatever similar help they needed, and handle the needs of the campus. For example, if the Chi Omegas or the Chess Club wanted to 'beautify' the campus one Saturday, Mimi might suggest that an ornamental bridge in the gardens needed painting. If the Recruitment Drive Committee wanted to meet in the Executive Conference Room on the same night the Campus Entertainment Committee wanted to use it, Mimi settled that, somehow, with a characteristic combination of tact, common sense, and steamrolling.

Apparently there was a lot more involved, but these were Mimi's main functions. She also served on several committees herself, simply because she was a Houghton and therefore had a strong interest in the college.

I heard a lot about Mimi's job in the weeks following the rape. My fund of small talk seemed to have dwindled away. Mimi filled in the gap while I waited for a new crop to grow. Cully chipped in with anecdotes about the iniquities of his predecessor, who'd given students some rather strange advice, to hear the stories Cully told. Now that I could observe Cully from a more detached point of view, I discovered he had a deep-buried sense of humor and a lot of patience.

Although all of us may have been thinking of what had happened to me, and who might have done it, my two housemates never discussed it unless I brought it up. Cully and Mimi listened whenever the terror and anger got to be too much for me. I tried not to drag on them, to leech them; I only went to them for help when I couldn't stand my own company anymore.

A week after Cully moved in, I walked in my sleep. He found me looking up the staircase from the foot of the stairs, trying to raise my leg to mount them. I only half-woke when he told me gently to go to bed. I obeyed in a stupor; I only recalled the incident the next day when he cautiously asked me how I was feeling. I don't think I ever walked in my sleep again. But sometimes when I went to bed very tired or anxious, I would wake about three o'clock with my heart pounding, sweating in the chilly night. Most of those nights I could go back to sleep. If the fear or the rage didn't keep me awake.

The detectives dropped in again after a week, to ask me if I'd remembered anything else. I had nothing to tell Mr Tendall and Mr Markowitz. They didn't seem to expect much.

Charles's lawyer friend didn't ask me out again. I was not surprised, and not much hurt. Charles himself was very awkward around me when he came to pick up Mimi or to eat supper with us. He treated me like Mad Aunt Letitia taking an outing from her attic; he humored me. But at least, as I kept reminding myself, he was trying to be kind.

I tried, too, even though it nearly cost me my expensive new dental work. I ground my teeth together frequently. The depth of my irritation did surprise me a little. I'd been halfway to liking Charles Seward before I'd been raped. (Everything was divided into two phases for me – before the rape and after.) Now Charles's mere presence filled me with uneasiness. Don Houghton's, too. I couldn't understand it. Don was sweet; he suffered through acute embarrassment to tell me how sorry he was I'd been 'hurt.'

Other men didn't affect me that way, so why Charles and Don? What did they have in common? At odd moments I wondered, but I could never figure it out. I dismissed it as a fluke.

Barbara and I met in her office on a Thursday afternoon, which was a free afternoon for both of us. I'd been compiling my list in odd moments. Sometimes in the middle of a class a name would hop into my mind, and I'd surreptitiously whip out my pieces of paper and write it down. The list was dismayingly long, despite the brevity of my life in Knolls. I'd met so many men the times I'd stayed with Mimi years before. There were so many male students in my classes.

Barbara's list was even more staggering. She knew almost all the male faculty members and at least a couple hundred students. She knew fewer townspeople, but she'd met some, of course, in her years at Houghton.

I guess the same thought crossed both our minds as we stared blankly at the little pile of paper: Our project was impossible. Swiftly I tried to imagine factors that might make our failure less sickeningly disappointing. The depth of our outrage would fade with time. It had to; human beings who wanted to remain mentally healthy could not carry such a crushing load. The rapist might get caught tomorrow, go to trial, get a heavy sentence . . .

But Barbara, who had managed words on paper for years, had other ideas. 'Our old friend process of elimination,' she said, her crisp midwestern vowels snapping clearly. 'Okay!' She pushed the brown frame of her glasses back up her snubby nose. 'How old was the voice?' she asked me.

It was like a pop quiz. 'I would say – thirty or over,' I answered slowly. 'Past youth, way past youth.'

'Same here. There, we've eliminated the students, except for the overage ones.'

I began to feel more optimistic. 'I only know two students my age or older,' I said. 'Two vets. Dan Kirby and Paul Scotti.'

Barbara closed her eyes. 'Don't know Paul Scotti,' she said finally. 'Dan Kirby's in my Victorian Prose class.'

'Then we have one name.'

'And we've eliminated about two hundred fifty men.'

'In one fell swoop.'

We'd both had the foresight to list students separately. Barbara threw away two sheets of her list and one of mine. 'What else do we know that could eliminate some more names?'

I pinched my cheek to help me think. 'White. Since we talked about that before, I presume you didn't list any blacks.' Barbara nodded. 'Heavy . . . and not extremely tall or short. That should knock out a few people.'

'The short part, anyway. I thought he was average or maybe a little taller.'

'And you were standing up, so you'd know better than I would. Strike the shorties and the very skinny men.'

Excluding the students except for Dan Kirby, my list consisted of twenty-six names. Barbara said hers reached fifty-one. This purge of too-short, too-thin men pared my list to twenty, Barbara's to forty-two.

'Compare, now they're manageable,' I suggested, and handed over my list. I watched Barbara's pen move down the columns. It hesitated over some names, drew a decisive line through others.

'Cully Houghton's not on your list,' she said at one point. 'He's on mine.'

'He was with me when you were raped, Barbara.'

'Oh. Okay.' A line, thank God.

At last she threw down her pen and lifted her glasses to rub her eyes.

'How many?' I asked anxiously.

'Nine,' she said. 'Just nine. That match.'

I hadn't thought the list could be narrowed so quickly. At first I felt elated. Then I felt sick.

'Let's check before we meet again, to see if either of us forgot anyone. For example, did you include your postman?'

'Oh,' I said slowly. 'Mr McCluskey. No.'

'But I don't know him. So he cancels out. Anyone else?'
I shook my head.

'Then let's stop. I can't stand much more of this.'

'I know what you mean.' It had its own peculiar ghastliness, our little project. I began to gather up my things. I asked, 'Did you know the dectectives before?'

Barbara's hand froze in the act of passing my marked-down list back to me. 'Oh my God,' she said. 'I knew John Tendall. Yes.'

'I met him at a security lecture he gives at every orientation,' I told her bleakly. 'I just now remembered.'

Barbara rubbed her forehead. She added John Tendall to both our lists. Ten names.

Jeff Simmons, college president
Jeffrey Tabor, cashier
Don Houghton, businessman
Charles Seward, lawyer
Ray Merritt, salesman
Theo Cochran, registrar
Randy Marquette, English professor
J. R. Smith, English professor
Dan Kirby, student
John Tendall, detective

'We've both got to think,' she said, as I stuffed the piece of paper in my purse. 'We're doing the best we can,' she added obscurely.

'I'll call you as soon as I'm sure I've got every single name on there,' I said.

She smiled up at me. She looked small and frail behind her big littered desk. The deep auburn of her hair made her face seem even whiter.

'We're doing the best we can,' I agreed. And it did seem to me quite an achievement. In thirty-odd minutes we'd managed to establish that our assailant was one of ten men. In making those sweeping eliminations we were able to do what the police could not, because we both were convinced that the man who raped us knew us. Now we couldn't even try to persuade the detectives who were handling our cases. One of them was on the list.

In fact, what the town was doing at this time was figuratively holding its breath and waiting for the next rape, though none of us realized it until afterward. Heidi Edmonds had been raped in early August. Barbara had been raped in early September. I had been raped in the latter part of October. And there were the rumors from Cully's policeman friend, rumors of at least two victims who hadn't gone to the police. Cully confirmed one rumor on a night when Mimi and I were wondering out loud if the attacks were evenly spaced.

'There was one in late August,' he said, and gave each of us a look to assure our silence.

'He must be counseling her,' Mimi murmured over the after-supper dishes. We would never mention it to Cully again. But among his books I noticed several new ones on rape and the treatment of offenders and victims. So it was true that Barbara, myself, and Heidi Edmonds had an unknown companion or two – or three, or even four.

'We should form a club,' I told Barbara bitterly one day as we sat in damned-together closeness at a table in the noisy student center. 'Think how we could narrow down the list!' The count still stood at ten, though we'd rummaged our brains for men we might have forgotten initially.

Barbara didn't answer. Stan Haskell had just come in, and her eyes were following him with a mixture of anger and grief. He was with a young anthropology professor who had the kind of quiet pleasant looks Barbara had. Stan picked women of a type. Surely the rapist did too? Perhaps Barbara and I should concentrate on what we had in common, what our near-fatal attraction was, rather than on our list. There was a pattern, I was convinced. There had to be a pattern, a reason. But maybe we two were too close to see our similarity. It might take a less involved person to spot it.

As I walked home a few minutes later I was praying, an infrequent activity for me until recently. I was praying that some nice man would ask Barbara out. Then, self-engrossed human that I am, my thoughts shifted to some reading I had to do, and from there to a letter I'd gotten the day before from my mother. She'd hinted heavily that she and Jay Chalmers weren't getting along too well. And she'd written it sober, I could tell. A couple of months ago, she'd been able to hold off until after church. I had already written her back, the longest letter I'd sent Mother in years. I hoped. I was afraid to hope.

I climbed the stone steps to the front yard, then the wooden steps to the front porch, with an ease and absence of pain that pleased me. Almost well.

'Mimi?' I called. She sometimes came home to lunch, walking for the exercise; so she might be in the house even if her car wasn't there. I hadn't glimpsed the bumper from the street, as I could if the car was parked behind the house.

'I'm up here,' she called from her floor of the house. She came down in a clatter, dark hair bouncing on her shoulders. She was carrying Attila by his middle, so she was angry. The cat had a guilty, smirky look about him. His big green eyes went from my face to Mimi's with false affection: I adore you, don't punish me.

'This durn cat turned over my bath powder, and now I'm late,' she said breathlessly. She handed the culprit to me. I gave him a severe shake, but then I hugged him. I'm a born sucker.

'You want me to get it up off the floor?' I offered.

'No, I got it. That's why I'm late. I'm going to run over to Alicia's instead of walking back to the college. She's due at the same meeting in' – Mimi glanced at her tiny silver watch – 'five minutes. I've got to run. I'll cut through the backyards, maybe I can catch her going out the door.'

Carrying a straggling Attila, I followed Mimi through the kitchen. I put the cat out and then opened the refrigerator to see if there were any pears left.

'Her car's still there!' Mimi called back triumphantly. She thudded down the back steps. She would cross through old Mrs Harbison's yard to Alicia's back door.

I'd washed a pear, dried it, and turned to lock the back door behind Mimi when I heard the sound. I knew immediately it was coming from Mimi, though I'd never heard her scream before. I dropped the pear, ran out the back door, flew down the steps, and crashed through the hedge. I glimpsed Mrs Harbison looking out her kitchen window as I sped across her grass. 'Call the police!' I shouted, and saw her begin to turn.

Mimi was screaming no longer: She was stock-still on the steps to Alicia's glassed-in back porch. She was holding the door open with one hand. The door was smeared with something like rust.

I didn't want to see what Mimi was seeing. I checked my pace abruptly and stood gasping four feet away. Mimi's head turned slowly and her eyes met mine. The brown of her irises stood out shockingly in her face, which had turned a dirty gray. I felt my scalp prickle. Against my will, my feet moved until I stood beside my friend.

Alicia's eyes were also wide and staring. Her face was even grayer. She lay in a crucified sprawl on the floor of the porch. We didn't need to check her pulse or breathing; even I could tell she had been dead for hours. Because I couldn't bear to look at her, I raised my eyes and stared through the length of the house. As though I was locked in a dream, I slowly recorded the fact that Alicia's front door was ajar, its dead bolts pulled back. And I thought, Barbara and I are right. Alicia knew him, too. She let him in.

We had to wait for the police. When the patrolmen arrived, they asked Mimi to check briefly to see if anything was missing. I didn't suppose for a minute that the police really thought the killer had been a panicked burglar. But I guess they had to be sure. After all, it was the first time the rapist had actually killed anyone.

The sunshine was horribly bright in Alicia's living room. It shone with autumn gilding on the blood spots on the pale gray carpet traced with golden color the rusty handprint on the newel post. I wondered how this house, lavished with Alicia's care, could tolerate her death so easily; how the sun could bathe the evidence of her last moments with such gracious light. Her mortal fear, the annihilating terror I knew so well, had remained behind her: I felt it.

She had fought for her life every inch of the way. She had almost made it. Almost.

The trail of her last moments led through the house. Spots of blood on the carpet inside that open front door. The handprint on the newel. One of her slippers. A knife scar from a thrust that had missed her and scored the wall. Splotches of blood trailing through the kitchen. And finally her body, collapsed inside the back door, blood from her hands smeared beside the locks as she'd fumbled to work them; had unlatched them but had not been able to get out that door. Alicia had nearly made it out into the yard, where she could have hidden in the shrubs until her screams brought help.

I had seen Alicia's intact underwear under her

bathrobe, pinned askew by her fall. So she'd been spared rape but she'd lost her life, oh Alicia! Her terror and desperation were as thick in the house as a fog. I was frightened for myself, in the part of me capable of selfish thought. It was too soon for me to tolerate this. But I had to, since Mimi was still upstairs.

My old companions Tendall and Markowitz appeared at the back door, surveying what lay there before crunching around to the front door on the gravel of the driveway. Then Alicia's body was hidden from my view by the police technicians who gathered around her.

She would have hated them seeing her as she was.

The detectives came in the front door, taking care not to touch the knob or sill. They weren't surprised to see me. Someone must have filled them in. They nodded but were too engrossed in their job to pay me much mind. I stared at John Tendall to watch his reaction, so I could report to Barbara; he was on the list. He simply looked preoccupied and professional. He had thick gray hair, meticulously groomed. With his deep tan and flashy sports jacket, he looked like a smalltime hood rather than a police detective. Markowitz was just as finicky with his hair – he favored sculpted waves of the Jerry Lee Lewis school. He was beefy and pale, with sharp eyes staring from a blank face. They were both workmen absorbed in a technically tricky job.

I was increasingly concerned about Mimi. The police shouldn't be keeping her so long. She needed to get out of this house. Just as I rose to look for her, she appeared on the stairs. Her face was a horrible color now, even her lips; white as the dresses we'd worn when we graduated from Miss Beacham's – Mimi, Alicia, and I. Mimi was shaking so hard she looked like she had palsy. One of the patrolmen had to help her down the stairs. I instantly got myself to the foot and waited there with arms uplifted, as if to receive an infant. I had no more grief to spare for the handprint on the newel post. Alicia was dead. Mimi was alive, and Mimi was going to collapse very soon.

Even as I had my arm around her and we turned to go, Markowitz was asking if Mimi knew how they could get in touch with Ray.

'Call Ray's mother, Mrs Ralph Merritt,' I said briefly. Later I wondered how I'd managed to dredge up that long-buried name.

We had to leave by the front door, of course. There were neighbors standing on their front porches looking at the police cars. People in Knolls were as curious as people anywhere, but they were ashamed of it. For a few seconds no one came to help me – not out of fear of involvement but for fear of seeming nosy and meddlesome. Finally old Mrs Harbison (who could consider herself a member of the situation, so to speak, since she'd called the police) hobbled down to give me what assistance she could. It was enough. As soon as the old lady saw I could manage and that Mimi was safely deposited on one of the couches, she left after one quiet question.

'Is Alicia dead?'

I nodded silently. I remembered what I'd long ago learned from Mimi: Alicia had given Mrs Harbison a ride to church every week. Alicia had called the old lady every time she went to the grocery store, to see if Mrs Harbison needed anything. Now the old lady was shaking her head from side to side, and tears began trickling through the papery wrinkles as she turned to leave.

Mimi was crying convulsively, unable to speak or move. When I thought I could leave her, I called Cully at the college. Ten minutes later he came into the house like a whirlwind. He folded his long arms around his sister and held her to him.

I was unnecessary, and I needed to be by myself. I sat in

the kitchen breakfast nook with my hands folded and my legs tight. I stared out the bay window into that lovely serene yard, at the last blowsy rose blooms. The blooms bent their heads waiting for the executioner frost. Time passed.

Cully came to sit opposite me. He blocked my view of the roses. 'I found some tranquilizers left over from her breakup with Richard,' he told me.

'Good.'

'She's asleep.'

'Good.'

I poured Cully a cup of coffee heated up from the morning. I put it in front of him gracelessly and sat down again. He stared blankly for a moment at the steam rising from the cup, as if he couldn't identify the drink. He lit a cigarette and smoked it, and drank the coffee.

After a while I got a cup for myself.

'She fought hard,' I commented. I imagined a pin lying in front of me; I would pick it up, if I could, and stick myself with it, to raise some feeling. I was only a loose-knit bag of perishable bones and skin.

Cully's hand covered mine, which lay fisted on the table. I looked at the black hair that grew in a pattern on the back of his hand. If I was ever called on to identify Cully's body, I thought, I would know it by that pattern.

'She fought, that's why she died,' I said. 'I was too scared to lift a finger, so I lived. He knew her. He knows me.

I was so alone. I opened my mouth and words came out, but I didn't know what they would be. The cool clean autumn air came through the window over the sink. It was polluted with the scent of those last rotting roses. That smell would be with me for the rest of my life.

'Look at me, Cully,' I said, though he had been looking at me all along. It was I whose eyes were lowered. I raised

310

them now. 'I'm not beautiful anymore, Cully. Look at my face.'

His own face was full of pain. He looked paler than ever, the lines from nose to mouth deeper.

'It could've been me lying there, Cully.'

'No.'

'Dead, Cully.'

He was on his feet and he hauled me off the bench with a violent yank. He kissed me. His fingers wound in my hair as he pulled my head back.

While, two doors away, the ambulance came to cart off what remained of Alicia, while Ray Merritt drove home to find his wife butchered, while the police took pictures and scattered fingerprint dust over Alicia's beautiful furniture, while Mimi slept a silent drugged sleep, Cully and I made sure we were alive, alive, alive.

On Saturday morning, when Mimi got up after sleeping in spells throughout the previous afternoon and night, Cully had left to get some warmer clothes from his apartment. The bite in the air that morning was a definite warning of winter. I got one of my heavy blankets out of the hall closet and put it on the end of the bed, after I'd pulled on my new winter bathrobe. My emotions were in chaos, a nauseating mixture of joy, grief, and fear. The joy was temporarily banished by the sight of Mimi's face when she stumbled down the stairs and asked me for some coffee.

She was shivering with cold and looked white and drained; but Ray Merritt was as close a friend as Alicia had been, and Mimi was convinced she should rush to his side. It took me a long time to dissuade her. I think her own weakness finally did the trick. I could tell there was something pressing her, something besides grief and shock; but I wasn't about to ask her what it was. She would tell me when she chose.

After two hours and four cups of coffee, Mimi quite abruptly told me she thought Charles Seward, her young lawyer, was the rapist. 'Because,' she explained wearily, 'when we went out on a date last week, and then one time before you were raped, we really had a wrestling match in the car. I hate to talk about it. It sounds so – high school. But this thing last week. When he stopped in front of the house, he just – grabbed me, and then he was just all over me.'

Charles Seward was on our list.

'Ah – you didn't want to do it?' I asked hesitantly.

'Not in front of the *house*.' Mimi summoned some outrage. 'Not in the damn *car*. I mean, I've always assumed that sooner or later I'd sleep with Charles, but not then. I've been jittery about what happened to you and Barbara, and when he grabbed me like that, I got scared all of a sudden. I kind of yanked backwards, and he grabbed harder. It was much worse than the little tussle we'd had before, right before you . . . anyway, I really got scared. I hauled off with my free arm and whacked him in the face. That calmed him down. Which was good for *him*. Because next I was going to grab for his *balls*!' Mimi managed a shaky smile, and I did too.

'Mimi, did he ever say anything about what was happening?'

'Not then, because I got that car door open and got into the house as fast as my legs could go,' she said flatly. 'He called me the next day, and I hung up on him. I'm sure he has plenty to say; I don't know if I want to listen.'

We eyed each other. 'Do you think – really, truly – that it might be Charles?' I asked dubiously. If Alicia had lived to help Barbara and me, he would have been on her list, too.

'I was scared to death,' she answered indirectly. 'My God, what if it *is*? A man I've been dating for months, someone I really care for. What kind of person does that make me, by the way, that someone that creepy would want to date me?'

Mimi's nose turned red, her eyes watered, and a couple of tears trickled forlornly down her cheeks. She used her napkin to blot them. She resembled an abandoned kitten far more than the lioness her mane of hair usually suggested. Mao jumped in her lap and wailed for attention. Mimi hugged the little cat with a passion that startled the animal, and turned all her attention to tickling Mao's chin.

I had realized that the man who'd assaulted me was someone I knew, but I'd realized it in an abstract way. I hadn't really felt it in my gut. The fact that Alicia – who had told us only two weeks previously how tightly locked she kept her house, who had told us how frightened she was – had opened her door to her killer was the strongest possible confirmation that Barbara and I knew our incubus in another guise. Now that I had a name, Charles Seward, to fit into the nightmare, I did feel it in my gut. I pictured Charles's face above me in the darkness, Charles's hand holding the knife. A man, not a demon. Not 'it' but 'him.'

'Should you tell the police?' Even I could hear the doubt in my voice.

'What?' Mimi asked angrily. 'That I had a tussle with my date in a car? When I was upset and nervous anyway? Can't you hear them soothing me down? "Now, now, Miss Houghton"!'

Of course I could. 'And it might not be him, anyway,' I muttered. Charles felt wrong, somehow, no matter how uneasy I'd been around him lately.

'Of course it might not,' she agreed, still with that edge of hysterical anger.

We fell back to gazing into our coffee, lost in separate

trains of thought. There was a knock on the kitchen door. I jumped, and Mimi almost dropped her mug. Mao sped toward the living room with a startled yowl.

The knock sounded again as we looked at each other, shamefaced. Shaking her head, Mimi rose to answer. There were no clear panes in the kitchen door. We were going to have to quit opening it blindly, I decided, even as Mimi twisted the knob.

The man at the door was Charles Seward. Mimi's back stiffened; I heard her breath whistle in. Her fear, rational or not leaped across the room and infected me. There was a sharp snap. I looked down. My fingers had broken the handle of my coffee cup. Suddenly the tableau seemed surrealistic: Mimi frightened at the door, her face searching for the right expression; I at the table in my bathrobe with coffee trickling down it; and a young lawyer at the door, not menacing but surely – sheepish.

'Mimi, please let me talk to you, please just listen to me for a minute.' Charles spotted me sitting in the breakfast nook. His hands made a quick gesture of helplessness. 'Nickie, please – I need to talk to Mimi alone.'

Ordinarily I would've vanished instantly. This wasn't ordinary. Old Mrs Harbison next door couldn't help us if she wanted to, I thought quickly. The Carters on the other side were gone; I'd seen them pull out in their car. There wasn't any telling when Cully would return.

I gauged the distance to the knife rack above the counter, all the way across the kitchen, and wondered if Mimi could slow him down long enough for me to reach it. At the same time, it was almost impossible for me to believe I was contemplating a situation in which I would have to stab Mimi's boyfriend.

But when Charles took a step forward, my muscles tensed to move. At that moment, as if on cue, the front doorbell rang. My breath came out in an explosion of relief. 'I'll get it, Mimi,' I said in an odd bright tone, as if Mimi were an unstable child.

I almost ran, but restrained my pace to a brisk walk. I perceived that we were trying to make the scene *normal*; both Mimi and I were eerily trying to pretend that we supposed nothing lay behind Charles's appearance except a man wanting to make up with his woman. Why were we doing that instead of screaming bloody hell and attacking Charles? Was this some form of passive defense, pretending Charles meant us no evil so he would take our cue and do us none?

I peered through the panes in the door . . . Theo Cochran. I hadn't exchanged more than a few words with Theo since the party. I was so anxious about the situation I'd left in the kitchen that it didn't surprise me at all that Theo was calling at Mimi's rather early on a Saturday morning. I swept the door open and ushered him in with an enthusiasm that must have bewildered him.

'Come right on back,' I babbled. 'Mimi's out in the kitchen and we're having coffee. Come have a cup with us.'

'Well, thank you,' Theo said with evident surprise, pulling off his jacket and gloves. I shut the door and sped past the registrar to lead the way to the kitchen, moving so swiftly he had to hurry to keep up.

Mimi was still blocking Charles's entrance. When she heard our steps behind her, her shoulders sagged. Charles's expression of gaping astonishment changed to one of frank resentment as I came to stand by Mimi. I abandoned poor Theo in the middle of the floor. When Mimi felt my shoulder touch hers, she said quickly, 'Thanks for dropping by, Charles. I'll – be in touch later.' She took a step forward, forcing him to retreat onto the porch. Then, with a horribly social smile, she shut the door in his face. We stood there shoulder to shoulder until we heard Charles's feet cross the porch and descend the steps.

Behind us Theo Cochran shuffled, reminding us that he was there and waiting. Mimi recovered first and turned to him with a dazzling welcome. 'How nice to see you,' she said shrilly. 'Have a seat, if you don't mind sitting out here in this messy old kitchen. I'll get you a cup of coffee; or tea?'

'Thank you, tea,' he murmured, and slid into the place I had occupied on the bench.

Mimi grasped my hand for a moment, squeezed it, then went to fetch Theo Cochran his tea.

Theo explained his multiple mission. As registrar, he was automatically a member of the Recruitment Drive committee, which was supposed to have met the day before when Mimi had gone to pick up Alicia. There had been a quorum present without them, so the committee, of course not knowing anything of Alicia's death, had proceeded to vote on a number of projects. Now Theo's thoroughly bureaucratic soul was in turmoil. He realized, I heard him tell Mimi, that this was an awful time to come to see her, but he'd really come to talk to her as a college official and a member of the committee; some of the measures passed had been most important. Now a new member would have to be appointed . . .

I overheard most of this from my room, where I'd scrambled into my clothes and then thrown the door back open while I was changing my sheets. I didn't really trust anyone right now, even proud, portly Theo (he was on the list), and I was worried, after I caught the drift of the conversation, that Mimi would be angry and grieved all over again at Alicia's demise being discussed in terms of committees and resolutions. I needn't have worried. When it came to the college and mention of the word *committee*,

Mimi became all business. Theo's visit was even therapeutic for her. People might perish, but Houghton College kept rolling on.

I didn't listen to the ensuing discussion or what they decided. Changing the sheets had put me in mind of more interesting things. I wondered when Cully would be home. I was half-afraid to see him again. He'd been gone this morning before I was really awake.

Their voices jogged me back to earth. They had risen and moved closer to my door.

'. . . to tea,' Theo was saying. 'Sarah Chase has been trying to get you this morning, but our phone's out of order, so when she found I was coming over . . .'

'Thursday? I'll call her, Theo, I know we'd love to come; but of course I have to find out about the funeral.' Mimi's voice was thinning again now that she was thinking of Alicia. Theo should leave.

'I'm sorry, again, for intruding,' he said. 'I tell you, I'm mighty worried about Sarah Chase. I wouldn't let her go out at night to her bridge club, but another woman picks her up and brings her home. It's terrible how this seems to be happening to Miss Beacham's graduates. Had that occurred to you?'

'What?' Mimi was startled. They were almost outside my door now. I looked up sharply.

'Well, Nickie, you know, and now Mrs Merritt. It's made me kind of extra anxious about Sarah Chase, as I'm sure you can understand.'

Barbara hadn't gone to Miss Beacham's.

Theo's back was to me. He happened to look in the open door of the former dining room, now Cully's room. I saw his shoulders stiffen at the sight of men's clothes dumped on the bed.

'I think Theo must be something of a prude,' I remarked after Mimi had shown him out.

'Oh, you noticed. He didn't say one word, but he kind of snorted,' Mimi said with a grin. 'Someone'll tell him it's just Cully. Wouldn't Theo have made a perfect English butler?'

I pictured the registrar in a swallow-tailed coat, and laughed. Mimi settled herself on the foot of my bed and relayed Sarah Chase's invitation. 'Isn't that sweet?' she said. 'Tea! Thursday afternoon, okay?'

I thought about my class schedule. 'Fine with me,' I said. 'But . . .' I turned back to my vanity and fussed with my comb and brush. 'When's the funeral, I wonder?'

'Tuesday. There's a delay because of the autopsy,' said Cully from the doorway. My heart gave a ridiculous lurch. 'But Mimi, I'm afraid, has to attend the inquest this afternoon. The coroner called before you two were awake.'

'Inquest,' Mimi said. The remainder of the spark that had animated her during Theo's visit, as she'd gotten to talk about normal life instead of violent death, was extinguished. She was face to face with Alicia again. 'I expected Ray to call me himself. Maybe this morning. But I guess . . .'

I guess we have to go to the funeral home, I told myself reluctantly. It seemed to me we'd been through enough; but after all we were alive. We had to pay for that, I supposed.

'I think the body will be at the funeral home by Monday morning or evening,' Cully said. 'I saw Alicia's aunt at the filling station. But the inquest this afternoon will be real short. Don't worry about it, Mimi.'

She seemed to wilt under my eyes. I sat beside her on the bed. We huddled together holding hands like children. Cully folded down on my left.

'But why Alicia?' Mimi whispered.

I decided to take that literally. 'Exactly.' Mimi needed

something to think about, and I needed another view-point. 'Why me? Why Alicia? Barbara? Heidi Edmonds?'

Mimi straightened. 'Right.' She understood me instantly. 'Why you all, out of all the women in Knolls? You're beautiful, Nickie. Alicia was attractive in her own way, but no one would say she was beautiful. That girl this summer, she was just an average-looking girl. Barbara's plain, really, unless you know her.'

'Alicia's lived here all her life,' Cully muttered. 'Nickie just came back here, hasn't ever before really lived here.' His eyes narrowed with concentration.

'As Theo said, Alicia and I, at least, are connected through Miss Beacham's,' I observed. 'We went there.'

'That's so,' Mimi said. 'He did mention that. I went to Miss Beacham's too.' She shivered.

'Along with Theo's wife, as he was saying,' I thought out loud. 'But I don't think Heidi Edmonds went there, did she? You would've known and told me so, Mimi. And Barbara didn't of course.'

'Strike that pattern.'

'Cully, isn't there bound to be a pattern?' I touched his sleeve.

'I think so, but I can't be sure,' he said. 'I've never had a patient with a record of rape offenses. I've never studied it before. I am now doing extensive reading on the subject,' he added grimly. 'There are all kinds of classifications of rapists, with all kinds of motivations, of course. Rapists most often do follow some kind of pattern, but it might be something as vague as simple availability, or women who look under twenty-one, or women who have gray hair.'

'Well, we weren't all equally available,' I pointed out. 'Heidi Edmonds was in the open, and Barbara was in her apartment and he had to break open the back-door lock.'

'Which was as flimsy as anything can be and still be called a lock,' Cully interjected. 'No expertise required.'

319

'He broke in here via the window. The open window. Just a screen to remove. Even I could do that,' I observed. 'Alicia, well, obviously he used some trick. What on earth would make Alicia open the door at night – I presume she was killed at night? – to someone when Ray wasn't at home?'

'It was at night. Her aunt told me Alicia had called her mother at ten-thirty Thursday evening,' Cully said. 'Alicia said then that she had a breakfast meeting scheduled for eight the next morning. She never got there.'

We all thought about Alicia unlocking her front door at night.

'Ray!' Mimi said suddenly.

We turned horrified faces to her. For the first time, I thought about Ray being on the list. But oh, not now; now that Alicia had been killed, surely we could strike him?

She said hastily, 'No, no! I didn't mean he could have done it! I mean that she'd open the door if someone told her something had happened to Ray.'

'Or to her mother,' Cully suggested.

'Not even for that. She'd have been suspicious right off the bat. Her mother lives with Alicia's older brother, and the brother would've called if anything was wrong with Miss Celia. It *had* to be something about Ray. She's always been scared to death he'd have a wreck on one of his sales trips.'

'Even then,' I said slowly, 'I think it would have to be someone she knew. Or a policeman. Even if the man at the door said he was from the police, when she went to the door she wouldn't have seen a uniform through the peephole. So she wouldn't have opened the door, right?'

'Not if he said he was a detective,' Cully said.

I thought instantly of John Tendall.

'I think she would've been suspicious of any stranger, no matter what he told her he was,' Mimi said firmly. 'She had a good head on her shoulders, even though she didn't sound like she did half the time. She was very much on the alert, remember? She was really scared. She'd have been on the lookout for a ruse like that, I'm sure. Maybe not; maybe at the words "Ray is hurt, he had an accident, let's go to the hospital," she would've thrown open the door to anyone. But I don't think so. I think the only thing that would have made Alicia open that door was recognizing someone she knew.'

Chilled and frightened, we hunched on the bed. The picture in my mind was in their minds, too: 'Alicia, honey, I just hate to tell you this, but Ray's been in a wreck just out of town. I happened to go by and the police asked me if I'd get you to the hospital.' Yes. The combination of a familiar face and an urgent summons would have added up to enough to make Alicia open the door.

'Okay. Recap,' Cully said briskly to break the mood. 'The access to each of you varied in difficulty.'

Yes, Professor. We nodded.

'You don't have physical traits in common. Not all blonde, not all blue-eyed, for example. One married; the rest single. But you're all connected with the college. Two students, one teacher, and one committee woman.'

'Yes, I guess you could call Alicia "connected with the college,"' Mimi said slowly.

But so, to some extent, was everyone on the list. 'All white. All kind of upper middle class,' I offered.

'That's the loosest tie imaginable,' Cully said.

'But it's something. It looks like the Miss Beacham connection goes down the drain with Barbara,' Mimi said, 'but I'll ask Theo to check Heidi's record sometime next week to make sure she didn't go there.' She scrambled to her feet. The talk had done her good, as I had hoped. Positive action, mental or physical, healed Mimi like aloe on a burn.

Cully slipped his arm around me. I leaned against him. Mimi looked from one of us to the other. 'It finally happened, huh?'

I caught myself actually ducking my head, and Cully (I peered at him sideways) looked embarrassed.

'It's about time,' she said brusquely. 'Well, I better go get dressed. What time's the inquest Cully?'

'In a couple of hours.'

She patted me on the arm and whisked out of the room. We looked at each other a little shyly.

'Well,' he said finally, in a tone almost as brusque as Mimi's, 'I'm scared to death of you, you know that? Rachel bruised me pretty thoroughly. It won't be easy for me, for a while. But I can't be less brave than you.'

Not exactly a romantic declaration. But I was satisfied our night together hadn't been a fluke triggered by emotional overload.

From the thunder of the pipes I could tell Mimi was running a bath upstairs. Cully's hand touched the nape of my neck, brushed it with long fingers. He rose and shut the door.

10

The next day Barbara and I had another grim little meeting. This time I went to her apartment. Like her office, it was crammed, but even more pleasantly – full of plants and books and clear, mild colors.

'Do you like it here?' I asked as she made some hot chocolate in her tiny kitchen. The building was a four-unit cube tucked in between private homes on a dead-end street. Someone with an empty lot had decided to make a little extra money – prezoning, of course!

'It's okay,' she said as she got mugs from a cabinet. 'I like having other people in the same building, now. I never liked that before.'

We settled in the little living room with our steaming mugs. We talked of this and that, awkwardly. Apparently Barbara was as reluctant as I to buckle down to our task.

'I'm getting almost too frightened to go on with this, Nickie,' she said abruptly. 'I don't know if fear douses the rage or just replaces it. I can only hold so much.'

'I've about reached my capacity, too,' I admitted. 'Everything's changed since Alicia was murdered.'

'We'd better do it before we lose our courage. Let's try to take one more step.'

We seemed to gather ourselves in unison before we hauled out our creased bits of paper.

'The list,' Barbara said as clearly as if she were reciting poetry. 'Jeff Simmons. Charles Seward. Don Houghton. Randy Marquette. Theo Cochran. Ray Merritt. Dan Kirby. John Tendall. J. R. Smith.'

'What happened to Jeffrey Tabor?'

'I remembered Jeffrey was definitely out of town the night of Mimi's party. That's why he couldn't come to it. I didn't just take his word for it,' Barbara said with a faint smile. 'I asked his friend who shares his apartment.'

'So that leaves nine.'

'Did Alicia know J.R., Dan, or Randy?' Barbara asked.

'I don't know, Barbara. How could we find out?'

She looked rather daunted. 'Well, we can't ask them, can we? Gosh.'

'Let's see. Dan's new at Houghton, and he commutes from Hill Run, he told me. He just got out of the army. I think his wife's family is in Hill Run. He's from Arkansas. So the chances are very slim that Alicia knew him.'

Barbara weighed that. Then, after an emphatic shove at her glasses, she crossed Dan Kirby's name off her list.

'Minus Dan,' she said. 'Eight.'

I scooted down in my armchair and laced my fingers over my stomach. Barbara twirled her pencil between her fingers as though it was a miniature baton. We both brooded over other possible eliminators. So suddenly that I jumped, Barbara grabbed her telephone and dialed.

'Hi, J.R.,' she said. 'This is Barbara Tucker. Fine, thanks . . . and you? Good, good. Listen, how'd you come out in that poker game?'

J.R. answered at length. Barbara rolled her eyes in exasperation, then instantly switched to a smile so the words would come out right when she spoke. 'Great! Thirty-four dollars, huh? Did Randy play? Oh. Oh, Cindy won't like that, you're right!' Barbara widened her eyes at me significantly. 'You played that late?' she burbled into the phone in a very un-Barbara-like manner. Again a mumble from the other end. Then Barbara was nodding at me vehemently, and I took the list from the coffee table and drew lines through two more names.

'No, I don't want to learn to play right now. Just curious, you'd talked about it so much. Right. Well – sure, give me a call sometime. We'll do it. Sounds like fun. English professors need all the extra income they can get, right? Bye, now.'

J. R. Smith was a jovial individual who taught me Archetypes in the English Novel with a kind of infectious zest. I was glad he was apparently cleared. I looked at Barbara expectantly.

She was a little pink in the face. 'I guess I'm going to have to learn how to play poker,' she said, and looked not unwilling. 'I remembered J.R. was having a bachelor party for Randy Marquette Thursday night, since Randy's marrying – well, he married – Cindy from the admissions office Friday night. The poker playing was over when Randy fell asleep on J.R.'s couch at four in the morning. Considering the liquor, I don't think either of them could've gotten back up to go out after that. And there were only six men there, since not everyone's willing to meet Friday classes with two hours' sleep and an A-one hangover. So I think that if one of them had slipped out for any length of time it would have been noticed.'

'Sounds like it,' I agreed. 'Besides, there would have been blood, with Alicia. To clean off.' I took a deep breath. 'So,' I said as evenly as I could. 'Six.'

For a full hour we tried to think of other qualifiers that would eliminate one of the six. We couldn't come up with any. We even left Ray on the list.

'By the way,' Barbara said as she walked with me to my borrowed car, 'I take it you haven't mentioned this project of ours to anyone?'

'Not *hardly*,' I said, like one of my young classmates. 'The only people I would tell are Cully and Mimi. And since their own father is on the list . . .'

She nodded. 'Not that I really think for a minute that someone sweet like Don Houghton, or for that matter someone as dignified as Jeff Simmons, our mighty college president, for God's sake, could ever do something like what was done to us.'

'That's just it! Do we know *anyone* on that list who acts anything like the disgusting beast who did that to us? Who could knife Alicia to death?'

Barbara knew the answer too well to say it out loud. If we were right, the beast had to be there, lurking beneath a civilized skin that covered someone we knew.

We looked up at the clear cool sky. It was sweater weather in the afternoon, coat weather in the morning – my favorite season. This would have been one of the best years of my life, if only . . . For a second the filth was magically washed away. I drank in freedom with the air. Then I tensed my forefinger against my thumb and thwanged my cheek. No point in going down *that* dead-end street. Hip-pity hop, back to wonderful old reality.

Barbara was too used to my habits by now to comment on my cheek-thumping. 'Six,' I reminded her before I drove away.

She just looked forlorn.

Probably because of her family's far-flung influence, Alicia's autopsy had been concluded and her body released to her family – and Grace Funeral Home – on Sunday. We decided to pay our respects the next evening.

I was dressed and ready, and Cully was in the shower, when Mimi caught me alone in the living room. She looked uncharacteristically drab in the plain dark dress she saved for funerals and funeral home visits.

'Don't tell Cully my idea about Charles,' she said without preamble. 'It's not like we really know anything. And to tell you the truth, Nickie, I'm worried about what Cully would do if he believed Charles was the rapist.'

Cully the rational, a vigilante? Farfetched. I stared at Mimi with dismay and a crawling suspicion. This was awfully like manipulation. Was she using Cully as a lever to keep me quiet, to protect her lawyer?

I didn't suspect Charles because of that bizarre episode in the kitchen the previous Saturday. I suspected Charles because he was on the list. But I couldn't tell her that, and I also wanted to find out what she was aiming for. 'What if it *is* Charles, Mimi? We can't possibly let him do it again. Think of what this man has done.'

'We don't *know* anything,' she hissed. The shower had been cut off; Cully would hear us if we didn't keep our voices down. 'I may have just gotten scared Saturday morning for nothing. If Charles gets hauled in on suspicion and he's innocent, the mud will stick and he'll be ruined. Besides, don't you see, I know Charles. And I can tell you don't like him, even though you've tried not to say anything.'

My heart plummeted. This was the fruit of those years before I'd gained more tact, more wisdom, in my relationship with Mimi. She couldn't discuss her feelings for Charles with me with complete honesty. There was some mystery here that she didn't think she could share with me, because it was between her and a man she loved.

'I know he couldn't, wouldn't, do that to a human being.' How often had Barbara and I thought of that, in scanning the names of the men on our list? 'Besides, if he was the rapist, he wouldn't have just tussled with me in the car. He would've raped me. I couldn't have stopped him. Nick, I've thought about it ever since. We were just scared and maybe hysterical that morning. That was my fault. That whole weird little episode was something we made up.' She twisted her fingers together. She looked at me and said, sadly, 'Don't ask me to tell you what I know, Nick. But since from the look on your face I can't persuade you any other way, I have to tell you that I *know* Charles didn't do it.'

That crawling suspicion came a little further out of its hole. Mimi had never, never lied to me, in fourteen years. But she was acting so strangely. I was totally bewildered by this whole scene. I couldn't have answered her if I'd known what to say. To my relief Cully entered the living room then, with the car keys in his hand.

As we rode through the dark streets of Knolls, I pondered. All Mimi was asking was that we keep those moments when Charles was standing at the door from Cully's knowledge. Maybe she did fear that now Cully and I were lovers he would feel obliged, in true southern fashion, to avenge his womenfolk's ordeal if he knew the identity of the rapist; for the ordeal had very much been Mimi's as well as mine. I had deep doubts about Cully ascribing to that attitude.

There really was no hard evidence indicating Charles was my assailant. There was no hard evidence against anyone, unless the police had dug up something; and they were hardly likely to tell me if they had. All I had was the list. And Mimi was definitely right about another thing: The panic we'd felt that morning when Charles came to the door could easily be written off to the tension and fear that had permeated our lives for so long.

So whatever she knew or didn't know, Mimi was right. I would not tell Cully about that stupid little incident. As we drove through the night silently, I whittled away at the knot of pain and confusion she had caused me, until it was only a canker of uneasiness.

I looked across the front seat at Cully. He glanced my

328

way at the same time. The normal austerity of his face vanished in a smile that made him irresistible. I hoped I wasn't using Cully as a kind of emotional aspirin. He would be willing. He was, after all, a wound healer.

Grace Funeral Home was housed in an old mansion with pillars. It was a freshly painted, carpeted, well-kept-up place. Ordinarily, I'd have rather admired it for the gracious air it gave to a grim business.

Ray Merritt and Alicia's mother, Celia Anley, were standing close to the door to receive mourners. Ray was gray and ghastly, Mrs Anley so rigid she looked like a mannequin. Mimi quivered when she saw them, and I knew she was afraid of what they'd ask her. Neither Ray nor Celia had been permitted into the house until it was cleaned by good and loving neighbors. Cully had told us that; he'd heard it from Alicia's aunt at the filling station.

When Ray's eyes met mine I knew I shouldn't have come. I had lived through it. I knew without doubt that he was wishing I'd died in Alicia's place. If the attacker had to kill, Ray Merritt wished the victim had been me, not Alicia. At that second, Ray Merritt was struck from the list, at least as far as I was concerned. He'd never liked or trusted me. If he had been the rapist, I would have died instead of Alicia, without doubt. I started to extend my hand, saw Ray wouldn't touch it if I did, and quickly moved on to Mrs Anley, whom I'd met years before. Alicia had had at least one brother, but I knew she'd been the only daughter her widowed mother had.

'I'm so sorry.' I felt I was expressing regret that I was alive, rather than sorrow that Alicia was dead.

'Bless you, Nickie,' Mrs Anley said.

She remembered me, then. I waited for the chill of condemnation I'd seen in Ray's face. Instead, Mrs Anley hugged me and led me aside. 'Don't mind Ray,' she told me quietly. There were traces of Alicia in the shape of her mouth. Though Mrs Anley had become very heavy, the likeness was there.

'He doesn't know what he's doing right now,' she continued. She sighed. She gathered her thoughts. 'There's a choice,' she said slowly, not looking up at me anymore. 'Not always. But for Alicia there was a choice.'

I was mystified. I shifted nervously, twisted the cuff of my navy dress, and waited.

'From what I've heard . . . you chose to endure it, and live through it. My daughter' – she spoke slower and slower – 'chose to fight. I'm not saying she chose to die, but she chose to take that chance. It proved to be the wrong choice, for her . . .' I had bent lower and lower, to catch her near-whisper. Suddenly Mrs Anley was finished, and she turned to resume her place by Ray.

I stared after her. How much 'choice' had I had? I simply hadn't been able to move. I'd been awakened from a heavy sleep, precipitated into a situation already established. I was sure Alicia had wanted to live fully as much as I had. But if it comforted Mrs Anley to believe that Alicia had had some freedom of will in the matter . . . Then I was enlightened. Mrs Anley was *proud* that her daughter had fought so hard. That was the only warm feeling left to Alicia's mother: pride, that her daughter had gone down fighting every inch of the way. Death before dishonor.

Cully and Mimi were comforting Ray, who'd begun to cry in the unpracticed way of men, with great heaves of his shoulders. I was standing conspicuously by myself. I felt, ridiculously, that everyone in the room was looking at me sideways. The One Who Got Away.

With a rush of relief I spied old Mrs Harbison, our next-door neighbor, standing by an archway leading to another room. I scooted over to her as swiftly as I could manage, hoping to blend with her into a clump of mourning. Poor old lady, she was sandwiched between houses evil had visited. She was wondering, I discovered, if it might come to her house next. She told me that right after she left the funeral home she planned to depart for a prolonged visit to her married daughter in Macon. I told her I thought that was a great idea.

The open archway led into another, smaller, room. I hadn't looked in, since I was concentrating on Mrs Harbison. Now the old lady inclined her head and said, 'You ought to go see her.'

I had no idea what she meant, but I turned obediently and stepped through the archway. And there, to my absolute horror, was Alicia in her coffin. I thought I was going to scream. I flinched backward, but Mrs Harbison had a firm grip on my arm and steered me forward relentlessly. The old lady had no doubt that I wanted to see Alicia 'laid out'; in her time she must have seen so many people die that viewing the faces of the dead was simple routine.

All too soon I was by the gleaming coffin looking down at Alicia. Her face was colorless and smooth and still. Of course . . .

For the first time the absolute immobility of the dead struck me. The complete absence of movement, even the tiny movements of breathing, seemed so remarkable to me that I couldn't turn away. I wondered briefly if I should, after all, have gone in to see my father. And I wondered how the mortician had managed to fix Alicia up. I felt an eerie professional curiosity about the makeup he'd used. Why had Ray wanted the coffin open? Why on earth had the family consented to lay Alicia out in front of anyone who cared to take a look? It seemed the worst invasion of privacy I'd ever witnessed. I was appalled; but I was also spellbound. She'd looked so awful when I'd last seen her: mouth open, eyes wide, legs sprawled, covered with blood. What I was seeing now, I forced myself to admit, was better – and, after the initial shock, strangely comforting.

Here was no woman frozen in final pain and fear. This was a serene Alicia: clean, her hair arranged, her face turned to one side to cover a scalp wound I remembered. She had the dignity she'd had in life. She was presented as she would have wanted. But I swore to myself on the spot that I would put something in my will about closing my coffin.

I was only vaguely aware of Mrs Harbison wandering away. When I finally looked up from the face I'd last seen smeared with blood, I met Don Houghton's eyes. His face was smooth and still and white. I shuddered. He looked at me steadily, with an unwavering disregard of what lay literally between us. 'It's always a shock, isn't it?' he commented.

Maybe it was the carefully dimmed lighting, maybe it was the overwhelming presence of death, or my own horror at seeing Alicia – but he didn't seem to be the same Don Houghton I'd known for all these years. Not the same man who'd taken us to the zoo in Memphis, the man who'd borne so patiently and lovingly with his difficult wife. I would rather have looked at Alicia's corpse than at the face of this stranger. When I lowered my eyes, I observed as if from a distance my own hand gripping the rim of the coffin so tightly that my knuckles had turned white. I snatched my hand away.

This man is also on the list, I thought. There was only one list in my life, a list of names. And this man, the father of two people I loved, was on it.

'In the midst of life . . .' Don quoted ponderously.

I glanced up involuntarily. He was looking down this time, at Alicia. 'I always liked that girl,' he said simply. He walked around the coffin, passing within two feet of me as he went through the archway.

Thank God Cully is so tall. I spotted him immediately and flew to him like a bird homing to its particular tree. He was engaged in low-voiced conversation with a group of college people: Barbara, the Cochrans, Jeff Simmons, a couple of familiar faces I couldn't label. I jerked at Cully's coat. He swung round with a surprised look. When he saw my face, he mumbled an excuse over his shoulder and moved me away.

'I have to get out of here,' I said through clenched teeth. He saw I meant it, and quickly asked Theo to get Mimi home; and without waiting for an answer he whisked me out the door and into the parking lot just in time. I sped to a clump of bushes on the far side, and I vomited.

'Romantic, huh?' I gasped between heaves. He wisely kept his mouth shut. I loved him so much for that that I could have kissed his hands. But love and throwing up, fear and throwing up, don't blend. In the end, all you think about is throwing up.

That night Cully's training paid off in spades. He didn't ask me any questions on the way home. He just murmured soothing things about a hot bath and bed, exactly what I'd been dreaming of myself. I leaned back against the car seat in a jelly of exhaustion. Things gradually quieted down internally.

It wasn't just the eerie conversation with Cully's father that had upset me so violently, or Mimi's painful withdrawal, or Ray's hostility, though all had contributed. When I'd looked down at Alicia's still face, I had seen my own. I had seen my longer, thinner hands folded on my waist.

It had been a vile moment, worse than a glimpse of my mother dead drunk, worse than the leer I'd seen in my stepfather's face; worse, even, than my rape. During that long ordeal, I'd known my enemy. He was right there on me. Now I didn't know who he was, whether he was observing me, or whether his hatred of me was spent or active. I'd finally reached the end of my rope. My reserves of courage were exhausted. My almost-faded bruises seemed to take on new life. My gums around the loosened teeth ached. I thought I tasted blood in my mouth again.

As I brushed my teeth in the blessed solitude of the bathroom, I decided it would suit me just fine if nothing ever happened to me again in my life. Nothing more distressing than misplacing my keys, nothing more elating than successfully matching some drapes to a rug. Yes, that would suit me just fine.

To make myself feel better, I let myself dream dreams I normally would have dismissed from my mind. Would Cully ask me to marry him? Given the example of my own mother's remarriage, the misalliance of Elaine and Don Houghton, and Cully's and Mimi's washouts, it was amazing that I wanted to contemplate marriage. But the dreams fed you as a child are almost impossible to dislodge. Those dreams can be very comforting when just being an adult is a burden.

As I soaked in the bathtub under a mound of bubbles, I conjured up a vision of myself in candlelight satin and a picture hat (I'd worn a wedding outfit like that in a show once), marching down the aisle to meet Cully – who was in a tux, of course. The whole tableau was fuzzily framed by an old-fashioned church full of flowers and people who wished us well. Mimi was beaming by the minister, her arms full of flowers – but not wearing a hat like mine, I decided judiciously; Mimi would look like a fool in a picture hat . . .

By the time I was ready to switch off the bedside lamp, Cully tucked in beside me, I had designed Mimi's whole outfit and selected my china and silver. Cully's love for the wounded, his air of remoteness, had completely vanished in my vision – as had my memory of the years I'd knocked on the doors of his awareness in vain.

As I sank into sleep, Cully's breathing even and quiet beside me, I almost fantasized myself a virgin again for the wedding night.

The funeral was scheduled for Tuesday at two. When I got up that morning it was raining, a cold autumnal rain. I let Mimi give me a lift to my first class; I didn't want to start the day soggy. I had been debating whether or not I should go to the service. I decided, after slogging between my second and third classes, that I couldn't. I'd already come up with a rebuttal to the argument I expected from Mimi. But when I got back to the house and announced my decision she only nodded.

Cully had an appointment that would keep him in his office till the last minute, so Mimi left alone. She was drawn with exhaustion: Her eyes looked hollow. Her emotions had been burned away by their intensity. Our conversation, what there was of it, was strained. We all needed time to heal. I wondered if we would have it.

The house was silent except for the patter of the rain. After I watched Mimi's car back out of the driveway, I tried to settle at my desk with a stack of work. I was doing well in most of my classes so far, particularly well in my English classes. I'd been so afraid that what I'd been through would ruin my grades that I'd actually been working much harder. Desperate concentration helped keep the wolves at bay.

I was supposed to read *Macbeth* for my Shakespeare class. It was fortunate that I was already familiar with the play, because I couldn't bury myself in concentration. I tried the devices that usually worked, but nothing seemed to help. The cats were having a running (and vocal) battle, both irritable at being trapped inside by the rain. I kept imagining Alicia's funeral and feeling guilty I hadn't gone, if for no other reason than to bolster Mimi. We might be estranged, but love is a habit as well as an emotion.

After I'd run through all my rational reasons for feeling restless, I discovered the true one. I was alone in the house for the first time since I'd gotten raped.

When I realized that, I closed my Shakespeare and began to piece together a conspiracy. If Mimi wasn't home, Cully was; if neither of them was in the house, it was while I was at school or studying in the library. Since I hadn't consciously been avoiding an empty house, it occurred to me that the other two had been orchestrating their departures and arrivals to ensure I wasn't alone. In an instant I was sure of it.

Well. I was alone now. I listened to the drip of rain off the eaves, and stared out the side window into the soaked vegetation between Mimi's and Mrs Harbison's empty house. I shivered a little and pulled my sweater closer around me, doubled over my breasts. I couldn't sit there at the desk a moment longer; not with my back to the silent room.

I prowled the house. Attila had curled up to sleep in my clothes hamper, but Mao drifted at my heels. Upstairs, downstairs, from the kitchen to my bedroom. Back into the living room. All my favorite colors were there, my own harmony in the rugs and furniture; but I took no pleasure in it, in the fineness of the workmanship and wood. I stood at a front window and peered out at the houses across the street. They looked forlorn and dismal in the steady mist.

A man was slogging down the opposite sidewalk, his collar pulled up and his head covered with a plastic-treated rain-hat. I eyed him with idle curiosity, not recognizing him as any of the regular neighborhood walkers. A persistent cuss, to be taking his constitutional in this weather. Only when he was exactly opposite my window and had turned to look at the house did I recognize that the man was John Tendall. I started to open the front door and call to him to come share tea or hot chocolate – that's how desperate I was. Even flashy Tendall, the detective, whom I associated with that horrible night, seemed preferable to the hush of the house. I caught myself with my hand on the doorknob.

'You fool,' I said out loud. 'That's right. Just ask a man into the house when you're alone. A man on the list, yet. Real intelligent.' My fingers dropped from the knob. 'Smart, Nickie Callahan.' It made me feel a little sick, calling myself a fool because I'd been prepared to be friendly, been at the point of extending the trust one automatically feels toward familiar people.

Come to think of it what was John Tendall doing walking in the nasty chilly rain? Especially when almost every other resident of a certain segment of Knolls was sitting in the church a few blocks away? I'd turned to sit at my desk, but now I moved again to the window to watch. Tendall had paused to stare at Alicia's house. Then, as I watched, he trudged away through the rain.

Maybe Tendall, the dedicated detective, was pondering the crimes. Maybe he'd wanted to stare at my house and Alicia's to refresh his memory. Maybe he was revisiting the scenes of his crimes.

My thoughts began the same old round. Barbara and I called each other, or saw each other, almost daily. We were still trying to come up with a way to further narrow our list, which remained at six. I'd told her I thought Ray Merritt was out, but she argued quite rightly that we had to have something more substantial than a gut feeling to drop him from the list. We'd temporarily reached a dead end. Maybe I should try again from the other end.

Back to the same old question. What did we, the victims, have in common? A young, inexperienced student. A college professor of thirty-plus. A former model, now writer-to-be and struggling student. An efficient young matron.

Already eliminated: build, hairstyle, access, age. Could be eliminated: Let's see. Income. Background – Alicia's and mine similar, but Barbara's father was a small-scale farmer and her mother a nurse, and Heidi Edmonds's father was a minister, I recalled. Oh – religion? No. Alicia had been a Baptist, I was an erratic Episcopalian, Barbara a Lutheran.

But there had to be a pattern, a rhyme and reason. This violence, this hatred, had a specific focus. I had to know that focus for my own peace of mind. I might tell myself and everyone else that I was blameless. And I was; of all the usual things rape victims are accused of: leading men on, wearing sexy clothes, being alone outside at night. As if such harmless behavior meant the victim should expect to be raped in consequence. As if lack of wisdom, incaution, merited such a punishment. But always at the back of my mind was the niggling idea that maybe I'd offended somehow, had trodden over delicate ground. In some innocent way, some blind way, I'd aroused that violence, and I wanted to know how.

I couldn't recall any disagreements I'd had with anyone in Knolls since I'd arrived. No arguments, aside from classroom discussion, came to mind. Those were hardly heated enough or long enough to provoke a reaction of that intensity, and they'd often as not been with other women in the class.

When Mimi and Cully finally pulled into the driveway in their separate cars, I was ready to talk. I wanted to hear voices and ideas other than my own. They wanted to talk, too; anything to wipe out the memory of what they'd just witnessed. They had taken the afternoon off to attend the funeral, so they were home for the day.

Cully kissed me. 'You were right not to go,' he said, and went to the kitchen to bring us all some wine. We settled in the living room. I asked him what he'd heard from his policeman friend about the progress of the investigation.

'He hardly tells me everything,' Cully warned. 'But I reckon they've checked all the obvious things. Men registered at the motels on the nights of the crimes. Drifters. Anyone in town or close by who has a record of violence or sex offenses. So far, almost everyone they've checked has an alibi for one, or all, of the incidents. The people who don't have alibis seem to be in the clear for other reasons: extremely short, which doesn't tally with anyone's impressions, or mentally deficient, which doesn't either. Or something. Thank God, Ray's in the clear. He was miles from here with witnesses at the time Alicia must have died.'

So casually, another name was gone. That left five: Jeff Simmons, Charles Seward, Don Houghton, Theo Cochran, John Tendall. I had a fact for Barbara.

'No one's seen anything strange on any of the nights the guy's been at large,' Cully was rambling on. 'That's not too surprising when you consider how early this town goes to bed. No cars parked where they shouldn't be, no fingerprints, just physical evidence collected from—' He stopped short.

'From me and the others,' I said quietly.

'What physical evidence?' Mimi asked suddenly. She'd been drinking her wine very fast, in silence. 'I don't want to upset you, Nickie, but I don't really understand what that means.'

I focused on a snag in my hose. 'What they got off me, with a kind of sticky-feeling pad,' I said after a moment, 'was a pubic hair that was not mine. And – saliva samples,

I think, and – semen.' My fingers plucked the snag into a run.

'Some men secrete their blood type in the semen,' Cully told Mimi quickly in a blessedly matter-of-fact way. 'Some men don't. But getting a blood type is a good corroboration. This man was a secretor, as it turns out. And from Alicia, I believe, they got some skin and blood from her fingernails, since she fought.'

'I haven't noticed anyone going around with a big scratch across his face,' I said. But I'd watch from now on. What would Alicia have grabbed for? Not his face, dummy. His hands. His knife. Of course. I'd seen what shape Alicia's hands were in, the palms . . .

'But none of this is any good, is it?' Mimi said abruptly. 'Until you catch the bastard. To match all this evidence up with. It can't help catch him, right? It'll just help nail him if he *is* caught.'

'That's right,' Cully said.

The rest of the day was just something to get through. Neither Mimi nor Cully could come up with anything we victims had in common. I lay awake long after Cully had gone to sleep. I was facing the fact that the man who had harmed me would probably go free. Quite possibly he would go forever unpunished for his violation of my life and body.

Then I had an idea so galvanizing that I sat up straight and drove my fist into my pillow. I shook Cully by the shoulder.

'Hunh?'

'Cully, wake up!'

'You okay, Nickie?' He rubbed my shoulder.

'I'm fine, Cully. Listen – did your police friend tell you what blood type the guy is?' I held my breath.

'What? Oh. Yeah. Let's see.'

Dammit, Cully.

'Not a big help,' he mumbled finally. 'O positive. Real common.'

'Go back to sleep, sweetheart,' I whispered. 'Everything's okay.' He was snoring in two minutes, but I waited ten before I crawled out of bed to call Barbara.

I knew she'd be awake.

11

Thursday morning began marvelously. Cully woke up feeling frisky. Hugging my wonderful plan to me, I was glad to respond. The room was cold. Cully and the bed were warm. My first class had been canceled because of a conference my professor was attending, so I didn't have to be at school until 9:45. Everything was going beautifully until I giggled when Cully's fingers brushed a sensitive area. In mock reproof, he lay a hand over my mouth.

I was instantly blind with fear. I struck his hand with all my strength, my breathing seemed to stop, and there went my heart, racing racing for the end, oh God I'm going to *die* . . .

'Nickie! Nickie!' Cully's face was over me, white and shocked. 'Oh my God, honey, I forgot! I'm sorry!'

I managed to gasp, 'Wait. Wait a minute.' I fought desperately to control my lungs.

He had frightened me so much that for a few seconds I hated him. His black hair rumpled from sleep seemed ludicrous rather than endearing. For an abysmal moment I thought: What is he doing here? I don't know this man. There was no sap left in me, nothing left that wasn't burned and shriveled from the blaze of fear and hate.

'I'm not going to hurt you,' he said very quietly.

I stared at him. I believed nothing.

'I'm not going to hurt you.' Then for the first time he said, 'I love you, Nick.' But he said it in his 'calming' tone, professional and even. He put his arms around me, to cancel out that voice. I shuddered. 'I wouldn't hurt you for the world,' he whispered. And I began to warm. I located myself correctly in the day and scene. Weak daylight was sliding from behind drawn curtains. This was my Cully.

'I care for you,' he said. He kissed me on the neck. I stared at the ceiling over his shoulder. Very slowly, he began to caress me again. I responded as best I could. I was trying very hard not to disappoint him, not to disappoint myself. When we finished, it had only been an exercise to me; to prove to myself I could still do it. I hadn't had a problem with sex before, and had counted myself lucky. The nightmarish flashback had been triggered by something as small as his hand over my mouth.

Cully kissed me very gently and adjourned to the bathroom. I lay wondering how many more such incidents were lying in wait for me. After a while, Cully came out and got dressed without talking. We both had a lot to think about. He sat on the side of the bed.

'Cully, I don't think I'll ever get over it,' I said bleakly when I saw he was waiting for me to speak. Then I was furious with myself. I'd cried for help, knowing he couldn't resist that. I would not become an object of pity to my lover.

He had been badly frightened, too, so now he was ill at ease with me. 'I wish I could stay here with you now,' he said to me directly. I searched his eyes. 'I can't. I have appointments this morning I can't break.' And he hadn't had his morning run, either. 'But you're not alone, Nick. I'm with you.'

'You're with a lot of raped women right now,' I said as lightly as I could. Underneath the blanket, I dug my nails

343

into my palm. Maybe you're pretty sick of coming home to another one, Cully.

'Nick,' he said, and pulled me up and put his arms around me. We sat like that until he felt me relax against him. 'I'll be thinking about you all day,' he told me.

I thought he meant it. Those were good words to leave me with. They infused some warmth into the outer edges, the area where I dealt with other people; and some of that warmth seeped a few layers deeper, to where I dealt with people I cared about very much. But my core, in which I lived as a solitary homo sapiens – that was still cold, still alone, and would be for an incalculable length of time. I had a mission to accomplish.

In that silent chilly room, I knew for the first time I would never be the same woman I'd been. Unconsciously, I'd been expecting to feel a 'click' someday; after the police caught the rapist, when I was sure Cully loved me, or just any old time. And I'd imagined that after I felt that click I'd be just the same as I had been before that dark night. I'd forgotten what had frightened me so much when Barbara got raped: my conviction that what had happened to her was *irreparable*. Until this moment, I hadn't applied that to myself. 'Dumb old Nick,' I said out loud and with immense sarcasm. And I slapped myself hard.

At that instant I quit waiting for the click.

Before I could brood any longer, I jumped out of bed. I moved briskly as I dressed and gathered the books I'd need. Just feeling my body moving and working revived that incredible wonder at being alive. As always, I outlined my day while I brushed my hair. A 9:45 class. Out at 11:15 for the day. A meeting with Barbara. A paper due in – I squinted at the calendar by the dresser – a little over a week, right before Thanksgiving. And all my midterms were over except the one a dilatory professor had scheduled for Tuesday. So I needed to spend some time in the

344

library studying before Mimi and I went to tea at Sarah Chase Cochran's in the afternoon. Also time to write my mother a letter, another fabrication that would omit all the important things. She'd sent me a thank-you note for the birthday present I'd mailed her, a sweater and blouse, and in it she mentioned that she'd gone out to dinner with some friends of my father's to celebrate. And again she hadn't mentioned Jay. Instinctively I throttled the rising hope, as I had for the past month. No point in dreaming about a sober mother, a mother without Jay.

Jay would just love it if he knew someone had 'gotten' me. What I should have done all those years ago, I decided, was rocket out of that bathroom with . . . well, no, not a plunger, not heavy enough . . . but *something* . . . and bam! Beat the tar out of him!

It pleased me so much to picture Jay cowering (or even quite battered) that I wished passionately I'd had the guts at seventeen to do it. The fantasy was so vivid and satisfying that for a few happy minutes I felt I *had* done it. Even the bite of the November wind couldn't diminish my smile. It was the first time in ages I'd gone to class with a real smile on my face.

Despite the morning's humiliation, despite the beast still at large, in spite of everything, I suddenly knew that in some mysterious way I was going to win.

'You take – let's see . . .' out came the ragged list, which never seemed to leave Barbara's purse. 'Um. Don Houghton, that'll be easier for you. Charles, likewise. I have Jeff Simmons and Theo. I don't know what to do about John Tendall.'

'That'll be the hard one,' I said soberly.

'I don't know. I think Jeff Simmons is worse. I spent fifteen minutes this morning, when I was supposed to be grading papers, trying to think of a way to ask the

Houghton College president what his blood type is.' Barbara wrinkled her nose and her glasses slid. I pushed them back up before her hand could reach her nose. She looked at me comically, and we both laughed.

'I feel good,' I confessed.

'Me too.' Barbara took a bite from a cookie. 'I don't know why. What we're doing is dangerous.'

'Not unless *he* knows about semen containing blood secretions,' I pointed out. 'Not the world's best-known fact. Out of all of them, only Tendall will be aware of that, I imagine.'

'It *would* have to be the most common blood type,' Barbara said ruefully. 'I'm O positive myself.'

'I'm A negative.'

'The school has a blood drive every year. A mobile van comes by. Stan went with me last year to give. His type is O negative.'

'Even though he was never on the list, I'm glad,' I said after a moment. 'That would have been too horrible.' It had gone without saying that Stan couldn't have leaped out of his car and beaten Barbara to her apartment.

Barbara looked straight ahead. 'Yes,' she said. 'So we work on our five.'

'You think the blood van went to the police department?' I asked.

She thought. 'I seem to remember that it did,' she said uncertainly.

'Stay here a second.' I fished a dime out of my purse and went to the phone booth in the student-center lobby. I flipped through the tiny Knolls phone book.

'Police Department,' said a bored voice.

'Detective John Tendall, please.'

Click click. Buzz. 'John Tendall speaking.'

That flat voice called to mind some unpleasant memories. I screwed my eyelids tightly shut. 'This is Elsie

Smith from the blood bank, Mr Tendall,' I said rapidly and nasally. 'We have an urgent call for B negative blood. Can you come in and donate?'

'There must be some kind of mix-up,' Detective Tendall said. 'You people need to get your records straight. My blood type is O positive.'

'Oh. Oh, my goodness,' I fluttered, 'I've pulled the wrong card. Thanks anyway.'

'All right,' Tendall said, and hung up.

I returned to our table and reported to Barbara in triumph.

'Good for you!' she said, and grinned.

'But he's still on the list.'

'What if he'd said, "Okay, I'll be right down"?'

We laughed before we simultaneously realized that if Tendall was the guilty man, his discovery that the blood bank call was phony would've put him on the alert.

'But I'll take my laughs where I can find them, nowadays,' Barbara remarked, and I had to agree with her.

'What if they're all O positive?' I said dismally.

'Then it'll be my turn to think of something,' Barbara said. She folded her list. 'Having worked down from a few hundred to five, I'm not about to give up.'

'That's the spirit. Yea, team!'

We clumsily punched each other on the shoulder like hearty men, and went our separate ways.

'White gloves, do you remember?' Mimi smoothed back her mane and smiled at me before she returned her attention to driving. The Cochrans lived close to the college, she'd told me, but on a little suburban loop behind the big houses that faced the college.

'But we carried them, we didn't wear them.'

'I still have four pair tucked away under my night-gowns,' she confessed. 'One pair has little pink rosebuds at the wrists. I can't imagine when I'll ever use them, but I just can't bring myself to throw them away.'

'I threw mine in the fire one night when I was trying to liberate myself from southernness.'

'Why on earth would you want to do that?'

'Now, Mimi, you know there was a lot of garbage we had fed us along with our grits and pralines.' A figure of speech – neither Mimi nor I would touch grits with a ten-foot pole; though pralines were another matter.

Mimi pursed her lips thoughtfully as she mulled this over. 'Oh, sure,' she admitted. 'But you know, we're a dying breed. We've got to preserve what we are. You never hear a real heavy accent anymore, except every now and then, like Alicia's. You never heard anything like the way Grandmother said "water." Six syllables, at least. It's Johnny Carson's fault.'

'*The Tonight Show*? Johnny Carson is responsible for the decline of southern accents?'

'Sho 'nuff,' Mimi said with a wild grin. 'Have you ever heard Johnny Carson say "water"? Nothing to it!'

Mimi was still expounding on her latest theory when we pulled into the driveway of a very modest ranch-suburban house, the kind you don't even have to enter to know the floor plan. She stopped in midsentence to glare at a stamped metal eagle, her particular abomination, which was nailed above the front door.

Sarah Chase Cochran met us at the door with a kind of subdued frenzy of hospitality. Over her shoulder, I glimpsed Barbara looking rather relieved to see us. I was surprised to see her until I remembered she didn't have any Thursday afternoon classes to teach.

Mimi was playing hooky from her job. She'd told me that she put in so much phone time and committee work at night and on weekends that she felt perfectly justified in leaving her office a couple of hours early every now and then.

'I'm so glad to see you,' Sarah Chase was saying. 'It seems like I never get to see you all anymore, so I just thought well, I'll have Mimi and her friend over to tea so I can get to sit down and talk to them.'

I perched on the lumpy plaid couch beside Barbara and answered the usual questions, posed to me in a gracious stream – how I liked Knolls, did I miss New York, how I felt about coming back 'home,' how wonderful it was that I was living with Mimi.

Then Sarah Chase began catching up on Mimi's activities – she must have already covered Barbara – and I had time to look around me.

It was the kind of house only a strong personality can vanquish. Sarah Chase's wasn't strong enough. From the green shag rug to the smell of polish and cooking, from the decent bargain furniture interspersed with inherited antiques to the truly beautiful silver tea service that Sarah Chase lugged in presently with considerable effort, it was the kind of milieu that hopes to state, 'Just here temporarily, soon moving up.'

But Sarah Chase and Theo were somewhat beyond the age at which they should have moved up. The Cochrans were a few rungs behind on that invisible ladder, and Sarah Chase knew it. She was facing it with dignity. I wondered if it was their daughter's awful illness that had kept the Cochrans down, that had given Sarah Chase the look of someone who's beaten but won't leave the ring.

On the fake mantel stood a picture of a girl I assumed was Nell. She was a plain child but had a liveliness about her face that made her attractive. I wondered if Nell was in the house. I recalled the frozen look on Theo's face when Barbara had mentioned Nell's illness at the party, and decided not to risk asking.

But Mimi braved it. Mimi is awfully good at expressing grave concern. She has a special look for it that isn't insincere though it's predetermined. I have accidentally glimpsed the same expression on my own face, in mirrors. So I guess we learned it. The brows draw in to form a pucker above the nose, the mouth assumes a sober line, and one looks directly into the eyes of the object of concern.

'She's back in the hospital,' our hostess said with a tiny shake of her head. 'St Jude's, in Memphis. Of course, we don't expect . . .' Her voice trailed off.

Didn't expect Nell to live? Didn't expect miracles? Didn't expect Nell would ever come home again?

With my new empathy for suffering, I felt a fraction of what Sarah Chase and Theo must have been enduring. Their only child was in the process of dying and they were helpless. I glanced at Barbara and saw from her expression that the same thing was crossing her mind. We had a raw surface for pain. We understood helplessness. In a minute, Sarah Chase would see that empathy too. Though I barely knew the woman, that silver service somehow told me that she'd hate to be the object of raw emotion.

I plunged clumsily into school reminiscences. Soon we were dredging up little anecdotes from our years at Miss Beacham's. Sarah Chase told us, with more sparkle than she'd yet shown, how it felt to be a student there and at the same time be related to the founder. The Founder.

'I remember taking Theo to meet Aunt Martha for the first time,' she said with a little smile as she handed around the cookies and nuts again. 'My Lord, was he scared! And in awe, too. Of course, my whole family talks about Aunt Martha like she was God Almighty. I think we nieces and nephews thought she *was*, when we were little.'

'How did you meet Theo?' Mimi asked smoothly. She

was determined to keep up this line of talk, since it was obviously cheering to Sarah Chase.

'Well, we were at college together. My whole family is in education, so naturally,' she said, with a deprecating wave of her hands, 'I was going to be a teacher too. And Theo wanted to be in the administrative part of education . . . we were in a lot of the same classes. It just kind of happened.' She shrugged and smiled and looked almost pretty.

'Is Theo's family in education, too?' Barbara asked gamely.

'No, he's a first,' Sarah Chase responded a little too brightly; so I knew that Theo had pulled himself up by his bootstraps.

I began to admire Theo Cochran. I knew what it was like to start out at the bottom, unknown, in a profession that depended a great deal on grace and favor and contacts. Mimi was fond of Theo, though she thought him a fuss-budget. He'd modernized Houghton's record system thoroughly, and was adored by the ladies who worked for him.

There are lots of good people in the world, I told myself. That was all too easy to forget nowadays. I compared my grievance against fate to the one Theo and Sarah Chase bore. For once, the violence that had been done to me seemed petty. After all, I'd survived it, and it had been over in maybe fifteen minutes. The Cochrans' ordeal might drag on for years.

'I tried to call you Saturday morning about the faculty Christmas party,' our hostess was telling Barbara. Mimi looked startled; then she gave a shrug and turned her attention back to the conversation. It did seem a little early to start planning for Christmas. We hadn't even had Thanksgiving yet. But when a large party was being planned, which

351

had to take place before the faculty scattered for vacation, I supposed you couldn't start too soon.

Barbara was explaining she'd been out shopping. 'Where's it going to be this year?' she asked. There followed a logistics debate on the amount of food, liquor, and tables necessary, which degenerated into a discussion of the character of the faculty wife who'd planned the party the year before.

Theo came in just as they'd settled the whole thing. I was wondering what the other committee members were going to say when Sarah Chase and Barbara presented them with a fait accompli. Mimi, forgetting to mind her expression, was looking faintly bored and stealing glances at her watch.

'Good afternoon, ladies!' Theo said cheerfully. He kissed Sarah Chase with surprising vigor and looked at us (grouped graciously around the silver) with considerable satisfaction. Whatever else we were – Mimi, Barbara, Sarah Chase, and I – we were bona fide ladies, modern version; and there we were, sitting properly around Theo's living room chattering. I understood his pleasure now that I'd seen his home and knew more about him; but that obvious satisfaction made me want to say something shocking or sit with my knees askew. I pinched myself surreptitiously for penance.

'All quiet at the college?' Mimi asked too brightly. She had been getting ready to leave and now felt obliged to stay a few more minutes.

'Yes. Even if Mimi Houghton played hooky this afternoon, the walls were still standing when I left.' Theo filched a cookie off the plate, and Sarah Chase smiled at him and shook her head in mock admonishment. The affection between them was alive and touching.

'Oh, by the way,' Theo told Mimi, 'I checked this

afternoon, and Heidi Edmonds didn't go to Miss Beacham's.'

Mimi and I absorbed this without surprise or comment. Barbara looked bewildered. I made a sign to her that I'd explain later. She responded with a look indicating she had something to tell me. I wondered if she'd extracted Theo's blood type from Sarah Chase.

'Oh, I'm so relieved these awful things aren't related to Aunt Martha's school in any way. Theo had thought of it, and he told me you'd thought of it too,' Sarah Chase said.

Mimi thanked Theo for checking. 'I know it was a long shot, but we were just trying to think of anything we could.'

Theo looked sober, almost grim, and I knew he was thinking that Sarah Chase was out of the pattern and perhaps safe, since there was no Beacham's tie-in. He put his hand on her shoulder and kept it there. Poor old Theo, with all his troubles. It would be a pleasure to mark his name off the list.

'Listen, what are you all doing for Thanksgiving?' Mimi said to switch the subject.

'We're driving over to Aunt Martha's,' Sarah Chase answered. 'I'm afraid this is our Thanksgiving to keep her company. She has nieces and nephews to the feast on rotation.'

Mimi and I had to laugh at the thought of Miss Beacham marshaling her relatives as she'd marshaled the girls in her care.

'What about you, Barbara?'

'Nothing in particular. It's too long a drive to go home for just a couple of days.'

'Well, come have your turkey with us,' I urged her.

'Okay. I'd love to,' Barbara said happily. I realized

she'd been dreading a lonely holiday that would remind her at every minute of Stan's defection.

'Be prepared to eat more than your share,' Mimi warned her. 'Cully and Nick are going out to a party the night before, so they may not be in shape to really dig in!' Mimi turned to Sarah Chase. 'Are you sure you can't come?' she asked.

'I wish we could; it's sweet of you to ask, isn't it, Theo? But Aunt Martha's Thanksgiving is a command performance. We'll be leaving early Thursday morning and coming back Friday. We get to pick up Nell at the hospital in Memphis. We got permission. She just loves Aunt Martha; whenever Nell's in the hospital, Aunt Martha goes to see her every day.'

With that amazing piece of information, Mimi and I widened our eyes at each other and rose to take our leave. I was glad to go. I was oddly restless and uneasy. Maybe the thought of Nell Cochran oppressed me.

Barbara got up hastily, too, and after a search for her handbag (which had worked its way under the couch) we were all out the door in a flurry of 'Enjoyed it' and 'Please come see *us* next time.'

A chilly mist brushed my face and made my hair go limp as we walked to the car. Barbara shuddered and stood for a second looking at the sky. A Scottie was lifting his leg against her car tires. She sighed. 'Thanks again for the Thanksgiving invitation,' she said gratefully.

Mimi had slung her purse onto the front seat and had one leg inside. 'Listen, why don't you come over Wednesday night before Thanksgiving?' she asked Barbara suddenly. 'Since Nickie and Cully are going out, I'll need help wrestling with the damn turkey. I have the worst time getting the legs out of that metal brace, when I'm ready to pull the innards out. And we can share some wine.'

'Okay,' Barbara said after a moment's hesitation. She

was obviously afraid that Mimi was only asking out of pity. 'What time?'

'Seven-thirty, I guess.'

'I'll bring the wine, and you have to let me know what I can cook and bring for the Thanksgiving table,' Barbara said firmly.

Mimi gave her a brilliant smile. 'Sure I will,' she said. 'I look forward to it, the whole holiday.' Then Mimi scooted out of the weather and into the front seat. I folded my longer legs and got in more slowly.

'What was it that surprised you when Sarah Chase and Barbara were talking about the Christmas party?' I asked Mimi curiously, after she'd negotiated the driveway.

'What?' she asked blankly.

'You had a pretty strange expression—'

'Oh, that,' she interrupted. 'Well—' Suddenly the Scottie shot across the road in front of us, I gasped, Mimi slammed on the brakes, and we began to skid on the mist-slick blacktop. We screeched to a stop about a foot from a mailbox. The Scottie scampered across a lawn, quite unhurt, and Mimi swore for half a minute while belated adrenaline made my mouth taste metallic.

'You better get one of those bumper stickers,' I advised when Mimi had started driving again. 'One that says "Warning: I brake for animals."'

'Might not be a bad idea,' Mimi said dryly, and then, glancing at the sky, added, 'Oh hell, look at that rain.' It hit the windshield as if someone had thrown a bucket of water at us.

The heavy gray of the sky, the wind, and the cold rain turned the day into one of those classic early-winter nasties.

Cully was already home. He opened the kitchen door as we scurried from the car. The kitchen light silhouetted him in the doorway; and the sight of that tall thin outline

355

filled me with a rush of love that made me a little short of breath. I found I was too thankful for the warmth Cully and I had begun to share to ask any more questions about motivation or permanence. I came out of the cold rain into the warmth and comfort of the kitchen. 'If I were watching a movie, I'd call that symbolic,' I murmured to the cats as I hung up my coat.

It was certainly our week for being entertained. Mimi had to answer the phone just when Cully was saying that Elaine and Don had invited us over for Friday night. I nodded assent glumly. I'd seen Elaine a few times since our confrontation a few weeks before, but though we'd made our outward peace, we were both well aware we just plain didn't like each other.

I passed Cully another biscuit, and reflected idly that Mimi must have taken her call upstairs, since I couldn't hear her voice in the hall.

'Are you all right?' Cully asked me. 'After this morning, I mean.'

His concerned face reminded me of the awful flashback. 'I'm fine,' I said firmly. 'There may be something else lurking in the woodwork for me; I don't know. But to tell you the truth, I feel better now than I have since it happened.'

'I hated to leave you today. I'll make it up to you tonight.' There was a slight hint of conspiratorial wickedness in his thin mobile lips that made me tingle.

I gave him a parody of a lewd wink; he laughed.

'Are you going to be around this evening?' I asked as he began clearing the table. Since he was gone so often in the evening, tending to his private practice, he'd slipped into the habit of clearing the table and putting the leftovers away, so all the dishes were lined up to wash and dry.

'No, two appointments. I should be home around nine.'

Mimi didn't get off the phone until Cully had been gone about ten minutes. She went directly to the sink, turning on the water with unnecessary force.

'What are your folks doing for the holidays, Mimi?' I asked, after I'd told her about our Friday night dinner at their home.

'Oh, I forgot to tell you. Ever since Cully and I graduated from college and went our own way, they've been spending Thanksgiving in the Bahamas. It's a yearly rite now. They thought about canceling their reservation after we both got divorced, but when Mother mentioned it a few weeks ago I told her they should go on and go. She and Daddy were looking forward to it, and we can perfectly well have our own Thanksgiving.'

Thanksgiving has always been my favorite holiday, so I was glad to have dinner with Elaine Friday night instead of sacrificing the big feast. Mimi seemed to be in one of her 'fond of Mother' moods, so I didn't voice my relief. It occurred to me that Mimi might be so fond of her mother right now just because she wouldn't have to spend Thanksgiving with her. I'd have been jumpy about spending a whole day with Don, anyway, since he was on the list. I hadn't seen him since the weird scene over Alicia's coffin. I shuddered when I thought about it, and told my thoughts to move right along.

I went on drying dishes mindlessly, content not to think for a while. Gradually I became aware that Mimi was quiet, too. We usually talked during this unpleasant chore, to make it go faster. Things had gone so well between us that afternoon that it had almost seemed as though nothing had ever gone wrong.

'Cully gone to an evening appointment?' Mimi asked.

'Yep.'

'He's probably meeting another woman on the sly,' she said bitterly.

That kind of nastiness, out of the blue, wasn't typical of Mimi. It was so ugly and unexpected that I put down my towel and stared at her. Surely she wasn't brooding any longer about Richard's defection to the long-haired lady in Albuquerque?

'I'm sorry,' she said curtly. 'Male junkies.'

'What?'

'I once heard a lecture by a woman who worked for *Ms*,' she explained, 'and she called women in our culture "male junkies." She said most women's magazines were about how to attract, keep, and entertain men. Or – having caught and kept – how to entertain and feed those men's children.'

'Was that back when you were in college?'

'Yes, but we still are, Nick. We still are! Look at the way we were brought up. Every woman, but especially southern women. All brought up that way. You remember teen magazines? Everything down to how to tie your hair ribbon – for your *date*. If you disagreed with him, you were supposed to keep your mouth shut. Unless the disagreement was about whether he could stick his hand up your skirt. Then, and only then, you were supposed to disagree. That was why you had to carry change in your purse, to call your folks when he dumped you out of the car for resisting him.'

This was the woman who'd saved four pair of white gloves? 'From the magazines I've read lately, that seems to have modified quite a bit,' I said mildly.

'Yes, maybe. But the old way is almost impossible to shake. You have to fight it all the time.' Mimi scrubbed the pot she was holding as if she were indeed fighting it. 'It's been impossible for me to uproot, just like monkey grass when you let it take over the garden. You pull it up one place, it comes back another. Propitiate, manipulate, never confront. And forgive, forgive, forgive! It's like a knee-jerk reflex!'

'Yeah, but you know what you do in a knee-jerk reflex, don't you? You kick at the guy with the hammer!'

That made her laugh. But I could still see the traces of regret around her mouth when I went to my desk to start studying. I'd known that Mimi's two aspects warred between themselves, but I'd never seen it get this intense. I was worried about her. But I concluded that, as always, Mimi would tell me what was on her mind when she chose. I couldn't figure out if she was angry with someone else or with herself. Both, I decided.

Barbara called about eight-thirty. 'I didn't have a chance to tell you this afternoon, but Jeff Simmons's blood type is AB,' she announced. 'It took me thirty minutes' conversation to work around to blood types in some semblance of a normal manner.'

'So. Four,' I said slowly. 'I thought you might've found out Theo's from Sarah Chase.'

'It seemed like an abuse of hospitality,' Barbara said. 'If we'd met anywhere else but her house. I just couldn't.'

'I see what you mean,' I said. But I wondered if we'd make any more progress if we let the smaller scruples stand in our way. I listened to Mimi's footsteps moving around her bedroom overhead.

'Are you really determined?' Barbara asked suddenly.

'I was just wondering if I could ask you the same question.'

'It's more awful, isn't it, the more we go on? Sometimes I'm tired of being so angry. Sometimes I just want to put it all away in a drawer somewhere. But then, when I really remember . . .'

'I know.' I took a deep breath. 'Should we go on?' I honestly didn't know how I felt. One day, one moment, I was up, hot on the trail. The next I was down, wanting only, as Barbara said, to shut it all away in a drawer, to begin to forget.

'I don't know. I just don't know.'

'Maybe we should finish what we've started,' I said.

'Like cleaning our plate of something we don't like to eat?' There was the faintest tinge of amusement in Barbara's voice.

Maybe I was being childishly stubborn. I pulled off my reading glasses and rubbed my eyelids. I searched around for a principle on which I could base a decision. Instead, I thought of Mimi, who in this continuing siege of fear and suspicion was being driven further and further away from me. It would put the nail in the coffin of our friendship if Barbara and I discovered somehow that Mimi's father or the man she loved was a rapist and a murderer. On the other hand (and I rubbed my eyes until I saw flashes), if Theo or John Tendall were to attack Mimi – after all, she was the same kind of woman . . .

I had a glimmering, then, but I let it slide away as I slogged down my original muddy path of thought.

. . . and if she got raped, then . . .

So I found the principle. 'Other women,' I said succinctly.

'Sure,' said Barbara. 'How could we live with ourselves?'

'So that settles that.' I wasn't exactly pleased with our final decision, but I was relieved to have it over with.

'What if all the rest really do have O positive? I was just joking this morning, but they might turn out to. What do we do then?'

'Hell, I don't know. We line them up and ask them to drop their pants.'

Dreadfully, we both began snickering.

'That was pretty sick,' Barbara said when she'd wound down. 'But we'd have a chance of recognizing the one.'

'Like you said today, I take a laugh where I can find it, now.' I heard Mimi at the head of the stairs. 'So you've got one more to go, and I've got two. Let's get to work,' I said hurriedly. 'See you.' I hung up.

'Nick, I'm going out for a while,' Mimi said. Suddenly she seemed to recall something, and looked concerned. 'When's Cully coming home?'

I glanced at my watch. 'He should be here any time. He said about nine, and it's almost that now.' I realized what she was worried about. 'Hey, I can be alone and not go to pieces,' I told her gently.

'Oh. You figured it out.' She grinned. 'We thought we were being so clever about it.'

'It took me a while,' I assured her, and grinned back.

'Nick, you know how – well, I'm sort of proud.'

'Yes, Miss Mimi Houghton.' I was still smiling, but I could feel my smile begin to wane. Her face had turned completely sober.

'You know I told you I knew Charles isn't involved in all this.' She gestured with her hand to indicate me and the direction in which Alicia's house lay.

I nodded, trying to keep my face expressionless.

'I did that all wrong, but what I said is true. I'll tell you all about it, when I can stand to.'

'Okay, Mimi.' What else could I say?

Then she was out the back door to her car. I was shaking my head as I locked the door behind her.

The Houghtons' dining room had changed very little since the night I'd met Cully more than fourteen years before. Elaine bought the best and took care of it. Just as she'd picked the best husband for her and had taken excellent care of him, I decided during the delicious dinner. I could have carried the idea further and further and my understanding of the family would have profited from it, but I called myself to order and reminded myself of my mission.

It wasn't easy to find an opening into which I could insert the odd subject of blood types. The gleaming wood of the table, the heavy sheen of the silver, the flowers in the crystal bowl, all reproached me for my tawdry problem. It hardly seemed possible that the rich striped upholstery of Elaine's chairs would consent to hold the bottom of a woman who had been raped. But that was just as real as the table or the silver, I told myself sternly. I braced and waited for the right opening in the conversation. Don himself provided it.

'Honey, have you heard how Orrin Sherwood is?' he asked Elaine.

'Not too good,' she answered with that ominous little shake of the head that means death is in the offing. 'That wreck was just a terrible thing. His wife won't even leave the hospital to lie down at home for an hour or two. She says Orrin's got to see her face if he opens his eyes, Miss Pearlie told me.'

'I didn't hear about that! What happened?' Cully asked. 'Orrin's worked for Father for, oh, twenty years,' he told me. Elaine frowned slightly.

Don proceeded to describe the circumstances of the wreck, which I barely heard, poised as I was to spring.

'. . . and he'd lost a lot of blood, way too much.'

Thanks, Don. Ready, set, go. 'I guess that's what they wanted the blood for the other day,' I interjected. 'They called this boy in one of my classes, he was telling me. The hospital was short of that blood type. He went in and gave.'

'Gosh, if I'd known that, I'd have given some,' Don said with deep chagrin. 'I do wish they'd said something while I was at the hospital! Orrin and I were in the army together, and it seems to me we found out then that we had the same blood type. What type was the boy, the one who told you this, Nickie?'

'He didn't say,' I managed to get out, feeling worse and worse.

'Let's see . . .' Don thought, his fork poised in midair. Elaine waited patiently, her face turned to him with apparent interest. 'I think I'm just plain old type O, universal donor,' Don decided. 'So Orrin must be something else, since the hospital surely wouldn't run out of O.' He was really sad at missing the opportunity to help his friend. My heart sank. Another type O.

'Aren't we all?' said Cully. 'I know I am.'

'Oh, it's been so long since I had you two, that's the only time I had mine typed,' Elaine reflected. 'Your daddy and I had to find out about that Rh factor. You know, it causes trouble for the baby if the parents are different.'

Mimi nodded to show she was listening, but she looked faintly bored. Then she brightened. 'Charles,' she said happily, 'can't give blood. He faints at the sight of it.' She seemed happy just to say his name.

During the inevitable exclamations this quirk of Charles's engendered, I told myself rapidly that even if Don did have O blood, so did John Tendall. And probably Theo, too. But that peculiarity of Charles's bore out Mimi's assertion that Charles could not be the rapist. All of us had bled to some extent.

'Is it just his own blood, Mimi? Or anyone's?' I asked, just to be sure.

'Oh, anyone's. It's been embarrassing to him for years because he likes to hunt so much, and if someone he's with cuts himself, Charles has to look the other way.'

Why the hell hadn't Mimi told me that earlier, instead of going through all that hocus-pocus about swearing not to tell Cully we'd suspected Charles? Then I caught on. She'd come out with this quirk of Charles's so unselfconsciously that I had to conclude she herself hadn't made the connection between Charles's horror of blood and his now-certain innocence. She'd been thinking of some other exculpating fact earlier, something she wanted to keep secret. Of course, the result was the same; Barbara and I could scratch Charles from our list. That left three, and one of those three was Don. The odds that he was the rapist had just leaped appreciably.

As Mimi and I cleared the table, I tried to keep my mind blank. I was able to join in the conversation just enough to keep my preoccupation under wraps. But after an hour, when we were all in the living room and Elaine was carrying in coffee and dessert, an awful line of logic insisted on screaming out in my mind.

Mimi had thought – briefly, and for whatever reason – that Charles might be the rapist. So she wouldn't see him. Now Mimi would see Charles. So he wasn't the rapist; Mimi said she *knew* he wasn't guilty.

How could Mimi know he wasn't the rapist?

She knew who *was*.

But why would she keep silent about it? Who on earth would Mimi protect from such a charge?

Her father, Don.

The whole room blurred before I caught myself. I felt sweat break out on the palms of my hands. I set down my coffee cup with a loud chink. Elaine glanced at me reprovingly before she resumed her conversation with Mimi. She didn't know how lucky she was; I'd almost dumped both cup and coffee on the carpet. I grabbed control of myself with a tremendous effort. I shot a quick look at Don, sitting on a love seat beside Mimi, opposite me.

I was thinking, quickly and desperately. I was probing

the raw gash, trying to remember. Trying to dig out fragments so the wound could be closed. What could I remember? I'd told the police I didn't know anything about my attacker. I hadn't seen him. But I had to be able to remember something, something else, something that might eliminate Don. Okay. Calm, now. Calm.

I remembered. He'd been heavier and shorter than, say, Cully; but that category included many men besides Cully's father.

He hadn't really been very strong. Otherwise, the damage inflicted would have been worse, far worse. I touched my face; I remembered. Don was hardly in good shape, and he must be at least fifty-five, probably older.

No beard on the attacker. None of the men on our list had one.

I had to yank myself out of the stream of my memory. Cully was eyeing me in a dubious way, his dark eyebrows humped together. I found I was on the verge of bursting into a laugh that would have been very unpleasant to hear; I'd wildly imagined asking Don to lie on top of me to see if it felt familiar. I mashed that laughter into a smile and offered it to Cully. He looked startled, as well he might; it must have been ghastly.

The worst thing about these few minutes of horror was that they passed in Elaine's living room. Everything in the room was civilized, conventional, expensive. The man who fit into this room simply couldn't do such a thing.

In a kind of suspended animation, I turned to Cully and asked him to give me some details about the party we'd been asked to for the night before Thanksgiving.

'One of the psych professors is throwing it,' he said, relief evident in his voice. He was grateful to me for apparently snapping out of a bad mood. 'He lives just three blocks away from Mimi's. It's a costume party.'

'What? Right after Halloween?'

'It was going to be on Halloween, but he caught the flu or something.'

'What on earth can we go as?' It was wonderful to work out this little problem. I had managed once again. I was on top of this situation. I could do it. Maybe Cully's father had raped me and killed Alicia, and I was trying to think of a costume to wear to a party. Hell, I could do anything.

'I think you ought to go as either the Sugar Plum Fairy or Wonder Woman,' Cully said. It was such an amazing thing for Cully to say, and the smile he gave me was so crinkled and sweet, that I almost kissed him.

'Grandmother's trunks are still in the attic, and heaven knows what's in them,' Mimi called from across the room.

It dawned on Elaine that Cully and I were going to a party together, that I was his date. Her eyes narrowed in irritation and jumped sharply from her son to me and back again. Cully caught the look, casually took my hand, and with a bland face continued the discussion of what was likely to be unearthed in the attic.

I shuddered to think.

I got through the rest of the evening. It was so unreal to think that a person I knew and loved could have raped me that I couldn't accept it either emotionally or intellectually.

I shot secret looks at Don every now and then, and on the outside he was just as nice as always. His face was just as amiable, his bald patch just as shiny. His conversation was certainly just as bland. As he discussed the vital need for a new traffic light at one of Knolls's intersections, I couldn't remotely imagine that mouth uttering the foul words I remembered.

I was more confused than I had ever been in my life.

I will never know how I did it. I don't think all of me was in my body that night. I think part of me just got up and left. What remained handled it. I did get through the rest of the evening.

12

What could I tell Barbara? I didn't think I'd see her until Monday. She had a date with her fellow professor, J. R. Smith, on Saturday. She really was going to learn how to play poker. Cully and I were going to a nearby state park on Sunday, to shuffle through the falling leaves and have a change of scene.

I surprised Cully with the enthusiasm of my leaf shuffling. I bounded, I sang, I talked about my classes, I told him I thought my mother was improving. I was a one-woman band all day. Cully was obviously a little puzzled by my frenetic mood, but he tried gamely to enter in. I even tried to lose myself in passion; and for an amazing hour among the leaves I succeeded.

I told myself over and over that Don was leaving town Monday night, for a whole week. If nothing happened before he left, I'd have a week to think, a week to decide what I must do and who I should keep faith with – Mimi or Barbara.

I lay awake most of Sunday night, waiting. Those hours of torment were the penalty for my indecisiveness. Every second Monday morning, as I sat through my classes or walked down the halls, I was terrified that someone would come up to me and begin, 'Oh, Nickie, did you hear about the girl last night . . .'

By midmorning, when Barbara met me in the student

center to tell me Theo was type O like Don and Detective Tendall, it hardly seemed to matter. I was glad she was in a hurry to get to a conference with a student. To preserve at least a partial faith, I told her about Charles's weak head for blood. But I didn't mention Don.

At three o'clock I knew the Houghtons' flight had taken off from the Memphis airport. I was sitting in the library snapping the point off my pencil and sharpening it again, to the discomfort of the students around me. Their faces became even more guarded when I shut my eyes and said a brief and silent thanksgiving.

Now I had time.

That night, I buried myself in the paper due that week, and in studying for one remaining test. I finished the paper. Cully laughed at my reading glasses and typed my paper for me while I studied.

'Your handwriting is terrible, but your paper is very good,' he told me, and I felt myself turn pink with pleasure. I dived back into my books, as much to dodge thinking as to make a good grade.

I trudged home after Tuesday's test, my eyes watering in the sharp wind, and found Detective Markowitz waiting on the front steps. It was almost as if I'd conjured him up. With the test out of the way, my mind had been running around and around my dilemma.

'You're looking better,' he said approvingly. 'How you feel, darlin'?'

'I feel a lot better, too,' I lied. It would have been the truth a few days ago. I smiled at him. He still looked tired and world-weary, but there was an air of cheer about him that I enjoyed. It was quite a change.

'I swear, I had no idea you was such a beauty,' he testified as I unlocked the front door. I told him to come on in.

After he refused coffee or cola, I perched on the couch and asked him what I could do for him. 'Something new?' I said hopefully.

'Well, not much, but something,' he said. I had known there was a reason for that cheer.

'Fact is, we've eliminated a mighty lot of people. Now, you might not think that's much,' he said as he saw my face fall, 'but in police work, that's a lot. It's not like in the books. The sooner we get suspects out of the way, false suspects, the sooner we can get at the real one. And I've worked so hard and so long on these cases that I just decided I'd be happy about that.'

Even as he told me this, his little manufactured happiness vanished. 'I've got a daughter myself, you know,' he said quietly. 'We're doing everything we possibly can, honey. So I decided to drop by, again; I know it's hard on you, having to think about it—'

What else had I been doing?

'—but I thought I'd ask, one more time, if there was anything, *any tiny thing*, you've recalled since we last talked to you. The last time I saw you, it was still just a week after. I thought maybe you might have thought of something by now, now you've had time to calm a little.'

'Well,' I said hesitantly.

He pounced. 'Something?'

I knew I was going to let him down. 'This is going to sound stupid,' I began. 'I don't remember anything specific, but I do know there's something to remember. It hasn't come to me yet, though.'

'I see,' he said doubtfully.

'There's an impression I got,' I blundered on. 'But it won't come to mind yet. I told you this was going to sound stupid.'

'No, no,' he said politely. 'Call me, any hour, any day. I'm in the book. If you remember. Now, as long as I'm here, would you feel like going over the thing with me again?'

There was nothing I felt less like doing. But of course I said I would.

'I couldn't tell how tall, because he was bending over the bed,' I started out. 'But not extremely tall, I think.' I looked at my feet to concentrate better. Markowitz's brown eyes were too eager. He was on edge and desperate to get something definite out of me. I didn't have anything to give him.

'He was pretty heavy,' I said. I bit my lip. 'He was white. He didn't sound very young. Not a kid's voice.' I rummaged through my memory. I had thought my film was so exact, but it had been skipping things lately, thank God. 'Nothing else,' I said finally. 'I just can't form any other conclusions. It was so dark, and with the pillow over my face . . .'

'Sure, sure,' Markowitz said hastily. He didn't want me crying on him. He reached up to check his Jerry Lee Lewis hairdo. It was a weary gesture.

Then I had it.

'He was *bald*!' I shouted.

The detective's head snapped up. His brown eyes glittered from that blank face. 'What?' he said intently.

'He was bald,' I said more slowly. I had it now; I remembered. That nagging feeling, like an itch beneath a cast, was gone.

Markowitz looked as though he wanted to turn me upside down and shake the information loose. 'How do you know?'

'My arms . . . when he . . .' I took a deep breath to brace myself. 'When he lay on top of me, my arms were crossed over my bosom, and the top of his head brushed them, and I felt scalp, not hair.'

371

The detective actually grabbed my arm. 'Are you sure?' His voice was little more than a whisper.

'Yes.'

Markowitz leapt to his feet. Excitement was jolting through him like an amphetamine. He walked to a window, ran a hand over his hair again, put both hands in his pockets, took them out. His hair was so carefully waved that it looked like a toupee. I wondered suddenly if his partner Tendall did indeed wear a toupee. That thick gray hair, so carefully styled . . .

'How bald?' He swung to face me.

'What?'

'Completely bald? Or just a little hair combed across the scalp? Or bald on top, with hair around the sides of his head?'

I tried to make the memory more specific. I closed my eyes. I actually crossed my arms over my breasts.

'I don't know. I can't remember any more than that,' I said finally.

Markowitz accepted my word, to my surprise. It seemed he was so excited at finally having a real clue that he could barely wait to get back to the police station to tell his partner Tendall. And he was proud, I could tell. He'd come back to see me that one additional time, without real hope, just because he was a good cop, and a desperate cop. I didn't tell him that if he hadn't had the habit of running his hand over his hair, I never would have remembered.

Markowitz said goodbye hastily and absently. From the front window, I watched him actually do a little dance step before he got into his car. Then he turned and waved.

I walked back to the bedroom and threw myself down on the bed. Now I understood why I'd felt so oddly uneasy around Don and Charles. That evening at Don and Elaine's, when I'd seen the lamp shining on Don's bald head, I'd remembered there was something *to* remember. Charles's hair was clearly thinning. He combed long strands across, but tanned scalp shone through. Thank God, Cully still had lots of hair.

But when I thought about it, I realized I'd met a lot of men in some stage of baldness since I'd come back to Knolls. Barbara's friend – ex-friend – Stan. Theo. And I realized I could've saved Barbara her half-hour conversation with Jeff Simmons, now that I pictured his luxuriant blondness. I had to laugh when I visualized dignified Jeff Simmons skulking through the Houghton gardens in his three-piece suit. We had actually suspected him! I caught myself up sharp; I gave myself a slap. How could I laugh?

I could laugh. I gave myself permission. My responsibility was over. I'd done everything, every humanly possible thing, to help catch the man who'd attacked me and killed Alicia. The police wouldn't go by our list. The police wanted facts. And I'd dredged up the very last fact I had. They had the blood type. They knew about the baldness. They'd listened to us when we told them the rapist knew us.

My part in this was over, I swore. My appointed role was that of victim. I'd been the very best little victim I could. I was sick to death of being a victim. I was turning in my pain, crawling out of the bog of suspicion and doubt. I would flounder in it no longer.

I shut a long narrow drawer inside me. The corpse it held was not quite dead; but I slammed the drawer shut with my own kind of ruthlessness. Maybe it would die for lack of air.

13

The next day, the day of the party, I hummed to myself in the bathroom all afternoon, doing things to myself I hadn't done since I moved to Knolls. Facial treatments, creams, the whole battery of makeup I'd considered never using again, all came out of boxes and tubes I'd stuck far back in my vanity.

After applying them, I felt a cool sheen slip over me, the sheen I'd worn like armor in the city. It didn't fit as well as it had. But I could still wear it. The New York Nickie had had her points. She'd had that wonderful gloss of safety most people don't even know they possess until they lose it. She hadn't been a victim.

For the first time in weeks, I consciously examined my face in the mirror. Today it seemed important; maybe the most important thing about me. I examined every pore, every wrinkle-in-the-making, as I once had done daily. I did my exercises, which had also been neglected lately. My muscles ached afterward. Cully the jogger would be proud of me.

I recalled all the warning stories I'd heard about what happened when you dropped that daily exam and tone-up. I could hear a friend (another model) relating with horror what had happened to a comrade of ours who'd married months before; inexplicably, she had wed an upstate farmer. 'In weeks, Nickie, just *weeks*, she's lost all her muscle tone,' Cicely had told me in a voice filled with outrage and fear.

Loss of muscle tone; oh my goodness gracious. A fate worse than death. I snickered at the mirror and went on with my work.

Through the bathroom wall, I could hear the *thunk* of Mimi opening the oven door in the kitchen. She'd forgotten to make cornbread for the dressing and was worried about leaving it out all night to stale, since Mao and Attila had shown themselves partial to cornbread in the past.

Cully had gone to the college to catch up on his paperwork. Most of the students had left for home the day before. His secretary was at home making her own dressing. He was looking forward to the peace and quiet, he'd said, when I'd asked him if it didn't make him feel uneasy to be alone in the empty psychology building. He had looked at me rather strangely. Of course, men weren't supposed to be afraid. They didn't have to be.

I pulled my thoughts away from that dreary track. Was I going to begrudge Cully the fact that he ran no chance of getting raped?

Back to frivolity. Maybe I should turn gay. I'd known plenty of women in New York who liked their own kind, at least occasionally. But the idea had never appealed to me, even at times when I was depressed over some romance that had failed. I pictured myself waltzing into the kitchen and putting the move on Mimi, and laughed at the thought of the look on her face.

She overheard. 'What's so funny?' she called from the kitchen in an aggravated voice.

'Nothing!' I'd tell her sometime when she wasn't worried about sage and poultry seasoning. I felt a little uncomfortable being invited to a party Mimi hadn't been asked to; but she had told me, almost too vehemently, that she wouldn't have gone if she'd been asked. I had raised my eyebrows.

'I've only met the guy once, and I didn't like him,' she had said lamely. 'And his *wife*!'

Aha. 'What about her?'

'I hate her,' Mimi had said to my surprise.

To answer my stare, she'd advanced the story that the woman kept a photograph of her father in his casket – on her bedside table.

How on earth did Mimi know that? Something in her face had warned me not to ask. But I'd told her about the time in New York when I'd gone out for a drink with the photographer who'd said my eyes were like opals (I'd always love him a little for that). He'd confessed to me after several Scotches that when he'd first opened shop, he'd made some money that way. 'You'd be surprised,' he told me earnestly, 'how many people want pictures of their loved ones in their boxes.' Then he'd made me swear to keep his former sideline a secret.

I mulled over that odd story as I unrolled the special pouch that held my arsenal of brushes. I decided that we all carry our dead with us. My hostess-to-be just carried hers openly and visibly.

Nickie the philosopher.

My left nostril is a fraction larger than my right. I painted it even. The work of art complete, I slithered out to the kitchen in a lounging robe I saved for great occasions, a gorgeous thin slinky thing. The big room was in a state of chaos. Mimi was determined that our Thanksgiving feast be full and traditional. She'd hauled every spice out of the rack so she could pick up what she wanted instantly. A heap of sweet potatoes was piled on the counter, and the turkey was perched to thaw in the drain rack.

Attila was prowling around the fringes of this bounty,

hoping to snitch some of it. Mao was curled up on top of the microwave staring at the turkey as if it were a live bird she was stalking. Mimi was crumbling the still-steaming corn bread, a pained expression on her face. She glared at me as I opened the refrigerator.

'Now, Nick, don't get drunk tonight, you hear? You can't have a hangover tomorrow. You won't eat much if you have a hangover.'

'Okay, Mimi,' I said meekly. 'Can I have a sandwich now?'

'Yes, ma'am,' she said, and suddenly grinned. The old warmth was back. 'I reckon you might find some food around here.'

'What would you recommend?' I asked seriously. 'The peanut butter and jelly or the leftover meat loaf?'

'Oh, boy, a meat loaf sandwich. Make me one, too, will you? Heat it up in the microwave, with cheese all over it.'

I began rummaging through the refrigerator. It might take me hours to come up with the meat loaf, the shelves were so jammed. 'You'd think,' I muttered, 'we were expecting an army instead of just us and Barbara.'

'Well . . . Charles is coming.'

I froze with my hand, finally, on the meat loaf. I felt the tension radiating from Mimi. She thought I was still worried about her protection of Charles, but actually I was struggling to slam a mental drawer in which a corpse had just moved and groaned. 'Okay,' I said, when I could. I heard her sigh behind me.

Cully hallooed from the door then, so the moment passed. I unearthed the serrated knife to slice some of my homemade bread for our sandwiches. Cully wanted one, too.

'When's Barbara coming over?' Cully asked as we sat on the benches in the breakfast nook wolfing down our food.

'Seven-thirty, eight,' Mimi said indistinctly. 'We're going to set up the dining table in the living room, and we're going to figure out when the turkey has to go in, and she's going to grip the bird while I reach in to get the innards out. I don't think I got him out of the freezer soon enough, to tell you the truth. I think the cavity's still frozen.'

'Wear rubber gloves,' Cully advised. 'That's what Rachel always did.'

Oh, great.

The phone rang when I was halfway to the counter to either make another sandwich or throw the meat loaf at Mimi and Cully. I picked up the receiver on our brand-new kitchen wall phone. (Mimi had gotten tired of standing in the hall to talk, and had had the old one taken out.)

'Hello? May I speak to Nickie?'

'Mother?' I felt age sit on my shoulders. I felt the stillness behind me as Cully and Mimi quit eating.

'Baby? Guess where I'm calling from!'

Oh, not the outskirts of Knolls, please no. She'd come to see me at Miss Beacham's like that, once. She didn't sound drunk. But she sounded uncertain, shaky. I felt my face settle into tense lines.

'I don't know, Mother. Where?'

'Well.' I heard her take a deep breath. 'I checked myself into a center for alcoholics two weeks ago.'

'What?' I felt dizzy and sat on the floor with a bump, taking the telephone receiver with me. I drew my knees up. 'You what?'

'Sober for two weeks,' she said, and began crying.

'Oh,' I said wonderingly. 'Oh, Mama!' All the years sloughed off. I pounded my fist against my knee for joy. 'Mama! Really? Really?'

'This is my first phone call,' she said. 'They don't let you

378

make a phone call for two weeks, until they can be sure you won't plead to be taken home.'

I noted the call had not been made to Jay.

'Where is he?' I didn't have to specify who 'he' was.

'Gone.' Her voice was very controlled. 'I waited till he went out of town. I'm really kind of a coward, Nickie. I'm glad you're grown up now. Maybe you can understand. I waited till he was gone. Then I filed for divorce, and I changed all the locks on the doors, and then I packed a bag and I headed here after I called my doctor. I was so drunk I barely made it. In fact, I drove over some bushes at the entrance. But they took me.'

The tears trickled down, tracking the work of hours. I gestured frantically at Mimi and she passed me a napkin to blot them. I felt the cold linoleum of the kitchen floor bite into my rump through the thin bathrobe. The muscles in my rear were cramping. I didn't care.

'Are you there, honey?' The frail voice was scared again.

'You're wonderful,' I said. 'Oh, bless you, bless you.'

'Hardly wonderful,' said my mother, with a ghost of amusement in her voice. 'Fourteen years too late. Not wonderful. And it's not over, by a long shot.'

'You'll make it,' I told her fiercely, trying to will my hope through the telephone line.

'For the first time, yesterday I really began to think I might,' she whispered.

'You will.' I paused. 'Have you heard from him?'

'He can't call in,' she said smugly. 'I won't come to the phone.'

'Yahoo! Good for you, Mama!'

'I have to go, Nickie. It's a long road out of these woods. Don't expect too much.'

'You think you might be out by Christmas?'

'I don't know. I hope so. Maybe I'll feel strong enough by then.'

'If you are, I'll come home,' I promised. I took down her phone number and address at the center.

'That'll give me a goal – Christmas,' she said, and chuckled. I hadn't heard that chuckle in so long I barely remembered she used to do it all the time.

'I love you.'

'I hope so,' she said. 'Bye bye, Nickie.'

'Bye, Mama.'

We both hung up very gently.

Mimi smilingly passed me another napkin.

My fitful good mood, which had been artificial earlier, now had some basis in fact. I almost danced as I got ready for the party. I only dance when I feel secure; my dancing resembles nothing so much as a frog leaping from pad to pad.

'Now I know you're human,' Cully remarked as I capered from the bathroom to the closet to extract my costume. I swept by him in a particularly daring maneuver and gave him a kiss on the forehead.

'Did you ever doubt it?'

'At one time,' he admitted.

'Why?' I stopped cavorting and looked at him.

'Oh . . . you never admitted anything was wrong.'

Well, well, well. I sat down at the foot of the bed with a thud. 'Explain.'

He folded his fingers together and looked at me with his lips flattened. I got a glimpse of what his patients saw. (Or did he call them 'clients'?)

'You were so beautiful,' he began, and I winced. It always came back to that in the end; my blessing and my curse. 'You were intelligent. You did very well at school, even while your home life was falling apart. Mimi told us what was happening with your parents, eventually; but you never said anything—'

'I was ashamed,' I interrupted.

'I can see that now, but at the time – I was inexperienced, too, you have to remember – it just looked like it wasn't touching you.'

A very different view of one of the most anguishing periods of my life. I'd been so afraid of tainting the smooth Houghton household with my sleazy problems. Faced with the cold perfection of Elaine, who could openly discuss having an alcoholic mother? I told Cully this.

'I can understand it *now*,' he emphasized. 'But then, I was only a kid, too. I was busy being a mighty senior in high school, then a lowly freshman in college, and every time you came to see Mimi I would go through torment. You just seemed far too perfect for someone like me. Then you went off to New York to become exactly what you wanted to be. Brave. Beautiful and brave, smart, successful. Making a lot of money. I met and married Rachel. Then you came to Mimi's first wedding looking like a woman from another planet, your clothes and face were so sophisticated.'

'Cully, I got drunk as a skunk at that wedding.'

'It was the first time I thought you might be a real human like the rest of us,' he said with a grin. The pursed lips and steepled fingers were gone, and he was Cully my lover, not Cully the observer.

'Did you lust after me?'

'You bet. Wet dreams.'

'Yahoo.' We grinned at each other, and I licked my lips in a parody of lasciviousness. I smoothed his mustache with one forefinger. He bit the fingertip.

'I saw your face everywhere I went for years. I used to buy magazines if your face was on the cover.'

'But you came to see me in New York, with Rachel,' I said carefully.

'All the feelings I had for you were so indefinite, you seemed so unattainable, that it didn't seem to have any bearing on my real life, my life with Rachel.'

Good. I didn't want to hear that his marriage had broken up over a fantasy, even a fantasy of me.

'Your apartment was beautiful. Your life was full of glossy people. You were on top of everything.'

Of course I had wanted to seem on top of everything, because Cully and Rachel were coming. I told him that too. He shook his head ruefully.

'When Mimi told me you were coming back here, I just couldn't believe it. I couldn't believe you had suffered any setbacks, any defeats. I let my adolescent picture of you go on and on. That never matured. The rest of me grew up, but not the part that held that image of you.'

'And then . . .' I murmured. And then I got raped.

It hung in the air around us.

I pounced on Cully and nipped him on the throat. I messed up his hair, something I knew would aggravate him. 'No more introspection,' I commanded. 'It's time to party.'

Cully made a gorgeous Robin Hood. I'd found an over-sized plain green shift up in the attic. Mimi vaguely recalled an aunt of hers leaving the shift behind after a visit to Celeste, and never asking for it again. Belted in, it made a fine tunic for Cully, coming down more than halfway to his knees. He had a pair of high brown boots he wore in the woods, and I made him pull on a pair of green tights of mine. Underneath his tunic, he wore a green flannel shirt. I'd made the hat, which sported a feather, from bits and pieces of green felt and an old hat of Celeste's. Cully had borrowed the bow and arrow from his friend on the police force, who practiced archery.

Naturally, Cully wanted me to dress as Maid Marian. I wondered if she had drooped around in the forest in long dresses waiting for Robin to return bragging about his exploits, or if she'd dressed up in tights, too, and aimed arrows right along with the best of the Merry Men. I finally decided that having donated my green tights to Cully's costume, it would be too much trouble to corral enough green for my own. I decided to go as a good fairy, since I'd found the perfect dress in my own closet. It was fluffy and white, scoop-necked and flouncy and romantic as hell. I'd worn it in a show and bought it on a whim afterward. It dated from a romantic revival by some designer who never made the grade.

I had spent the morning constructing my crown from cardboard and glitter and putting together a wand from a cardboard star and a fly-swatter handle, also liberally be-glittered. I curled my hair furiously and fluffed it out into a blonde cloud, then painted two pink spots high on my cheekbones. I'd even unearthed some gold nail polish.

When Cully and I were ready, we presented ourselves to Mimi, who smelled strongly of sage and cranberries.

'Good fairy, please turn this frog into a prince,' Mimi requested in a piping child's voice, pointing at Cully.

'Poof!' I said obligingly, in the most dulcet voice I could manage. I waved my wand. 'Young frog, you are a prince for this evening only, a limited-time offer.'

'Ping,' Cully responded, widening his eyes and standing up straighter to enact his transformation.

We all laughed like hell, Mimi having drunk a couple of glasses of wine while she was cooking, and Cully and I high on being in love.

Barbara came in before we left. She looked perkier than I'd seen her look for months, color in her cheeks and a little bounce in her walk. I thought she'd enjoyed learning to play poker. She was wearing boots and had a scarf wound around her neck. She warned us it was getting colder outside by the minute. 'But I love it. It's like home.'

'Fairy Clarabelle will waft us to the party on her magic broomstick,' Cully said with a straight face.

'You better warm it up before you get on,' Barbara commented.

'Think we ought to take the car?' Cully asked me. 'I didn't want to, since there won't be much room for parking and it's only three blocks. But I don't want you to freeze in that thing.'

I told Cully I thought I could endure three blocks' worth of cold, so we set off on foot.

Once guests have unlaced themselves enough to put on costumes, you have the makings of a pretty uninhibited party. I decided that about two hours later as I leaned against the kitchen counter chatting with my hostess Sally (the lady who allegedly had the corpse photograph on her night table – how *had* Mimi known that?). We agreed on this matter – costumes equaling letting one's hair down – after great deliberation. I'd had one glass of wine too many, and my hostess had had about three too many. Our conversation was rather erratic.

We rambled into a heated discussion on whether men or women had originated the idea of witches. Sally thought women labeled 'witches' were persecuted by men to express their general fear of women, and I thought women claimed to be witches to attain some power in a chauvinistic society. Since our conclusions were the same – witches had gotten a pretty raw deal – we ended the discussion pleased with each other.

At long last my hostess perfected her tray of sausage balls. I offered to help by carrying it into the living room;

and that's how the accident occurred. The house was old, with floor furnace grates; and as I passed through the hall, my heel caught and broke in one. Miraculously, I managed to keep the tray upright even as I slid to the floor.

'Poor thing,' my new friend Sally observed. 'At least the sausage balls are okay.'

I thought that was a callous point of view, but fortunately hadn't enough breath to tell her so.

Several gentlemen (a mouse, Hitler, and Tarzan – who must have been freezing – among them) helped me to my feet, one of them feeling me up in the process. I couldn't identify the culprit until I saw the leer on the mouse's face. I didn't know his name and couldn't recall seeing him before. With a gracious smile, I leaned forward to his ear and whispered, 'You bastard.' The leer disappeared in a hurry, replaced by a shocked reaction to my unladylike language.

I decided it was time to find another glass of wine and Cully. After reassuring my rescuers that I wasn't hurt, I coasted through the big old rooms looking for him. I'd last seen him in the company of a lean dark woman he'd introduced as his high school sweetheart (rather tactlessly, it seemed to me). She had giggled like a maniac and ducked her head in a way that made me positively loathe her. I'd debated opting for northern directness and telling her to buzz off, but instead had fought fire with fire and given her the sweetest smile I could construct while remarking that since those high school days were *so* long ago, she and Cully surely must have a lot to talk about. Of course, I'd removed myself immediately thereafter, and I hadn't spotted Cully since.

I didn't see him now. My vinous sense of well-being was evaporating as my coccyx began feeling the effect of the slide to the floor. Lurching around on one heel wasn't making it feel any better. I wanted Cully to appear, fired with great concern, and beg me to tell him I wasn't damaged. He didn't. I couldn't spot Miss High School Sweetheart either. I decided after some careful thought that my attitude could best be described as 'piqued.'

The shoe situation had to be remedied. I considered lasting through the party by taking both shoes off, but my host and hostess had not gotten around to renovating the floors yet, and the wood looked splintery. In a spurt of independence, I decided I would walk back to Mimi's and get another pair of shoes, and then return to find Cully frantic with worry over where I'd been. A neat consolidation of motives.

'Sally, I'm just going to run home and get another pair of shoes,' I informed the hostess.

She nodded vaguely and said, 'Suit yourself, Mike.' Crossed wires, there.

With some difficulty I found my coat, checking out a couple of bedrooms before I located the one that held all the wraps. By sheer chance I noticed Cully and the dark-haired woman weren't in any of them.

It had gotten colder outside. I didn't want to go bare-foot in temperatures like these, but trying to balance on one high heel was impossible and dangerous. Someone at the party had mentioned that just north of us there was freezing rain and the rain was expected to reach Knolls in a couple of hours. This was unseasonable for the area; the Thanksgivings I remembered were chilly but sunny. Winter was paying a premature visit.

I wasn't so brave and didn't feel so smart once I had gone a block in my bare feet. They began to sting with cold. Maybe I should return to the party and wait for Cully to walk me home for the shoes, I thought uneasily. But that wouldn't make my feet any warmer. I belatedly realized I should have hunted down Cully with more determination, and sent *him* back to the house for my footwear, since his shoes were intact. I paused on the sidewalk, shivering, and almost turned back. But I'd gone nearly a block, and I knew exactly where my replacements were stored in my closet. Besides, Cully might be busy with his *sweetheart*.

I gritted my teeth and proceeded. I was half a block from Mimi's when the lights went out on the entire street. The freezing rain to the north, no doubt. 'Oh hell,' I said to the black night to the silent block, to the tension that suddenly leapt from the core of my awareness. I hadn't known I was afraid. But I knew it now. I was alone in the night and unsheltered.

Obviously I couldn't stand still. I wrapped my coat more tightly about me, clenched my teeth, and started forward. There wasn't even much light from the moon or stars; the gathering clouds of the oncoming storm were obscuring them. I could see darker shapes in the darkness. That was all.

Because of the gloom, I overshot the steps leading up to the yard. I slapped myself lightly in punishment. 'Stupid Nick,' I muttered. Then my bare foot met the gravel of the driveway that led around back. That might be for the better, really. If I'd gone to the front door, Mimi would have had to blunder through the length of the lightless house to let me in. The kitchen door would be easier; she was sure to be in the kitchen with Barbara. Maybe they'd already gotten the candles lit.

That was a cheering thought. But since I'd had it, I was twice as dismayed to find the kitchen windows as lifeless as the rest of the house.

I patted my way past the cars, narrowly avoided falling into the bushes flanking the back steps, and crept up them with my hands extended. I was clutching both the shoes in my left hand to leave my right free. I heard a car go by in the street. From all the whooping and hollering, I gathered that a group of teenage revelers were excited by the black-out.

I padded blindly across the porch and had the great good fortune to encounter the knob of the kitchen door on my first try. I pushed it open, wondered for a second why it wasn't locked, and stepped inside calling 'Mimi!' . . . and the lights came back on.

I gaped for one long, dazzled second. Mimi was crouched by the breakfast nook and she had a screwdriver in her hand, gripping it fiercely with its business end jabbing upward. In front of her – *So ludicrous* flashed through my mind – was Theo Cochran.

He had a knife in his hand.

'Watch out!' Mimi screamed.

Confused by the sudden light and Mimi's shout, Theo had half-turned by the time I threw my shoes at him. They missed by a mile (I never could hit the side of a barn), but they provided a distraction. He dodged quite unnecessarily and then tried to decide who to attack.

Mimi settled that by a simple act of heroism. She flung herself at him.

In the middle of chaos, I frantically looked for a weapon to use in the struggle. Mimi was gripping her screwdriver in one hand and grasping his knife wrist with the other. In the shattered seconds I was frozen with shock he wounded her with a twist of the blade, and I saw blood well on her arm.

'No,' I said very definitely, and grabbed the only heavy thing that came to hand: the Thanksgiving turkey, slath-ered with butter, resting on the counter by the sink. I grabbed the legs in their metal brace, darted across the linoleum, swung the turkey back, and brought it crashing in an arc against the side of Theo's head. On impact, the greased turkey flew out of my hands and skittered grotesquely across the floor.

Theo staggered, let go of Mimi to right himself.

She instantly stabbed him with the screwdriver, and from his grunt I could tell he was hurt, but I didn't think that blunt end would penetrate enough to wound him seriously, so I wrapped my arms around his chest from behind and bit him in the neck as hard as I could. I didn't let go even when we hit the ground. Each of my hands grasped its opposite wrist, and even the pain of falling wasn't going to loosen that hold. On the way down I caught a glimpse of a form huddled on the other side of the kitchen by the refrigerator. He's killed Barbara, I thought. I'm going to kill him . . . and then I realized that Theo was trying to stab at me backhanded and there was nothing I could do because I was pinned under him.

I bit harder, my mouth filling with salt, and he screamed but kept on trying to stab me. I caught a flashing glimpse of Mimi circling, and wondered how long it would be before he finally succeeded in gashing me. Then an extra weight and a flash of tawny fur landed on Theo's chest. He screamed louder and Attila took off for the open back door in sheer panic. Mimi seized the instant to fling herself on Theo's knife arm. I heard her grunt when she hit the floor, I released my mouthful of neck to breathe and quickly sank my teeth in again.

Over Theo's shoulder I saw Barbara stir – she wasn't dead, then – look around dazedly, and begin crawling in the direction of our struggling heap. I wanted to shout, to tell her to arm herself, but with my mouthful I couldn't, and, as it turned out, Barbara had a neater solution than a knife.

She crawled on top of Theo and pinched his nostrils shut, then put her other hand over his mouth. I heard her hiss as he bit her, I felt him writhe to get free, but I didn't loosen arms or teeth, even when the pressure of his weight on top of me – I'd felt that before – and of Barbara's body lying across my locked arms began to make me dizzy. Barbara, I thought fleetingly, we were on the right track all along. I gave up too soon.

With the respite Barbara afforded her, Mimi scrambled halfway up and knelt on Theo's knife arm, and after a few seconds he had to let the knife go. I spied Mimi's hand snaking out after it as it slid to the linoleum.

Theo wasn't struggling so vigorously, now. Barbara was making sure he didn't get any air. He was on the receiving end of death, and he must have known it.

We would have let him die, I think, if only out of fear that if any of us let go he could attack again. But Cully came in the door at that moment to find three women and a suffocating monster in a heap in the middle of the kitchen floor, the Thanksgiving turkey upended under the breakfast table.

I didn't know it, but Theo was turning a strange color by that time. I could hear the funny noises, but I wasn't sure who was making them. The weight of two bodies was rendering me semiconscious at best. I was only capable of praying desperately that some end to the situation would come soon, and of keeping my grip around Theo's body and in his neck. I didn't even know Cully was there until I heard him say, 'Mimi! Mimi! You can get off now.'

That didn't sink through clearly. I didn't think it was safe to relax our attack yet. I tightened my hold with all my remaining strength.

'Barbara, he's dying,' I heard Cully say quietly. 'Let go.'

'No,' said a voice I barely recognized as Barbara's.

'Mimi, call the police, if you can.' But I heard Mimi already at the phone before he'd finished speaking.

'Barbara,' Cully tried again, urgently. 'Nickie's being crushed.'

'Oh,' Barbara said in a dazed voice, and at last I felt a

weight shifting. 'Son of a bitch,' she said, and I didn't know if she meant Theo or Cully.

'Nickie, are you all right?' Cully asked in a careful voice that irritated me immensely.

I had to unclench my teeth from Theo's nasty neck to answer. 'I'll tell you right now,' I said viciously in a trembling voice, 'I'm not letting go till the police are here.'

'Nickie. He's unconscious. I think maybe he's dead, or almost.'

'Good.'

Mimi's face appeared, in my limited field of vision. There was a smear of someone's blood on her cheek. 'He really is, Nick,' she told me expressionlessly. 'I think it's really okay for you to get up.'

I trusted Mimi's judgment more than Cully's. Mimi had no mercy either.

'How?' I asked practically.

'Oh,' she said, with the slow diction of complete exhaustion. 'Well. Cully's holding the knife on him,' she explained carefully, 'so I'll just kind of shove him off.' She tried. 'Nick.' She bent down to me again. 'You have to let go, first.'

Reluctantly, painfully, I unclenched my hands, then straightened my arms. I heard a shuffling noise as Barbara came to Mimi's aid. Slowly the weight toppled off me. I felt as if my pelvis had been crushed. I drew in great draughts of air and tried to pull my knees up. My legs trembled, but I managed. I raised my hand and rubbed it across my mouth, which was completely numb. My fingers came away smeared with blood.

'You look a sight,' Mimi said, and a smile twitched across her face.

'I reckon I do.' I absorbed that face, then slid my eyes over to Barbara's. I made my stiff lips move upward.

'Vampire,' Barbara said succinctly. She tried to answer

my smile, but couldn't manage. 'We were right, Nickie. We would have had him in one more week.'

They were helping me up when the police came through the door like a cavalry. When they pulled off Theo's gloves and I saw the network of nearly healed scratches on his wrists, I thought of Alicia, who'd fought all alone.

14

None of us quite felt up to eating the turkey, so we ended up having ham for Thanksgiving. And we held the feast in the evening instead of at noon. After being up almost all night, we had slept late.

Cully had to do most of the cooking, since Mimi, Barbara, and I were too sore; besides, Mimi's arm gash was bandaged, and so was the bite on Barbara's hand. Charles was pretty incompetent as a chef's aide. He turned up about one o'clock and made a laudable attempt to be useful, but it became obvious he'd never chopped an onion before.

Before he got there – while Barbara was still asleep in the upstairs guest bedroom and Cully was rattling pots and pans – Mimi finally explained about Charles. She had been aware all along, of course, of my bewilderment at her shift in attitude. As it turned out, she'd had some hurt and confused feelings of her own to handle.

'I really was just being hysterical that morning he came to the door,' she said through stiff lips. 'I infected you with it.' She was curled up at the end of my bed along with Attila the Hero. 'I did finally talk to him when he came by my office at the college, and we had a long showdown on the phone.' I remembered that evening; I'd had to wait for her to help with the dishes.

Mimi took a deep breath. 'Because of our weird

393

behavior the morning he came by, he thought I already knew what he was going to confess to me; otherwise I guess he never would've told me . . . This is going to sound like a soap opera, Nick. Charles thought I was so upset with him not because of the tussles in the car but because I'd somehow found out he'd slept with Sally, the woman whose party you and Cully went to last night.'

Oh dear, oh dear. Right after Richard's defection to the woman in Albuquerque. Mimi's pride.

'Of course I didn't know anything about it. But when he asked me to forgive him, he also told me which night he spent with Sally; it was the night Alicia was killed. So he was guilty of screwing another woman, but he wasn't guilty of something far worse. Sally's husband was on a hunting trip, and she invited Charles over – she'd dated him years ago – and things just went from there. He was mad at me when he went to see her. For various reasons.'

Uh-huh. Mimi wouldn't go to bed with him. And that must have been an extremely thorough confession, because that was how Mimi knew about the picture on Sally's bedside table.

'I was hurt and disappointed. I'm still not over that. We're going to have to have a few more talks,' Mimi said grimly.

'Why didn't you tell me?' I asked bluntly.

'I just couldn't. I knew you were thinking some kind of awful thought, I knew you were upset, but you know how critical you've always been of the men I've dated. I just couldn't face your saying, "I told you so." I knew you didn't like Charles anyway.'

'You're right,' I admitted. 'I wouldn't have been able to keep my mouth shut on that one.'

So that little mystery was cleared up; not exactly to my satisfaction, but at least to my understanding. I couldn't feel fond of Charles, but I promised myself on the spot that I'd try to like him better. He had arrived like a shot the night before when Mimi had called him, and had wanted to sleep across the door to her room to guard her! It was a good thing the police had taken Theo away before Charles arrived. I had never seen anyone more ripe for violence. Mimi had finally gotten him to go home, but with a great deal of difficulty.

'You know, Mimi,' I said to change the subject, 'the day Charles was over here, the day we were so scared? And we thought Theo's coming saved us?'

'We let the wolf in.'

'He came to get you, Mimi.'

'I thought so. I remembered that day, when I was trying to go to sleep last night.'

'He had gloves on when he came in. He only took them off when I answered the door and asked him to have coffee with us in the kitchen – when he knew there were two of us here.'

'But in broad daylight?'

'Right after Alicia, he must have felt pretty powerful. When he failed that day, and he saw Cully's things here – remember what a prude we thought he was? – he must have realized he had to plan better. He probably had to scramble to think of an excuse for stopping by at all. And he came up with two. The committee meeting Alicia missed, all the stuff they'd passed. And coming to tea with Sarah Chase.'

Mimi nodded as I pulled myself up straighter in the bed and reshuffled the pillows behind me. She said, 'Last night I also recalled Theo telling me that same morning that Sarah Chase hadn't been able to call me because their phone was out. But when we went to tea, Sarah Chase was telling Barbara she'd called her apartment Saturday morning. It was such a little thing, I can't believe I wondered about it even for a second. I was about to tell you when that Scottie ran in front of the car, and it just went out the other side of my mind.'

'He almost made a big mistake that day, Mimi. I can't believe he thought he could just walk in here on the spur of the moment.'

'Well, he did. We let him in, didn't we? I don't think he planned it at all. You know what I think? I think he said, "I just got that bitch Alicia, here I am driving by Mimi Houghton's house, let's see if she's alone. I've fooled everyone so far, they'll never catch me." He was drunk with power. That's how I see it.'

'He failed. So he tried again.'

'Ugh, ugh, ugh. I can't talk anymore now.' Mimi, though covered in a blanket, was shivering. 'I think I'm going to go climb in a hot tub and soak. Barbara'll want to bathe when she gets up, so I better get in and get out.'

I slept for another hour after she left. I was only vaguely aware of Cully coming in the room, looking down at me, and pulling the covers up higher around my shoulders. His long thin fingers touched my cheek. I smiled and slept.

Our little group was quiet over the ham and sweet potatoes. I think we were all preoccupied with our own thanksgivings of one kind and another, and, more prosaically, we were very hungry after the excitement.

When we'd all settled in the living room with glasses of wine in hand, Barbara said, 'Well, I guess we should talk about it.'

'I'd like to know,' I said, 'what happened before I got here last night.' I hadn't heard Barbara and Mimi give their statements to the police. I'd been too busy giving my own.

Mimi pursed her lips and launched into her account. I remembered her telling the story about Heidi Edmonds the night I'd arrived in Knolls, so long ago.

'We were just fiddling around in the kitchen,' she said. 'We got the sack of giblets out of the turkey and put the brace back on the legs. I boiled the sweet potatoes and mashed them; Barbara put in the cinnamon and raisins and found some marshmallows. Attila was on top of the refrigerator waiting to see if he could get some turkey when we weren't looking, and Mao was asleep on the couch in the living room.' Just where the little cat had been, still asleep, when the whole thing was over.

'I guess Theo was outside looking in the windows only *after* I sent Barbara upstairs to look for some Kleenex. She was sneezing – she's allergic to cats – and the box I keep down here had run out.'

'So he didn't know Barbara was here,' Charles said.

'No,' Mimi answered. 'He thought I was alone.'

I felt Cully twitch beside me.

'He rang the doorbell, the kitchen doorbell, not the front. I looked through the peephole Cully put in last week, but a fat lot of good that did me. Because when I saw it was Theo, I let him in.'

Alicia had let him in, too. After all, it was *Theo*. Good old bureaucratic Theo, who was actually on our list but whom we *still* didn't seriously suspect!

'He looked funny, but I didn't pay any attention at first,' Mimi continued. She barely knew we were there. Her hands were still, for once, clenched in her lap. 'He asked if Nickie and Cully had gone to the party. Remember?' she asked me. 'He heard that when we were leaving his house that day we had tea. But he didn't hear me ask Barbara over for Wednesday night, because I asked her when we were outside in the driveway.'

I wondered how it had felt to Theo, to see two of his victims and a third potential one sitting in his living room with his wife. He must have enjoyed it. I recalled his pleasure.

'Fool me; I said oh yes, that Nickie and Cully had left at least an hour and a half ago. I assumed he'd been working late at the college, like he did often, to clean up something before he and his family left for Thanksgiving. I kept waiting for him to bring up some point he wanted to talk about but he didn't . . . I began to get uneasy then, I think. I hadn't really worried earlier, because it was still early in the evening and all the other attacks were pretty late; except for Heidi Edmonds, and she was in such an isolated place. But I did feel a little funny. I went on and turned away to pour him a glass of wine, at the kitchen counter, and he came up behind me. And grabbed me. And put the knife to my throat.'

Mimi took a deep breath. Charles put his hand on hers, but she shook her head very slightly and he removed it. I put my own hand over my eyes to cover them. I felt Mimi's fear.

'Of course then I knew what he was,' Mimi said, and fell silent. Cully rose to refill our glasses. When he sat down again he put his arm around me.

'Even his voice was different,' Mimi said very coldly. 'He whispered. He told me what he was going to do to me. It was as nasty as you can imagine.'

Barbara and I could imagine. Barbara and I knew. A couple of tears wetted Barbara's face and she made no move to wipe them off.

'And he told me why,' Mimi continued.

I leaned forward. I wanted to hear.

'It was because we were successful,' Mimi said to me directly. Then she flicked her eyes in Barbara's direction. 'Successful,' she repeated.

'He said that?' Barbara asked incredulously.

'Successful,' I whispered.

'That was what it boiled down to,' Mimi said. 'What he actually told me was that we were arrogant women who had everything in the world and needed to learn a lesson; the world would go better, he thought if all these damned bitches learned a lesson,' she said tonelessly.

'I don't understand,' Barbara said.

'Because of his daughter – Nell – being so sick, do you think?' I asked. I knew I must look as dazed as the others. Charles's mouth was hanging open.

'That was probably part of it,' Cully said. 'And you told me his wife comes from an academically prominent family. He hasn't gone very far for someone his age – to them. Stuck as a registrar at a little southern college, with a dying daughter and a wife he knew could perceive exactly how he was situated on the ladder.'

'But she loves him,' Barbara protested. 'You know Sarah Chase would never say anything to him about—'

'But she knew,' Cully interrupted. 'Even if she never said anything, he may have been convinced he knew what she was thinking.'

'Oh, sweet Lucy,' Charles said disgustedly.

'And the added pressure and grief of Nell in the process of dying,' Cully went on. 'While all of you were going on with your lives, your rich lives. Alicia was loved and prominent, Nickie is beautiful and talented, Mimi is prominent and respected and pretty. Barbara had just gotten tenure, and she was in love. And that little freshman girl, that first one . . .'

'A little one, to practice on,' Charles said with more acuity than I'd given him credit for.

'Exactly – the girl who'd done everything in high school, right, Mimi? The girl who had a future in anything she chose, an achiever of the highest promise.'

'But he was always so polite to everyone, the women who worked for him thought he was great,' Mimi said. 'I can't understand how he could . . .'

'The women who worked for him were *under* him, had

no ambitions to go anywhere else or do anything else but clerk in the registrar's office until they retired,' Cully explained. 'It was easy to be courteous. They were never going to top him. They weren't stealing his daughter's future. And it was easy to be polite to you all, too. Look at the power he had over you, just by knowing what he'd done.'

'I'll never understand it,' Charles said simply. 'Even if I heard him talk about it, I wouldn't understand.'

'I don't want to,' Barbara retorted instantly. 'I don't want to even begin to comprehend a mind that sick.'

'That was all speculative, anyway,' Cully the psychologist said cautiously.

I'd been thinking. 'Mimi, he planned to kill you too, last night,' I said out loud. 'Or he wouldn't have let you see him. He must have found out he enjoyed killing women even more than seeing them walk around with his mark on them.'

Mimi nodded once. Charles took her hand, and this time she didn't shrug him off.

'What happened after he grabbed you?' Charles asked when the hush became too oppressive.

'Oh.' Mimi pulled herself out of a grim reverie. She looked at Barbara.

'I guess he was so involved in cursing Mimi that he didn't hear me come down the stairs,' Barbara said obligingly. 'And I hadn't heard the doorbell because I had my head stuck in the closet looking for Kleenex.' She sneezed right after she said the word, and we all laughed weakly. 'I clumped down the stairs, as usual, but he didn't hear me until I came into the kitchen. I was just saying "Mimi, I found them" and pulling one out to blow my nose, and I looked up and saw—' Words failed her then. Only the reminiscent shock on her face told us what she had felt when she saw a trusted friend and coworker holding a knife to Mimi's throat.

Mimi picked up. 'But it distracted him, I felt him jump. And I pulled away as he turned to Barbara. He went after her right away. Then the lights went out.'

'Oh, shit,' Cully whispered.

'Well, it gave us a second. I knew where the screwdriver was because I'd had to use it to lever the brace off the turkey's legs, like I always do,' Mimi explained. 'A knife would've been better, of course, but I grabbed what I could.'

'I'm just lucky he didn't stab me,' Barbara said thankfully. 'He bumped against me just when I was turning to run out the front door to get help. And I feel like a coward, that I wasn't going to stay to help Mimi, but it was the only thing I could think of to do.'

'The only smart thing to do,' Mimi told her promptly, and Barbara looked relieved.

'Well, since he caught me as I was turning,' Barbara continued, 'I slipped and whammed my head against the refrigerator door handle, I think, and then against the floor when I fell. Two bumps. So I was just about unconscious.'

'I heard Barbara fall,' Mimi said. 'I thought he had stabbed her and it was all over for her. I was trying to get to the kitchen door and go out the back. See, Barbara, I was going to leave you, too. I kept remembering all those thrillers I'd read where they tell novice spies or whatever to stab from underneath, so it'll go under the ribs instead of bouncing off, so I made myself hold the screwdriver that way and was listening to find where he was—'

'And then the lights came on and I was there,' I finished.

Mimi then described our epic struggle to Charles. He looked half-proud and half-horrified. He'd certainly never see Mimi in exactly the same light again.

Barbara asked, 'But why did you happen to come in just then, Cully? We could have handled it by ourselves, but I guess it was good to have someone untwine us.' I heard the undercurrent of resentment. I knew, then, that we had all resented Cully's arrival, his resolution of what was, for all of us, a personal struggle.

Cully looked surprisingly sheepish. As well he should, I thought, suddenly remembering Miss High School Sweetheart. With so much going on, we had not yet discussed her. Possibly we never would.

'I missed Nickie at the party. Then someone told me her shoe had broken, and I figured she must have come home to change, so . . .'

He'd really thought I'd gone off in a fit of jealousy. If he'd only been worried about the broken shoe, he'd have called the house rather than set out in pursuit.

'Does anybody know if Theo's confessed?' Charles asked.

Barbara shrugged. 'I don't know if he has or if he will. They'll test samples from him along with the evidence from all of us. Something will match up, even if he doesn't confess.'

'And he told me he'd killed Alicia. I guess that'll be admissible in court,' Mimi said. 'Though you never know. Think about it and give me a verdict, Charles . . . Listen, gentlemen, I'd like a fire. Why don't you two bring some wood in? I got a pickup load from Mr Rainham yesterday.'

After Charles and Cully had slammed the kitchen door on their way out, we three looked at each other for a long moment.

'We would have killed Theo if Cully hadn't come,' I said finally.

'Yes,' Barbara agreed.

Mimi stared into her glass of wine. 'How do we feel about that?' she asked her chenin blanc.

Barbara extended her thin hand and waggled it to and fro. 'A little of this, a little of that,' she said almost casually. We smiled at each other. Mimi smothered a laugh.

'We would have had to live with it,' I said consideringly.

'Look at what we have to live with now,' Barbara said in a savage voice.

'Alicia,' Mimi pointed out.

'Sure, Alicia,' I said. 'But after the first satisfaction was gone, wouldn't we have felt . . . on his level? We might have felt horrible right then, when we looked at him.'

'After our blood stopped singing,' Barbara murmured.

'When the rage was gone,' Mimi whispered.

'It's just as well, I think,' I concluded.

Barbara ventured, very hesitantly, 'Do you suppose, Nickie, that Cully's going to be able to live with seeing you with your mouth all bloody?'

If we had not been sharing this moment of close communion, she would not have asked that. Mimi would never have mentioned it, under any circumstances. But in this moment it was acceptable; a valid question.

'In all fairness, I wouldn't like seeing *him* that way. I mean, it's a pretty vile sight.'

The others nodded.

'I just don't know. We'll have to see. It may have been too – maenadlike – for him to handle.'

'The women who ripped apart anything in their path, in a kind of holy madness, one night out of the year,' Barbara reminded Mimi, who had been trying to remember.

'Oh,' Mimi said, flaming up. 'You mean maybe we should have sat there nice and quiet and been killed?'

'Maybe if one of us hadn't acted, if just one of us had submitted, the others would have, too,' I said.

'It doesn't bear thinking about,' Barbara murmured, after trying for a moment.

'No,' I agreed. 'We shouldn't. We won't.' We would try not to, anyway.

'Sarah Chase and Nell,' Mimi said. 'I wonder.'

'If Sarah Chase knew?'

'Oh my God, no!' Mimi protested in horror.

'That was what *I* was wondering,' Barbara said calmly.

I nodded. It had crossed my mind, too. How on earth had Theo explained to Sarah Chase that she was going to have visitors for tea? There was a slim chance that Sarah Chase really had intended to invite us. In that case, maybe he'd told her he'd bumped into Mimi and me by chance, that Barbara was the only guest she'd have to call herself, but . . . Surely even the dimmest woman would smell something fishy?

'Not *consciously*,' Mimi said vehemently. 'She just couldn't have had all three of us over that day. She just couldn't.'

I had to agree with Mimi. 'But Mimi, we can't go see her or call her,' I said firmly, for I knew that that was what Mimi had intended to bring up. She would see the obscenity of it in a second.

'No,' she admitted. 'I – no.'

Charles and Cully reappeared carrying armloads of dry oak, and proceeded to build the fire with much unnecessary hustle and bustle and advice to each other. They felt the pressure of our silence as we thought our separate thoughts and each viewed her own movie. The film was getting grainy and worn, the soundtrack fading, at least on mine. Perhaps I wouldn't have to watch those scenes much longer. Mimi was gazing at the bandage on her arm;

she'd had to leave the sleeve of her blouse undone to allow for its bulk.

I had put on a dress, in honor of the day and my survival. Cully had zipped it for me that morning; my arms were too sore for the job. He hadn't kissed me then, even though I'd scrubbed my mouth till it was raw, inside and out, the night before.

He bent now, as he passed the couch, and gave me a quick kiss – on the forehead. He and Charles were going out for more wood.

I rose with my empty glass in hand. I walked to Barbara, stooped over her chair, and kissed her. I went to Mimi on her couch, sat beside her, and kissed her. She held me for a minute.

Then I went to the kitchen to get some more wine.